W9-CKR-635

# Bait

C. J. SONGER

HarperPaperbacks
*A Division of HarperCollinsPublishers*

# HarperPaperbacks

*A Division of HarperCollinsPublishers*
10 East 53rd Street, New York, NY 10022-5299

This is a work of fiction. The characters, incidents, and dialogues
are products of the author's imagination and are not to be
construed as real. Any resemblance to actual events or persons,
living or dead, is entirely coincidental.

A hardcover edition of this book was published in 1998
by Scribner.

ISBN 0-06-101424-9

Cover illustration © 1999 by Phil Heffernan

First HarperPaperbacks printing: September 1999

Printed in the United States of America

Visit HarperPaperbacks on the World Wide Web at
http://www.harpercollins.com

❖ 10 9 8 7 6 5 4 3 2 1

# 1

"He's been kidnapped?" I asked.

"*Kednahp?*"

I hate taking Mike's phone calls. There's always a problem, and he's never around and nobody just leaves a name and a number.

"Kidnapped," I said. "Someone's stolen your son?"

"Stolen?"

Like a parrot, like an ignorant bird. And then the caller came back eagerly, avid: "Yes, yes, es good. 'Kednahp,' you say, for 'take es not yours.'"

It's not what I usually say.

"Mr. Haroutunian—"

"Es kednahp," he said firmly, "so Mike, he must come."

As if that settled everything. As if *now* I'd produce him.

People should really learn English.

"He's not here," I said for the ninety-fifth time, "and I have no way to reach him, okay?"

"But es kednahp! Kednahp!"

"Right," I said. "Have you called the police?"

"Politze!!"

I wasn't expecting absolute horror. I'm not what you'd call a great fan myself, but I don't go into convulsions. He was whirling, though, dervish, furiously spitting out phrases: police were no good, only *Mike*, Mike must come—Mike had said, Mike had *promised*—where was our *honor*?! Why wasn't I sending Mike over *instantly* to protect him and recover the *boy*?

Honor, for Chrissake.

"Hold on," I said, "just a minute, okay?" and I pushed down the hold button before he could spew any more. Stared at the light for a couple of seconds, but it kept right on blinking. Not going away on his own.

Mike will do things sometimes because he likes to be helpful, likes people to like him. And the way we're set up, it's an odd kind of business. We sell security systems out of Beverly Hills. John Gill Corporation, that's us. Mike Johnson, Meg Gillis. Mike is the front man, because, let's face it, would *you* buy security from a female? And a lot of it is contacts—who you know, who'll recommend you—and Mike's good at that. He's got the look, too, from his years in the uniform—capable, polished, a little bit dangerous—so people will call wanting him to do favors—bodyguard, background checks, that kind of thing. Sometimes he will. I don't know all the side jobs.

Don't always ask.

I jabbed at the other line, dialed Mike's home number. He hadn't been there all morning when I'd been actively looking, but it was worth another try.

I let it ring twenty times. Mike wasn't there or he wasn't answering, and it could be either.

Because sometimes, you know, he makes nice-sounding promises—yeah, sure, babe, I'll be there, kiss, kiss—and he won't be, like not coming in to the office to help me today. He forgets all about it, kind of loses the train, or he thought you meant *next* week, which sort of ticks off the clients, real and potential, which is why I spend a lot of my life on the phone.

I punched at the blinking button.

"Mr. Haroutunian?"

"You-y-y—not—" He was stuttering, twittering. Panicked?

"I didn't call the police," I said, "I was trying to reach Mike."

He only heard "police," I know he did—it was a mistake to have used the word. He yawped something Iranian, and then he was sucking those shuddering breaths, the heart attack kind.

"It's okay," I said, "take it easy." I was reaching for the file drawer next to me, thumbing, while I said whatever I could think of into the receiver. No damn folder under "H," nothing immediately visible under any other letter.

I stood up and ransacked the top of Mike's desk, dragging the phone cord with me. No Haroutunian, no notes on him, nothing, not even Mike's usual small scraps of paper, and I was going to kill the son-of-a-bitch when I found him.

"Mr. Haroutunian, what's your address there?"

"A-a-ahdress?"

"I want to send somebody," I said fairly patiently, "and your file's not in the office right now. So if you'd give me your address, please—"

"Nobody, nobody!"

"Mr. Haroutunian—"

"Nobody! Only Mike—*Mike* must come," and I think this was just about right where we'd started.

"I can't *find* him, okay? You want to tell me—?" but it was useless, so stupid—I wasn't going to get anything from this guy over the phone. Damn Michael anyway. I don't know what else made me say it. "Listen, Mr. Haroutunian, how about if *I* come over?"

There was a second of fumbling silence as if I'd stunned him or he'd dropped the receiver.

"No," he rushed loudly, "no, must be Mike—" and then he choked, just cut off, and I thought, ah, Christ, he *has* had a heart attack. I couldn't even call 911 because I didn't know where he was. Damn man had a phone block on, cutting out the caller ID.

He pulled himself back, though. Heavily on.

"Yes," he said, "yes, you must come," and there was something about the way he said it, sort of despairing, that snapped me right to attention.

"Mr. Haroutunian?"

"You get Mike," he said. "You come. Please."

I'm ten times a fool. I always have been.

"Where?"

It was an address in Beverly Hills, the old section in one of the canyons where there was lots of new money. Mike had gotten a few contracts up there recently. People with money tend to like attention, expect it, even, and Haroutunian could be one of them.

"You don't want the police?"

"No politze!" It was panic I heard, unmistakable fear.

"Are you okay?"

"You hurry," he said, and then I was listening to a dial tone because he'd hung up on me.

People will do that.

They get in a rush.

They're excited or hurried and the button goes down.

A disconnect, very simple.

Doesn't have to be wrong.

I had no way to call back, though, didn't have the guy's number.

Didn't have *anything* to go on, exactly—just the address he'd given and a very old instinct.

Recognition of trouble.

"*You come*," he'd said, "*hurry*," as if I were his only last hope for salvation. "*Get Mike*," and I couldn't, didn't know where he was. "*Please*," like a breath, like a prayer.

Supplication.

I carry a Colt .45 on my person sometimes. Didn't have it today. Sat there reckoning chances, responses. I don't look like much, which I find very useful, kind of small, just a female, but I can take out most men in close-quarter combat because I don't maybe care about fair. I figure you outweigh me, it's a built-in advantage, and that's all the fair you'll be getting, okay?

I can move when I have to.

Doesn't mean that I have to be stupid each time, be one of the fools rushing in.

"*No politze*," he'd said, and my ghost whispered, "*Meg . . .* ," a warning, reminder. I could still hear that anguished "*Where is your honor*?!" but if I'd *had* any, foreign-man, it was long hell and gone. I was already standing, reaching, outstretched for the phone.

911.

No, I didn't know what it was, I told them.

Yeah, maybe kidnapping.

Sure, I'd meet the officers there.

I hurried a little bit. Not a whole lot. A feeling it'd be best if the cops got there first, and not quite knowing how long it would take them. There was more traffic on Santa Monica than I'd been figuring, weekend shoppers, so I used up ten minutes just getting through town. I hung a left off of Sunset, another on Loma Vista and found the right cross-street.

Cruised the lane.

People in Beverly Hills tend to build to the reach of their property lines—very big mansions on very small lots—real estate costing what it does, don't you know. Makes for all sorts of domains, odd styles, jostling each other, cheek by jowl, but somehow you still get a feeling of privacy. These people won't be hearing each other, no matter how close the houses—there's too much room inside.

Money always makes the best insulation.

Haroutunian had a little more land around his, what they call "grounds" in the lifestyle magazines. It was a two-story house, plantation style, Gone-With-the-Wind, set back on the lot to make it look more impressive, white with fake shutters, a circular drive. Tiers of blank windows blindingly reflected what was left of the sun. There was a police unit already in place outside the wrought-iron gates, with two officers standing purposefully on the front steps, fronting a small dark man in the doorway.

Haroutunian. He was shaking his head emphatically,

gesturing. I left my car across the street and walked up the drive. Big house. Well-kept lawns. The cop on the left had been watching me park, and he called his sergeant's attention to me as I approached. I thought the guy had noticed me already, just something, but he turned as if he hadn't, and gave me his attention, very undivided. I don't know what it is about uniforms that makes people look wider. Imposing.

"I'm Margaret Gillis," I said.

His name tag was Reilly. Sergeant Reilly. He was taking his time surveying me, six-two or six-three, maybe two-twenty-five, very thorough, sort of thoughtful, and normally I don't care, people can look all they want to, but there was something in his gaze, something in the four of us standing there, nobody moving or saying quite much.

"What is it?" I said.

"What *should* it be, ma'am?"

Gentle. Cultured.

Christ.

"Look, Sergeant, the name is Gillis, Meg Gillis, and I called in about fifteen minutes ago on Mr. Haroutunian's son."

"I have no son," the dark man said clearly.

Cut me with a fork. "You have no son," I said stupidly, and then, as stupidly, said the only other thing I could think at the time:

"And you speak English."

# 2

Well, Haroutunian may not have spoken a *lot* of English,
I couldn't really tell. The English he did have was very
accurate and extremely concise: he didn't have a son, no
one had been kidnapped, he didn't know Mike, and he
didn't know me.

Didn't seem to want to, either.

I didn't have any problem with that at all, and I'd
have backed out of there in a hurry, but the sergeant was
politely disinclined to let it go.

A thorough man.

Efficient.

He'd called in another unit after hearing my story,
had gotten its two guys inside. Haroutunian hadn't been
excessively willing for them to go in, but the sergeant
had talked to him quietly, low-voiced, both of them
standing on the wide, white front steps, glancing over at
me: "crazy female," you know, and "I'd just like to
check, it won't take very long." Haroutunian was looking
harassed about then, fairly tense, but there were four
cops there, largish cops, and I pretty much knew how he
felt. I was feeling that touch tense myself.

I hate being taken.

I used to have to deal with this stuff all the time: *"Hey, girl, what's the matter—you got no sense of humor?"* and I didn't, okay? Not for jackanapes things.

Stood there containing it, and hating the world.

Hating *myself*, because I'm really too stupid. I could have come in alone and checked this thing out, been embarrassed in private, not standing with egg for the PD to see.

"How long'd you work?" Reilly said.

He'd come up beside me, was on top of me almost, soundlessly moving, face expressionless, blank—and he might have been meaning "at the office today," but I couldn't think so. It hadn't sounded quite like that and he was watching my eyes.

I know when I'm caught.

"Nine years," I said.

"That's a long time."

It was, yes.

Had been.

Nine years as a cop. I'd thought that I'd buried the tics that betray me, but apparently not deep enough. He'd picked it up somehow, because I hadn't mentioned it—and now I had to explain *that* part to him, too.

"It was a while ago," I said, "nothing I'm current on, so I don't try to claim it."

He absorbed it. Nodded. I'd called him "Sergeant" when I'd first walked up, read the chevrons—not something your Average would have known. Made me doubly stupid for keeping it quiet.

"Your partner, too?"

"Yeah," I said wryly. "Mike, too."

Two used-to-be cops. It put my story and my answers on a whole different plane.

"Any reason that someone would call you like this?"

"No," I said.

"Partner?"

Mike and his goddamn circle of friends. "I don't think so," I said.

"You don't sound very sure."

Maybe I didn't. This sergeant didn't know any more than I did that the cops in the house had come up with nothing, it just felt like it, okay? All the blank windows staring down and the time ticking by.

"Look," I said, "I don't have any idea what's going on, and I don't want to start guessing, all right? As far as I know, it's nothing to do with Mike and me."

"The guy asked for your partner."

"Yeah," I said. "So? Mike's the salesman. Lots of people have our card with his name and the number."

Not the private number, though. The card's only got our main number on it, and the call had come in on the private line. That's why I'd answered it, really. It's the number Mike tends to give out, of course, because it's the number he tends to remember, but I didn't have to tell Reilly that right at this moment. Not until I'd checked it with Mike.

"Someone who knows him," Reilly said.

He wasn't looking at me, he was staring across the driveway at the house, at the windows, following his own train of thought. Following it out loud, though, for me to react to, and I probably was, almost certainly was, clenching that bit. Too goddamned rusty.

"A lot of people know Mike," I said. Shrugged. "I

could call the station, ask for *you*, Sergeant. Doesn't mean you're involved."

"Yeah."

He was silent, too silent, and I'm inclined to get edgy. Curbed it.

"Something?"

And he was too damned observant—was making sure that I knew it.

"I'm just ticked," I said, "thinking about it."

And I *might* have been stewing, you know, might not have cared that he saw me, might very well have been angry for the fuss and the cross-examination, for looking like a fool in front of Beverly PD.

In front of this sergeant, who was watching me now like he had a right to, like a big man deciding.

"Why'd you call *us*?"

Why hadn't I just come myself, he meant, me with my background—why hadn't I checked this thing out before stirring the ants up? And I could have flipped him an answer, could have said almost anything, because I was definitely sliding towards that kind of mood. But this man was a cop.

"It sounded real," I said flatly.

Reilly might have asked more, kind of looked like he would have, but his two guys were coming out the front door about then, shoulder to shoulder, dwarfing Haroutunian still standing there on the steps with the officer, Thompson. Haroutunian was small anyway, five-six or five-seven, and surrounded as he was by the uniforms, he seemed a lot smaller.

Darker.

More nervous.

"Nothing," the one guy, Escobar, called.

"No boy's things?" I said. "Toys? A skateboard or anything?"

Reilly okayed it with a flick of his eyes.

"No," the cop said.

So much for that theory.

"You willing to come back with us?" Reilly was easy, offhand. "I'd like to go through this more thoroughly, not fret Mr. Haroutunian any more than we have to."

Any more than we *had*, he meant. He was good. Very good. Asking me civilly, nicely enough, but clearly expecting that I'd come along. It was late on a Saturday, four-thirty, five, and I was pretty damn tired. Pretty fed up. I *could* have said no, could have said I had other things, have the dicks come and talk to me Monday if they want to pursue it. We work out of Beverly Hills, though. Do a lot of our business. I didn't need to be disobliging anyone on the force there, much less a sergeant, and he knew it the same way that I did.

"Yeah, sure," I said. "Glad to."

He was still looking down. Had maybe a small smile edging his eyes, maybe half of a nod, and then he was leaving it, shifting smoothly aside to meet Escobar coming up on us.

I'd *called* them, you know?

That goddammit instinct.

The one that keeps steering me wrong.

# 3

The Beverly Hills station is part of a triangle: the library's one leg, the PD's the second, and a multilevel parking garage stretches across the back to make up the third. You have to enter the station from *inside* the triangle, on the second-floor level. Eliminates drive-bys.

The public gets in by a pedestrian bridge that juts out from the second floor of the parking structure. It joins the curved eastern wall of the station and runs along it like an exterior balcony, a ramp, with the public door to the PD two-thirds of the way up the incline. The ramp continues its rise to the end of the building, then drops down some steps and bridges back in a great looping circle through the middle of the triangle to end up right back where it started on the second floor of the parking structure. There's an offshoot of the circle just past the PD that stretches over the parking driveway. It lets you cross safely above the in-and-out traffic and then down a flight of stairs to the library. The whole thing's a graceful design, very elegant, sweeping, befitting the city. Byzantine arches in designer colors, teal and hot pink. Thick cement. Leafy palms.

I drove myself there from Haroutunian's house, signaled all the turns. Pulled into the parking garage and parked while they followed behind me, while Reilly got leisurely out and strolled over, waited for me to climb out of my car. While the officer, Escobar, took the unit on down and the sergeant escorted me in.

He paused halfway up the ramp, turned slightly out towards the railing.

"It's a nice view," he said casually.

It *is* a nice view. There's an open-air courtyard about three stories down, shaped by the parking structure and the base of the PD. It looks like an ancient amphitheater, scrubbed from the lions and white in the sun, concentric circles of cement steps, descending. A quiet little place to eat lunch, hold a riot.

A long way to fall.

"The mountains," he said, touched my arm, redirected me.

You could *just* see a mountain through a gap in the buildings. It looked distant, obscure.

"Yeah, it's nice," I said.

I might have been edgy, might have been broadcasting. I didn't like the feel of whatever this was and this guy had me every way, coming and going. Knew it. Stopping oddly to chat.

Watching me, thoughtful. Not even responding.

Testing.

And then he was stepping back for me to precede him, arm curved politely, not quite touching, behind me. Ushering mode. Moved us on up the incline. Held the door for me like a natural service.

There's an overhead camera there, aimed at the

ramp. Eye spies everywhere linked to the Command Center, makes things secure.

The lobby inside is really a hallway, slightly more open, with the public staircase filling the center, coming down from the third floor above. The far end of the hall rounds off to the right past floor-to-ceiling display cases that hold police patches from other agencies. I don't know if they'd been given up willingly. The front desk officer is stationed at the near end behind a podium, not where *I'd* be comfortable, no glass, no cage, no particular place to duck, but then this is Beverly Hills: they'd have you on film if you came in and shot the place up.

Reilly flapped a casual hand at the guy as we came through the doorway. Paused us inside it.

"The Record Bureau's upstairs," he said. Nodded sideways towards the curve where the hall disappeared. "That's one of the meeting rooms there, but I think they're in doing a press conference now."

It was useful information, life-enriching, and I'd opened my mouth to say so when "Come on," he said easily, "I'll show you around." His arm was behind my back again, lightly but touching this time, firm, pressing me towards the cop at the podium and the door that leads into the station.

Or it might have been me. I might have looked like I needed the handling. I clamped very hard.

He and the desk guy were sort of nodding in passing.

"They still going at it down there?"

"Yeah," the guy said. "All the brass. Doing video clips." He was looking at me, and Reilly shifted between us, digging a wallet out of his pocket. It felt like protection, him covering me, but I didn't know the desk guy, sure didn't know Reilly. And then he was waving the wallet at a plate on the wall, unlocking the door, showing me in. Door closing behind us, that good solid clunk, as if I might be there a while.

Police stations are buildings, places of business like anywhere else, just walls and concrete. With reinforced steel, of course, and double-lock doors and everything bright from the overhead lighting. That faint tang of metal in the recycled air. Filing cabinets, desks. Guns. Bars. I used to belong in places like this, used to walk in and out, safe with my badge and my shield. Friends. I don't anymore.

"You want a soda?"

I wanted very much to be gone.

"No," I said tightly, "and I don't need the grand tour, okay?" There were people at the end of the hall coming at us.

"We'll go in here, then," he said, and opened a door right beside me. It was a Beverly Hills kind of conference room, state of the art: TV, VCR, a big maple-wood table, deep-plush blue chairs. He moved us through the door together, shut it, just the two of us in, but it was a reasonably-sized room. I went away from him into the space, and he stayed put, watched me do it. Said very gravely, "Your choice of seat."

My choice of nothing. I took a chair at the far side, with my back to the wall. He was reading it, reading me, and I wanted not to be so delinquent, but some things just *are*, you know? He settled himself across the table, looked quizzically at me.

"You nervous, Ms. Gillis?"

I'm always like this. "It's a lot of fuss for a phone call," I said.

He could have soothed me a story—I was geared for it, actually, expecting—but he just nodded very coolly, surprised me. "We've been having some problems," he said.

"People making phone calls?"

"People harassing Iranians."

Like by having the cops show up. "I don't know about that," I said. "I just reported the call."

"Mike get a lot of these calls?"

"No," I said.

He was sitting there watching me, and I'd been too quick.

"Okay," I said, "what kind of calls? From strangers? Yeah, he does. People pass his name all the time, we get a lot of cold calls. From Iranians? No, he doesn't, not to my knowledge, but that doesn't mean anything—he makes contacts wherever he goes. He could have picked this caller up anytime. We've been pretty busy this week and we haven't touched base much—is that what you wanted to know?"

"Yes," he said calmly. Did seem to be satisfied. "So you weren't surprised at this call?"

"I thought it was a panicky client," I said. Only partly a lie, because I'd really thought it was one of Mike's panicky side jobs, but Reilly was taking it, nodding.

"Explains why you went there."

It didn't explain it at all and I figured he knew it. You don't go haring off to an unknown's house on the strength of a half-garbled phone call.

"It explains why I called the police," I said steadily. "I

*went* because your dispatcher asked me to go."

I watched it mean something to him, watched him absorb it, but I was studying the wall when he flicked back to me, waiting for him. He observed me a moment.

"They call you Meg?"

"Yeah," I said.

"All right if I use it?" Well-mannered. Courteous. Break down those formal barriers between us.

"Yeah, sure," I said. I can be courteous, too.

He wasn't ignoring it, exactly, my not being responsive, but there are times when you press people and times when you don't. It's a delicate business, this measuring stuff, gauging the degree of resistance.

And then the door was opening beside him, and Reilly was turning his head, turning to see. It was Officer Escobar, looking surprised, which was a very nice job indeed.

"Oh," he said, "you're in here."

There was a guy behind him, and then they were both coming in. The guy was a Somebody. Had that air, that arrogance, rolling on through.

"Joe," he was saying warmly, aiming at Reilly, "I heard you were working today"—bright attention switching to me—"but I can see that you're busy."

Reilly was rising. "We've just been talking. Did you need the room?"

"No, no. No." Something passing between them. "Ray was going to hook up the VCR for me. Tape myself on the news, eh?"

The VCR was on a shelf to my left. A TV. It might have a cable hookup. He might not have anything like it at home.

I was watching Escobar because he'd driven with Reilly back to the station. He was the link, if there was one. He was leaning quite casually against the now-closed door. Saw me looking and smiled, a wide bandit smile, friendly and gleaming.

"This is Meg Gillis," Reilly was saying, a civil intro-duction to the Somebody and, really, only because we were all still there. I stood up, reached a hand. The Somebody came in to meet it, shook briskly.

"Frank Abbott."

No honorific.

"Lieutenant?" I said, and Abbott looked that half-tick sharper, brows raising.

"She's an ex-cop," Reilly said, so Escobar hadn't car-ried that message or else we were getting it into the open. No hidden anythings here.

Except whatever they were running on me.

The lieutenant was taking a brusque, friendly inter-est. "An ex-cop, eh? Where're you from?"

I wasn't from anywhere now, but I told him. Went through the "who do you know?" type of quiz, and yeah, there were a couple of names. Abbott looked pleased.

"He's a good man," he was saying of one guy. "I heard he retired," and it's hard to give one-word answers when people are chatting so civilly, just being pleasant. Gracious. Easing you through. Very effective technique, makes you feel like a fool.

He was large, the lieutenant, not especially tall, but wide, massive, portly, and you'd write him off as a hearty old fat man if you didn't look at his eyes or his smile. Smile like a shark. Teeth. Purpose.

Me and the rest of the fools bleeding on the beach.

"So what are you doing with Joe here?" he said, as if Joe and I were an item, as if that's what he thought. As if he were old Father Christmas and my sweet winking uncle rolled into one.

I waited to see what Reilly would say, but apparently nothing. "He's asking me questions," I said. "I reported a kidnapping call."

Abbott was taken aback, bush-brows snapping together. "Really?" And then he had to hear all about it, us being acquaintances, practically kin, so we settled ourselves into various places while I went through the story again. Bare-boned it this time because I was ready to be done.

"Well, that's really something." Abbott, shaking his head. "Your partner—what's his name?"

"Michael Johnson."

"That's it. You've checked with him?"

"I've been *here*," I said.

"That's right, that's right." Looking to Reilly. "Going to follow up on it, eh?"

Reilly wasn't looking anywhere. "I thought I would," he said. A quiet man. He'd faded into the walls the whole time I'd been trotting my story for Abbott, so that you wouldn't even have known he was there. Watching me. Listening. Not like Officer Escobar, who was shooting me another of his dark angel smiles.

Pretty free for a Patrol guy in uniform. Nobody rushing him to get back out on call. It *could* have been end-of-watch, I guess. I didn't know how Beverly ran it, what kind of shifts, but I wouldn't normally expect that an officer would hang around on his own time for something like this—or that a lieutenant would let him. It wasn't even Escobar's call, come to that, because the guy at the scene writing everything down had been Thompson. So *Thompson* was the officer dispatched on the call. With Reilly, of course. Reilly, a sergeant. Escobar and his partner were just there as the backup. The search team that Reilly'd requested.

"You probably want to check Haroutunian, too," I said. Said it nicely but clearly, gathering myself up as if I thought I was through, as if I had no more claim on their time. They were busy guys, you know, working, still on the clock, and really, my part was over. "Might want to see why somebody named him."

"Yeah." Reilly was nodding, thinking, and I was half a step closer to the door. He noticed me, marked it. "I'll walk you out."

He could do that. Somebody had to, back through the mantraps, you can't just stroll out on your own. I'd have been easier with Escobar, whose interest was clear, but at least they were letting me leave. You can't always be sure.

And nobody'd come back with the obvious question: "why would someone name *Mike*?"

"Lieutenant," I said, shook the hand he was reaching. Abbott smiled widely, engulfing my grip.

"We'll hope to see you around, Ms. Gillis."

You bet. I retrieved my fingers, nodded politely at Escobar. "Officer."

He nodded back, mindful of Reilly now at my shoulder, but with a gleam barely hidden, a "see you soon" kind of glint that said "maybe I know you."

He didn't.

People think what they want to.

I walked along with Reilly down the hall, and my shoulder still only came to his chest but this time at least he was keeping his distance, keeping his arm to himself. Until we got to the lobby, that is, the actual parting, and then he was sort of detaining me there, holding the inside door open.

"I'll call you later," he said, very casually, "if there's anything else. You going home now?"

As if "home" were a place we both knew. The front desk officer was three feet away, writing diligently, not paying us any attention, and this was where we'd come in, my buddy Reilly and I. Touring the station. Not me being *brought* in. Not being interviewed. Just Reilly impressing the hell out of me, showing the little lady the place where he works.

I can play.

"Yeah," I said. "I thought I'd go home."

"Good." He was smiling down at me for the first time, like maybe he meant it. Appeared to notice the desk guy, turn a little self-conscious, restricted. "Go slow."

Like the wings of the wind.

"Oh, you know *me*," I said deliberately, curving in close, "I just can't seem to do that," and then I was moving pretty fast out the front door, didn't turn around, blow him kisses or anything.

God has this way of giving fools rope.

# 4

We sell security packages, Michael and I—rotating cameras with computer linkups, that kind of stuff. We'd set up shop in Beverly Hills because it was convenient, handy to a lot of places and people who might like to purchase expensive security systems. There are stores all over Beverly Hills, and, of course, it has its moneyed citizens. We're a quick hop from Century City, where there are towers of offices, lots of small businesses. East is Hollywood and Sunset with its film-producing clientele. West is Santa Monica's beaches.

Mike does the bulk of the selling, the "smile-and-sign'em," and I do most of the follow-up. I'm the one who schedules the contractors, the site visitations, oversees installation, the billing, etc. He'll do some of that, sometimes, but I'm actually better at it. Mike spends a lot of time chatting.

Any partnership, that's how it goes—you find out what works and you use it. Mike's always been golden. He can talk to anyone anytime and make them feel good, even back in the days when we were arresting them. He enjoys people, likes it. Views life as a game.

I don't know how I view it.

I left Beverly Hills PD by way of their bridge, stoking myself up a fine head of steam. I shouldn't have jacked Reilly there at the end, but I didn't care. Drag me in on my day off, make me sit through this farce. I was going to run Mike to earth and flag this thing by him, going to see that damn shrug, hear that "hell if *I* know," and *then* I was going to put this damned day behind me, never drive down their street again, set foot in their door.

Part of me's Gaelic.

I made my way down the ramp to the parking garage, and the Gaelic part of me, the "grand wind blowing" part, the "all for the fine gesture" part, came out of the sunlight and saw that my car wasn't there.

It was not where I'd left it.

The damned thing was gone.

And I could swear all I wanted to, look around like a fool, picture it parked in twenty different places, but there was the hole in the pavement, there the column and the Ford that was next to it, and there was definitely a shiny red Lexus instead of the 'Ru that I'd put there.

Someone damn playing games.

Escobar's meaningful glimmer. That "see you soon" nod.

It didn't take me two seconds to cross back up the ramp and less than one second to get the front desk officer's attention. He had a welcoming smile.

"*Reilly*," I said. "I want to see him now."

"I'll have to check—"

"He's expecting me."

The officer didn't like me after all. He picked up the phone to call, but he made quite a point of turning his head and lowering his voice so that I wouldn't be able to hear. That was okay—I was framing my own speeches and pacing in front of the display cases, and I didn't really care what he was saying to Reilly.

"Someone'll come out. You want to have a seat?"

"No."

"Someone" was Reilly.

"This is nice," I said before he could get through the doorway, "very cute. You want to tell me where you had my car towed now?"

Reilly blinked, seemed to process it.

"I didn't have your car towed."

A literal man.

"Where'd *Escobar* have it towed, then?"

The overhead lights sketched the lift of his eyebrow. He paused, looked across at me. "To the best of my knowledge," he said very evenly, "we haven't towed your car."

"It's not there, Reilly."

"Did you lock it?"

Jesus H. "You think someone *stole* it?" I said. "You think someone happened to come through the parking garage stealing *four-year-old Subarus*?" I didn't need this, didn't need any of it. The desk officer was listening, but the whole world could hear.

Or not.

"Never mind," I said tightly. "I'll call it in stolen when I get home and maybe by then you'll have discovered it in one of your tow yards, okay?" I whirled for the door. I'd call a cab from the library or walk back to the office because I sure as hell wasn't sticking around here.

"I think you should talk to me," Reilly said, and wasn't that just the point? I threw him a look and kept going.

"Find Escobar," he said to the desk guy, and then he was coming after me. He moved very quickly for a big man because he'd caught up to me before I hit the bend to the library, had gotten around me.

"I think you should stay."

He had me cornered at the bottom of the first flight of stairs, not totally blocking me in by the railing but close, too close—I was all but breathing with him. I could move him aside, but that would be assault on a peace officer, and maybe they were looking for that.

"Get out of my way, Reilly."

"A few more minutes," he said reasonably. "Talk to me." He'd seen me sizing him and the son of a bitch was amused. There was an understanding sort of smile in his eyes—meant for me, to lure me—but he didn't understand *anything* and I was not in the mood.

"Listen," I said viciously, "*stuff* it, okay? Keep the friendly advice because you don't even know me."

His face went quite hard.

"I knew your husband," he said.

Charlie.

Christ, Charlie.

It was a thousand things searing—anguish, betrayal. I wasn't expecting it, wasn't prepared, and maybe I stepped back from him, maybe I did, because there was a column suddenly jamming my spine and he had a hand on my elbow, seemed to be holding it.

The man moves through the darkness. A whisper—the *woman?*—and he turns, half turns, instinctively reaching, the holster snap stiff in his hand. It is dark, there are people—*two of them?*

*three*?—and the night splits apart, rips, muzzle-
flash blinding. There is pain, wrenching pain,
twisting up, slamming sideways. "Meg," he
thinks—*does he think*?—but the fingers are slipping, splayed fingers, blood-slicked, and the rest
is so simple: he falls—topples, really—cement
there to take him, scraping what's left of his face
on the ground. "*Meg*," the snarl of an engine, car
engine, and somewhere, not far off, a woman is
screaming . . .

"You all right?" Reilly asked.

I was fine.

"I'm sorry," he said very quietly, and I wanted my
arm back, wanted him gone.

Vanished.

Removed from the earth.

"I'm sorry," he said again. People can never think
what to say. He let go of my arm but didn't otherwise
move, and we were our own little universe there by the
railing. I watched maybe five cars come up to the stop
sign, pass under our section in the afternoon sun, and he
wasn't doing anything else, wasn't pressing or speaking,
just standing there, blocklike, waiting for me.

"It was a while ago," I said, finally. "A couple of
years. Your guys didn't tow my car?"

"No."

"And you don't know anything about it?"

"No."

I believed him then. He didn't look any different, so
what it came down to was his knowing Charlie, but that's
the kind of thing that influences you.

Influences *me*, anyway.

"What's going on?" I said, and Reilly was matter-of-fact, noncommittal.

"Looks like someone stole your car."

"*Don't* you," I said, "*lie* to me. This whole thing's a piece: you bringing me in for a phone call, bringing me in under cover."

He was very still.

"I thought," he said slowly, "that you wouldn't want your name all over the station."

Because of Charlie, he meant. Handling me with gloves on because of Charlie, and the pain was the fuel, always has been. Launches me. Aimed me at him, very directly. "What the hell do *I* care what a bunch of cops think—a bunch of cops that I don't even know? You brought me in because you're working something, plainly and simply, so what are you—Vice?"

"STU," he said.

Special Tactics. The elite corps, the bully boy squad.

"Escobar, too? He's one of your guys?"

"Yeah."

With Reilly as the goddammit sergeant. It was worse than if he were Vice, because at least that had limits, I could tell the parameters, but STU works all kinds of things. It could be *anything* they were looking into—STU goes where it wants, at their captain's discretion. He had Escobar. Probably four or five others.

"Is Abbott IA?"

Reilly was looking distinctly closed, but I could find it out ten other ways and he knew that I knew it.

"Detective Division."

Not IA—not Internal Affairs—so why were they

keeping me covered from cops? Reilly wasn't leaving me time.

"I want to know about your partner," he said, and that was pretty damn straight.

"You mean, the connection to the phone call? I have no idea. You'll have to ask him—"

"Where *is* he?"

"I don't know," I said. "He could be anywhere. It's a weekend."

"Where's he usually go?"

"Tahoe," I said. "Vegas or Reno. The Colorado River. He's got a mother in Bakersfield, a brother in Redlands, and friends across two or three states." Reilly was looking that hair-bit tight as if I were being deliberately difficult. Maybe I was. "I'm just saying it depends, okay?"

"On?"

On whether he went off looking for fun or whether he'd already lined up some fun to take with him. What the fun wanted to do.

"On the girl," I said. "Mike's very agreeable."

"*Is* he?"

I didn't care for the emphasis. "Yeah," I said shortly, "he is. What was Abbott doing in today?" On a Saturday, when lieutenants go golfing.

"Drug bust. Press conference."

Maybe. Grabbing the glory. Something Reilly hadn't known, do you think, when he'd invited me back?

To run me past Abbott.

"When are you expecting to hear from him?" he was saying, meaning Mike.

"Monday," I said. "Nine o'clock, at the office."

"Not until then?"

"No."

He didn't bother to look like he even believed me.

"I don't know that he knows anything about this," I said, and Reilly had those damn steady eyes.

"Someone picked up his business card, decided to call?"

Okay, not likely. I knew it was feeble. There was something in the waiting-for-it way he was standing, though, so very righteous, that ticked me off majorly. This whole thing was wrong, and I've always been willing, always had my own mouth, so "No," I said back to him, "I'd expect one of *your* guys had his number in a pocket and decided to call."

That one went home.

"You've been having some problems here, Reilly? Someone bored on the console or something, been making some phone calls?"

He was that kind of still.

"Yeah, I thought so," I said. "Don't be looking at my house for spooks."

"Why would they involve *you*?"

"No particular reason," I said. "They might've just called Mike for something, got *me*, and decided to have them some fun. Jack me around, you know? Some of the guys don't like female cops, even when they're *ex*-female-cops."

He knew what I was saying. Wouldn't admit it, I'm sure, but his eyes knew exactly. "Yeah," I said straightly, "I put up with a whole bunch of things in my time, and this feels like more of the same."

"Why Haroutunian?"

"Why not?"

He was shaking his head.

"Okay," I said fairly, "I don't know that it's *me* they were jacking. *You're* the one who brought me back, introduced me to Abbott."

That caught him big-time. I hadn't meant anything by it much more than a jab, but he was fastened on me and I could see it revolving. He and Abbott. Me being what had brought them together today. Me and Iranians and problems with harassment.

"If I was somebody looking to see if you two were checking for cops," I said very slowly, "I'd know it now."

"Yeah," he said.

Sort of grim.

An uncomfortable moment watching him work it, and this was where I'd come in, you know? Phone calls and cops. Loyalties. Tugging me which-way.

"Mike'll be in Monday," I said. "Maybe he'll know something then."

"Yeah."

Maybe he wouldn't. I stood another long minute watching him thinking, containing, tamping down whatever it was. Couldn't stand there forever. I touched him finally, touched his arm, and saw him switch over to me.

"You going to put in a Stolen report on my car?"

"Yeah," Reilly said. "We'll have to do that."

He didn't seem to be rushing. I was still backed into the column with him standing in front of me, and there was really no way to get out or around him.

"What?"

"You'll have to go in," he said slowly. "Have to sign it."

Into the station. I didn't want to do that, really did

not, but I could see that he wouldn't want to leave me out here while he went back in to get forms.

"I'll go as far as the lobby," I said. He could like it or lump it, but he was just looking, so maybe it needed something else added. "I've had enough of police stations to last me a lifetime, Reilly." Had enough of cops, too, but I didn't quite say that. Probably didn't have to. He was nodding, stepping back so that I could turn without bumping him, so that we could go in together, and there was that one other thing. "Am I still your girlfriend?"

He regarded me thoughtfully.

"Yeah," he said. "For the moment. That all right with you?"

As if I had a choice.

"I get naggy," I said.

Half-smile forming, very grave eyes.

"Well, you're a female," he said.

# 5

I let him drive me home. It's not the kind of thing I'd usually do, not what your mother would advise you, but there it is—I did it. We'd walked across the bridge to look at the Lexus still sitting in my spot, and then had gone down to chat with the parking attendant—a wasted exercise, really, because I always leave my ticket on the dash so I don't forget it or lose it and have to pay the full go for being ticketless. Meant that whoever stole the 'Ru had only had to hand the attendant the ticket and the money to be no more memorable than everybody else who was doing it. Subarus don't generally stand out. One of the reasons I like them.

It didn't escape me either that someone could have saved themselves even *that* small outlay of cash if they'd just driven the 'Ru down a few levels and taken the cop exit out. You'd have to have the Kingdom card for that, of course.

It hadn't been towed. I asked the guy straight out and there hadn't been a wrecker there all day. Reilly didn't say anything, but he had a look like he could have.

I didn't care.

And then we'd gone back up to the lobby. I'd

flumphed myself over to the far end by the badge cases, standing with my back to the world like the malcontent girlfriend while Reilly talked quietly to the front desk guy, and came back with a Vehicle Stolen form in his hand. Did my best to look aggrieved and petty, which wasn't much of a stretch. Wouldn't look at Reilly while he asked me the questions. Signed the damn thing. He paused on his way to return it, and looked down at me. "You'll need a ride home."

There was no way in hell.

"I'll be fine," I said.

"You have someone to call?"

"I'll get a cab."

"To Burbank?"

He'd been paying attention, knew where I lived. "Yeah, to Burbank," I said. "It's not the edge of the world. Cabs come and go there."

We were over by the windows, by the goddamn display cases, miles from anyone able to listen, and he was looking across the lobby at the front desk officer, not quite focused on me. "I can give you a lift," he said slowly. "I'm done here now."

It might just have been part of the cover, to make it look better—you know, the girlfriend's car gets stolen, you're getting off work, you don't really send her home in a cab. I was done being part of this, though.

"No," I said.

"I have to go right by there. No reason for it to cost you."

No reason for him to keep offering.

"I'll be okay," I said.

He nodded. Understood it. He wasn't moving away,

though, not leaving, just standing there like a lumpkin, a very large block, and I knew that he was thinking of me on the bridge, our three fragile minutes.

Outside, when he'd said he knew Charlie.

Dammit.

Goddammit.

Ego and pride. Mine used to mean a lot to me, but I no longer equate self-worth with throwing kindness back in people's faces.

"I'm sorry," I said tightly. "Are you really going to Burbank?"

He flicked a glance at my face. "Going to Glendale," he said, "but it's not much to stop off the freeway."

That was true enough. "You live in Glendale?"

"Yeah."

People live there.

"Whereabouts?"

"East California. California and Louise."

Apartments. "Over by the PD," I said. "Been there a while?"

"A couple of years."

Divorced.

He was looking at me again, eyebrow quirking, not precisely amused but something damned like it.

At me.

At my inquisition.

"So did you want a ride?" he said.

I didn't, you know. I just couldn't.

"No," I said, "but thanks, okay? I appreciate it, really."

"All right."

He was tranquil this time, accepting, and I couldn't

have told you what it was—the quality of his tone or the way he was standing. I stared at him.

"You're going to be *following* me?"

He was between me and the desk, looking down at the report in his hand. "I thought I'd be sure you got home."

Because someone had stolen my car. Because he'd known Charlie. Because it *wasn't* just phone calls and harassment, apparently, that he and Abbott were checking.

Because it was cops.

"Christ," I said. I stared at the window frame, tried to figure it differently, but it all came back to me being stupid. I wasn't carrying, and he'd at least have a weapon. Might be protection, supposing I needed any. I didn't *think* that I did but you can't just ignore things. Well, you can, but you shouldn't—I knew that part, too. It just galled me, okay, that he was standing there placidly, waiting for me to see reason. Said not quite graciously, "Well, I guess if you're going there anyway, I might as well let you drive."

"Yeah," he said. Didn't seem too surprised. Left me with a magazine he cadged from the desk guy, and went in to change. He said something to the guy on his way inside, with a nod back at me, and I'm sure it was along the lines of "she's flighty and rabid, let me know if she books." Christ on a stick. It *would* be a cold day before I came here again.

He wasn't long, ten minutes maybe. Jeans and a loose-fitting shirt. Set off his chest, but then, anything would've. Arms. Wasn't bothering to hide himself now, I guess. Took me down to his truck.

I'm not nervous around guys much. I've worked with too many, seen 'em passed out and drunk, seen 'em crying or smashing in walls. Leering. It's all how you handle it. Reilly was different. I couldn't tell what he was working or *when* he was working or precisely what it was he was wanting. Seemed content to be driving me home.

He had an '84 minitruck, rusting and beaten, which wasn't what I'd have expected. I'd have thought maybe a Bronco or Blazer, but a lot of the guys have a travel car, for mileage rather than drive. Keep the good one at home. Or sometimes they're car buffs, restoring and putting in power.

Not on a Toyota, though.

Nobody'd bother.

He was making sergeant's money, so it meant he had kids, was likely supporting the world. It also meant I was taking my life in my hands, but if we could make it through the twists on Coldwater Canyon, there was hope that I'd get home alive. The brakes had that thin screeching sound which indicates rotor replacement, supposing there was anything left by the time we got down. I figured Reilly'd need his concentration for driving, so I drummed aimlessly on the armrest and tried not to think, tried not to listen a lot to the engine.

"The clutch needs some work," he said.

The clutch, the transmission, the lifters, the valves.

"You much of a mechanic, Reilly?"

"Not much." He said it idly, so I guess it didn't bother him any. He was downshifting for the turn onto Coldwater with the engine balking and I had to find something else to dwell on before we got to the top of the hill. I was watching the mirror on my side, not obviously, I think, not compulsively, and there might have been something following us, a light Ford, I couldn't be sure. We'd be single-trailing it anyway up Coldwater, not many places to pass, and me, I would have gone less directly, taken an alternate route, but Reilly was driving. Couldn't outrun anyone in the Toyota anyway, I guess.

Should have taken the cab.

"When'd you leave the department?" he said.

It was small talk, nothing, taking my mind off. Civil of him, maybe, because maybe he'd noticed me sitting there tense in the seat. Minitrucks are small and he was taking up a lot of the room, wide shoulders, right elbow brushing whenever he shifted. I was up against the side of the door, not locked. Seat belt.

"Two and a half years."

He did the math. Nodded. Didn't ask anything else, for which I was grateful. It was getting dark outside, the sun finally setting, the little lights glowing like points on the dashboard. I worked nine years with Charlie. Managed almost half a year more.

Cops die. It's a fact of the job. You think that it never *will* happen, not to you, not to yours, couldn't, but you gear for it anyway, remind yourself, take those precautions, and every time you see a story in the newspaper, you read the accounts, you can't help it, every last little detail, but it's always someplace else, some *other* department. Somebody else's pain.

"No man is an island," but women are, have to be.

Islands with bridges.

Bridges to burn.

"Who do you know at the department?" Reilly said.

Startled me. We were almost to the top, to Mulholland.

"Yours?" I said stupidly, because he wouldn't mean mine. Collected myself. "Nobody now. I used to know one of your sergeants, Jack Williams, but that was a while ago." Reilly was nodding. Billy-Jack had gone to the feds, Springfield, or wherever—five years back? I couldn't remember. We'd worked some interagency Vice things.

"Anyone have a reason to know you?"

Meaning to phone me personally, to involve me. "Not that I'm aware of."

"You're sure?"

You can never be sure. "Yeah," I said.

He was nodding again, lapsing back into silence. Shifted fluidly to second. Left me alone the rest of the way down. I was watching the descent, the twists, the cutbacks, and he handled it well, kept the truck in the turns, which, considering the way it wanted to wander, was no easy thing. Made it *look* easy.

Damn guy could drive.

"What about Mike?" he said.

"What about him?"

I might have sounded too sharp. He was looking in the rearview mirror, casually checking, and the white Ford was still back there, a couple of cars, but then we were most of us aimed for the freeway, and once you're on Coldwater, it's the only way there.

"Who's *he* know?"

"I don't have any idea," I said.

He shot a glance at me sideways. And the problem was that he had a thing about Mike—I could feel it, could sense it. Pretty extreme for a guy who didn't know him. It occurred to me to wonder if Reilly'd always lived in Glendale, and why he was divorced. Not all of the women who've liked Mike have been single.

"I won't talk about him," I said. "I appreciate you giving me a ride home, but Mike's not the price."

He shrugged at me. "No price," he said calmly. "I was just wondering."

It was clever of him to have asked me while we were driving. A cab makes a natural sound booth, an intimate cell. And it was even more clever of him to back off, because we were still in that sound booth and now I felt guilty. Rude. Unnaturally suspicious.

Fortunately, I've learned to live with it.

"You have any friends, Reilly?"

He quirked me a smile, a very nice smile. "A couple," he said.

Not many. I leaned forward in the seat belt, fished around on the floor for my purse, for distraction. And it was a useless impulse, but I was praying to Something that Mike hadn't been stupid. There was no way he was mixed up in harassing Iranians, I knew that, I knew *him*—hell, he went through the Academy with me. But that didn't mean he ever saw past his feet. That didn't mean that if he knew you and you wanted him to hold a bag for you, he'd ask what was in it first. And there were cops involved. I was getting a really bad feeling, and the cop who was driving wasn't missing a thing.

"He have a key to your car?"

"Jesus."

"You signed the Stolen on it."

"Well, then, I can *unsign* it," I said. "You want to watch the road?"

He was silent, driving, and I was tired of being the goat.

"Nobody needs a *key* if they've got a slim-jim and a pair of pliers, Reilly. I'd have thought they'd have mentioned that to you somewhere in training."

He smiled at me again. Gentle, self-mocking. Mocking both of us, really.

"But I didn't believe them," he said.

# 6

I live in Burbank between the two freeways. It's an older house, owner-built in the guy's spare time, or as he got money, I think, set in a neighborhood of like-minded houses. They're small lots, but sufficient, particularly if you don't want to spend much time on the upkeep. We tend towards bushes on my street, lots of hedges, some trees. Slim patches of lawn.

It was full dark by the time we got there. We'd lost the Ford on the freeway—he'd gotten off at Tujunga, the interchange there, and I never saw him back on. Reilly had some notion of checking the house, I think—made that move of his shoulders as he pulled up and parked, was reaching forward to switch off the key, but I had my hand on the truck door, had it already open, my legs swinging out.

"Thanks a lot," I said. "I really appreciate it."

That lift of his eyebrow.

"You have someone in there?"

And I was tempted, really was, to say "Mike." Except I wasn't so sure about Reilly's sense of humor *or* his reason for asking, and I didn't want cops coming back in an hour with pieces of paper, searching the place. So I just smiled at him pointedly, shaking my head. "Nice try."

He was looking beyond me to the house. "You'll be all right?"

As if he were truly debating it. Things that go bump in the night. It was dark outside, harder to see, and the interior light hadn't come on in his truck. No lights at all in the house.

"I can manage," I said. "Thanks again for the ride." I levered myself up and out, and closed the door before he could say anything else. It's all pressure and mind games, you know. Vulnerabilities.

He waited until I was in the house, though, waited for lights to come on.

And I waited inside the front door, leaning against it, waiting to hear the transmission shifting, to know he was gone. He realized that finally, I think, put the truck into gear and moved off, but it was a long two minutes, listening for everything. For sound in the house or sound from outside. I had the Glock .45 from the hall in my hand.

No one was there.

The house was untouched.

I slipped through the rooms like a ghost, checking.

We have a large living room in the lower right corner, and then you have your choice of two narrow halls. The hall going towards the back of the house has the dining room immediately off to the right. The dining room has a connecting archway through the west wall into the kitchen, so you could shortcut that way if you wanted to, which is what we usually do. A few feet further up the hall, though, if you were to keep going, is the main kitchen doorway, also to the right. On the left side of the hall, the owner built three little rooms—don't ask me why. Too big to be closets, too small to be useful. We'd hung shelves in the one across the hall from the kitchen, made it a pantry. Squeezed a desk into the second and called it an office. Use the third one mostly for storage.

The hall ends in a back door and a porch we enclosed about five years ago. It's insulated, sort of, so it serves as a laundry room, with the washer and dryer off to the left and an old washtub/wringer Charlie'd found to the right. Also a freezer. Very picturesque. Lots of windows, hanging plants. We'd built a wooden deck out beyond it into the yard, so you have to cross the deck, go down three steps and over right to the driveway to get to the backyard garage. It's a separate building, old-time construction, wooden, side door and a window, a sink. Not really a two-car garage, more like one-and-a-half, and it mostly has tools in it now. Charlie's old Chevy truck. Odds and ends. Some of Mike's stuff.

To get to the bedroom side of the house, you'd go back to the living room and take the other narrow hall to your left. The first door down the hall is a very small den, the door on your right is a bathroom. The hall takes a sharp jog, sort of splits like a foreshortened "T," with the left end going into the front corner bedroom, just past the den. On the right side of the "T" split, turning towards the back of the house, the spare bedroom's on the left, and then straight ahead is the door to my bedroom. I have the suite. Bathroom, shower, walk-in closet. We'd talked about cutting through a door to the deck, maybe a slider so we could go in and out, but there's not really a spot for it. Have to go through the tub, which would be kind of awkward.

I searched everything, including the tubs, and there was nobody there.

It was dark out, pitch black, by the time I was done. Eight o'clock.

I found myself something to eat, some leftover pizza, and sat at the kitchen table to chew it. It's a big wooden table, solid, sturdy, and I don't use the dining room really to eat. Store stuff. Do the bills. Clean it up when there's company. Charlie and I never got very formal.

Tried to call Mike.

He's not perfect, okay? He has his notions, his half-baked ideas. You can never be sure when something will touch him, get him wrapped up and going, or when he'll be normal, sort of what you'd expect.

Weekends, for instance. *This* was a weekend. Weekends, Mike likes to be off. It doesn't bother me mostly, because he works hard and plays hard, and why the hell else would we own our own business if not to have control of our time? So he likes his weekends, and me, I've got nothing, so I put in the Saturdays alone when it's needed, doing books, or whatever, Miss Goody-Two-Shoes, unless something comes up.

Unless I get flamingly ticked off or something, like I'd been this past Friday.

Yesterday, in fact.

He'd had a long lunch and come back very scattered—yeah, yeah, he'd get to that, whatever, he'd said, it didn't much matter, or *I* could call the guy, maybe, later—and it was the one straw too many because he'd been like that all week. Half there and half gone, on some jig of his own.

So I'd pulled out the stops and I'd vented like crazy—this thing and that thing and ten other nothings—until he'd dammitall *promised* to come in today and help, at least sort his receipts, at least write down some numbers. I don't ask for much, but he's a partner, you know, it's not all just sales, it's not all just charming the pants off of people. And he'd had that look in his eye, that devil excitement, like he was already seeing his weekend.

"She can wait," I'd said snidely, "a couple of hours," and he'd flashed me that grin, that shame-faced "you got me."

"Sure, babe," he'd said, "I'll come in."

He hadn't, though.

And I'd expected he would. I mean, Mike and I get along pretty well. It's not that he hasn't forgotten before, and it's not that he'd do it to show me or anything, it's just—I don't know—that I'd thought he'd come in.

Had thought, when Haroutunian called, it was *him*. Saying, "Sorry, babe, I got hung up," or something, which was why I'd even answered the phone.

The damn private line.

Reilly hinting around, and seeing connections, seeing cops working. "*You'll be all right?*" And now my car missing.

I *really* wanted Mike to be home.

I tried calling his brother in Redlands, but no one was answering. Mike had bankrolled Sam into a house out there a few years ago, so he sort of has dibs on a bedroom. Sometimes, going in or out of Las Vegas, he'll stop for a quick change of clothes, and I'd been hoping to hear that Sammy had seen him. But Sam wasn't home, wasn't answering. He could be working or something, I didn't know. It was Saturday night, and he could be out, could easily be, dining and dancing. He has Michael's charm. It was possible, even, that Mike had stopped by and swept Sam out *with* him. They could both be quite happy in the middle of Vegas, and I had no way of knowing. Even calling hotels wouldn't do it, because there was nothing to say they weren't staying with friends or the chance-met acquaintance or had figured that Laughlin was better. Or Reno. Or skiing at Parker. Or the quick trip down Mexico-way.

I was tired. Spooking. Letting the sounds and the night and the company reach me. Mike didn't *have* to be anywhere. No one had come bothering me. It was Reilly getting my wind up, and he had his reasons—lots easier for him to push *me* to find Mike than to spend his man-hours looking himself. Frees up the forces, you know. Good police work in these budget-crunched times.

And it was for nothing.

Mike would roll in tomorrow, as he had fifty times, or he'd call me or something, and I was just wasting my night. It's at times like this that you want someone with you—not the damn cat, who was rubbing my leg off, and not all the ghosts, but a fleshed human being, some-one to talk to. Someone you know will talk back.

I tried Mike one last time, tried Sammy again, and then called it quits, tucked myself into bed. Beverly Hills would just have to wait.

They were patient.

They waited until eleven o'clock the next morning.

# 7

Sunday mornings, I like to sleep late, have a little breakfast, and putter around. I used to try to do church on Josh's weekends, but religion's more his mother's line. Caroline found God when He gave her directions to the freeway a few years after she and Charlie split up, and although I haven't noticed her going to church much on Sundays either, she does seem to feel that *she's* got the direct line to the Lord. Certainly there were a lot of anguished prayers after Charlie died and she discovered that Josh didn't inherit everything we had. I worked out a deal through my lawyer to continue paying child support as long as I got visitation rights— which wasn't quite what the Lord had in mind, apparently, but which He eventually counseled her to take. Josh mostly comes over every other weekend, and we usually do breakfast out instead of church. He's twelve now, almost thirteen.

Since this was an off weekend, I wasn't doing much when the doorbell rang. It was Reilly, larger than life.

"They found your car."

No "Hello, how are you?" Not much of anything, in fact. It wasn't that he'd been so open last night, but he was definitely impassive this morning. I couldn't read him at all.

"Where?"

"Point Fermin."

That's down the coast from LA. It's a small town on the ocean, sort of run-down and private, so it's a haven for drug dealers. It's not where I'd have thought they'd find my car. East LA or a Beverly Hills parking lot maybe, but not down the coast.

"There's a hold on it," Reilly said.

I looked beyond him, and there was an unmarked unit parked at my curb with a driver.

Escobar.

I looked back at Reilly. No one in uniform.

"Why don't you tell me about it."

"I was hoping that we could do this back at the station. There are a couple of things that we should discuss."

All very formal.

"I went to the station yesterday, Reilly. I don't feel any need to go there again."

"There was blood in the car," he said.

Maybe I *did* feel a need.

"Human?"

"Seems like."

"I'll get my things."

"I'll want to come in," he said.

He could come in—I had nothing to hide. Well, not very much.

"Yeah, sure," I said. Stepped back and he was moving in, filling the doorframe. Overwhelmingly large. "I'm going to call a friend of mine," I said very carefully, "my lawyer, okay? Just to have him on tap."

"You can call from the station."

"I'm going to call now," I said. "It's nothing personal, Reilly, but I want someone I trust to know where I'm going."

His eyes thought about it, what it meant and how much trouble it was worth to him, before he nodded.

"All right."

I eased half a trifle. Kept an eye on him while I went down the hall to the kitchen. He was following me closely, looking around. Noticing everything probably—seemed to be, anyway. One cup of coffee. The one empty plate, scattered crumbs, the spread-open newspaper. Only me, Sergeant Reilly, here all alone.

Louis' home number was in my address book, but, of course, it was Sunday. I got his answering machine and filled it in, telling it the time I was calling and why, stressing the fact that I'd already talked Saturday to Abbott and Reilly. Spelled out both names. Added Escobar for good measure. Told him to call Beverly PD if he couldn't reach me by the time he got home. Then I pushed down the tone button, didn't hang up the receiver.

"You want me to try Mike?"

Reilly very steady.

"Yeah."

Watched me dial the number. Nobody home. I'd been hoping, I guess. Felt very alone.

"I'm not riding in with you," I said. "I'm taking my truck, and you and the bandit can follow me."

"All right," he said peaceably as if it didn't much matter. Seemed a tad easier around the edges, as though he'd thought I was something and maybe I wasn't. Me proving out. Or he might have been playing me again, I don't know.

I found the keys to the truck in the bottom of the sock drawer. Hadn't driven it since Mike and I went to the desert last year, so it'd be my luck if it was out of gas or the engine wouldn't turn over. It was Charlie's rattletrap, big-block '62 Chevy—it seeped oil and transmission fluid and it drank gas like water, but there was nothing it couldn't tow. I'd kept it because it was Charlie's and I'd figured that maybe in a couple of years Josh would like to have it. Always supposing he could pass a driver's test by then.

Reilly'd followed me, of course, into the bedroom. No way around it. He didn't touch anything or comment, just stood in the doorway, looking. I didn't waste any time pulling my stuff together, though. I was already wearing jeans, which was good enough for Beverly PD, and I sure as hell wasn't planning to change. Grabbed my bag and the keys, and brushed past Reilly out the door.

He waited coolly while I locked up, and then strolled along behind me to the garage, waving Escobar back to the car. Escobar'd been by the sidewalk, kind of ready. I don't think I look particularly dangerous these days, so it was either that he was practicing or the car thing was bad. Special Tac guys *do* tend to practice a lot—the cowboy mentality and the type of work that they do. Always prepared.

I just wished that I knew about the car.

I got the garage door unlocked, the Chevy's door open, turned the key. It ground a few times, and then the motor caught, thank you, Lord.

"We'll follow you over the hill."

They could do that.

"Coldwater Canyon?" I said.

He was looking at the Chevy, one eyebrow half up.

"You think it'll make it?"

And for a second, just there, we were back and connected. Shades of last night coming down in his truck.

"Reilly—"

He closed. No other word for it. Closed tightly against me.

The car thing was bad, very bad.

# 8

It was quiet in the Detective Bureau, up on the third floor, not a lot happening, and I was feeling pretty restless. I'd been left unattended for about twenty minutes. The technique is called "Keep 'Em Waiting," and though I appreciate the psychology involved, I don't like being on the receiving end.

Reilly had a pile of papers in his hand, was on the phone at the other end of the room in one of the cubicles, not saying much. Taking notes, as far as I could tell. I'd already gotten up twice and paced, stared at the framed cartoon in Abbott's office through the big glass window. Felt like a kid in a store. You have to behave, but you don't have to like it.

I don't know where Escobar'd gone. He'd vanished about two minutes into it, said something to Reilly. We'd been clustered at one of the desks at the far end of the Bureau—not in an interview room, not buffered away. There wasn't anybody up there, but still, I didn't expect it. And then he'd reappeared, gotten Reilly to the phone, handed him files or papers or something, and was gone again somewhere. All very polite, "excuse us, this'll just take a minute," and I knew they had other things working, okay?—but what I *didn't* know was if any of this was legit, catch a witness while you can, it being Sunday, the best time to find people, or if this was all being done just for me.

Or a little of both, watch her stew.

I'd been stewing since we left the house. Since before. Since yesterday, probably, a nice easy simmer.

Controlled burn.

"I'm sorry." It was Reilly, looking austere. The man had cat feet, had come up behind me.

"Are we going to do this?" I said.

"Yeah."

It helps me to pace, not to feel so confined, so I kept on moving to Abbott's office, the glass window, the lieutenant's-eye view of the room. Returned.

"Who starts?"

"I will," he said. "You want to sit down?"

Twenty minutes too long. "No."

*He* sat. Lowered himself to the desktop so we were still at a height. Eye to eye almost, me standing.

"LAPD found your car at Point Fermin," he said. "Last night."

"What about the blood?"

"You don't want to know when?"

I guess, really, I did.

"Eight-thirty," he said.

So? Eight-thirty meant nothing, because at seven forty-five, he'd been dropping me home. I couldn't have made it from there down the coast if he was thinking I was some way involved. I didn't bother to hide the expression, and his own didn't change.

"You talk to your partner last night?"

To Mike.

"No," I said.

"Yeah?"

He didn't believe me. My phone had been busy, but I couldn't think how he'd know it.

"I tried to call him a couple of times," I said, "but he wasn't home."

"That didn't worry you?"

It might have, a little. I stretched nonchalantly, gave him a shrug.

"I wouldn't even have bothered," I said almost truthfully, "if this thing hadn't come with his name. Mike *lives* on his weekends, goes where he wants. I told you already."

"Does he have a key?"

I wasn't following him. "To what? To my car?"

Reilly's eyes lidding down. "Yeah," he said, but there'd been half a second.

"No."

"You're sure?"

Mike could have gotten my spare from the office. It's not what I should have been thinking, so I'd already been around this sergeant too long. "Yeah, I'm sure," I said.

And Reilly was sitting way back on the desk there, looking quite gentle.

"Does he have a key to your *house*, Meg?"

The working cop mind.

"No," I said.

"You have a key to his?"

"No." That wasn't strictly true because I knew where to get one, but it wasn't on me, and it wasn't his business.

"You want to tell me about the Porsche?" *Mike's* Porsche, and the way he was jumping, all over the place, I was feeling too wary.

"What about it?" I said.

"How long's he had it?"

"A couple of months."

"Six?"

Reilly'd been looking it up. "About that," I said.

"He pay cash for it, Meg?"

There was a joke. Nobody in our league has the cash for a 911 Carrera.

"DMV doesn't show a legal owner," Reilly said.

I stared at him while I tried to think. "No legal owner" meant Mike was the owner of record. No credit union. No finance company.

"DMV doesn't always get things right," I said. "Or maybe he paid it off already."

"In six months?" That skeptical eyebrow. "Business that good?"

Hardly.

"We're doing okay."

"You're not driving a BMW."

"Neither are you," I said, rather pointedly, "but then, Mike doesn't have an ex-wife keeping him poor."

He hunkered back some, considering me.

"Yeah, that's true," he said equitably. "I sometimes take side jobs to make up the check."

I probably was frozen.

"Yeah," I said somehow. "A lot of cops do."

"Ex-cops, too," he said. He was looking past me down the Bureau at someone approaching, but that peripheral vision's a killer, you know, and I'd say Reilly had it in spades. "I don't know if it's worth it," he said very casually. "You've got to declare it, pay the taxes and everything."

He didn't have to draw me a map. Undeclared moneys paying for Porsches, and the IRS coming around with a searchlight. Us doing stuff we weren't quite legal for.

"Yeah, it's a pain," I said. Turned to look. It was Escobar, almost dancing. Filled with an inner excitement.

"Sorry," he said cheerfully, "got a line on that doper. You just about done here?"

"Just about," Reilly said.

*I* was done, certainly. Crisped to a fare-thee-well. Burned.

"You want to tell me about the blood, Reilly?"

"Oh, we don't know about that yet," he said very blandly. "LAPD's lab is still working on it. It'll probably be a couple of days."

It probably would be.

"A *lot* of blood?" I said, as opposed to "some smears."

"Yeah."

"But no body," I said.

He was regarding me gravely.

"No."

Of course there was no body. If there'd been a body, I'd have been talking to Homicide, not hustled in here to be STU-toyed-with. He could have asked me all this at the house. I took maybe a breath.

"You know where they're holding my car?"

"Why?"

"I have to notify the insurance company." It sounded okay for a reason. Reilly didn't *have* to tell me, but it wasn't exactly vital information. It's not as if I could steal the car from the tow yard. He must have been deciding the same thing.

"It's at the San Pedro tow yard. Eighth and Main."

"Thanks."

He was thinking something.

"I'll walk you out," he said slowly. "I've got to go do this thing with Ray and I don't know how long it'll be."

As if he wanted to keep me. Probably did. To keep chipping away.

"Yeah, okay," I said. Through the lobby again. Shades of yesterday. He was standing up, waiting for me, and I don't know how I kept forgetting that he was so big. Deceptive, I guess. Something he used. I smiled nicely at Ray and he grinned back at me broadly. *Liked* bad girls, you know, and he figured I was one.

Maybe I was.

"Come on," Reilly said.

We were almost to the stairs when I thought of something else. "Was the car locked when they found it, Reilly?"

"Why?"

I didn't have any trouble looking impatient. "Because if they had to break a window or something, I'll have to get it fixed before I can drive it, and I'd like to start setting things up. I'm assuming they'll release it to me pretty soon."

"Yeah, a couple of days." He hesitated. "Everything was locked," he said at last. "The field sergeant got in with a jimmy."

It was what I wanted to know. I had a careful thief, someone who locked doors behind him. Habit? Or just didn't want anyone stealing the car before it was found.

And he was somebody fairly careless with blood—or else he wasn't careless at all. There were a lot of possibilities and I didn't like most of the ones that were occurring to me.

I stopped at the top of the stairs and looked up at Reilly.

"Anybody seen Haroutunian lately?"

There was a perceptible pause.

"He doesn't seem to be home," Reilly said.

# 9

I hit more traffic than I would have expected going south on the 405 freeway. I was going south on the 405 because I had to do *something* and there was no way in hell I could go snooping around Haroutunian's. Not with Reilly already looking in that direction. Not when I had no business being there.

Haroutunian didn't *have* to be missing, of course, any more than Mike was. He could be out for the day, off on a trip. Having Sunday brunch with his family and friends so he could tell them all about the excitement I'd given him yesterday. Lots of things. And he was a solid citizen. Moneyed. Beverly PD wasn't going to stir up a rat's nest just because he wasn't home when they called. But they'd be keeping more than an eye out for him to get back, and they'd be checking pretty heavily into Mike and me in the meantime, just in case. They'd already started. That's why they'd brought me in this morning.

So that's why this afternoon I'd wasted a lot more time trying to find Mike. I'd called just about everyone I could think of, starting with Sammy. He was finally home, but Mike wasn't there, and I couldn't bring myself to say that he might be in trouble. "Have him call me,"

I'd said, "with his damn lost weekends," and Sammy had laughed. I know them both pretty well.

I'd gone through the list of other friends and old girlfriends. Nothing and no one who knew where he was. There was one guy who'd thought Mike was hunting because of something he'd said at a party last weekend, but he couldn't pin it down and I didn't think it was anything. Maybe I was wrong.

I didn't call anyone from the department. Maybe I was wrong about that, too. It's that I kept thinking about the eyebrows and the rumor mill and the likelihood that Mike would be back safe and sound tomorrow and embarrassed as hell that I'd started something. I wouldn't appreciate it if I were him. Can't even go away for the weekend. Anyway, I didn't call them.

So I'd drawn a blank everywhere, and it was stupid and probably a major waste of time, but I was driving down the coast. Give Mike time to get home. Give me something to do. Give my mind something to work on besides where the hell he was and fifty million other questions, like this business about the Porsche. It just hadn't come up, how he'd paid for it, I'd never even thought about it. I mean, he'd been busy showing the thing off, its trick turbo and the gear ratios, and I'd figured he'd financed it, leased it, whatever—a bravura gesture because work had been slow. We weren't hurting, you understand. We were chugging along nicely on the fees from the earlier accounts, but we weren't raking in the kind of new cash that would pay for a 911. Certainly not out of pocket, no matter what savings plans he had going, and Mike isn't all that big on rainy days.

I wished I could think of a reason for Reilly to have

lied about it, but he couldn't have been sure I wouldn't check. And he couldn't have been sure I wouldn't have already known all about it because maybe I'd co-signed the damn thing, which would have blown his bluff right out of the water.

Unless he'd been fishing.

Trying to see what I knew about Mike's affairs, how involved I was. And it was kind of a safe bluff, now that I thought about it, because I wasn't likely to ask any of our old friends from the department to run a make on Mike, not when they all knew him, too. Maybe I had somebody else I could call, but it would still be awkward to check on my partner. And what was the downside for him if I *did* find out? "Oh, sorry, guess I made a mistake" while Abbott sat in his lieutenant's chair and smiled.

Did I think Reilly was capable of that?

Yes, I did, I certainly did.

Did I think Mike could have bought out his car?

Six months ago, I would have said no.

And *that* was what was propelling me down the coast, that nagging disloyalty, that uncertain feeling. "*Side jobs*," Reilly'd said, as if maybe he knew. "*Ex-cops, too.*" Mike and his "hey, man, you have any problems, you give me a call."

So I was chasing my doubts to San Pedro, looking for truth on a Sunday afternoon. Maybe I'd find it at Eighth and Main. I didn't think Reilly would have bothered to call them about me—tow companies generally have strict procedures regarding access to cars, and it was a whole jurisdiction away. But tow yards get awfully busy on weekends. No one would let me near the Subaru, of course, but someone might tell me where it'd been found.

It was maybe an hour to San Pedro, and what I noticed most was the traffic. Even for a Sunday, there seemed to be a lot. Lots of people coming and going. Buses. Taxis. I turned off on the 110 and took it on down.

The tow yard was a massive junker place, full of smashed auto bodies waiting to be reclaimed. I could see my Subaru sitting behind the barbed-wire fence of the Impound section as I drove up. I parked on the street and walked over to the main shed. It wasn't a hotbed of activity. One old man was nodding over the counter with its telephones, but otherwise the place was empty, the wreckers and their crews out on calls. Maybe this was better. I tried to tamp down my rising lucky feeling.

"Excuse me," I said, and brought the old man to life. I flashed him an apologetic smile and looked distract-edly around. Harmless Little Woman #6. Charlie would have had a heart attack, but then he knew me pretty well. "I'm sorry to bother you . . ." I let my voice trail off, rousing fatherly instincts or something similar.

"What can I do for you, honey?" A sweet man.

"Well, they told me my car was here, and I . . . that is, do I just pick it up?"

"You gotta have a form," he said promptly. "Didn't they give you a form?" He was already reaching for a clipboard on the wall next to him.

"Oh, no," I said. "The officer didn't say anything about that when he called."

He shook his head over police department ways and

put the clipboard back. Nothing about bureaucracy surprised him, I guess—he'd been around long enough to have seen it all. "It's policy, though. Can't give you the car without you givin' me the form."

"Oh, I didn't expect you to do that. I just . . . *why* didn't the officer tell me? I probably wasted the whole trip down, then."

Yep. He guessed I'd have to come back on Monday when the regular guys were there. That was the trouble with young kids filling in on the weekends, they just didn't know what they were doing.

Well, yes, the officer *did* sound kind of young, I thought. I hadn't really gotten his name, though—Corski, maybe, or Barnes?

The old man was more knowledgeable than I. "That'd be Borchard. Damn, you'd think *he'd* have it straight."

"Well, I don't want to get anyone in trouble or anything. He was in kind of a hurry and maybe I didn't get it right. This whole thing has just been a nightmare. Oh," I smiled at him ruefully, "you must hear that all the time."

He was puffing and blowing a little, and I could almost feel Charlie behind me, rolling his eyes. If there was one thing that Charlie'd hated, it was that I could come in and "do the pretty" and get away with it. Jealousy, I'd always said. Just because *he* couldn't do it.

Meanwhile, the yard man was assuring me that yes, he'd heard just about everything a body could say. Seen most of it, too—why, I wouldn't believe some of the wrecks they'd dragged in here.

I let myself look a little bit anxious. "Oh, Officer

Borchard didn't say anything about my car being wrecked."

"Well, now, which one is it?"

"It's the silver Subaru. He told me they found it last night."

Frowning and pursing his lips. "That one? You won't be getting that one out tomorrow, no sir."

"*Is* it damaged?" I tried to look as if I were reckoning the deductible and it would break me.

"Well, not damaged, not exactly." He leaned across the counter and lowered his voice. "Blood. Homicide."

"Blood?!" I was shocked. Appalled. "*My* car?"

"Yep." Slapped the folder next to him. "Got the report right here."

"Are you sure there hasn't been a mistake? Because Officer Borchard never said a word about this." It was a calculated risk, but he took the bait.

"No mistake." He opened the folder and flipped pages until he came to the one we wanted. "Says right here, 'Homicide.' "

"Oh, my God." I turned the book sideways and talked feverishly while I scanned the page. It was just the recovery sheet, the CHP 180 with none of the gory details, but across the front was stamped IMPOUND— HOMICIDE INVESTIGATION and it had the only information I wanted—the street where they'd found my car. I was memorizing the address even as I babbled at the old man. "Homicide—oh, my God—and you said 'blood.' There's blood in the car? What am I going to do? Are there bullet holes? Oh, my God."

No, he was a little regretful, but he didn't think there were any bullet holes. It was locked up tighter than a drum, but he'd have heard about slugs. Blood all over the back seat, though—puddles of it, pools. The cops had been telling him. I looked properly impressed, asked how long he'd been working there. A long time, it seemed. I let him reminisce while I thought.

No bullet holes, no body, presumably no weapon yet, because Reilly hadn't asked me about any of mine. Blood, though. Definitely blood. Puddles of it. Pools. Driven down from Beverly Hills? Or had someone shot a dealer here in Point Fermin and left him in the back seat for a while?

It didn't have to be just Beverly Hills or here, of course. They could have driven to Watts or Inglewood or anyplace else in the LA basin to shoot someone before driving him over to Point Fermin. Or been shot themselves and driven home before somebody else dumped the car. I wished the hell I knew how long the 'Ru had been sitting there, or that I regularly checked my mileage.

The phone rang like the Trump of Doom or the school's-out bell. It broke the yard man in mid-stride about a homicide from the sixties and gave me my release. I thanked him quickly and promised to call the detectives before I made the trip down again.

"No point in wastin' your time, y'know," he said, and then to the insistent phone, "I'm comin', I'm comin'" as he turned to pick it up. I skated out the front door. Behind me, I could hear him telling someone he didn't have a wrecker he could send until later, and then I was clear.

It took me six minutes to get to Paseo del Mar and find the cross-street from the report. It was fairly isolated, right on the cliffs, so it was a good area for people dumping things. A few houses on the land side of the street were boarded up. The others looked desolate, shuttered. Uninterested in me. People tend not to notice what's going on around them when they've lived somewhere a while or have a reason to mind their own business. I'd guess the few residents here were used to cars driving by, cruising. Hard to tell whether it'd be young lovers or a drug dealer scoring and you wouldn't wander up to a parked car to find out. Not if you had any sense.

I stopped on the ocean side and got out. You could still see the tire marks from the police activity last night. With any kind of luck, they wouldn't have obscured everything, but then I wasn't really here for luck. I didn't expect to find anything. Homicide teams are pretty thorough and they'd had the time to do what they needed, so we could rule out the gun in the bushes or the small scrap of shirt cloth leading to the body below. In fact, I'd better *not* find a gun in the bushes because there was nobody who'd believe that I hadn't just placed it there. "And what were you doing at Point Fermin, Ms. Gillis?" "Just felt an urge, your Honor. That female intuition they rode me about on the force."

Right.

So I sat on a rock at Paseo del Mar and looked down the several hundred feet to the ocean where it swirled at the foot of the cliffs. A long drop. At this particular point, a clean drop. Not much below to snag a small scrap of shirt cloth if you were strong enough and could hold a body out far enough before heaving it over. I didn't know *whose* body, of course, or how heavy, but you'd still need considerable strength to hold something out like that and chuck it.

You'd also need to know that this place was here. Not many people with a body in Beverly Hills would drive down the coast looking for a convenient chucking place. Not when there are trash bins every fifty feet. Not when you could just head up Mulholland.

So we had somebody with upper-body strength who knew the area, who'd made a point of leaving my car bloodied and locked where a body could have been tossed into the ocean.

And because it was bothering me, I took a thought out and looked at it in the daylight, on the edge of the Pacific Ocean in the warm California sun. I thought about Mike, whom I've known for thirteen years, who got me through some of the roughest days I've ever faced. Mike, who before he entered the Academy and my life, was a boy in Long Beach, just five miles down the coast. My friend Mike, who works out regularly and is proud of his strength, who takes foolish risks because they're there, who six months ago went out and bought a Porsche with money I didn't think he had.

Sell-out? Or set-up? I knew what Reilly thought. He was taking the pieces and making the puzzle fit. That's what police work is all about. Most of the time, it's the simple answer, the straightforward connection. If you hear a dog barking, you don't look for a cat.

But I knew Mike.

And I'd heard dogs barking before.

What it came down to, very simply for me, was whether I could picture my friend Mike in a jam that would have him heaving a body off this cliff. And the answer, the simple answer, was no. It didn't matter whose body, and it didn't matter how heavy, because no,

Mike would never have done that. Simply, straightforwardly, unequivocally no.

People are always saying, "I never thought he could do that—he was such a good neighbor," "a quiet boy," "an honors student," "a regular guy"—and he's the one over the freeway shooting at cars, or abusing young kids, or chopping his wife. But *somebody* knew. *Had* to have known. Known the potential, anyway. Known he got ugly when he drank or he free-based or he snorted cocaine. Just didn't want to say, didn't want to be interfering, didn't want him to leave if a little more love made it right.

Love doesn't make things right. It never does.

Anyway, that put it straight for me. Reilly and Company could keep collecting pieces but I wasn't going to help assemble them. When it came to sell-out or set-up, I was putting my money on someone constructing a frame. Reilly had all but admitted that he had a dirty worm in his apple there at Beverly Hills, and the way I figured it, the worm had gotten wind of Reilly investigating or had just plain gotten the wind up, and thought he'd throw Reilly off the track by throwing him me. Us. Mike and me. Mike, anyway, because the call came in for him.

And there I was sitting in the damn California sun, when that thought came up and hit me like a wave of relief, like a blessing, unexpected and cheering. I hadn't known I was worried—Reilly hinting, Mike missing, and me just so blind, refusing to see. But *that* was the answer. The *call* was the answer. *Because whoever had set this thing up was expecting Mike to be at the office on Saturday.* We hadn't arranged that weeks in advance, it was a last-minute thing, me throwing him my grand "the least you can do is come in and help" speech Friday afternoon, kind of late. So it had to be somebody Mike had been talking to Friday *night*, which meant he'd be able to remember who it was—and come tomorrow, this would pretty much be over.

And the *best* part, the good part really, and I never thought I'd be saying it, was that Mike in his inimitable way had totally messed up this frame.

Because whoever had planned this hadn't expected any more than I had that Mike would forget me and head out for the weekend. Mike was supposed to be there, Mike was supposed to answer, Mike was supposed to head into the trap. Only he *wasn't* there—they caught *me* instead—and then the frame didn't fit.

Reilly might have brought Mike in, but he'd never have offered him a ride home. So Mike wouldn't have had an alibi for last night, not like the one *I* had, unimpeachable. And Reilly wouldn't have been giving Mike any of that "knew your husband," "benefit of the doubt" stuff if the blood had been found in his Porsche instead of my Subaru. He was already prejudiced against Mike, for whatever reason, so Mike would have had a lot of explaining to do, which Mike doesn't always do well. I can smile and overlook with the best of them if I have to, but you start impugning Mike's honor and he gets a little touchy. Men are like that.

So by virtue of Mike's just being Mike—irresponsible, careless—he'd planted a major spike in what looked to be as tight a set-up as I'd ever seen. I *hoped* he had, anyway. Surely did hope so.

I needed to get home, needed to find out if Mike was

back so I could check all this out. I wondered briefly where they'd gotten the blood. Because there wasn't a *body*, you know. Just blood, puddles of it, pools, the guy'd said. A hospital, maybe, or a lab. Any clinic. You could bribe a disposal service, hell, flash the badge: "we need this for evidence, keep your mouth shut and we won't bring you into it." Someone who'd steal a car parked across from the police station wouldn't draw the line at scattering tainted blood. I hoped LAPD's lab was being careful about AIDS.

I took a last quick look around the area, trying to picture it at night. Not a place I'd choose for a date, but then I'm not romantic. Give me those old creature comforts every time.

I climbed into the truck and cranked it over.

It's a couple of miles back to the heart of San Pedro. You could walk it easily if you couldn't hitch a ride, and from there you could go all kinds of places. Bus service looked to be good between here and LA. Or you could get a limo to LAX, and from there fly to Frisco or Vegas, or catch another limousine to an uptown hotel as if you'd just gotten off of a plane. If memory served me, there was even a van that would drop you at the Beverly Wilshire Hotel. That was always supposing you didn't have an accomplice waiting down the road to give you a lift. There were too many possibilities and I wasn't a police force. What was I going to ask anyway? "Did you pick somebody up at the airport last night?" "Anyone get on your bus in San Pedro?"

"Yeah, right," Charlie's ghost said over my shoulder, and it was time to be getting on home.

# 10

The phone was ringing when I got in, but it was Louis, my lawyer, wanting to know what was going on. I filled him in as best I could, leaving out most of the guess-work, but telling him about my trip to San Pedro. He wasn't thrilled.

"So that's 'false pretenses' and 'obstructing justice' and whatever else they feel like filing."

"I didn't obstruct anything, Louis. And it wasn't 'false pretenses'—I am the owner of the car, I didn't lie to the man about that. Didn't try to take it, or bribe him, or anything else. Just asked a few questions, got a few answers, that's all."

"Do you know where Mike is?"

"No." I hesitated, but Louis is my lawyer and a friend for quite a while. "He was a little pumped up on Friday."

"Is he mixed up in this?"

The million-dollar question. "No," I said, because there was no way Mike could be, there was just no way.

Louis huffed for a moment, which usually means he's thinking things he doesn't want to tell me. "I'm not a criminal lawyer, Meg. Pesconi's moved on, but I've got someone else who could handle this if you need it."

I knew what he was offering, and why. Louis is another part of my life. "Mike'll clear it up tomorrow, Louis. Thanks, though."

He said a few civil things before he hung up. I dialed Mike's number and let it ring. Not home or not answering. It was five thirty-five.

Same story at six, seven, and eight. Also at nine-thirty. There was no law that said he had to get in early on a Sunday night, and no guarantee that he'd end up at *his* place rather than the girl's. I was just very edgy. The cat was staying out of my way, and I'd straightened every room in the house. Finally, at eleven, I went to bed. Mike still wasn't home.

By the time I got to the office next morning, I was really out of sorts. No Mike, though I'd tried him three times. The phone rang while I was in the shower and I almost broke my neck getting it, but it was someone wanting Monica. He didn't have an Iranian accent, but I made a note of the call anyway.

I drove by Mike's place on the way in, same as I'd gone by there yesterday, but the 911 still wasn't in his parking spot, so he either hadn't made it back yet or he'd already been and gone. The odds were best that he was just waking up somewhere else. I went on to the office anyway in the hope that he'd breeze in from wherever he'd been staying and we could talk before Reilly hit the door. Reilly struck me as the punctual type. Mike wasn't. Meanwhile, I busied myself turning on the coffee-maker and getting the messages off the machine. The third one was Mike.

*"Yeah, babe, it's me—where the hell have you been? I'm tired of dialing your damn number."* His voice was thin, strained, not

like Mike at all. "*Look, I'm not going to make it tomorrow—something's come up and I've got to check it out.*" There was a little pause, a click. "*If anyone comes looking for me, just tell 'em I'll be back in a couple of days, okay? And, um*"—his voice hesitated—"*you be careful.*"

It took me a moment to remember to breathe. I hit the playback button and listened three, four more times. Mike's voice, uncharacteristically tense. I couldn't have told you what I was looking for—background noise, someone else breathing, a threat. There was nothing. Just his voice. Just the message.

Mike hates answering machines. He'll call back twenty times before he'll talk to one. I'd had to fight with him about installing this one on the main line because I couldn't see paying an answering service every month for the calls.

And here I had a message, on that machine, from him.

I took his words apart, strung them back together, looking for something, anything. Nothing. Just his voice, torn, anxious, troubled, with a note I hadn't heard for a long time, had never wanted to hear again.

And what the hell was I going to tell Reilly when he came tapping at the office door?

I stared at my coffee cup for a long time, but no answers came.

Reilly didn't knock, just swung the door open, expecting a reception room, I guess. He wasn't surprised to see me, but he would have noticed the truck outside. There was a weasely-looking little man with him, both of them plainclothes. Casual.

"Good morning," Reilly said.

No inspiration had come in with them, only the cold knowledge that I couldn't withhold the tape. I didn't even say hello, just leaned over and punched the playback button one more time. I didn't look at either of them while I went to get more coffee. Reilly had the grace to keep his mouth shut.

The little man had his pad out, taking notes, but this was Reilly's deal. He still hadn't said anything when the tape was over, so I punched it off.

"You guys want coffee?"

Black for Reilly, none for the little man. He looked the herb-tea type to me, but we didn't have any, so I didn't offer. We waited for Reilly to speak. He was sitting back in one of the reception chairs, contemplating the steam rising from the cup in his hands, both hands holding, very peaceful, slow, and I didn't trust it for a second. Finally he looked at me.

"That was your partner?"

He knew it was. He had to get it, though, have me say it. "Yeah."

"Know where he was calling from?"

"No."

He nodded thoughtfully. "Heard from him otherwise?"

"No."

"Any idea what he's talking about?"

"If anyone comes looking," Mike had said, but did he mean Reilly? The little man was kind of intent from the other side of Mike's desk. "No," I said.

Reilly took a reflective sip from his cup. Well, I was all but killing the conversation. The little man started to say something and Reilly shut him up with a look. No flies on Reilly.

"Meg," he said gently, "you know we're going to have to call around on him. It'd make it easier if you'd cooperate."

I knew that. I'd known it since I'd first heard Mike's voice on the tape. It's just that "cooperate" sounds so much like "collaborate" and I couldn't get the Judas-taste out of my mouth. "I've already called almost everybody, Reilly. I don't think you'll get any farther than I did."

"Probably not as far." His smile was small but genuine. "Nobody knew anything?"

Everybody knows *something*. "Mostly they were surprised I was looking for him."

"No idea where he was, though?"

One guy thought he'd gone hunting.

It hit me then, the thing that had been bothering me about Mike's call, the reason I'd been listening for anything wrong. I knew I was staring at Reilly, but I couldn't see him, I was seeing a pool of blood in the back of my car and Mike's face on Friday. I guess I was standing, I don't really remember moving, but I was sure enough up against the wall behind me and the little man was half out of his chair in alarm.

"What was the blood type?"

They'd have it by now, surely they'd have it.

Reilly was just sitting there watching me, not edging a muscle.

"*Tell* me," I said.

He didn't have to, you know. Something flickered behind his eyes and then,

"O positive," he said coolly.

Half the world has that type, including Mike. It proved nothing, disproved nothing. This whole damned thing was a coil, snarled in on itself, and I didn't know where it had started or what it concerned. Mike, though. Me and mine. Reilly was watching me like a man with a snake, and the hell of it was I could almost trust him. But there were cops involved, he'd said as much himself, and he was a clever man, clever enough to tell me that. I was starting to think again. If we were being set up, it wasn't by an amateur, and there was no question that Reilly was a pro.

He and Abbott.

Double-teaming.

I had to have time. Focused on the little man. "I don't know you," I said.

He was taken aback, his face twisted like a walnut, wary. "Mitch Harris," he said too quickly. "Mitch the Snitch," I bet they called him.

"You're with STU?"

"Well . . . yes." He was half glancing at Reilly, not sure he should have told me. Reilly was impassive.

Two STU men. Nobody from Homicide. I sat back down a little closer to my purse and shrugged at them ruefully, at my foolishness, leaping around like an idiot. Tried to smile. Reilly looking right at me and the smile slipping. Too rusty. "I'm sorry," I said. "I don't mean to be jumping. This whole thing just has me spooked."

"You had a shock," Reilly said. "Apparently. What was it?"

"It's nothing," I said. "Somebody told me they thought he'd gone hunting, and I had this flash suddenly, an accident, but it doesn't explain how the blood got into my car. I wasn't thinking it through."

"Mitch," Reilly said quietly, "would you wait outside?"

He had instincts like a goddamn bat and I couldn't afford to be one-on-one with him. "That's okay," I said. "I'm all right now."

Reilly wasn't listening. "Mitch?"

Mitch gathered himself up fairly quickly and paused by Reilly's chair, said something low. Reilly nodded without taking his eyes off me, and then Mitch was gone, out the door, and it was just the two of us, across the desk. Reilly was right-handed, holding his cup that way, and I maybe moved some to face him, swung the back of my swivel chair left, stretched my legs sort of more to the side. No reason to sit with them trapped underneath me.

He was observing me, each little movement. Makes you very self-conscious.

"You going to tell me?" he said.

I took kind of a breath. He really was *big*, occupying the chair. Three feet away from me, over the desk. "Yeah, sure," I said. "I can give you a list of the people I called, their numbers and everything."

"That would be helpful."

I try to be, sometimes.

He leaned in to put his cup on the edge of my desk, to free up his hands, I guess, for the notes, and I don't think I moved, didn't shove back or anything, but *something* caught him, got his attention. He leaned in more deliberately, an extra inch, testing, and then, yeah, I readied, couldn't help it, just that little bit set, but he was easing fluidly out again, resettling, stretching his shoulders, his neck. Looking peaceful.

Cowlike.

As if something had cleared.

"I talked to some of your people yesterday," he said

casually while he fished out a notebook, a pen, from his left shirt pocket under his windbreaker. "They're mostly of the opinion that if you're involved in something, it's because of Mike."

He'd called my department. I'd known he would, of course, but he hadn't wasted any time about it. I wished I knew who all he'd been talking to. People who knew me, or people who knew me *well*.

"I'm not involved in anything, Reilly."

He was watching me, gauging. It was my own stupid fault because I never should have talked to him in the first place. As far back as Saturday, I shouldn't have. Now he had a standard to measure me by.

"You want to give me that list?" he said.

I gave it to him. Didn't have all the phone numbers, not with me, but it wasn't about names and numbers, you know, it was about me cooperating, taking that step down the road.

"So Mike hunts?" he said.

I stared at him blankly, and then I remembered. Hunting accident.

"Yeah, sometimes he does."

Why you shouldn't lie, because he'd already read me, was letting me know it, those so-steady eyes.

"You're not going to tell me?" he said.

I gave him my best honestly-confused face. He nodded. Tucked the pen back into his shirt pocket without any haste, tucked the notebook. Rose.

"If you change your mind," he said evenly, "you can reach me at the station."

Fair enough. I knew where the station was. I watched him turn and head for the door and wasn't terribly surprised when he stopped and turned back. He had something deliberate to say.

"I talked to Dave Yarrow some."

I could feel the icy fingers starting in on my heart. Not just anyone, then. He'd found *Dave*. "Was it interesting?"

"He said you were good, that they'd tried to get you to stay."

"They don't like to lose females," I said. "It's bad for the stats."

Reilly wasn't listening again. "He asked how you were."

"I'm fine."

"He seemed to think you might not be."

The fingers had my lungs now, closing them off. I'd shot with that man once, been under fire, driven backup more than a few times. Drank tequila with him out in the desert till we were stone-blind and maudlin, toasting the sons-of-bitches we knew. My old man. His. Not even Charlie knew all the things that I'd told that man with my head on the sand and the stars coming up crosswise.

"Maybe you should go talk to him, Meg."

Maybe he could die.

I don't know what I looked like to Reilly, but he'd gone very hard. Hostile? Something else. "All right," he said tightly, "have it *your* way." He was already turning back to the door, hand reaching out for the knob, and I recognized the set of his shoulders. Angry. At himself, seemed like, mostly. I have that effect.

"Have it *your* way," he'd said, but my way wasn't going to get what I needed. It was worse than that, actually, because with Reilly walking out, I didn't have anyplace else left to turn. He'd been at the department asking about me, so there weren't many people I could call now for help. And I didn't know anyone at Beverly PD—didn't know who to talk to, who to trust, who wasn't tied in. I had to talk to somebody, though, somebody official and somebody soon, because if Mike had gone hunting, then he was in trouble, and the only trouble I could think of came from Beverly PD.

"Reilly."

He swung around at the word, aggressive, unfriendly. I shouldn't have started, should have just let him go.

"What?"

Sixteen feet from me, one hand behind him, and I didn't even know where he carried his gun. Stupid— very stupid—but sometimes you look for truth, and sometimes it swallows you whole. If he were going to take me out, he'd had plenty of chances on Saturday.

Unless, of course, he'd had a reason to leave me.

"Why didn't Homicide come here this morning?"

He looked straight at me. "It isn't a homicide yet."

So there still was no body. It was possible then that STU would be working it, particularly since Reilly'd been in on the call. I chose the next words carefully. "I keep running into you."

"It's my case," he said, fairly tightly. "What else?"

He had the notion of what I was thinking and it wasn't sitting well with him. Okay for him to doubt *me*, I guess, but not the other way around. That was reassuring, too, in a backwards kind of way. Honest men don't like you questioning their motives.

"How long have you lived in Glendale?"

His eyes narrowed, trying to see it. "Two years."

Wouldn't know Mike from there, then. "And before?"

He looked at me levelly. "Canyon Country."

It's a ways north of Mike's usual stomping grounds. Not likely that he'd known Reilly's wife. Possible, of course, depending *where* she'd worked or *if* she'd worked, but I couldn't really ask that and it wouldn't do me much good anyway. "Why'd you move to Glendale?"

It was a private matter. His eyes considered and decided. "I knew a woman there."

Well, we all know people. Some of them are women.

"Am I going to sit down?" he said. "Or are you just wasting my time?"

He could sit.

"Mike left the message on Friday," I said without looking at him. "Friday night, I'm pretty sure." And Saturday, I'd gotten a bogus call, been sent on a wild-goose chase while my car was stolen. While somebody lost a lot of blood, O positive, in the back of my car. "The thing is," I said, and I was trying to keep my voice steady, to be detached, "Mike hates answering machines, so I didn't even think about it on Saturday, didn't take off the messages or anything." I should have, though—Jesus, I should have, even if it *was* a weekend and I didn't want to be there, even if I hadn't come in to run the damn office.

"He could have called last night," Reilly said. He'd moved back in to the chair, was settling opposite me, filling my field of vision.

"No." I stared at the desk, all the piled-up folders, because it was easier than looking at him. "I was home last night. All night." I wasn't home in the afternoon, though, and I felt a brief surge of hope, but Mike would have called back. And by yesterday afternoon, there was already blood in my car and people looking for Mike and I hadn't known enough to say that he'd be back in a couple of days. Hadn't known enough to be careful. "Look," I said, "Mike wouldn't normally have bothered with the machine, so it follows that it was important and it was sometime when I wasn't around. It also tells me that he thought he wouldn't be able to call for a while, or he would have just called back later. I mean, if it was important enough that he talked to the machine, he wouldn't have worried any about waking me up."

Reilly wasn't saying anything.

"Okay," I said, "it's sketchy, but it feels right. I wasn't home Friday night, so he couldn't have reached me. And he was supposed to be here Saturday, so the message still fits his 'not coming in tomorrow.' "

There was a raw kind of silence.

"What?" I said.

"He was supposed to be here?"

I guess I hadn't quite told Reilly that.

"Yeah."

"Not just *you* working, then?"

A flat tone, clipped. His face quite removed.

"No," I said.

He wasn't saying anything.

"You'd have taken it wrong," I said. "He just goes, okay?"

"When he's supposed to be working?"

I sketched a hand. "He forgets. I don't usually ask him."

"When'd you set this thing up?"

I'd already been lying. "Friday," I said.

Friday to Saturday. He let the silence speak volumes.

"Look," I said, "you can check it around. Mike is *legend* for forgetting, okay? And he had a *date* Friday night, something hot, something special—" I could hear my own voice sounding wrong, for Christ's sake—sounding, God help me, piqued.

Reilly's eyes very clear.

"You sleeping with him, Meg?"

"No," I said.

"Not?"

He'd been at the department. Everybody there minding everyone's business.

"No, I'm not," I said flatly.

"You've been partners a long time."

Yeah, we had been.

"We work well together," I said very evenly. "Mike's never minded me being a female." We were eye to eye, then, drawing lines. "The point is," I said, "he had a date Friday night. Somewhere in there, he must have told someone that he'd be coming in, because somebody called Saturday and was sure that he'd be here. *I* thought, when he didn't show up, that he was just having a good time, Friday lasting the weekend, but now it doesn't look quite that way."

Didn't look that way at all.

"I don't know what he's checking," I said. "Don't know what came up. I don't know if it's something with the girlfriend, or your problem at the department, or what. That could be the connection, though, Reilly. He knows some of your cops."

"Who?"

"I don't know." Not useful, but true. I don't hang

much with cops, particularly ones I don't know, but Mike likes to gather and bullshit. War stories, that kind of stuff.

"Never said any names?"

"Steve, maybe. Andy, Dan. It was always 'I'm going out with Joe for lunch,' or 'I was talking to Al.' Like that. I don't remember him saying last names."

"You never met any of them?"

I shook my head.

"Meg," he said, but his intuition was off this time.

"I didn't, Reilly. I left all that to Mike."

He stared thoughtfully over my shoulder. I *should* have met them, should have gone at least once to some of the bars, but who knew?

"The thing is," I said, "if he got wind of your guy, of there being a harassment problem out of Beverly PD—heard something over a beer, say, or was even approached—he's likely enough to go after it."

"It's not *my* guy," Reilly said mildly. "Why wouldn't he have gone to the department?"

Because he was ripe.

Because he was restless, maybe, and bored. He's good as a salesman, very fine, but he'd been a cop and it marks you—galls you after a while.

"No evidence," I said. "Thought he could get some."

Reilly was rubbing a thumb at the side of his jaw. "That's the hunting connection?"

"I think so. The friend I was talking with couldn't remember what Mike said exactly, but he was surprised when I called so it must have been definite. It's just that hunting usually means women to Mike, so I didn't make anything of it."

"And you think he ended up in your car?"

He had lazy eyes, hooded, looking at me. Because I'd gone leaping around like a crazy person asking about blood types. Because Mike was my partner. There was a little distance between us, suspect and suspector. "No," I said steadily. "For a minute, I did. But whoever called Saturday was looking for Mike, so they didn't *have* him. If I'd come in and taken the messages off the way Mike expected, then I'd just have shined them on when they called. 'Sorry, Mike isn't here. Sorry, he'll be back in a couple of days.' I never would have gone over to Haroutunian's and none of this would have happened." Only Mike hadn't known that I wouldn't be Old Reliable, that I'd come in Saturday in a flaming bad mood, with a hangover and an attitude. I looked at Reilly.

"Whoever called didn't want me, they were asking for Mike. So they didn't *have* Mike then, they were trying to track him. Now, even if they found him in the next hour or so while you were waltzing me around at the station, why trail me downtown and steal my car? If they had him, they had him. If they were going to kill him, they could have just done it, there or wherever, they didn't need my car for that. It's an extra risk, a foolish risk, and what's the point? It's not to send me a warning, because I don't know anything about anything, and even if they thought that I did, it's a lot simpler to follow me home and do me. I mean, if you're killing people anyway, what's one more body?"

Reilly was listening to me, eyes intent and alive.

"It comes back to the game plan," I said. "Mike had something to do this weekend, and he left me a message to clam up and stay put. I didn't get the message, though, so when someone came looking for him, I offered to help. They didn't want *me*, Reilly—it was 'no, no, must be Mike'—and then they changed their minds. 'Yes, you must come, you hurry.' Maybe they thought I'd make a good hostage or they could get something out of me, but in any event, I show up with the cops. Stupid bitch, and now they're in a bind because you're taking me down to the station. God knows what I'm going to say to you, what I might know about them, and they still don't have Mike. But they can reach *me*. They can discredit *me*. They know where *I* am—I'm at the station. If I disappear or get killed after telling you about crooked cops, that blows everything, because you wouldn't stop looking then. But if I'm embroiled in suspicious circumstances, like my partner missing, car full of blood, and me with no alibi, that's going to distract you some. That's going to buy them some time."

"You have an alibi."

Because he'd driven me home. "Not for all of it," I said. "Even this tape doesn't get it because it might be a message I've held on to for weeks. You don't know."

He smiled at me then, full on. Nice and wide, Sergeant Reilly approving. "You're right—I *don't* know. So where do you think Mike would be?"

Jesus. "He could be anywhere," I said. "What's the scope of this thing?"

He looked at me quizzically.

"Well, you said 'harassing Iranians,' Reilly, but it's obviously more than some guy making phone calls. Are we talking a Brotherhood here?"

A unit. A cell. Aryan or otherwise.

"I don't think so," he said. He was focused beyond

me, on the city map on the wall. Reflecting. Calculating how much to feed me, what would keep me in line. Had that hand sort of rubbing again on the jawline, and then a decision. "You going to be here all day?"

Not going to tell me anything. Standing to leave, retucking the pen.

"Yeah," I said. "I've got to handle things, cancel the appointments. Why?"

"I'll try to call you later." He was looking down at me, a long way down, so I stood up, too, to lessen the distance. Formal again. Back to our roles.

"I'll want the tape," he said.

From the answering machine. I turned without speaking, popped the plastic top open. Retrieved it for him. I'd have to replace it. Reached to hand it to him over the desk and he was watching me funny.

"What?"

He nodded as if I'd answered something. "Dave told me you were quick. Used to pick things out of the air, he said."

That sounded like Dave. I could feel myself tightening, but Reilly wasn't exactly a dullard himself. Testing. "Only when the air's thick," I said.

He nodded again, conversationally. "Told me to watch you. Said you could be friendly, easy to work with—five minutes and people would think that they knew you. Take 'em weeks to find out that they didn't."

Or years, apparently, but I'm not that hard to understand. Just do me right. I smiled at him stiffly. "Dave's always fancied himself a psychologist."

He let it go. He'd be back on the line with Dave probably, if he had the time, but there wasn't anything I could do about it. "I'll call you," he said, and opened the door. It was bright outside, sunlit. I moved after him to lock up and I could see beyond him to the parking lot where Mitch-the-Snitch Harris was sitting in an unmarked in one of our spaces.

"Why'd you bring the weasel, Reilly?"

Man had a quirked sense of humor to match that damn eyebrow. Had a personal glint, leaning in kind of close.

"Escobar was looking too good," he said.

# 11

He bothered me. It was stupid and annoying and a host of other things, but Reilly bothered me—I could feel him in the room. I took his coffee cup and washed it out, set it to dry on the sink in back. Rearranged the reception chairs in front of my desk. Finally sat at Mike's desk to get a different angle on things. Not *much* of an angle, it's true, but something—not the front of Reilly's chair, anyway.

My first priority was the business calls. I didn't know how long Mike would be gone or what he could deal with when he got back, but I had to tell people something, so I called the names in the appointment book and shuffled them all to next week. I hoped I had everything Mike had set up, but I couldn't count on it. He tends to work off of napkins.

The accountant was kind of ticked, too. We were supposed to have had the books to him Friday, but I'd called and put him off, and since I hadn't finished them Saturday, I had to call him again and reschedule. I figured he'd come up with a charge for his trouble. Finished the rest of the nonsense, the bills. Stared at the telephone, the receiver.

I could call people, you know. *Do* something. I didn't know what shifts or details anyone worked anymore, but I could find out. Still remembered some numbers.

But—

It was *me* calling, asking about Mike.

That would raise a lot of eyebrows, a lot of questions, and Mike still goes back there. I don't much—well, I don't at all, actually, not to visit or anything—hell, I don't even go into town—but Mike does, and he'd have to live with it. *And* he'd gone away on his own. Left me a message about it. Not as if somebody'd kidnapped him.

Which reminded me of Haroutunian, and I wondered how *he* was doing, if he was home yet. I'd forgotten to ask Reilly.

So I doodled on a piece of paper and tried to think of things to say to people I hadn't talked to in a while, and basically kept putting it off. Mike's a resourceful guy. Mostly is, anyway. He wouldn't appreciate me stirring things up and he'd told me to stay out of it.

Well, he hadn't, actually—he'd told me to be careful. "Something's come up and I've got to check it out." *What* came up? Where'd he *go*? Why wasn't he *specific*? I'm an ex-cop, not a damned mind reader.

So since I'm not a damned mind reader, I did what an ex-cop does. I went through Mike's desk. Forget about invasion of privacy, betrayal of trust. I started methodically at the top, and worked down through the drawers, ignoring the candy wrappers and miscellaneous junk, looking for scraps of paper with names and phone numbers. There were a lot of them, stuffed every which way, but I sat holding the one for Haroutunian for quite a while.

Natural enough for Mike to have it if we had a contract with the guy. We didn't, though. Haroutunian had *said* that we didn't and I had no file. Natural enough for Mike to have it if he was *trying* to get a contract with him. But Haroutunian had said he'd never heard of us— didn't know me, didn't know Mike. And here Mike had *his* name and phone number, and the Haroutunian who'd called had had ours. Our private number. Not the public line, from the ads or the business card, but the number Mike tends to give out.

And if I'd thought about it since, which really I hadn't, I'd have figured that Mike had given that number to the guy or guys on Beverly PD who were trying to find him on Saturday. That could still be true, I guess. It's just that I'd been thinking Haroutunian was a blind. I'd been thinking he *wasn't* connected, just someplace to send me so that they could pick me up.

Couldn't leave their district? Wouldn't have time before somebody noticed? That argued a patrol car, a regular beat. Also someone who was working on Saturday.

But now I had *Haroutunian's* phone number in *Mike's* handwriting in *Mike's* desk. And the thing that spoke to me loudly and clearly was that if Haroutunian *was* involved somehow, as victim or perpetrator, then that went a long way to explaining Saturday's phone call. If Mike wasn't supposed to have this piece of paper, for instance. If someone, some cop, had been indiscreet around him on Friday and then realized it. If Mike hadn't had a chance yet to call Haroutunian, which would answer why Haroutunian had said he didn't know him, and which would explain why things went so suddenly to hell on Saturday. Find Mike before he can call. Find the number. Containment. Jam that cat back into the bag.

You don't learn anything by sitting around wondering, so I picked up the phone and dialed. It rang fifteen, sixteen times. No one answered, which meant almost anything. A wrong number, no one home, someone busy. Haroutunian hadn't been home yesterday, either. We'd seen him for sure Saturday afternoon, because they'd have gotten identification, Reilly would have done that, and Saturday night my car showed up bloody. Wasn't home Sunday.

I drew a few more arrows on my little piece of paper, but there was nothing else to do. I called Reilly.

I got transferred around to the STU office. Nice-sounding guy to answer the line. Professional. Courteous. Sergeant Reilly wasn't in, but he'd be happy to take a message. It was just that I didn't know who this guy was and I didn't know who Reilly suspected, how close. Tell him to call me? I didn't have to talk to Reilly *himself*, though, not really, and he was probably busy.

"Tell him it's Meg Gillis, okay? Wondering if Haroutunian's back."

I had to spell "Haroutunian," so maybe the cop wasn't heinously involved. I hung up and went back to tossing Mike's desk.

Something was wedging the bottom drawer shut. I finally managed to pull enough junk out so that I could get my hand in under the crossbrace and feel what was blocking the track. Thickish paper, wadded up. I worked it around, ignoring scraped knuckles, until I could push it down into the drawer and release the top catch. The drawer slid into my hands.

I was looking at a photograph of Charlie and me, torn in half and crumpled now, ripped down the middle but very recognizable, taken just before he died. We were on the pier at Santa Monica, laughing at the camera, lovers caught in an intimate pose. Charlie's arms were around me and I looked so happy, carefree, while the seagulls soared over our heads.

I'd never seen this picture before.

I don't think I moved for about a minute while I held the snapshot in my hands and tried to have it make sense. I remembered the day all right. Mike was the cameraman, and we'd all taken Josh to the beach. Mike was between girlfriends or she'd stood him up or something, and we'd spent part of the afternoon at one of the outside wharf bars under a blue-and-white-striped umbrella.

But Mike had never shown me this picture, not in all the dreadful days after. I couldn't imagine what it was doing in pieces in his drawer.

The phone rang and I answered it mechanically. It was a nice lady from my insurance company, returning my call. I gave her the particulars about the car, including the fact that I wouldn't be able to get it back for a couple of days. She was as helpful as could be, reminding me that my policy ran to a rental car if I wanted one. I was in the process of turning her down, more to get her off the line than anything else, when it occurred to me how very visible Charlie's blue truck was. So tell me, I said, how do I get this rental car? A nice lady, a helpful lady. Two minutes later, I had a rental agency's number and five minutes after that, I was all set up. They'd even deliver the car to the office for me.

Well, that would be great, I said, but a client was taking me to lunch soon, so perhaps they wouldn't mind
dropping the keys off around the corner with the building manager. I'd let him know they were coming, and
they could leave the car parked by his office so he could
keep an eye on it. No problem at all, they'd be happy to
oblige. I called Ed, the manager, and went back to my
picture.

People say the dead die, that they go, but I don't
know that—they seem always to be with me, one way or
another. Charlie was smiling up at me as if he'd never
gone, never *would* go, and I'd believed that was true.
There were hard tears, hot in my eyes, but you can't
change the past, you can't undo or redo, can't call back
the words. I traced his face lightly, the lips—his arms
warm around me in the cold ocean wind. What had he
told me, what had he whispered before he turned me to
Mike? I couldn't remember, but you could see I was
blushing, so it was something outrageous, unbearably
him. God, that was a day. Jesus, it was fine. Before my
world went to hell and ashes and everything was lies.

I had to quit this, had to put it away. I knew why Mike
had this picture—a memento, a keepsake—and it wasn't
important, it just wasn't, to anyone but us.

*"You sleeping with him, Meg?"*

I knew what Reilly would make of it, what *any* cop
would, but he would be wrong. There was nothing else
in the drawer particularly interesting, so I piled the rest
of it back. Mike's a hoarder, but I've always known that.
Not many secrets about Mike.

Except Haroutunian.

That one hadn't come up.

And the picture he'd torn in half.

I looked at the paper again—Haroutunian's name and a phone number. Dialed it a second time. Still no one home.

It didn't have to be *Haroutunian's* number, of course. It could be his name and somebody else's number who knew about him, but when I looked Haroutunian up in the phone book, he wasn't listed, so that didn't help. There was an "M. Haroutunian," no address, different number. Nobody home there either. I was trying to remember. I was pretty sure that *my* Haroutunian had said "Youssef," which didn't necessarily mean anything if it was a set-up call, a lie, but the operator who answered 411 admitted that there was a "Y. Haroutunian"—she just wouldn't give me the number because it was unlisted, which is what people pay extra for every month. I thought about bluffing my way through, but I wasn't a cop anymore and the procedures had probably changed. And if I was a cop, I could have just looked it up in the backwards phone book, or if I even had a cop friend, he could do it for me, which sort of came back to Reilly.

I stared at the phone.

Reilly'd checked the man's ID, so he'd have gotten a phone number and everything else for the report. Driver's license, that sort of thing. He'd know the man's name. Maybe he went by Joseph instead of Youssef, maybe Youssef wasn't right. Reilly's first name was Joe, that's what Abbott had called him, so maybe I'd flashed on that. Joe, Joseph. The mind working in mysterious ways. I wished I knew when he'd call me back. I hate waiting around.

Haroutunian as victim. Maybe so. He'd been kind of nervous, really. Not desperately, maybe, mostly pokered-up dignity, but then all the cops were there. Thompson and Reilly. Escobar. People get nervous around cops. I do, and I know how it works. Of course, I also know how it's supposed to work, and where the hell was Reilly?

Because you'd *think*, this being kind of late Monday morning, that the weekend reports would have been copied and distributed by now. You'd think that somebody working the STU desk would know where his sergeant was, out doing a field investigation, and why, and in connection with which case. You wouldn't think I'd have to spell "Haroutunian."

I stared at the side of Reilly's chair, but I was seeing other things. Haroutunian's face as he stood in the doorway. "*I have no son,*" he'd said, "*no son,*" and he was looking at Reilly almost beseechingly—like "*Get this crazy woman out of here, haven't I been through enough?*" Only maybe it was "*Am I doing this right?*" They'd been there before me, Reilly and Thompson. They'd had time to talk to him.

I'm not good at trusting people, really I'm not.

*Reilly'd* answered the call, made sure he was there. Gotten his own men in.

And *Reilly* was the one telling me about it, saying they'd had problems—harassment, maybe worse, maybe even by cops. That would get me going, enlist me a little, make me willing to cough up Mike if I knew where he was. He'd implied that Abbott was keeping the lid on, a secret investigation, but how likely was that, really? You might do something like that under orders from the

Chief, but who's going to bypass Internal Affairs on their own?

Okay, Abbott might. He had the balls for it, and maybe IA was implicated somehow. Hell, maybe he *did* have the nod from upstairs but nobody'd thought it was any of my business. Who was I going to ask? Reilly? The Chief? "Hello, sir, my partner and I are suspects in the possible disappearance of a possible Iranian harassment victim, and I was just wondering if you could tell me what your cops have been doing?"

Right.

Which left me nowhere. Reilly was around too much, taking too much of a personal interest. There was reason for it if they thought this was a cop ring, harassment becoming a homicide. They'd sit on it then, they'd sit on *me*, because I was a lead, maybe their only lead.

But still.

If Mike was alive and healthy and off investigating something, I could mess him all up by asking questions—particularly if I were asking in the wrong places, trusting the wrong people. Mike's a resourceful guy, all right, but that doesn't mean much against a Magnum.

And if he'd already met that Magnum, which I had to stop thinking about, then I wouldn't help him now by going to the guy who'd maybe pulled the trigger. Not if there were cops involved.

I couldn't even report him as missing other than what I'd said to Reilly. They were already looking for him for questioning, and now we had a goddamn tape on which he'd said he was going away for a few days. He wouldn't qualify as missing till next week, maybe not even then.

And then I remembered that *Reilly* had the tape.

Okay, I said to the Charlie-half of the picture, what do I do? Can't just sit around and hope Mike shows up. Can't just trust Reilly and wait for him to find him. I was picturing blood again, pools of blood, and God, I was trembling. I had to quit this. I could feel Charlie beside me . . . Some gang, they'd said, a drive-by shooting, but they never found out who, never told me.

I hadn't been home Friday night because I didn't trust myself alone. "Anniversary" is such a strange word; it sounds like presents and parties and fifty happy years. It has nothing to do with blood on the street and a man lying there, nothing to do with the doorbell ringing at three in the morning, always at three in the morning.

My hands still worked. I watched the fingers bend and flex.

Three years. Mike hadn't forgotten either, although I'd thought that he had, thought that he'd just forgotten the date. I hadn't reminded him, hadn't said one damn word, but it had been in his voice on the tape.

If I'd only been home.

If I'd talked to him.

If pigs flew.

I couldn't do anything about the past, but I could damn well guard the future. It all came down to trusting Reilly. I stared at Charlie's picture for a long, long time, and then I did what I should have done in the first place. I called the department.

I called everyone I could think of, everyone I could reach, there or at home. Casually, easily, chatting a while because that's how you do it, and then, "Oh, yeah, I ran into this guy this weekend, Joe Reilly, I think—you know him?"

And when I was done, it came down to this: nobody knew Reilly. None of Charlie's friends. They'd never even heard Charlie mention him.

Well, it wasn't quite true that *nobody'd* heard of him. I did find one guy who knew Reilly, all right—as a Beverly cop who'd called Saturday asking about *me*.

Saturday.

Not Sunday.

Saturday afternoon.

# 12

I collected the rental car from the manager about four-thirty. I'd been back and forth to the truck a couple of times but I couldn't tell if anyone was watching. It seemed likely, and I wasn't in the mood to guess. I'd already dug Mike's keys out of their hiding place and this time I went out through the storeroom window and crossed the alley to the other building. Ed was looking a little frazzled, but his secretary found the rental key and pointed me towards the car. A Ford Taurus. Well, at least it had air-conditioning, something to be thankful for because the Santa Ana winds were coming up again and it was as hot as the desert.

And the other thing to be thankful for was that the Taurus was parked in the lot around the corner from our building. Not visible.

I took the scenic route to Burbank, letting the traffic flow past. Rush hour, everyone in a hurry. No one seemed to be following me. I drove once around Mike's block for the heck of it, and Mitch-the-Snitch-the-Weasel was on the corner, reading the paper in his car across the street. I kept going.

By the time I worked my way back, it was after six. I'd

left the car a few blocks over and made a stop at the mini-mart. I had my hair pulled into a bun, sunglasses on top, toting a sack of groceries and munching on a hot dog as I walked through the back parking lot at Mike's place. The print shirt I'd bought was maybe a little loud and kind of baggy, and the makeup too much, but I hadn't been interested in fashion.

There was a man in jeans and a tee shirt by a '95 T-Bird. Finished washing his car, I guess, polishing his hubcaps. I didn't pay him any particular attention, just another resident coming home with dinner on her mind. He glanced up at me and kept polishing. Shiny hubcaps.

The building next to Mike's has the laundry room on the ground floor. It's more convenient than dragging your clothes out to a Laundromat, and since it's only a few steps away, nobody bothers much watching the tubs spin. If somebody's wash is done but they haven't picked it up yet, you just pile it on the folding table and dump your own stuff in. Very casual. Very trusting.

I turned in there and watched the hubcap man through the dirty little window. He was still polishing, not as energetically, but there were no moves to grab a radio or talk into his shirt, no indication I'd been burned. I borrowed a few items from the several piles, socks and things that you wouldn't miss right away, and stuffed them in the top of my bag. Then I trudged across the courtyard, fumbling for my keys, still intent on dinner but with the laundry at least out of the way. Hope John and the kids weren't home yet so I could have a drink. Behind me, the tempo of the polishing had picked up, but I couldn't sense anything else. It was forever to Mike's building.

I said hello to a lady coming out the door, who nicely held it open for me. "Isn't this awful, this heat?" I said, and she agreed that it was. Two residents chatting. She didn't seem to recognize any of the socks. Then I was inside.

I was pretty sure they wouldn't have anybody in the building, just front and back entrance, but I hung on to the character anyway and shuffled on down the hall. Mike's door was the middle one on the right. I passed it and went through the far door to the stairwell, climbed the stairs. There's another window partway up, on the landing, and by standing on tiptoe I could just see down to the parking lot. The hubcap man was taking it easy and no one else was around. I pulled out Mike's key and left the bag in a corner of the landing.

I wasted another minute or two easing the stairwell door open and looking through it. No one in the hall. Luck like that wasn't going to stay with me, so I went down the hall and put the keys in the locks, top deadbolt first and then the door handle. It turned and I pushed in.

Something was blocking the door.

I couldn't think, and then I pushed harder. Whatever it was gave as far as the chain. *The goddamn door was chained from inside.*

"Mike?"

There wasn't an answer, there wouldn't *be* an answer.

There was blood on the wall.

I couldn't breathe. I was taking in chestfuls but the lungs weren't working. The damn door was shaking in my hands or maybe I was shoving it—I couldn't think, I wasn't thinking. There was a sound behind me, and it was Mike's neighbor, an old lady, I couldn't remember her name.

"Call the cops," I said, I think I said. "There's blood in here. *Burbank*," I said to her, "go call the *Burbank* cops."

She fled to her apartment. The door kept moving and I was still shoving but I couldn't break the chain, get it open. Mike. Michael. Too many things and too much time, buddy, don't do this to me. I was cracking wide open and I couldn't stop it, couldn't control. There was blood on the wall.

It was the smell that brought me back. Someone was cooking onions down the hall, and it hit me then, that I could smell onions. Mike's door was open as far as the chain would go, two inches, three. There's no mistaking the smell of a dead body, not if it's been there any time at all—and there was nothing. I pressed my face to the opening and breathed again, deeply.

Onions.

That was all.

Somehow, then, I was kneeling on the floor. No body, my mind chanted over and over, no body here. But part of me was remembering where *another* body hadn't been found, and how it might have gotten from here to there last night with the use of my car. Beverly to Burbank to Point Fermin—to dump *Mike*? *Why*? Christ help me, *why*?

"Are you all right?" Mike's neighbor was back and what could I say? "I called the police and they'll be here soon. Are you all right?"

Was she talking to me? Was she nuts? Why wasn't she hiding in her apartment till the cops came? Didn't I look violent, crazed? "It'll be okay," she was saying, and she meant well, but I couldn't think. What was I going to tell the Burbank police? How much? How little? The Weasel would be in as soon as he saw the units and how the hell could I stop him? The pipeline to Beverly. The brother-hood.

*No body*, I thought again, like a curse, like a benediction, but what else was in there? Blood on the walls and what all would they find? I had to get in, had to know. There must be someone who could vouch for me, someone I'd known or Charlie had known.

"Did you hear anything this weekend?" I said. "Fights or anything?"

The neighbor, sixtyish, seemed very worried. "I wasn't home, I'm sorry, I went to my sister's in Claremont. Can I get you something?"

"No," I said. "Thanks."

"They'll be here any minute."

I knew they would. I just didn't know what to tell them. The minimum, I thought. Keep it reasonable, simple. Enough to start a Missing Persons on Mike whether Reilly'd done that already or not. Not much the Weasel could say about it then, and it would be official somewhere anyway. Something on record.

I pulled the pins from my hair, releasing the bun and brushing it straight with my hands. Trembling hands. "Could I have a glass of water?" I said. "It's just so hot."

"Don't you want to come and sit down?"

I did, actually. "I don't want to be any trouble. I mean, they'll be here soon . . ." I let my voice trail off and plucked at my shirt indecisively. She was a good-hearted woman, grandmotherly, and she knew I'd had a shock.

"You come on," she said. "I'll leave the door open, and they'll be looking for me anyway. You'll feel much better in the air-conditioning."

"If I could just splash some water on my face," I said meekly, and followed her next door.

Her bathroom was right inside the door like Mike's was, same floor plan, reversed, and she left me there while she went to get ice water from the fridge. I stripped off the Hawaiian shirt and scrubbed at the makeup. I'd put the shirt on over my tee and was wearing jeans, so the tee was okay. I didn't look underdressed or disguised, just a whole lot more like myself. There were voices in the hall.

Simple, I said to the eyes in the mirror, keep it simple. I left the shirt hanging from the inside hook as if I'd forgotten it and went out to talk to the cops.

Two of them. Both Burbank.

No Mitch.

Lying low? Keeping his cover? There were a number of reasons why Beverly wouldn't have told Burbank they were running a stakeout in their territory, and I didn't like the most obvious one. How could I ask, though? "Hi, did you see the Beverly cops outside?" The Burbank guys were approaching me. Andrews and Sullivan.

"Hello," I said, "I'm Mike Johnson's partner. He's supposed to be away for a few days, but the door's chained on the inside, and there's blood, I think, on the wall." I wasn't as controlled as I'd meant to be, but they'd gotten the picture. Sullivan was already down the hall examining Mike's door.

"It was like this when you got here?"

"No, I opened it. He left me his key."

It was still sticking out of the bottom lock, which was stupid of me because now it was gone, but I wouldn't be able to get in there anyway. Not with a police seal on the door.

"Something on the wall," Sullivan confirmed.

"Did you hear anything when you opened the door?" That was Andrews, talking to me.

It was the crucial question, the hinge. Say yes, and they'd kick the door now. No, and they'd do it by the book with me shepherded away while they called their field sergeant and went in. God, I wanted to say yes, but these weren't rookies I could bluff my way past and there was no way in hell a pair of seasoned cops would let me take a look. Yes would just get me the prime suspect position if I didn't have it already.

"No," I said. "I don't think there's anyone in there. The blood's dried and I didn't smell a body."

Ah, Christ, I thought instantly, but it was too late—Andrews and Sullivan were already exchanging looks. How did *I* know what a dead body smelled like? Sullivan was disturbed. "I'll check around out back."

"If you ladies could just give me some details—" Andrews said, drawing our attention away from his partner, who was disappearing out the front door. We went through the who-we-were-and-where-we-lived routine while he made precise little marks in his notebook. I couldn't hear anything from outside, which didn't mean that Sullivan wasn't talking with Mitch or the hubcap man. Andrews wanted to know why I was there.

"Checking the plants," I said.

# 13

Basically, I skated. I said all the right things as sincerely as possible, "sirred" and "yessirred" and produced identification. The neighbor, Mrs. Arcuni, had seen me there before, and that didn't hurt—"Oh, yes, she's Mr. Johnson's partner, such a nice young man"—and they didn't find a body. That was pretty well crucial. If they'd found a body, the game would have been up. I didn't mention that I used to be a police officer, was careful about that, but they knew Mike had been one as soon as they entered—he has brag stuff all over the walls. Trophies. I didn't say anything about Reilly or Beverly Hills.

We'd waited the two minutes for the field sergeant to get there, Sergeant Harbin—someone who didn't, thank God, seem to know me—and they'd cut the chain lock while Andrews kept us busy at the end of the hall. Another ten minutes and I'd figured my time was running out. Mitch was going to show, or Reilly'd be calling, and that was going to do me. They were all cops, you know. Easy enough to detain me at another agency's request, routine enough for Reilly to ask them to do it. He'd just have to mention what had been happening this weekend, and Burbank wouldn't be letting me go anywhere anyway. So when Sergeant Harbin emerged from Mike's apartment, I touched Andrews' arm. "Excuse me," I said, "are you going to be needing me? I mean, to identify anything?"

I was probably looking pretty white—well, I still felt kind of sick—and Mrs. Arcuni, bless her, had been hovering. "You should be lying down, honey."

"No, no," I said, "not if they need me."

Andrews went to confer with Harbin, and they both came back. Harbin was an efficient man. "Were you just going home, Mrs. Gillis?"

"Yes, sir." I was planning to go eventually, so it wasn't really a lie. "That is, if it's okay. If you don't need me to stay."

They'd already checked my identification and I was who I'd said I was, lived where I'd said I lived, not ten minutes away. I seemed reasonable, and there was no obvious involvement in a crime other than discovering it—and, come to that, *I* was the one who'd had Mrs. Arcuni call the police. She'd said so. I took it a step further. "Do you know who'll be investigating this? Someone I could call tomorrow, just to see?"

Sergeant Harbin didn't know, but he'd give me the case number and then I could call the station in the morning. Probably the detectives would be wanting to talk to me. Satisfied honor for all of us. Mrs. Arcuni didn't think I should be driving, which was sticky for a minute, but I assured them I was fine. The last thing I needed was a cop driving me home.

I went straight out the rear door, sweeping through the parking lot. Hubcaps was gone. Pulled back, probably. Maybe out front with Mitch, but I wasn't going around the corner to check. Maybe Mitch was gone too, and I thought about it for a second, what it would mean, but I was skating on the thin edge, shaky ground, and the only alternative was marching back inside and throwing myself on Burbank's mercy, which, under the circumstances, was not the wise thing to do.

Not when the dried blood on Mike's wall looked to be several days old. Not when I'd told them that I'd had the key since Friday when Mike left the office. Not when my car had turned up Saturday, bloodied and locked.

Cops don't care much for coincidence. *I* never did.

Someone might have been following me the several blocks back to the rental car, but if so, he was very good. I was willing to believe someone was very good, so I spent an extra half hour dodging around the city of Burbank. I know it pretty well. By the time I got to the freeway, I was as certain as I could be that I was alone. They might be guessing that I was going to the office and have somebody waiting, but how many men were involved? How many could they call on? I might be going anywhere, and they couldn't have a lot of guys hanging around on the off chance.

Hell, they didn't need to be following me anyway, it'd be a precaution if they were even bothering. I'd have to surface sooner or later, and they could just reel me in. Self-convicted. Less than truthful. I knew exactly what Harbin would be thinking when he found out.

Christ.

I cursed most of the way to Beverly Hills, words I don't usually use, and some I made up. Like a chorus behind me, I could hear Charlie doing his Oliver Hardy routine, *"Here's another fine mess you've gotten us into."* Charlie did lousy imitations—usually when he was drunk at a party. "*Hello, I must be going. Ar, ar, ar.*"

Why hadn't I just closed the damned door and gone around to the front window? I braked hard to avoid a pedestrian with a death wish, and turned onto a side street near the office. "*Another fine mess.*" Mike wasn't there. Mike's *body* wasn't there. *Nobody's* body was there. A locked door, some sort of struggle, because there was blood on the wall and stuff blocking the door, but there was no injured person waiting, no body to be taken out in a bag. That was all I knew now, all I was likely to know for a while.

It was no good flaming because I'd lost my head at Mike's door. The truth is, I wouldn't have broken in anyway. When something looks this nasty, you don't play private eye like you never heard of the Penal Code. Because if Mike and I *were* being set up, for whatever reason, then someone might have been *hoping* that I'd break in, might have been waiting for it. I wasn't forgetting that Mitch and Mr. Hubcaps hadn't come in when they saw the Burbank cops. Had they planned to drop the dime while I was in the apartment? Was that why Hubcaps hadn't nailed me going in?

Christ, I could do this all night.

I didn't take any particular pains parking the rental car, just left it around the corner, locked. If someone wanted to watch me crossing the lot to Charlie's truck, they were welcome, although there didn't seem to be anyone around to be interested. I opened the driver's door carefully, standing in the vee of it, and unsnapped the .45 under the seat. It's my travel piece, a Colt Commander, and it wasn't much to slide it into my waistband

and pull the tee shirt down over it, blousing it out in the front. I fussed with my bag meanwhile, caught on the door handle, and then I made a point of remembering keys. "Where are the keys, dammit, can't find them, have to be in this bag somewhere," while I scrabbled around, and then "Oh, that's right, left them in the office. Should I get them? It's late, I'm tired"—a look at the office door—"yeah, I guess I should," and all very natural, nothing alarming, I closed up the truck again and walked the few steps to the office. I didn't feel any eyes, but who knows?

I shut the door behind me, locked it, reached for the lights. Only my office, nothing disturbed. Had the Colt in my hand, and I went on to the storeroom. Nobody lurking, just dust and shadows, so I turned on all the lights and locked the back window. The window I'd skinnied through three hours ago. Not such a long time. Not long at all.

I sat down at my desk, facing the door, and the .45 was in front of me, safety off, like a shield. Time I was talking to someone I trusted. Time I took Louis up on his offer. I dialed the number and it rang and rang. Louis, be there, be home. He was, Marie said, watching Monday night football. "I'm sorry," I told her, "this won't take very long."

It did, of course, it took forever. He wanted to know everything. "Just give me the guy's number, Louis, I don't want to keep you," but Louis is my mother and he wouldn't let it go. So I told him pretty much all of it, Reilly driving me home, Reilly on Sunday, Reilly this morning. Me with Mike's keys.

"They can make a case that you had access."

"Yep. Friday night, Saturday, anytime I wanted. And nobody saw the car being taken, so that's just my say-so, too. Maybe I had a friend drive it away. Mighty convenient that I claimed it was stolen, since it's turned up now, full of blood. Mighty convenient that Mike's missing, but I happen to have a tape. And then we have Reilly coming along and rattling me this morning, saying who-knows-what, it's just him and me here, my word against his. A few hours later, I'm there at the crime scene—maybe looking for something I left, something he'll remember he asked me about. And then it's 'So, Sergeant, didn't you have a tail on her?' 'Yes, sir, I did, but she deliberately eluded him,' and there's the cop who was outside here saying, 'Yep, she did—rented a car and everything.' It's circumstantial, Louis, but it'll hold. I've arrested people for less."

"You stay there," he said. "I'm going to call you back."

It was a long fifteen minutes. I fretted, I paced, I kept looking out a corner of the window blinds. I'm not good in small rooms. I don't usually think of the office that way, but tonight the walls were closing in.

"Here's the number," Louis said when the phone finally rang. "The lawyer's name is Bob McKenzie and he's expecting you tomorrow at nine. Now, for tonight"—he took a breath—"Marie's making up the extra bed—"

"No." I'd had time to think about that, too, to prepare for it. "They've been setting me up, Louis. Nobody's made any real moves on me, they're just looking for me to take the fall—I can feel it. I should be safe enough until tomorrow." And if I wasn't, I sure wasn't bringing trouble to his house. It wasn't a secret that we were friends, I'd already called him at home on Sunday in front of Sergeant Reilly.

"Meg, you need to—"

"Louis, I'm fine. You take care of your wife."

There was a silent struggle. Louis has a choice collection of phrases, but with Marie nearby, listening, he couldn't let loose. It wasn't nice of me to use that. He knew it. We both knew it. Finally, he gave in. "All right, then. Go straight home. Don't do anything else, don't *go* anywhere else. Call Bob, though, if they pick you up tonight. He's primed for it, and he'll let me know."

"Thanks." I was feeling kind of low, and Louis could tell, I guess.

"Don't worry," he said roughly, "it's still only circumstantial," but Louis is a corporate lawyer and he's not used to thinking with a criminal mind.

"It's worse than that," I said. "Reilly's my alibi for Saturday night, my only alibi. All he has to do is deny that he drove me home. His word against mine and he's a cop. Then it doesn't matter *what's* circumstantial, because then I had plenty of time to be going to Point Fermin and back."

He took in another breath. "Jesus, Meg, you should have told Burbank."

"Who would they have believed?" I said.

# 14

I was pretty well keyed up. It didn't make any difference, really, what I'd said to Louis about being safe, I didn't *feel* safe, and that was flat it. I drove back home watching all the mirrors, with the Colt snugged into its holster on the seat beside me.

I was thinking about motels. I had credit cards in my bag, and there were signs everywhere, but that would be one more thing against me in front of a judge. I wasn't a fugitive. Honest citizens can sleep where they want to—hell, I could drive to Washington if I felt like it, no wants or warrants out for me. But in a circumstantial case, it's the preponderance of evidence, the chain of events. "She told you she was going home, Sergeant Harbin?" "Yes, your Honor, she did." "But, in fact, she did not go home—is that correct?" "Yes, your Honor, it is. Furthermore, I'd told her that our detectives would be contacting her, but when they went to her house, she wasn't there and she was later discovered at a motel, presumably to avoid questioning." My "Well, I didn't feel quite safe at home" would look pretty thin next to that, next to the fact that I'd had the key, that my car had been used, that something had happened to my business partner. Bang goes the gavel, and Meg gets no bail, no matter how hotshot a lawyer this Bob McKenzie was.

So I was tense, I was edgy, I was seeing phantoms everywhere. Lights in the rearview mirror which followed me for two or three miles. A car speeding up beside me on the ramp. Two guys hanging around on a street corner near my house. I watched the drugs changing hands from down the block before I moved on. Old habits, old reflexes.

Old fears.

There was a light on in my house.

I noticed it in the kitchen window, a small patch of light spilling down the side of the house onto the driveway. Had I left it on this morning? I couldn't remember.

I was already swinging past the house, and I couldn't even remember this morning. Hand flicking out to turn off the light? Maybe. I've done it a million times, but I couldn't swear that I did it today. Couldn't swear that I didn't. Couldn't tell you that I wasn't being paranoid.

I moved slowly on down the block, pretending I was looking for house numbers while I studied the mirrors. There was a car or two I'd never seen before, but some of my neighbors have revolving friends. Nobody seemed to be sitting out. I turned right at the next corner, passed the black mouth of the alley, turned right again at the corner after that, and parked halfway down on the street behind my house.

I was trembling, kind of sick, kind of tired. Maybe I'd just left the damn light on myself. I could call Burbank. "Someone's in my house," I'd say. "I think there is, I mean." And I could wait and they'd send someone. They'd go through the house then, of course—legitimately, looking for a burglar. No need for a search warrant or anything fancy. When you open the door for the cops, you can't open it halfway. Whatever they see is fair game.

Someone had been to a lot of trouble already, though, to drag me in front of the police, to wave me in their faces, show me off. Because I did predictable things, like calling the cops, and maybe somebody'd remembered that. Maybe no one was sitting at my house waiting for me, maybe they'd just dropped in to leave me a present. Something special to open in company. Something a trained cop could find. Christ, I was paranoid. With reason, you understand, but paranoid all the same. I wished I could remember about the light.

"Hello, hotshot lawyer, it's late and I'm scared—do you think I forgot to turn off the light?" That would be good. I'm sure he'd come rushing right over. More likely it'd be "meet me at Burbank and we'll explain to the cops," and they'd still send someone out, still go through the house, although at that point they'd probably have woken a judge for a warrant because at that point I'd probably be in jail. Felony suspicion. Terminally stupid.

Because maybe it was Mike.

Maybe Mike *dead*, but I didn't know. Some hopes die hard, and there was nothing to say that the blood in the apartment was Mike's, nothing to say it was fatal. He could be hurt, he could be hiding, he could be waiting for me to come home.

I went over it again, the options, the possibilities. It all came down to my going in. If something was planted, I needed to find it, first and alone. If *nothing* was planted, then I'd left the light on myself, no harm, no foul. If it was *Mike*, and I was kind of hoping, trying not to, but hoping, then that would be best, that would be fine, because then I would know what was going on, then he could tell me, then we could plan.

I stuffed the keys into my back pocket so they wouldn't jingle and eased the passenger door open. It was dark on that side and with the tree for cover, no one should see me slip out. Christ. Oh, Christ. I hadn't done this in a long, long time.

You breathe, you know, and the chest pumps, the adrenaline goes, everything's heightened, the feel of the night. The Colt was hard against my hipbone, tucked under my shirt because you don't walk the streets with a gun in your hand. I made it to the far corner and turned. No one behind me. Nothing moving on the street.

You breathe. The blood flows. Makes it harder to hear with the pulsing, the hum. The alley was next, halfway up the block like an open door, waiting. Trash cans and shadows. A car.

A car.

I kept walking, crossed the mouth of the alley on the sidewalk without missing a step and angled left across the street. I got to the far side, turned up the block going away from my house, and went on to the next corner. Turned left there, walked over, and came back down the alley one block to the north.

The light was reasonable, not very bright, but enough. I couldn't see anyone in the car. It looked to be parked, tucked in off the asphalt near the Balfours' yard. I could go around again or I could go straight down the alley, my choice. I crossed the street and kept going.

It was a 1994 Buick Century. Two-tone blue, with a scratch down the side, but that's what you get for parking in alleys. No sign of a radio, no mugs, no wrappers. Didn't look like a city car. Didn't look like a stakeout. I hadn't heard that anyone was visiting the Balfours, but I hadn't been around much the last few days and it was possible. It's not that they have to check in with me anyway, it just would have been nice to know. Maybe I wouldn't go straight into my backyard after all. The windows off the porch give a pretty good view and there was a moon.

I let myself in through the Balfours' gate, watching out for their cats and their windows. Didn't need them calling the cops on a prowler, but I could hear their TV going, so they were probably safely in the bedroom. Jane likes to be comfortable. I stepped carefully through her garden, the roses, the peonies, and scrambled up over the wall. I dropped on all fours, lightly, knees flexed, stomach tucked, the Colt riding high. It was dark in this stretch of my yard, about eight feet of lawn between the wall and the house. I was facing the spare-bedroom window, and a long zag would take me around to the back door.

I pulled out the gun.

I could feel the adrenaline pumping me up and the day was like dust in my mouth. Just a look, I'd just go take a look, but I was trembling, the grip warm in my hand. This is what they pay cops for, to serve and protect, but *I* was the cops, I used to be, and the last time I'd been this hopped up, I'd broken the arm on a PCP mechanic who was trying to tear Jablonski's head off. Christ, that was three, four years ago. The night and the tension and the Colt in my hand brought it all back and I was going to be a basket case if I didn't get moving.

I stopped under the window but I couldn't hear anything. Maybe some voices deep in the house. With the Balfours' TV on, it was hard to be sure. I snaked up for a look and it was dark in the bedroom, just a small spill of light from the hall. I feathered around the corner to the porch. Faint light out the back windows, coming down the main hall from the kitchen. The rest of the house was dark.

The back door was locked, of course, and I wasn't going to pull out my keys. I have a spare for emergencies in one of the rain gutters, so I reached up warily, keeping my eyes on the door.

The key wasn't there.

My hand made the circuit again.

No key.

I stretched out my hand slowly, carefully, barely caressing the knob. It turned. Not locked. Not anymore. Mike knows where I keep the key, but he would have relocked the door.

I breathed on it and it opened. No voices. Just the sound of someone, *one* someone, moving around in the kitchen. A glass. The scrape of a chair. Make yourself at home, little honey, because I'm coming to see you. I slipped down the hall, my own hall, moving from doorway to doorway like a dream. The .45 was in my hands, safety off and ready, the wall of the hallway an inch from my back. Pied the kitchen doorway carefully, sliced the available view into sections, deeper each time, scoped it, as far as I could. Not enough, then, to see. I breathed and whirled through the open doorway, mov-

ing in to the right, tucked low, front sight focused, a hair
from explosion—and saw Josh, my stepson Josh, sitting
at the end of the table, terrified.

*"Jesus Christ, Joshua, what the hell are you doing here?!"*

His eyes shifted, just that one tiny movement, and I
was already turning, transitioning, gun back to my chest
in a Close-Quarters-Ready as the voice came behind me.

"You have a permit for that thing?"

Christ, goddammit, there'd been two glasses on the
table. I was facing him, then—facing the man.

Josh was speaking urgently, stuttering, scared. "M-
M-Meg, this is Sergeant Reilly."

"I already know Reilly," I said. "Is there anyone else
in the house?"

"N-no."

Right.

"You have a warrant?"

Reilly's face was starting to change. "No."

Behind me, Josh was confused, pleading. "But, M-
Meg, he knew m-my dad."

As if that was all the explanation he needed. It probably was. I said tightly, not lowering, "Getting a lot of
mileage out of that, aren't you, Reilly?"

His eyes were ice.

"But, Meg—"

I couldn't stand the sound in Josh's voice, part hero-
worship, part hunger. "He never knew your dad," I said
harshly. "He's a lying bastard who's using you." The
frost in Reilly's face would have stopped an avalanche,
but I was past caring. "I talked to a lot of people today,
Reilly. Contacted some of the guys—Charlie's friends.
Maybe it'll surprise you that none of them knew you. *I*

was surprised. So I dug a little deeper and finally I *did* find someone who'd heard of you—because you'd called Saturday asking about *me*. Saturday, Reilly. Not yesterday. Did you think I wouldn't check?"

Reilly was only a yard or two from me and I still had the gun in my hand. I could see him remembering that, felt him starting to size me.

"Don't try it."

"No," he said, but his eyes were calculating. I moved back the few steps to the wall.

"Past me to the table," I told him—to the table where Josh was still sitting. I couldn't risk the glance to see how he was doing, but he hadn't made a sound. I put all the urgency I was feeling into my voice. "Josh, come around the table, over here behind me," and I heard the scrape of his chair as he stood. "You go that way," I said to Reilly. "That way towards the sink. I want you sitting in the far chair where Josh was." Farthest from me.

Reilly moved carefully past me, hands where I could see them, his eyes never leaving my face. The night and the tension flowed around me like a current, my jaw ached, and it took Reilly forever to reach the end of the table. "Keep your hands out," I said, "and sit."

The frost was gone, only a watchful carefulness, a man under control. "All right," he said, and put his hands on the table, sat. I could feel Josh in the corner by my shoulder and cleared a step left. Lowered the Colt a fraction.

"Suppose we talk," Reilly said.

"Dealer's choice."

"All right."

"How'd you get in?"

"Josh."

It made sense. Josh knows where I keep the key. "He wouldn't let a stranger into the house."

Beside me, Josh stirred.

"I have a badge," Reilly said easily, protecting him.

"And the magic words." I couldn't keep the bitterness out of my throat.

"I *did* know your dad," he said sideways to Josh. "Your stepmom never asked me, so I thought she knew."

*God*, he was a dangerous man. Enough truth to make you doubt yourself. I *hadn't* asked, I'd taken his word—for that and a lot of other things. "Tell us about it."

"We worked on a task force out of Sacramento."

"When?"

"Twelve years ago."

Twelve years? Jesus, a long time. Charlie was divorcing and I hadn't really known him then. He might have worked Sacramento.

"What sort of operation?"

"A burglary ring. It was just a few months, but we were paired most of the time."

Charlie'd talked about a burglary deal he'd been tapped for. They'd needed out-of-town talent and he'd wanted to get away from home for a while. I couldn't remember much about it, though, vital things like dates and names.

"Who headed it?"

"A guy named Kusak. I think he's still there."

"Not something I can check tonight."

"No."

Impasse. Reilly was still watching me, but then I still

had the gun. He'd talked the edge off me, though, which was probably what he'd wanted. I could feel the cold aches and tiredness slipping in under the tension, and what was I going to do with him? It was a nightmare crawling, all of it, the blood and Mike and everything, and now I was holding a gun on a cop. With Josh beside me, right beside me, *watching* me holding that gun on a cop. Twelve years old. Christ. I thumbed the safety on the Colt, and put it carefully down on the shelf next to me. I didn't make any bones about leaving my hand by it, though, and Reilly's eyes were taking notes.

"You could call your station tonight," he said quietly. "Maybe somebody there remembers Sacramento."

It wasn't just his knowing Charlie, it was *everything* now, all of the questions, and still with that pull to him there in the flesh, being so reasonable, so much like a cop.

Hell, he *was* a cop.

This was more than an impasse, it was a total, absolute piece. I'd just given him anything he wanted to put me away. Plenty of cause now, including assault with a deadly weapon if that's what he felt like. I'd held a gun on him. I was a suspect in a case, he'd entered legally, and there was no question that I knew who he was or that I knew he was a cop. Couldn't claim that I'd thought he was a burglar or anything. Well, I could claim that, but I'd still be in jail with the charges filed.

And things happen to people in jails. Accidents. Suicide. I'd feel safe enough being there in the light of day—tomorrow morning, say, with the bail already arranged and a lawyer beside me raising hell so that people would be careful. A few hours to wait in a cell, a little bit of time. I could stand it then, but I wasn't going in tonight.

"God*dammit*," I said, and took my hand away from the Colt. Goddammit to hell and gone. Reilly was nodding rather grimly, like a man who'd been expecting me.

"Think you want to talk to me, Meg."

"I *don't*," I said fiercely, "I don't want to talk to you at all. What I want to do is call my lawyer." Which was a good idea except that McKenzie's number was in my bag and my bag was in the goddamn truck. It would have to be Louis, and hope that Marie was still up.

"Meg—"

"I'm away from the gun," I said. "I'm not offering you any harm or resistance. You just keep your hands where I can see them while I make the phone call."

He was very still, watching me. And, of course, he was closest to the phone, there on the wall, dammit, sitting right next to it, no way around him or through him. Couldn't make him move without the gun, not the way he was sitting, not the way things had gone. He knew it, his goddamn eyes knew it, were waiting for me.

"You want to be sensible yet?"

I didn't—Christ, I didn't. I wanted to smear his face all over the wall. "What?"

"I'm not here to hurt anybody. I want a couple of answers and then I'll go."

A couple of answers. "You're overlooking the gun?"

"Unless you make it a problem."

I didn't have to *make* it a problem, it already *was* one. He might be talking very calmly and coolly, but there was a muscle working at the side of his jaw, and I know what it is to come down from a situation. Facing a gun.

"There was blood at Mike's," I said, and maybe I was explaining it a little. "Blood all over and then you here with Josh. No warrant, no backup. Not exactly procedure."

"You want *procedure*?"

People talk themselves into jail. "No."

He was silent again and I hated it, all of this. Hated that he had the position and the authority to back it up. Color of authority. The badge.

"I think we need to work out a few things," he said slowly. "Maybe we've gotten some wires crossed."

And what was I going to say? "Hell, no, man, jam it"? "Sure."

"Why'd you leave the office?"

I shrugged at him. "Nobody knew you."

"*Dave* knows me," he said.

Yarrow.

"Seems to me I mentioned him this morning, Meg."

His eyes very cool, looking at me.

"Seems to *me*," he said, "that you could have found out anything you wanted to about me, if you'd tried."

If I'd called Dave Yarrow, he was saying.

If I'd only called Dave.

"*Hello, Annabeth, is Dave home?*"

"My partner's been missing for three days," I said harshly. "There's blood all over and you showing up every time I turn around. I'm supposed to call Dave Yarrow on your say-so? Take your word for *anything* because you knew Charlie twelve years ago? Charlie never talked about you, he never did, not to me or to anyone else I called, and what does that tell me—that you're good old trustworthy Joe? That if I just call one more person, a guy you specifically mentioned—went out of your *way* to mention—Dave Yarrow, in fact—I'll find out that everything's fine?"

He had a thumb rubbing at his jaw, the corner of his mouth, and I had time to remember where I was and why. Who *he* was and why. Time to remember Josh at my elbow, dammit, drinking the details in.

"Reilly—"

"All right, I see it," he said, and maybe he did, I don't know. His mouth was a straight line. "You want to go down to the station?"

"No."

"Burbank?"

I didn't want to go to Burbank with him.

"You're going to talk to me, Meg. There or here." He hesitated, and then, flatly, "You want that lawyer?"

He wasn't reading me rights, he was asking. I should call Louis anyway, do something, but it was late and I was tired. God, I was tired. His other hand was still on the table, curved towards me, and it's the little things, the stupid things.

"That's okay," I said.

He eased. Not very much, a hair, but his mouth wasn't as tight. "Come and sit down, then."

Leave the gun, he was saying. Move away from the Colt.

"Okay."

"Josh, too."

Of course, Josh, too. Wouldn't want him splitting the focus. "Come on, Josh," I said, and pulled out the middle chair for him, moving it closer. I took the end chair myself, nearest the gun, and then we were both sitting, facing Reilly. He looked enormously large and capable at the other end of the table.

"Suppose you tell me," he said.

I could have jerked him around, I guess, "Tell you what?" like I didn't know, but that would just piss him off and there was no point in doing it. He was still asking why I'd left the office.

"Your guy didn't know 'Haroutunian.' "

"What guy?"

"At the station. When I called."

"Dan?"

I didn't know who it was, hadn't asked. "The guy who took the message, Reilly. Answered 'STU,' but I had to spell 'Haroutunian' for him. I thought you'd all been working on this since Saturday."

"Not Dan," he said.

"He doesn't read the reports? Nobody talks to him?"

Reilly was scratching thoughtfully at the underside of his chin. "That's why you took off?"

"No, that's not why I took off," I said. "I took off because your guy didn't seem to know about the case, nobody seemed to know about you, and I was damned if I was going to be a sitting duck when you got back."

He was nodding. "Why'd you go to Mike's?"

I could have given him twenty answers, would have, but he was waiting on me, ready to roll. That thin line, and there was Josh to consider. "Someone had to check."

"There are other departments," he said. "You could have called Burbank if you didn't trust me."

Could have sent someone else, he meant. Had someone else do a "check the well-being." On Mike. Mike's well-being. Mike and his pack-rabbit habits and his god-damned paid-up Porsche Carrera. I couldn't look at Reilly so I stared at the table, my hands, and finally I gave him the truth. "I didn't know what they'd find."

"They found plenty," he said. "Why didn't you stay?"

Christ, *I* didn't know. It had all made sense at the time. Josh was shifting beside me, taking too long, and I guess I was losing what little control I'd had. "I offered to stay," I said. "They didn't want me."

"They didn't know."

That was true enough. Nobody'd known.

"Why didn't you tell them, Meg?"

If I was so scared, he meant. If I was so sure he was setting me up. He was watching me from across the table, always watching, and it was too late and I was too tired for this. "There was blood on the wall," I said thickly. "Blood everywhere and your guys hanging around outside. Nobody knew you, Reilly, nobody at all." I was holding my left hand down because it was trembling suddenly and it was damn-all I could do to focus on the table in front of me.

"*Guys?*"

It was the inflection, the emphasis, that caught me, held me. I stared up at him, at his face.

"Mitch," I said, "and the man in the back." I saw it then, his eyes and the way he went blank, with that peaceful expression spreading over him again like a mask. My voice was a whisper, hurting and dry: "You didn't have anyone on the back, Reilly?"

"No," he said, "I didn't."

# 15

Maybe I believed him.

Maybe I just *wanted* to believe him.

It was a hell of a time to be wondering which it was, with Mike missing and my kid there and the only man who'd been coming around lately sitting across from me at the table like he owned the chair.

"I want a description," Reilly said.

Well, yeah. "Male white, five-ten, -eleven. Kind of built, but not huge. Maybe one-ninety-five."

"Age?"

"Thirties. Thirty-two, thirty-three."

"Meg."

Too slow with the details. "Light-brown hair," I said, "sort of long. Not really down-and-dirty, but enough for casual undercover. Too long for uniform, not long enough for Vice. No facial hair. Not scruffy. No distinguishing marks that I saw. Fairly tan. He was wearing old jeans and a plain white tee shirt, no logo. I didn't notice his shoes."

"You're sure he was a cop?"

I just looked at him.

"All right," he said, but it wasn't all right. Too many things unresolved.

"You want some coffee or something? Some hot chocolate?" I was maybe leaning in towards Josh, my arm on the table, and Reilly's eyes flicked that way. Held. Returned to me.

"Sure."

Nice of him. "How about you, buddy?" I said to Josh. "You want something?"

Josh shook his head quickly, ducking down.

"Yeah, you do," I said. "You can even have marsh-mallows."

"I just had a soda."

So had Reilly, two glasses on the table. Or maybe water for him, keeping Josh company. "Okay," I said, "you don't have to drink. You want to get the cups for me and be handy, though?" I was already on my way towards the sink, moving, squatting down. The Brew-master coffeepot was in the bottom cupboard. Charlie'd gotten it that last Christmas and this seemed like an occasion to use it. I generally make instant in the microwave, but Reilly drank his black, so he might still have taste buds. I looked back over my shoulder. "What are you doing here anyway, babe?"

Josh was very small in the chair, his voice a thread. "I just, you know, wanted to see you."

He'd seen me last Wednesday, was coming over this weekend. "Well, that's fine," I said casually, on my knees, rummaging. "I didn't notice the bike, is all."

He flushed, darting a look at me. "It's behind the garage."

Why I hadn't tripped over it, then. Usually it stays where it lands on the back porch. "Thought maybe you'd gotten a ride."

"Nuh-uh."

Ridden over on his own. Not the first time by any means, but it cleared away the little naggy suspicion that Reilly had brought him. I smiled lightly at them both, social mode. "Well, you picked a heck of a night to come by. First Reilly, and then me popping in. Your mom'll be thrilled."

Josh was a silent lump, staring down at the table. Mom wasn't going to be thrilled about any of this.

"We'll work it out," I said. I was already into the cupboard, shifting the pans around, and it's difficult talking over your shoulder, so I stopped. I found the Brewmaster on the lower shelf behind a couple of large pots I never use. They're just something to keep the lids in unless you make a lot of spaghetti, and I've always thought it was a rip-off to sell them in sets.

"Yo, Josh," I said, dragging the Brewmaster backwards, "were you going to get those cups?"

He scraped the chair back obediently, but slowly, not moving much, kind of standing there like a block, and he knows where things are in the kitchen.

"The rack behind you," I said. "Cups?"

He flushed again, halfway between humiliation and something stronger, flicking a look at Reilly, and I'm no good with kids, never have been. I'd told Charlie that all those years ago. I didn't know the first thing about them, I'd said, so if he was looking for maternal instinct and the little woman to help him out, he'd have done better to kiss up to one of the waitresses at Bob's. Josh had scared me to death then, so small and so needing, and what the hell did *I* know about babies? But we did the best we could, tried to, anyway, and it was harder than I'd thought it would be to give him back after Caroline found herself. Couldn't keep a mother from her child, though. That's how the courts felt then, and maybe, after all, they were right. Caroline wouldn't come flipping in with a gun and then expect everyone to sit down and have coffee.

"It was a misunderstanding," I said, not looking at anyone. "Mike's in some sort of trouble and I'm kind of jumpy about it, that's all. There were those guys hanging around, and the blood, and I didn't know what to think when I got here and found you with Reilly. I guess I thought maybe he'd snatched you."

"You mean like kidnapping?"

"Yeah."

Kidnapping was interesting. Josh was coming alive again, looking at Reilly speculatively, wishful thinking, how he would have handled it if Reilly'd tried. Reilly looked steadily back at him, and then at me.

"You going to make that coffee?"

I was, yes. I gave him a fragile smile, apologetic, awkward, and buried myself in the fridge. Coffee on the bottom shelf, wedged at the back behind the jam and two boxes of baking soda. Mountain-grown best getting stale. I hoped it was still drinkable—I don't know the shelf-life of coffee and I couldn't remember when I'd put it there.

Josh had lifted the cups down and put them on the table. Three cups, so he was joining us after all. "I've got some cookies in the pantry," I said. "You want to dig those out for me? And you can get another jar of creamer while you're at it." I didn't wait for either of them because I was fishing around for the filters, left-hand drawer of the sideboard. It was too close to the Colt, right next to it, so I kept my hands very visible, obviously just getting filters, not trying anything, and then I was back across the room at the sink. Had to get a spoon from the drainer to measure the coffee. It's kind of a production, you know, when you haven't used something for a while, and I put in an extra spoonful to be sure. Reilly wasn't stopping Josh from leaving.

The pantry's the one of the three small rooms that's directly across the hall. There was nothing Josh could do from there, no way out. Reilly had a clear view through the doorway, but I didn't want anyone getting strange about it—we'd had enough strange already. Reilly wasn't saying anything, though, not stopping him or interfering. Taking me at face value, I guess. I put the water in the pot and plugged the damn thing in.

"I'm sorry about the gun," I said brusquely. Josh was coming back already, which was just as well. I didn't know what else I'd wanted to say to Reilly anyway.

Josh had a cellophane tray by the edges, looking disturbed. "They're not really cookies," he said, "just these wafer things. Is this what you meant?"

He was hoping for something different, I guess, something better, but that's what I had. Courtesy of the local booster club, the high school team. "We'll push 'em off on the sergeant," I said, and Reilly almost smiled. Definitely looking easier. The power of apology. The coffee smelled bitter and strong.

"Were we out of creamer?"

"I forgot," Josh said. He was already turning. Forgetting a lot of things.

"You didn't lock the back door either," I said, "and I

left it open behind me. You want to go flip the knob?" I was moving the cups to the counter, ready to pour.

"Oh, yeah." He was hesitating, damn the kid anyway, why couldn't he just get it done? "There was this guy," he said.

The room was very still. I could feel Reilly snapping to, and that wasn't what I wanted at all. "Joshua—"

"No, for real. I was going to tell you before, only—" His eyes slid between us uncertainly. Only I'd come in with a gun. Driven everything else from his mind. Christ.

"What guy?"

"He was at the door when I got here."

"Back door?"

"Yeah. Like he was trying to get in, like with tools or something."

Tools. "What time?"

"I don't know. Around five."

At five I was on my way over to Mike's or I would have been coming home. "One of yours?" I said to Reilly, and he was shaking his head, eyes very intent. Someone walking on my grave. Digging it. I switched back to Josh.

"Did you get a good look at him?"

"Yeah, I guess. The back of him anyway, 'cause I was coming in from the alley."

"What was he wearing?"

"Sort of a suit—like on MTV, you know?"

"Flashy?"

"I don't know. Expensive. Like with jewelry."

"Did you *see* jewelry? Chains?"

"I think so, yeah."

Not Mitch, then. It's not that it's so far from here to

Mike's, but he hadn't been wearing anything like a suit when I'd seen him there at about five-thirty. Or could he have changed? "Was he short?" I said. "My height?"

"I don't think so. Kind of taller. Well, maybe. I don't know."

Not six foot anyway. "Dark hair? Blond? Mustache? Beard?"

"Well, he looked kind of like Ricky's brother, you know? Only it wasn't him."

"Reyes," I said for Reilly, "a neighbor's kid. He looked like Eddie? Thin? Dark?"

"Yeah. With kind of a mustache."

"Eddie's age?"

"Older," Josh said.

"Like me? Like Reilly?"

"I don't know. I don't think that old."

Older than sixteen, but not ancient like me. Twenties, maybe. In a suit. Trying the door.

"Did he get in?"

"Well, no, 'cause I stopped him."

"You what?"

He flushed. "Well, I was coming in through the bushes, you know, just to see, but he must have heard me 'cause he started looking around."

"He *saw* you?"

"Well, yeah, I guess so. I said like 'hey' or something, and he looked at me real quick and then he took off down the driveway."

Spilled milk. Worse than spilled milk. And Josh so full of himself, so full of his age, coming in through the bushes like a goddamned guerrilla. "I'm going to say this one time," I said, "you had no business doing that. If something happens, you go to the neighbors right away, every time. Jesus Christ, Joshua, you know better than this."

"Well, he wasn't *doing* anything."

"He was trying to break in. He could have had a gun, you don't know."

"He just ran away."

"Because you were *lucky*," I said. "Not because you were so brave or so smart. Why the hell didn't you lock the back door?"

"I was waiting for you."

And that wasn't right. Except he'd have thought I'd be home any minute if he got here at five, because, me, I'm predictable, routine, nothing to me, no damn surprises, very easy to trace.

"Son of a *bitch*," I said. Even Reilly knew right where to find me, and who the hell else? "What were you going to do if he came back?"

Josh's eyes slid away, and I didn't need that answer either. *"Did you touch my guns?"*

"N-no."

*"Your dad's?"*

"I didn't, Meg, honest . . . just my BB gun."

A toy in his hands, and who-knew-who coming around, probably armed. Children die, you know. Die like the rest of us in fear and despair. For stupidity. "I'm going to break that thing in half," I said, "I'm going to burn it. You're too damned old for this nonsense and I'm not having any more of it. You go lock that door right now."

Josh went. Turned on his heel and ran—red-faced, humiliated, starting to tear. He'd stay for a few minutes, maybe longer, before he came back. Hating me.

"I'm going to send him home," I said. "Have him call his mom and get the hell out of this. Whatever business you have with me doesn't involve him."

"He saw someone breaking in."

"No," I said. "You can get a description, make your report, I'll talk to you till dawn, but Josh is out of it."

"I can't just let him go, Meg."

Gently. So nice. As if I were ten tons of stupid in a frail little female bag.

"Why?" I said. "You recognize the description? Got more than one dark Mexican on your squad?"

There was a noticeable pause.

"I've got two," Reilly said evenly, "but they weren't *here*."

"Where were they?"

He didn't have to tell me, but I was getting him ticked again. Pushing at him all the time. "Pete's in Cancún on his honeymoon. Lots of family there. It's a safe bet he's not hanging around Burbank."

Cancún's not that far. A plane trip. "And Escobar?"

We were eye to eye. "Escobar was sitting outside your office," he said.

Well, I'd known he had somebody there. He knew I'd known it. I shrugged at him. "So maybe he found out he lost me and came here."

"He found out at a quarter to five," Reilly said. "When *I* did." If I'd had any doubts that he was pissed, they were gone. He had that look on his face, that "try me" look, that thin-lipped, waiting-for-an-explanation-but-not-waiting-long look. "I thought we had an understanding this morning," he said.

Standing over me in the doorway. Escobar looking too good. "I don't owe you anything," I said. "You've just been using me to get to Mike. Part of the job, maybe, but I don't have to like it, don't have to help you. You think I'm going to tell you anything *now*?"

"Yeah, I do."

It might have been a challenge. It sounded like one. "How's your Iranian accent, Reilly?"

He didn't even blink. "It's lousy," he said, and waited. I could oblige.

"You know, *somebody* called my office Saturday, claiming to be Haroutunian. *Somebody* said that his boy had been stolen. It's not so hard to figure what I'd do, me being an ex-cop and all. (a) I call the station, (b) I go myself, (c) I do both, that old need to be of service. Now, I don't know what response time is in Beverly Hills, obviously very quick, but I wasn't exactly sightseeing my way up to the house, and you were *still* there ahead of me. Pretty damned efficient, I'd say. Almost as if you were waiting for it. Was that it, Reilly—were you waiting?"

"No."

"No?" I was pacing back and forth by the sink because I get like that, slamming the dishes away from the drainer, throwing the silverware into the drawer. "Aren't you the guy who let Haroutunian walk? 'Sorry to have troubled you, sir,' when you could have damn well brought *him* down to the station and cleared everything up. He still missing, Reilly?"

There might have been half a flicker. Obviously yes.

"*Right*," I said, "but you're not rousting his family and friends, you're just coming on to *me* all day long: 'I knew your husband, Meg.' 'Let me ask you about Mike, Meg.' 'Let me give you an effin ride home.' ''

Reilly had a kind of lock-jaw look about him. "You done?" he said, and I wasn't, not by a long shot.

"No," I said, "there's more. This business of you already at Haroutunian's house when I pulled up. It's not like anyone was showing *me* ID—*I'm* the one producing, *I'm* the one explaining, and I've just got to damn well take your word for it that this guy is even who he says he is. You know, my caller didn't speak a lot of English, hardly any, in fact, very hard to understand, but your guy's clear as a bell quoting Shakespeare. Same lines, too, over and over, like he doesn't want to go off script. But that's okay, huh, Reilly, because you've checked him out, you've gotten his bonafides, and why would I question *you*? What do you think—I'm stupid? Blinded by the badge?" I fumbled a glass tossing it into the cupboard and it smashed down into a couple of pieces against the counter. "Shit."

"Are you done?" he said again, and I was, yes, this time I was. "That's good." He was a big man, maybe I've mentioned that, and he was already coiled, but Jesus, he had some control. "You've gotten it wrong."

"Tell it to somebody else, Reilly."

"I'm telling *you*," he said. "Saying it for the last time so you need to listen."

I didn't need to listen, I needed to push him, push him hard. "Does that work for you?" I said scornfully, " 'Shut up and listen'? *I thought we had an understanding, Meg*—yeah, I *bet* you did. Did you reach an understanding with Josh, too? I mean, you had, what, half an hour? Long enough to tell a few stories about Dad, get a few

stories back. Is that how you made sergeant, Reilly—
working women and kids?"

He was two hundred and twenty-some pounds, rising and moving in on me, hard with it and feeling ugly,
and I was backed up before him, backed into the corner
like an absolute coward.

"You've got a nasty mouth," he said tightly. "You can
run it all you want to at somebody else, but when *I* say
'Listen,' that's what I mean." He was towering over me,
Jesus, he was big, and close, not two steps away. I couldn't
hope to take him, not a prayer, not a whisper, on my best
day I couldn't, and he was ready for me, waiting for it, waiting for me to be stupid and try.

"Please, Reilly," I said.

"Please *what?*"

Liking it. Liking throwing his weight at me. That
flash of satisfaction, grit. Sexual. Carnal. Grind the bitch
under, and me shrinking before him.

"Please," I said. "Reilly, I'm sorry." I was trembling,
maybe, more than a little. His chest wavered in front of
me, all I could see, and I was helpless, so stupid, my gun
on the other counter. Helpless, pleading like a goddamned female, reduced to a whisper. "Please, Reilly,
don't."

A pause.

A breath.

Exhaling out over my hair.

"God*damm*it," he said.

The way *I'd* said it when I'd put up the gun. Constrained by circumstance, the straits of the Code. He
took a step away and then another, distancing himself
from me, from the situation. A second breath, grim.

Disgusted, seemed like, at himself or at me, or even at both of us. "I should have just taken you in."

"Yeah," I said, "maybe so."

He looked at me sharply then, seeing my eyes, the way I was standing. Awareness flared through him, and temper, and Jesus, I thought he was going to come at me anyway.

"Have you been *playing* with me?"

He was speaking softly, very distinctly, and I could see the Abbott relationship. Blood brothers. Sharks.

"I had to know," I said.

"Know what? That I could crush you with one hand?"

"That you wouldn't."

"I would," he said flatly. "In a second. You couldn't have stopped me."

I opened my right hand where he could see it, around the knife I'd been holding, the one from the dish drainer.

He was still again, unreadable.

I opened the other hand, around the piece of glass from the counter.

"You'd have marks at least, Reilly. Something to explain."

He wasn't moving. A statue.

"Why?"

"Your Toyota's not outside," I said.

I moved very slowly then, no sudden anythings. Placed the knife on the countertop, easing it down.

"I was just showing you," I said carefully. "I'm not very good at trusting people, okay?"

"That glass is going to cut your hand."

I guess *he* wasn't good at trusting people either. Or maybe it was me. I tossed the shard of glass towards the table. There was always the coffeepot beside me an arm's sweep away.

"So this was to draw me in."

Reilly was speaking evenly—meditatively, almost— but he was positioned, taut.

"I'm sorry," I said. "I couldn't take any chances."

Something flickered and I braced, I don't know what for. He was still speaking softly, very gently. "You don't consider *this* chancy?"

I did. It was. "Reilly—"

"You think you're good."

"Not that good," I said. "Really."

He was nodding, slit-eyed.

Not listening.

"You think you can take me."

"I know I can't."

"But you can play these *games* with me." He was a step closer and I could smell it, the danger. I was shaking again, old habits, old reflexes. Standing low.

"I had to know," I said.

"You were holding a *goddamned .45 on me*," he said savagely, and all I had left was my voice.

"What was I going to ask? 'You here to do me, Reilly?' You'd have said, 'Yes'?"

He wasn't saying anything.

"There was blood all over Mike's place, Reilly, and you here alone with my boy."

"You could have called Burbank. Had Josh call them."

"You could have let me call my lawyer," I said.

He was silent another fierce minute, staring down at me, and then he took a breath and blinked, and I knew we were okay. "No," he said. "Then you wouldn't have talked to me."

And that was true enough. I wouldn't have. Couldn't even tell him he was wrong. I took a breath of my own, finally, shrugged at him. We are what we are. Sketched a hand at the pot.

"Did you still want that coffee?"

"*I'll* pour it," he said.

# 16

Sometimes things work out. We were back across the table, coffee steaming lightly from the cups. "What about Josh?" he'd asked, and I'd shrugged nonchalantly.

"Eavesdropping down the hall."

"Safe enough?"

"Well, he can't get to any guns," I said, "without passing the door behind me, so probably if you sit there and stare at it, you'll be okay."

"I was thinking about the neighbors."

"Don't want them to know that you're here?" I smiled at him, a regular smile, and it was odd to feel so free. Reaction, probably. A long, tense day. "I don't think he'll go for help unless I scream, so you just keep your distance and we'll be fine."

There was a considering sort of look in his eyes, a heartbeat's worth of pause, and I was turning red, I knew I was, *he* knew I was, but he only nodded and went back to sipping his coffee. Son of a bitch. Like I'd propositioned him or something.

"You don't want to call him in?" he said.

"He's okay for a while."

"I don't want him doing anything stupid, Meg."

Like *I'd* done, he meant. I wasn't feeling free anymore, I was feeling hemmed in and testy. "Then speak up," I said, "so he doesn't misunderstand anything, right? I still want to hear about the Toyota."

Reilly was weighing me, measuring. "I'm driving a city car," he said. "Two blocks over. I didn't want you spotting it and taking off."

I *should* have spotted it, should have driven the neighborhood looking for cars. Next time I would. And it was perfectly reasonable that he'd hide it from me, given that I'd already run out on him once. Twice if you counted Mike's place and Burbank, and I was pretty sure Reilly was counting—something about his tone. I guess I wasn't the only one feeling testy.

"I'm sorry," I said.

"Sorry's good."

"Fine, then," I said, "you're so clear on everything, you tell *me* what's going on."

He took another sip of coffee. Set the cup down very deliberately. Looked at me. "Where all'd you go tonight, Meg?"

"Mike's," I said. "The office. Here."

"Anywhere else?"

"No."

"Anyone see you?"

"Lots of people," I said steadily. "Anyone know that you're here?"

"Abbott. You want to give me a name?"

Of someone who'd seen me. Alibis. "I spent an hour on the phone with my lawyer, Reilly. He thinks I shouldn't talk to you."

He was nodding, ignoring it. "You call *him*?"

"Yeah, I did, actually. He called me back, if it matters." It didn't matter. They could always get the records from the phone company.

"An hour on the phone," Reilly said. "A half hour there, a half hour back. That's two hours, isn't it?"

I'd left Mike's place at seven, he meant. Hadn't gotten here till after ten. He didn't even need to be looking at the big clock behind me. "I wasted a lot of time ducking your tail," I said.

"My tail?"

"Whosever it was."

"Someone was following you?"

"I don't know. I didn't see anyone."

"But you suspected it."

"Yeah," I said shortly, "I suspected it." He already had me answering like a damn crook.

"Why?"

"Well, someone's been going to a lot of trouble," I said. "I didn't want to be run off the road and abducted."

He was nodding thoughtfully. "So you went back to your office."

Where anyone could find me, he meant. It *was* pretty stupid. "I needed my gun," I said.

"You left it at the office?"

I sure as hell wasn't going to tell him that I'd left it in the truck. "I wasn't expecting to find blood at Mike's."

He nodded again, letting it pass. "Why'd you go out the window?"

A trap working somehow, but the answer was simple. "I didn't want Escobar following me," I said, "or breaking into the office once he knew I was gone."

"You weren't afraid of being abducted *then*?"

I'd taken off, he meant, but I hadn't taken the gun. Ducked out the back window, but left the .45 behind. I could have shined him on, given him a story, but he'd keep working it because it wasn't logical, not a reasonable thing for me to do, and it was stupid of me to let it go on just for my pride. "The gun was in the truck," I said, "okay? I figured your guy would be watching it, so I left it where it was. I didn't want to tip anybody off that I was moving."

He let the silence run.

"Reilly," I said, "it's not that big a deal. I wasn't thinking things were desperate then, just that I'd do better to be ahead of you checking out Mike's place. I could always get a gun over here."

"Then why'd you go back to the office?"

To hide the rental car. To bring Charlie's truck home. "I thought it would be safer," I said.

He was silent again.

"Oh, for Christ's sake, Reilly, where was I going to go? Here? You had people all over, don't tell me you didn't. I needed a damned gun and I knew there was one at the office. I figured by that time you'd have pulled the guy there, shipped him here or to Mike's, figured you'd be tied up with Burbank showing your badge, and Mitch and the other guy would be lost on the freeways. If that wasn't true, then it wasn't—I'm not a damned mind reader, I'm just doing the best that I can."

"Not doing so well," he said.

Fine.

"First of all," he said, "I want to know why you went out the window."

I'd already told him five times. "Because I was spooked, Reilly. Because your cop couldn't spell 'Haroutunian,' because nobody knew you, because things were wrong and I reacted. Why the hell *else* would I go out a window?"

"A phone call from Mike."

He had me absolutely pegged. He was wrong, but he could have been right. I stared at him, seeing it. Me going over to Mike's. Skating out again. "To pick something up."

He was nodding.

"No," I said.

"Where'd you get the key?"

Trap shutting. Shut. Because I'd told him on Sunday that I didn't have one and Burbank had told him I did. He thought I'd been meeting Mike. "Mike keeps a spare at the office," I said. "It didn't seem like something to tell you at the time."

He didn't like it, and I mean *really* didn't like it, but "Look, Reilly," I said, "you're the same guy who was sitting there trying to scam me about Abbott, so don't get self-righteous at me. I was protecting my own."

"Your own."

"That's right," I said, "Mike. You don't have to like it, it doesn't have to suit you, but I've known him a really long time."

"You know he was using?"

It's a very old trick. "He isn't."

"They found a needle, Meg."

Something uncompromising about the set of his face. He didn't look like a man who was lying.

"A needle—," I said, "or a kit?"

"Kit."

A kit. Syringes. Ties. Warming spoon.

"Heroin?"

"Yeah."

"Mike wouldn't touch the stuff."

"Seems to have. His prints."

I was going to be sick.

"They found some bags, too," he said. "Empty. Traces of rock. Too much just for leisure, so we think he was running it."

A to B. B to C. "No."

"There was a cop on his place," Reilly said. "You saw him, you said so. Somebody's narc."

Mike running drugs.

"Someone broke in," I said. "They could have planted anything."

"With his prints on it?" Reilly was shaking his head. "Someone was looking, Meg. His place was torn up, emptied out—like a deal gone bad."

"Mike's not a dealer, Reilly."

"He left you a message to be careful," Reilly said. "Something he normally do?"

On the machine. On the goddamn machine. And *I'd* played it for him.

" 'If someone comes looking,' he said. He have a lot of people coming by looking?"

Not coming by.

Calling, though.

A lot of calls.

"He *isn't* dealing, Reilly."

"You want to tell me about the Porsche?"

I wanted to, yeah. Wanted to tell him I'd *loaned* Mike

the money or he'd found it or something, under a rock.

Rock cocaine.

"Reilly—"

"The guy Josh saw at your back door wasn't mine," he said. Definite. Final. Meaning who the hell else thought I was involved, was coming around. The guy was Latino. Mexican? Colombian?

"You said it was cop-involved," I said.

Reilly looked at me sharply.

"Saturday, outside the station," I said. "You told me cops and harassment."

"I said it *might* be. I don't think so now."

He didn't *want* to think so, though. Had his reasons, his blind spots. Like I had with Mike.

"If the cop in the back at Mike's place was 'somebody's narc,'" I said, "why didn't he come in when Burbank showed up?"

Reilly shrugged. "Didn't want to. Didn't need to. Might even be theirs."

"You can find out."

"I can do a lot of things," he said. "That isn't the point."

The point was No Return. The point was that he didn't want to be playing dodgeball with questions all night, didn't want my halfhearted, lukewarm response. Cooperation, that was the point. Me giving in.

Trusting.

Something I do so well.

"Burbank didn't know you were doing a stakeout."

It didn't seem to bother him. "You have cop connections," he said coolly. "I don't know who all you might know at Burbank."

Who might want to warn me, he meant. Warn Mike. Mike and his drug-running friends. It was reason enough as things go.

"Why didn't *Mitch* come in once they got there?" I said.

*That* caused a glitch, a hesitation. Hardly noticeable except that I was noticing everything.

"He was waiting for me."

I stared at him. "You personally?"

"That's right."

Reilly was everywhere. At my house, at the office, the station.

At Mike's.

And that clicked it for me, was the tumbler, the key combination, because he *had* said it was cops on Saturday, had thought so in my office this morning. "You don't trust your own guys?" I said, and his eyes lidded down.

Jesus H. Jesus H. and Mary, Mother of God.

"Let me see if I have this right," I said. "You and Abbott *aren't* really working together, but you *are* doing a little side job on police corruption. Some housecleaning, Reilly? Somebody point a finger at your squad?"

He didn't want to tell me, but I wasn't likely to stop now that I'd started guessing. The muscle on his jaw moved and set. "Possibly," he said.

Possibly. "And you're checking things out on the q.t. before Internal Affairs does."

"Something like that."

Exactly like that. Exactly the hell like that. Didn't want his whole unit grounded for a possibility. Have IA traipsing through, whiplashing his guys and basically shutting them down. He'd a lot rather it was Mike and some drug deal, independent of everything, nothing to do with his team.

"Did it occur to you," I said very tightly, "that Mike might know someone on your squad? That someone might have a really good reason to set him up like this?"

"It occurred to me."

"But you weren't going to tell me about *that* part, were you? You weren't even going to mention it."

"If there's anyone who knows Mike," Reilly said, "it's you. That's what I keep hearing. 'Ask Meg.' 'Meg'll know.' But so far, you don't seem to know anything about anything, which means somebody's lying. You want two guesses who?"

I didn't need two guesses.

"You're in it up to your neck," Reilly said.

His face was closed against me again, very hard.

"You want to make a deal, Meg?"

I didn't want to make a deal.

I didn't want anything.

We were back at the Point, and there was no way to go. I stared for what seemed like forever at the cups on the table, but there was just no way.

"I'll get Josh in," I said finally. "Give his mom a call."

"All right."

Crisp. Clipped. That was fine with him, then. "It may take a few minutes. I don't think she knows he's here—he hid his bike."

"You can use this phone."

The kitchen phone, so he could listen in. But he didn't mind me making the call. "I think probably," I said, "that we'll have to hang up the phone in the bedroom first. She hasn't been calling every fifteen minutes and it's pretty late. Usually she does that."

Reilly wasn't looking quite so iced. "You have a routine?"

"Josh has some problems with his mom," I said. Reilly didn't seem especially surprised.

"Actually," I said, "I was thinking she'd be ringing the doorbell by now to haul him back home, but probably she doesn't want to give me the satisfaction."

There was another little thaw, a half-glint. That one raising eyebrow.

"Would have interfered with my kidnapping plans."

Well, yeah, there was that. Didn't have to spell everything out for Reilly. I wished I didn't like him. I watched his thumb stroking the rim of his cup. Big hands. Not in a hurry. Just us in the kitchen and nobody wanting to end it, I guess. The way it had to go.

"What are you doing, Meg?" He didn't mean about Josh.

"I kind of thought you were taking me in."

"You don't want to negotiate?"

I didn't want to do anything.

"Someone's out looking for you," Reilly said. "They've already been here once, maybe more."

"My drug friends," I said. "Coming by for supplies."

"You think it's a joke?"

"I think you're working me, Reilly."

He was silent, looking.

"I've only got your word for it that this guy wasn't yours, only your word that they found drugs at Mike's. Sort of calculated to make me run for shelter, you know? The nearest strong pair of arms, and here you conveniently are." He didn't say anything, but his eyes were down. Acknowledgment? Admission? I couldn't read my way out of a paper bag right now, I was so goddamned tired and I shouldn't even be talking, shouldn't give him that much, but somebody had to, for Mike. "Mike wouldn't touch *drugs*, Reilly. Liquor, yeah—maybe a joint if it was there at a party, I couldn't swear he never did, but nothing to do with heroin or cocaine, nothing to do with selling it. I've been kind of blind lately, kind of absorbed—I'm not going to tell you I know everything, because I sure as hell don't, obviously don't, but I know the heart of the man, what he's made of. Mike's not the smartest guy going, not the quickest, and his morals aren't everything a mother would want, but he's never had any traffic with drugs. It's a set-up all the way, and a good one if you don't know him. The difference is that I *do* know him, and I'm not going to turn him over to a cop with a hard-on. I appreciate that you don't want it to be *your* guys who are harassing or dealing or whatever, but you're not jobbing Mike while I'm here to protect him. That's the way I see it. That puts us on opposite sides. It's not what I want, Reilly, but that's what it is."

He was thoughtful, very quiet, absently stroking the rim. I should have kept my mouth shut, not given him anything else to know me, to work me. Let him think what he liked.

"They say you were sleeping with him," he said.

"They" was Dave. Dave had told him. So much for impassioned defense.

"That was a question, Meg."

One he kept asking. I watched his hand going round. Long fingers. Thorough. I wondered if he was that thorough other ways, and the thought of it burned me. I focused on my own hands, the nails.

"Meg."

"People like to make assumptions," I said.

"Don't see you doing much to correct that." He took a deliberate sip of his coffee. I watched the cup coming down.

Dammit. Goddammit.

"Mike was my running partner at the Academy," I said. "We liked each other a lot, got along pretty well, and people just had to be busy, you know? Had to think they knew everything. It was easier to let them go on."

"Easier?"

"It solved a problem for me, okay? There was a guy who was hard to turn down."

"You try telling him no?"

"He was one of the instructors," I said. "He didn't want to be hearing no and I didn't want to be washed out of the Academy. There's always another class coming, but it's better if you have a good reason. Mike—" I swallowed. "Mike was a good enough reason. The golden boy, the wonder. Everyone understood if he'd gotten there first, they were all but expecting it."

Another sip. The cup like a barrier. "Did he?"

Get there first.

"No."

"But you told them he had."

"Reilly," I said, "I didn't have to tell them *anything*. Just had to be friendly, had to hang out with him, look a little self-conscious. Mike picked up on it, well, he knew pretty much, not totally stupid, and I guess he thought it was funny. Pumped him up some, his ego, and he liked the notion of himself as a savior, liked teasing me about it, saying stuff, making me blush."

"That was it?"

"Yeah," I said, "that was it."

"Just teased you a little."

Reilly was a cop.

"Look, Reilly, I'm not saying he didn't ever offer, and I'm not saying I never thought about it, but it didn't work out that way. There was too much going on, and I was just trying to get through the Academy in one piece. And then we got out and I met Charlie, and that was sort of it for me."

He took another pull at his cup. "Charlie understood all this?"

"Yes," I said baldly, "he did."

"It didn't bother him?"

"What was to bother, Reilly? We were all good friends, liked the hell out of each other. Sometimes I think he and Mike got along better than I did. And he *had* me, you know, it wasn't exactly as if this was current stuff, people whispering."

"Nobody whispered?"

Goddamn Dave. "People got used to us," I said.

"*Mike* get used to it?"

I was blindsided. "What?"

"You and Charlie."

Frozen in the field. In the glare of the lights, in the crosshairs. "Why would it matter to *Mike*?"

"Might have thought he had a claim."

Reilly didn't know about the picture in Mike's desk, hadn't been there yet, hadn't searched. I should have taken it with me, so honorable, but there's no room for honor when there's blood.

"Mike didn't have any claims," I said.

"Might have *thought* he did."

"Reilly," I said, "you can't have been checking up on the same Mike Johnson. I'd say over the past twelve years, there's been roughly a hundred women."

"Not so many the last three," he said.

My life on a platter. Everyone looking.

"He quit the force when *you* did, Meg."

"He was going to quit anyway," I said.

"Was he?"

I didn't know. Reilly was quite still, waiting.

"Mike's a romantic," I said very carefully. "I think for a while after Charlie died, he was thinking I'd be the honorable thing to do. Gunga Din and all that. I didn't see it at the time or I'd have made him stay." *Should* have seen it. *Should* have known.

"*Made* him stay?"

How the hell had I ended up with Reilly talking like this? "Talked sense at him," I said thickly. "Debunked his ideals." It hadn't been like that, exactly, or I couldn't remember it right. Michael so angry. Raging in the living room, our living room, punching the wall. Me like ice, numb. I don't know if I *could* have talked him out of it, don't know that I wanted to, what would have happened. Reilly was watching me and I'm usually better at keeping the past where it belongs. I started to say something, anything, but he was already homed in on me.

"Mike was going to quit anyway, you said."

I couldn't remember. I didn't know now if it was true.

"Was it awkward, Meg, all of you at the same department? You and Charlie having some problems?"

It doesn't stop, it *never* stops, the cop mind keeps working.

"It wasn't *like* that," I said. "Mike had some grand scheme going—thinking he'd make his fortune mining gold dust or something."

"And now he's selling security systems."

For me, he meant.

Because of me.

"It was a *plan*," I said. "We'd talked about it, the three of us. Something to do when we retired. We knew a guy with the franchise. It wasn't like I forced him."

"Quite a comedown from being a cop."

Yeah, it was.

"He's into something, isn't he, Meg?"

I should have made him stay. I watched my hands flex, watched the fingers move and my rings were loose, so Freudian, I'd have to size them down. Find a jeweler who could do that. Anyone, really.

"You need to talk to me, Meg."

"I don't need anything," I said clearly. "Don't need to listen to this, don't need to put up with it. If you're going to take me in, then let's do it because I'm not going to talk to you anymore."

"What about Josh?"

Another blindside. "What about him?"

"Somebody saw him, Meg."

At the back door. At *my* back door.

"Maybe you *don't* need my help," he said. "Maybe you can take a night or two in jail. You think Josh'll be all right?"

Christ.

"You're going to be watching him, Reilly."

"A kid?" He shrugged. "Hasn't done anything."

"To see who'll show up."

"You're telling me there isn't anyone."

He was a son of a bitch.

"You want to tell me something different, Meg?"

I wanted to tell him a lot of things.

"Josh for Mike," I said. "Is that it?"

"That would be coercion," he said roughly. "If you were cooperating, though, and the information seemed to warrant it, I could probably talk Abbott into posting a man for a couple of days. As a protective measure."

If they hadn't posted someone already. If that wasn't who Josh had seen. I had a flash of me walking into the Burbank station and just turning myself in. Sitting across an interview table with strangers and telling them anything, everything, all the way back. Spilling my guts and letting them do what they wanted, just to have it over, be done. Except that I'd be no closer to Mike, and then they'd all be focused on me. If they weren't already. If I didn't already have cops tripping over themselves on my doorstep. "Somebody's narc," but I didn't know whose. Didn't know why.

"I don't know you," I said.

He moved impatiently. "Know me by now."

Maybe I did. "Did you catch a lot of flak for driving me home?"

"Saturday?" When else had he driven me? "Not a lot."

Not a lot. That was good. I wouldn't have wanted him to be in any trouble for it, trouble at home, say, or at the station, where they take kind of a dim view of things like that. Fraternizing. You'd think it would have come up while they were checking out my whereabouts for when my car was being dumped. You'd think someone would have spoken to him about it. He was looking at me, sensing it.

"I had to write two supplementals," he said roughly. "You want copies?"

I did, really did. Signed and dated, with maybe a notary's stamp. I dug out a rueful smile. He didn't smile back.

And then he was going into his jacket, right hand to left upper chest

—*right to left, Christ*—

and I was frozen where I sat, frantically scrabbling, pushing away from the table, trying to heave it, upend it, *anything,* because I was too goddamned rusty, too slow, *and there was no room and no time.*

He stopped.

His hand stopped.

Frozen as *I* was, mid-reach. *Danger, danger* between us, and everything on the line.

"Notebook," he said.

He kept his hand where it was, still as my own. Brought the left one up slowly, very slowly—only using the thumb and two fingers—drawing the windbreaker back and away. I saw the straps of a harness, tan straps, the holster, the butt of a blue-steel Smith, but his right hand was over his pocket, shirt pocket, fingers on the ridge of a notebook, a field book, three by five.

"Notebook," he said again, and he drew it out, the shirt pocket clinging. And then he was using both hands, left to hold, right to strip, twisting the rubber band off and away, thumbing back through the pages, no wasted moves. Snapped the band on again to hold the page for me, and flipped the book across the table. I caught it before it slid to the floor.

I was looking at a page with Saturday's date. Saturday's date and the time, and a notation: "drove M. Gillis home. Jack Williams? Mike Johnson—key?" Reilly had a long arm already reaching to take the book back. Privileged information. Other notes.

"You can subpoena it," he said, "if the reports aren't good enough."

I smiled at him shakily. "*Two* supplementals?"

"Abbott wanted more detail."

So he *had* caught some flak.

"I'm sorry," I said. Always sorry, and he was ignoring it anyway.

"Are you going to talk to me?"

I knew what Louis would have to say about it, Louis and the hotshot Bob McKenzie. I was giving all this to Burbank in the morning, though, so maybe it wouldn't matter too much if I told it to Reilly tonight. Maybe it would all be okay.

"Can I send Josh home?"

"Yeah."

"Will you look after him, Reilly? Anyway?"

A moment's silence.

"Yes," he said.

# 17

Josh didn't come in when I called him, exactly—we had to go find him. He was standing behind the door of the storage room, hiding, a thin, stubborn stick. I love that boy, love him incredibly, but I was not in the mood.

"You're going," I said. "I don't want to hear about it. Your mom's probably already called the cops, and this isn't what I need tonight."

"You could tell her I know stuff. You could tell her I *have* to stay."

"Josh—"

"I *do* know stuff. I even know where Mike is."

"Babe—"

"He's at the beachhouse," he said.

Reilly was a block beside me.

"What beachhouse?"

"On Friday," Josh said. "He had a date."

There are things that I know about my stepson, things that I've taught him, things that have rubbed off by mistake. The fine art of lying, for instance. Weaving fiction and fact. Had Reilly and I been specific about Friday? I couldn't remember.

"You don't want to be fooling with this," I said.

He had those blue eyes of Charlie's looking back at me.

"I mean it, Josh."

"He *did*," Josh said. "With this girl."

"What girl?"

"Somebody."

"That's useful."

He flushed again, very aware of Reilly beside me, watching, listening. "Sue Something," he said.

Sue Something. "You know her?"

"No."

"Ever meet her?"

"No."

"See her?"

"N-no."

"So how do you know about her?"

"Well, I heard them talking."

"Them?"

"Him," he corrected. "Mike."

"You heard Mike talking to a girl you couldn't see?"

"It was on the phone," Josh said.

I was really very tired of phones.

"First of all," I said, "you don't spend that much time with Mike. The time that you *do* spend is when I'm around and he hasn't been making any phone calls that I know of—"

"It was Wednesday."

I stared at him.

"You were out talking to Mrs. Reyes," he said.

Last Wednesday. We'd brought Josh back from football practice and had chicken at the house. Alma was having a problem with her youngest boy, truancy, contact from the Juvie officer, and we'd ended up on the front porch for a while. "He called from *here*?"

"Uh-huh."

What were the odds? Mike calling from here for a date. For Friday. It's not as if he lives fifty miles away, not as if he doesn't have a phone. It was possible, though—I couldn't say that it wasn't. He'd had the time. "What'd he say?"

"Just that about Friday."

"*What* about Friday?"

"That he'd meet her at the beachhouse."

"He picked up the phone, said, 'Meet me at the beachhouse,' and hung up?"

"He was already talking," Josh said. "I just, you know, was washing my hands, so I heard him. Kind of loud."

Not really eavesdropping. "He knew you were listening?"

"Yeah. I mean, he must have heard me or something 'cause he said he didn't have time to argue and just be there."

" 'Just be there'?"

"Yeah."

" 'Hi, Sue Something, this is Mike, meet me at the beachhouse, I don't have time to argue, just be there.' That it?"

Josh's eyes were blinking. "Well, they were talking," he said. "Like Mike would say something, and then he'd listen, and then he'd say something else. It wasn't all together like that."

I couldn't tell. I've known Josh a long time, and I just couldn't tell right now. People could lie to me all night long and I'd never catch it, never even see the damned smoke. "Reilly," I said, "could we talk around the corner for a minute?"

He stepped back and into the hall without saying a word. "You stay where you are," I said to Josh. "We're going to be right back, so don't move."

He just looked at me, those eyes, and God help me if I could tell. Too old for this stuff. I turned straight into Reilly, his chest, and there was trust everywhere in this house. "You want to back up a little? Give me some room?"

"I want to know what's up."

"Down the hall, okay? We'll make a stab at privacy, anyway."

He'd been very accommodating, the long rein, but it was late for him, too. He was looking me over pretty thoroughly, deciding, and I tried not to seem like anything, tried not to set him off. "I'm not running a game," I said.

"Then tell me."

Not going to move. I didn't know if it mattered anyway, it was just kind of awkward talking into his chest. "He wants to stay," I said. "He'd say almost anything so we'd let him."

"Sounds real to me."

"Reilly, he heard everything we said in the kitchen, all but the last two minutes. He's not stupid. He's going to tailor it to get what he wants, which is not to go home."

"I don't mind him staying."

The hell he didn't. Did he? "Why?"

His eyes were noncommittal. "Easier for me. Just have to watch the one house."

That was true enough. Cheaper to requisition.

"Easier for you, too," he said. "Then you don't have to worry about him."

Had he picked up on that? He was looking at me, and it's a fine line, this helping-out stuff, when you're the prime suspect and also a fool. Damned if you say anything, damned if you don't. I stared at the pocket on his chest. "I just don't know if it's true, Reilly."

"Well, we'll find out," he said.

Calmly. Easily. As if we'd do it together. As if he wasn't already wondering what I might know about Sue Something and a beachhouse. I wanted to tell him I didn't, but it doesn't work that way. The more you volunteer, the more they think you know, and Reilly already thought I knew quite a bit. Was probably thinking now that I was trying to stall him, trying to keep Josh from talking, throw doubt on his story.

And the truth is, I would have done it in a second if I could have figured out how to get two minutes alone with Josh to find out what was what. Find out what Mike had said. Who the hell this Sue was.

"We'd better go make some calls, then," I said. "Clear the night."

We ended up in my bedroom because we did have to hang up the phone. Reilly wasn't going to send Josh, wasn't about to let me go, wouldn't leave the two of us alone while he went himself, so the three of us trailed down the front hall like ducks, happy ducks, Reilly bringing up the rear. All very polite, of course, no suggestion that there was any reason to doubt anyone. Just an easy "let's get the phone first" as he ushered us past the kitchen door.

It's just that I didn't want him in my room.

If he'd come in with a warrant, there'd be distractions, there'd be others, not this one-on-one peek at my soul. You don't think of your stuff like that, how revealing it is, until someone is standing there, looking, who's got no right to be. Or even if he *has* a right to, not like this.

But I wasn't in any position then—couldn't tell him to stay out, because what did that mean I was hiding? What if I came up with a gun? He'd look pretty stupid *dead,* wouldn't he, respecting my privacy?

So I kept my mouth shut and let him come in, didn't even try to block him, just hoped to God things were neat, tucked away. The bed was a mess, I knew that, with newspapers scattered all over. That's how I read in the morning, standing up, on the fly. And this morning, I'd really been racing, trying to get out, to find Mike, to get to the office before anyone else did. God, this had been a long day.

Reilly was being polite, though, relatively tactful. Standing back so I could flip on the overhead light, waiting for me to walk in. Spotting the phone off the hook on the dresser. "I'll get it," he said, as if it were the most natural thing in the world, to save me the trouble, save me the steps. Not a hint that he thought there was something in a drawer I might want to be pulling, or something I'd try to conceal. He was already moving towards it, skirting around the waterbed, so I couldn't have stopped him if I'd had it in mind, but, of course, I didn't, didn't need to. We were all just good people here, working together. Practically friends.

And then he saw the closet door.

Open.

He stopped short of the dresser, fixed on the closet, and I saw it then, too.

The shirts.

*Men's* shirts in my closet.

Hanging.

"They're Charlie's," I said, too quickly. "I haven't sorted through all of his things yet." He had an eyebrow raising, that goddamned flick, and yeah, it had been three years, and maybe I needed therapy, but it was none of his business. The shirts wouldn't fit Mike. He could check *that* all he wanted.

"You mind if I take a look?"

At the shirts. The goddamned shirts. "That's fine," I said.

He came smoothly around the bed again, cornering it, and I backed up with Josh towards the door. Reilly took up a lot of the room, or I didn't want to be close to him.

"Don't leave," he said. I guess he could have thought I was doing that. He was already thumbing through the hangers. Seventeens. Mike's a fifteen and a half or a sixteen, maybe, depends on the cut—works out to be pretty but not to be big. Reilly had his hands all over the shirts, the sweatshirts, and then he was looking at my half of the closet. The dresses. The tops. He wasn't touching anything there.

I should have gone down to the station with him. We'd be in an interview room then, bare walls and a table, nothing of mine to interest him, nothing to spark him, spark me. Which was why he'd wanted to keep me here. Push a little and prod, puzzle me out in my own surroundings. Even if they'd come through with a warrant and swept everything out of the house, they wouldn't have the information he had now. About me. How I react to things.

"You keep *everything*?"

The trick is to misdirect.

"Not everything," I said. "You want me to hang up the phone?"

I was already moving towards the dresser, which meant he'd have to come out of the closet or trust me, and trust wasn't high on the list tonight. He was sure enough in the closet doorway when I got to the phone. Ready, I'd say, to move in any direction, but waiting coolly, to watch me. That look in his eyes. Wary—knowing I was pulling him and not quite sure what he wanted to do about it.

I smiled at him nicely and hung up the phone. Crooked my forefinger at him like holding an invisible gun, pulled the invisible trigger. Bang.

Bitch.

The look changed, pretty *damn* sure what he wanted to do and it had to do with me and the bed and his hands on me, that force from the kitchen. He'd actually taken a step out of the closet, coming around, but Josh was there at the foot of the bed, and I was saying, rather breathlessly, "You hungry, babe? Eat any dinner?"

Josh was bewildered, suspicious, currents over his head. "I had some chips."

"Well, *that's* not enough," I said. "You come on and I'll fix you something in the kitchen. We'll let Reilly make his calls." Not afraid to leave you alone in my room, Reilly. Not worried you'll find anything, see? Innocent as the day.

"I'll go with you," he said, and there I was, trapped, not going to get Josh alone. I smiled ruefully, shrugged. Win some, you lose some, if that's what I'd wanted. Reilly was thinking about that, too, I could tell, whether that's what I'd wanted or if it was something else. Or if I'd been jacking him just for the hell of it. Manners all around, ever so nice, but he stayed where he was so I had to pass by him, following Josh out the door. Fell in behind me, *right* behind me, practically wearing me down the hall. Physical intimidation. Push me/pull you and that kind of contest. I shrugged again and slowed, letting him feel *me* pushing him back.

He was so clever.

Now he had a new puzzle to work on.

# 18

Abbott was kind of bent, I guess. Reilly'd called him first and he seemed to want to know things that Reilly wasn't going to tell him while I was around. I leaned a little deeper into the bottom of the fridge, but you don't become invisible that way. He was wanting to know why I wasn't in a holding cell, I'd imagine, and what the hell was this about Josh? Reilly was being very brief. Short. Can't say I'd ever heard him long.

"Because she's willing to talk," he said.

I guess that was true.

"You can tell him I want protection," I said. "You can tell him I'm fed up with the candy-asses running your department."

"Just a minute," he said to the phone, and covered it over. "You want to talk to him?"

I didn't.

"You sure?"

I was pretty sure.

Reilly nodded succinctly and went back to the phone. Another one of his "shut up and listen" deals. I got out the eggs. Josh was sitting at the table, taking both of us in, and he had that sullen sort of juvenile delinquent expression on his face. I didn't know what it was with him, didn't know what it was with *me*. Supposed I should figure it out sometime soon.

"Bill," Reilly said. "He knows what she looks like."

Someone to watch over me. Someone named Bill. I cracked the eggs into a pan. Sausages starting to spit.

"I don't think so," Reilly said. "We can always call them in later."

The rest of his squad? IA? Burbank? Mine not to ask those questions, mine just to go with the plan. Reilly's plan. I stuffed the bread in the toaster and he was done already, hanging up the phone. I had a couple of chatty comments I could have made, but it seemed like maybe I shouldn't. Something not right.

"Do we call Caroline?"

"Yeah."

So that was still on. Abbott, then, maybe. Maybe not liking things. Reilly was putting himself out quite a bit for me. I wished I didn't see it or didn't feel grateful, because that's a trap, too, one that'll get you. Reilly was doing his job.

"How long have you been STU sergeant?" I said.

"About a year." He stretched back in his chair. Nice stretch. Nice chest. All the time in the world.

"You know this Bill pretty well?"

"Yeah, I came on with him."

Tight little group. "How's he happen to know what I look like?"

"He was sitting with Escobar outside your office," he said.

Oh.

Okay.

Kind of dampens the conversation. I *did* feel guilty, and he knew it, was playing to it or testing it or using it like a ram to batter me, keep me in line. Payback. I wondered how long he'd hold a grudge. Charlie had been good for weeks sometimes, but it would always depend on his mood. Wished now I hadn't waltzed Reilly around in the bedroom.

"You going to make that call?" he said.

Yeah.

"It'll go better if Josh does it," I said. "You know, 'Please, Mom, I'm sorry, but there's this friend of my dad's here, which is why I *really* want to stay.' No mention of Mike, no mention of trouble, just you talking to me in the background. She's more likely to say yes if she thinks she's got an audience, an old friend of Charlie's. Wouldn't want to tarnish her image." Unless, of course, she was really ticked—I didn't know what words she'd had with Josh. I looked over at him and he was sunk in his chair, eyes on the table and that so-sullen mouth.

"You want to stay?"

He didn't look up. "Yeah."

"Then do it right," I said. " 'I don't know what I was thinking.' That kind of stuff. You do it often enough over here."

His lips compressed, but he did it right. Right enough, anyway. Got through the "sorry" part before he fell silent, whitening and listening to Caroline unload. I took the phone.

"Caroline? It's Meg."

"You want a drink?" Reilly said.

"What? Oh, thanks. No, not you, Caroline, I was

talking to Reilly—Joe Reilly, you remember him? Worked with Charlie up in Sacramento, he says, about twelve years ago. Maybe you met him then? He thinks he remembers *you*." Reilly was shaking his head no, he'd never met her, and Caroline was saying the same in my ear, but she was thawing slightly and she seemed to remember Sacramento, remembered Charlie working it, so that much was true.

"It's my fault about Josh," I said, "I wasn't thinking how late it was and tomorrow a school day. Can he just spend the night?"

Well, no, he couldn't spend the night—"Just a minute," I said, "I'm sorry, hold on. What was that?" and I pointed at Reilly, who said something obligingly garbled. "Well, she doesn't *want* him to," I said, and got back on the line. We played this back and forth for a few minutes, old spoilsport Caroline, until finally she wavered. "I can bring him back first thing in the morning," I said, "*well* before school. That way he can talk for a while and still get to bed. It's just kind of important to him, you know, the link with his dad." A neat touch, I thought. Caroline had spent months with a therapist trying to understand Josh's need for a link and why that link had to be *me*. To her credit, I might add. Credit where it's due. She at least struggles with her prejudice, and I don't always bother. Makes one of us a better person, and tonight it could be her.

"All right," she said reluctantly, "all right, he can stay."

That was great, I said, that was wonderful, Josh would be so happy. He *looked* happy, scowling at the countertop, but nerves'll do that, nerves and frustration, and maybe some hormones. Anyway, I thanked Caroline profusely and disengaged before the self-satisfaction and the virtue wore off.

Reilly had those eyes on my face. "You do this a lot?"

"You enjoyed it," I said. "Don't pretend that you didn't." I was feeling good, yes, I was, things working right, and Reilly a part of it like a well-oiled machine kicking back into gear. A long time since I'd done this, a mighty long time. "Josh-boy, you're on," I said. "Have some sausage, have some eggs, and tell us about this phone call, this mysterious Wednesday night deal."

"I already told you."

"That was when you were buying time. Was there really a call?"

"Yeah," he said.

Not meeting my eyes. Dammit. I handed Reilly his plate, handed him mine without thinking, fished out some forks and some spoons. "You were washing your hands," I said.

"Yeah."

"*I* was out talking."

"Yeah."

"Mike was already in?"

"Yeah," he said, the details just rolling on out. I settled myself at the table, Reilly to the left, and stared at Josh pointedly.

"Well, he *was*," he said. "You don't have to believe me."

"I believe you all to hell," I said, "but you have to give us something to go on. How did Mike sound? Was he nervous? Was he angry? Talking 'kind of loud,' you said, but what does that mean?"

"Angry."

"He didn't seem angry when I came in, and I wasn't out more than a few minutes."

"Well, I don't know if he was angry," Josh said. "Maybe he was just, you know, saying it."

"*Acting* angry?"

"Yeah."

"Joshua," I said, "buddy, you're not really thinking this through. I was there, okay? I know this house. I was out with Alma for what, five minutes? Ten? Not a long time. You guys went in together to wash up, set the table. So Mike *wasn't* already in the house, right? The two of you went in together. And the other thing is that the bathroom's a long way down the hall and around the corner from here. Hard to hear stuff going on in the kitchen, especially when you're running water to wash with. He'd have had to be yelling, so you'd think I'd have heard it through the open front door."

Josh was looking kind of white. Looking at Reilly.

"Josh?"

"He wasn't in the kitchen," Josh said.

I scrubbed at my face. "You're saying Mike called from my room?"

"Yeah."

It was the only other choice, and we'd just been in there. Hanging up phones. Association. "Mike doesn't have the run of the place," I said to Reilly. "I'm sure he knows there's a phone there, but it's not the type of thing you'd just go do. I mean, why would he? He could use this one and welcome, or he could wait until he got home. He only lives two miles down the road, and it's not like he was here all night."

"Here *late*?" There might have been an inflection.

"He was here an hour," I said flatly. "If that."

"Maybe he had to call her by a certain time."

"So then he says, 'Oops, babe, I gotta reach this gal—mind if I use your phone?' It's not a big deal, Reilly. He's done it any number of times."

Reilly was watching Josh. "What about it?"

"I don't know," Josh said. He was staring at his plate.

"Any part of it true?"

"He was in there talking. That's what I know."

"In the bedroom?"

"Yeah."

"And you were in the bathroom washing your hands?"

"I was going to," Josh said. "And then I did."

"After he heard you?"

"Yeah."

"Did he say anything to you?"

Josh looked confused.

"When he saw you," Reilly said, "did he say anything about it? About you hearing him?"

"No."

"Didn't mention it? Didn't say anything at all?"

"Well, he said, like, 'Hey, slick, so you're back already' or something."

"Back from where?"

"The car," Josh said. "He left his sunglasses."

"He asked you to get them?"

"Well, yeah. But I couldn't find them anywhere, so I didn't."

Reilly's face had that blank, kind of peaceful expression again, and I knew what he was seeing because I was seeing it, too: me out of the way, Josh on a fool's errand,

Mike sneaking in to make a call. The bedroom more private than the kitchen, less noticeable if someone came in. I wouldn't be likely to head straight for the bedroom, Josh wouldn't, and Mike could always come down the hall like he'd been washing up in the bathroom. It was a clean play, a good one, except for Josh and his tendency to listen in doorways.

"How long were you gone," I said, "getting the glasses?"

"I don't know. A couple of minutes."

"Where was the car?"

"On the side," Josh said. "You remember."

I guess I did. Parked in the driveway almost to the garage, so Josh would have gone out the back way. Not come by Alma and me in the front.

"Were you guys in the kitchen?"

"Uh-huh."

Start from the kitchen, fifteen seconds out the back door, another five to the car. "You look pretty thoroughly?"

"Well, sort of I did."

Open the car door, scan the seats, the floor front and back, the dashboard—a minute, maybe less. Josh was a kid. "You go straight back in?"

"Yeah."

"To tell Mike you couldn't find them."

"Uh-huh."

"But you heard him already talking on the phone in my room."

"Yeah." He was looking a little better, more color.

"So he had maybe two and a half minutes," I said to Reilly. "Maybe three. Why would he do it, though?"

"Seems like," he said calmly, "he didn't want you to know about it."

"Then why the hell call from my house?" I said.

"The time."

"Reilly," I said explosively, "he didn't even have to come back here. It was *his* idea to pick up chicken in the first place. Normally we'd have gone to the practice and gone our separate ways. I mean, sometimes we'll go out for burgers or something, but if he had this hellaciously important phone call to make, you'd think—" and I stopped, rubbed my face, my eyes. Because this was *Mike* we were talking about. Heedless, careless Mike. Everything falling into place, and Reilly looking at me, on to it.

"He forgets things," I said, and Reilly was there.

"Women?"

"Sometimes."

"Dates?"

"That," I said. "Or he'll show up at the wrong one's house."

Reilly's face was a mask. "So he could have been rescheduling. Wednesday to Friday."

"Could have been, I guess."

"Why would he hide it from you?"

"I don't know that he was hiding it from *me*," I said. "It was Josh he got out of the way."

Reilly had a thumb rubbing at his chin. "Why would he hide it from Josh?"

"Well, he's a kid," I said. "You know, you try to set a better example."

"Afraid he might say something crude?"

"Yeah."

"Might ruin Josh's image of him?"

It was always possible.

"It doesn't seem to have bothered him that Josh heard him," Reilly said. " 'Hey, slick, so you're back already' doesn't sound like a man who's concerned."

He was so damn perfect.

"On the other hand," he said, "he didn't even mention it to you. Picked his moment, Meg, while you were outside."

"You're making that a big deal," I said, "but he might have just remembered that he should call. Or you could be right about that time business—had to reach her by seven or whatever. I was stuck out there with Alma and he knew I wouldn't care if he made a phone call, no need to interrupt us to ask. And really, no need to tell me about it after. It's none of *my* business what he does."

"He was using your bedroom phone," Reilly said.

"Well, it's more private that way, if he didn't want Josh to hear."

"Did we talk about you lying to me?" he said.

Kind of a fraught silence.

"I'm not lying," I said carefully, "I'm pointing out some other possibilities."

"Why wouldn't he have told you about her, Meg?"

I should call for a lawyer, get somebody in. "Well, I think it's pretty clear," I said. "I was screwing around with him, he had a girl on the side, I found out about it and did him—is that what you wanted to hear?"

"I'll keep it in mind," he said. "Why'd he hide it from you?"

Like a goddamned shark, closing in. Wouldn't let a little blood in the water distract him. I needed time to think, time to sort it out, and he wasn't going to give it to me. Eyes right on me, reading me. Slicing right to the bone. He'd seen too much of me in action, and there was just no help for it.

"Mike has a thing about nice girls," I said. "That's sort of how he classifies me. Thinks he ought to shield me from the rougher facts of life."

"Yeah?" He didn't believe that either, but it was the truth. Part of the truth.

"If she was married," I said.

"Married?"

"Yeah," I said, "and if she was married to one of *your* guys, that would explain quite a lot."

He was hit, no doubt about it.

"What's your *wife's* name, Reilly?"

He fastened on me. Focused. "Ex-wife," he said. "It's Diane."

"Girlfriend?"

Another pause.

"No Sues," he said deliberately.

Plural.

"Any of *them* married?"

"Not that I know of."

I guess that was something, told me something. "How about your guys?"

"No Sues," he said again. "I'll have to check about the girlfriends." He was broadening the range as I watched him, cops he knew, guys he might have met. That's how it works. You start with a circle and move out. We were both very quiet, thinking. Josh was still as a mouse.

"It could have been," I said. "He's been keeping *some-thing* under his hat, and I just didn't ask, didn't bug him.

Something that jazzed him, like a kid with a secret. It could have been."

"He wouldn't have told you?"

"I'm kind of a prude," I said.

He wasn't saying anything, just looking at me. The things he would have heard. About me, about Mike.

"He doesn't drag it in my face, Reilly."

"Is that why you didn't ask him?"

Maybe. I didn't really know. Nothing conscious, anyway.

"Anyone else he would have told?"

"I don't think so," I said. "For someone so careless, he's pretty discreet." Self-preservation. I didn't say that out loud, though. I picked at my plate. "I mean, he's got the reputation, so guys are always assuming he's making it everywhere—a lot of ribbing, you know, if he's in a bar and some girl's looking at him. And he's *gone* plenty of places, it's not that he hasn't, straight across the room and out the door if he's interested, not really caring who's watching. But he doesn't *talk* about it, Reilly, not much, not the details. I used to think it was just around *me*, being careful of me, but actually, I think he tells *me* more than anyone."

"But not if they're married."

"No," I said. "Not then."

I was trying to picture it, see all the elements, see how they'd fit. Reilly'd be doing the same. He was staring into his cup as if it held answers, and I can tell you it didn't. The answers were inside us, each of us, both of us, our experience and our knowledge of the people involved.

Why he wanted my help.

Why I wanted his.

"It makes more sense than drugs," I said. "As far as Mike's concerned."

Reilly just nodded.

Mike with a woman. With a married woman, or a married cop's woman. Last Friday. Blood on the wall.

"Did they find any slugs, Reilly? At Mike's?"

"One. In the wall by the door."

"Caliber?"

"It's at the lab."

He wasn't going to tell me. It could have been Mike's, but then, really, it could have been anybody's. I was just hoping.

The door chain was on, but there's always the balcony from the front, off of Mike's bedroom, a four-foot drop, or a climb. If they'd come in *that* way, though, why chain the door?

Trashed, Reilly'd said. The place was trashed. Somebody looking, requiring some time. Or somebody planting the dope and *then* trashing, so it'd *look* like somebody looking. Also requiring some time.

Why the balcony?

Neighbors. Because then you don't have to drag anything, any*one* down the hall. Don't have to be seen. Just park your car on the street and load 'em. *Mike's* car.

"You have a bulletin out on the Porsche?"

"Burbank does," Reilly said.

My car, though. Stealing *my* car. Saturday. Someone bleeding in the back. Somebody *else*?

"Did they find any women's things?" I said. "At Mike's?"

"No."

Something, though. He was looking too blank.

They'd found something. "Did they do a prelim on the blood type? From the wall?"

"No."

Still waiting on a lab. So it could be anyone's, his or hers. Theirs. Mike with a woman. A married woman.

"Josh," I said, "they were meeting at 'the beach-house' for sure?"

"Uh-huh."

Would he have brought her back to his place? Been followed by her husband?

"So they could look at some pictures," Josh said.

I don't think anyone was breathing. *I* certainly wasn't.

"What was that?"

"Pictures," Josh said.

"You didn't say 'pictures' before."

He looked anxious, caught. "I forgot."

Everybody yelling at him. Doubting him. Me, anyway. What was "pictures"? Reilly was already taking it.

"What kind of pictures, Josh?"

"I don't know—just pictures. You know, like with a camera."

"Did he *say* 'camera'? 'Photos'?"

"I don't know. Just that's what I thought."

"Mike has a Nikon," I said.

"He have a video camera, too?"

Reilly'd been at his place, would have seen the equipment, all of Mike's toys.

"He doesn't hang around *motels,* Reilly, if that's what you're thinking. He just likes this stuff, likes to play."

"Maybe *she* didn't." His face was absolutely expressionless, but the room had changed.

"Oh, Christ," I said. "If she didn't want to play,

Reilly, then she wouldn't have to. Mike's not going to force anybody into anything. Not a woman."

"She didn't want to meet him."

"Reilly—"

"He 'didn't have time to argue, just be there.' Sounds forceful to me."

"Oh, come on," I said, "you've never had words with anyone? Never said 'just do it' before you slammed down the phone?"

"He's missing," Reilly said.

"And you don't want it to be your guys. We've been over this ground."

"When all of this started," he said very deliberately, "the rumor was blackmail."

Blackmail? I stared at him blankly. "You told me harassment," I said, "harassment of Iranians—" and then I stopped, stopped short because, for Christ's sake, there *was* a link, that I knew about, that Reilly didn't, that made everything make sense. There was a paper, a small piece of paper—the paper in Mike's handwriting, with Haroutunian's name on it.

"Josh," I said, "this is really important—when Mike said 'pictures,' did he say 'look at' or 'get'?"

" 'Look at,' " Josh said, "I'm pretty sure."

"Did he say 'negatives' anytime?"

"I don't think so."

Not negatives. Not that Josh heard.

"Pictures" could be anything, I didn't know. Could be porno flicks, could be "you and me, honey, and the Polaroid," could be a damned wedding album, because Mike did that sometimes. Played with his Nikon. Helped out a friend.

But he was missing, *bad* missing, blood, and what had he said on the tape? "Something's come up and I've got to check it out. If anyone comes looking for me, just tell 'em I'll be back in a couple of days."

And then he'd told me to be careful.

I hadn't been, really.

"He had a number," I said. "In his desk. I found it today." The voice wasn't mine, but it worked and that mattered. It was all that mattered right now. "Haroutunian's. The name and a phone number."

Reilly wasn't moving.

"I called you to run it. That's when you were out. I was thinking it might not be *Haroutunian's* phone number, that Mike might have jotted it down to remind himself—'call Jack about Haroutunian,' that kind of thing. If he'd heard some cop talking White Power or something, if he was checking into it. Because *you'd* said harassment, and Haroutunian had said that he didn't know Mike."

Reilly's eyes on my face.

"The way our business works," I said, "we get referrals. You know—you meet an old friend in a bar, get to talking, and he says that so-and-so might want a system because they just bought antiques, had some break-ins, whatever. Gives you a name, an address. A number. Mike tends to keep them that way, scraps of envelopes, corners of napkins. It helps him remember. That's the way this number was. I was thinking contracts, because it was at the office. And it was in *Mike's* handwriting—not perfumed, not a pretty pink pen." I cleared something out of my throat. "And because a *guy* called on Saturday, you know?"

Reilly knew. You get things into your head.

"But there wasn't a file," I said. "I usually do those anyway—Mike throws me the name if it leads anywhere, if the first contact looks promising, so we have some sort of record to follow up, do whatever." This was so hard, that ultrafine line. Drawing the truth without blackening Mike.

"Mike likes women," I said carefully, "and women like Mike. Which is sort of an asset for us because most of the time it's the wife who's home when you're calling to make the appointment. Going into their house, you know, to talk about security. It doesn't so much come down to the system as it does to the salesman. Mike—" I swallowed. "Mike looks very capable. Like you'd be safe with him. And he's very naturally sweet, kind of protective with women."

Reilly was keeping his opinions to himself, which was good. I couldn't tell him if he was going to be critical.

"It could be either," I said. "He met her in a bar and wrote down her number. Or it *was* a referral, and he called and met her that way."

"You're saying 'Mrs.' Haroutunian?"

"It adds up," I said. "Why Haroutunian didn't know him. Why Mike would have kept it from me." Thinking he could handle everything, so goddamned stupid.

"If she was in trouble," I said. "If she turned to him for help."

"PI work?"

With no investigator's license.

"As a favor," I said.

"He wouldn't have called the cops?"

You'd *think* so. You'd think he'd have done that. But then, you'd think the same of *me*. I've lived here nine years, six of them with Charlie, and I know every one of my neighbors pretty well. Well enough to chat, to make conversation, to do or ask a favor, so why hadn't I knocked on somebody's door when I saw lights that shouldn't be on in my house? I remembered the rush, the pumping adrenaline, swinging up over the wall and dropping into the yard, and did it come down that easily to wanna-be cop? To the damn horse and harness? I was staring at Reilly, but it was Mike I was seeing, my old friend Mike, heading down that same restless, alienated, wanna-be road, saying, "I can handle 'em, babe, I'm tough, I'm smart." There's always someone tougher, Mike, there's always someone smarter. Why don't we *learn* and call for backup, why don't we knock on a door?

"You all right?" Reilly said, and I was, you know, really. I just don't always look it.

"We need Sue," I said.

"Seems like."

One way or another. Find out who she was, which scenario. Find out where to start.

"Did you talk to Haroutunian today?" I said.

"No."

No? He was taking a sip, his eyes on the cup as he put it back down. "You didn't go by the house?"

"No one was there."

*No one.*

"Not even a *maid*?"

"Not today," he said.

People can take those vacations, give servants time off. They don't have to tell the police all about it.

"You check plane reservations?"

"There weren't any."

No reservations. Not in Haroutunian's name. "Reilly," I said, "you had this guy Saturday. You didn't get a work number from him, an address?"

"I got one," he said. Calmly. Composed. "He didn't show up there today. His assistant is very concerned."

That made two of us. Three. He had very straight eyes.

"Don't take off again," he said.

# 19

In the end, you do what you have to do. It doesn't matter about friendships or love or the look in someone's eye, it comes down to what has to be done. I sat in my kitchen and gave Reilly Mike. Gave him places and names, people, events—whatever I could think of that would help track Mike down.

And Reilly was perfect. Asked a question here and there as I talked, nothing offensive, nothing intrusive, very soft, very calm. Interested. Nonjudgmental. The kind of guy you could tell anything to, everything. *Working* me, and I let myself be worked, was grateful even—because if I'd had to do it any other way, I couldn't have said a word.

I focused on Josh every once in a while, hearing me giving up Mike, but he didn't understand it that way. It was just questions to him, exciting, adult stuff that he got to be part of, that he got to absorb. Something to talk about in corners at school. No reality.

Nothing was real. Except the Colt on the counter behind me, and the man across the table.

And the nightmare intensity of Mike being gone.

"You all right?" Reilly said, and I was, really. Shaking's normal for me when I've had too much coffee and too little sleep. Too many problems.

"Are we done?"

"Yeah," he said. Done enough for the night anyway—he'd have about a million more questions tomorrow. "You want to get Josh to bed?"

"I have to," I said. I don't know why getting up was so hard. Maybe because Reilly was sitting. I stretched under his casual eye to loosen the kinks and motivate Josh, get the feeling of movement back into the kitchen. "Come on, buddy, you can handle the plates."

"Okay."

He's a good kid, really. Insecure, but I don't have the answers for that, I'm just doing the best that I can. The popular psychologists would say I'm "enabling," and maybe I am. Maybe I *should* have just left him to his mom. But he's a piece of my heart, you know, and I couldn't.

I shuffled the food stuff into the refrigerator while Josh cleared the plates and Reilly tucked his pen away, shed his windbreaker. Peeled it right off, and then he was standing, rolling up his sleeves, the tan holster bucking under the left arm as the right hand worked, and then the reverse. Unsnapped his watch in one easy motion, the wrist twisting. Piled it on the table. Caught me looking.

"You cooked," he said.

As if, now, he had to wash.

"I'll just do them in the morning, Reilly. Maybe even put them in the dishwasher."

"This gets it done."

He was amused, wryly friendly, reading my caution,

and *I* didn't care—he could wash my dishes and welcome, anytime. Didn't make him more than a cop.

"Soap's under the sink."

"All right."

Josh though, looking at me quickly and as quickly away, alive to the nuances and carrying his own baggage.

Fears.

"Don't," I said sharply, "don't do them."

Reilly stopped halfway to the sink, the strap a black slash across his shirt, shaping his back. How many times had I been here like this—although usually the holster would have been slung across a chair, or left on the dresser in the bedroom. He was turning to face me, a question, and this was so stupid.

"I'm going in to Burbank tomorrow," I said.

"Burbank?"

"The PD. It's already arranged."

Comprehension. Something else.

"That lawyer," he said evenly. He wasn't moving his mouth much and he wasn't amused anymore.

"I have to talk to them, Reilly."

"Yeah." Starting to roll his sleeves back down. Crisp movements. Compact.

"Your being here tonight doesn't change the essentials," I said, but that wasn't what was eating him. It was that he'd put in a lot of time on me, put in the work, put himself out quite a bit with the lieutenant and his captain, and God knows who else, persuading them to let him run me, telling them I'd be worth all the effort, the expense of guarding me tonight, and here I was, walking in to another agency. Going to Burbank to hand it all over. Let him look like a fool.

"I *have* to talk to them," I said. "It's what was set up, what they're expecting. If I don't do it, there'll be trouble, and I don't need any more trouble with Burbank right now." Didn't need it with Reilly, come to that. "You can sit in if you want to," I said. "I'm not going to tell them anything I haven't told you, but that way you'll know."

He was refastening his watch, very cool.

"Who're you seeing?"

"I don't know. Whoever's handling the case, I guess. The lawyer was making the call."

"*Your* lawyer?"

"Not Louis," I said. "He set me up with a criminal guy."

Reilly was nodding, distant. "What time?"

And this was all messed up, but it was better, maybe, to have the lines drawn, to have it be business. "Nine o'clock."

"I'll drive you." He was reaching for his windbreaker off the back of the chair, sliding it on. I could have said no, I guess, but we both had to go there.

"I have to get Josh home by eight. I was going to leave about a quarter to."

"All right." Adjusting his cuffs.

"Thanks," I said.

"No need to thank me," he said very coolly. "I'm leaving a man inside here tonight."

I was slow, that heartbeat. "Bill's coming *in*?"

"Dan is. Dan Hibbard. Bill will be outside."

*Two* men. Very common, one in and one out. I just hadn't thought of it. He hadn't mentioned it. Wandering my house.

"I guess I won't get much sleep, then," I said.

"He's the guy on the phone this morning."

The one who hadn't known Haroutunian. Not involved, Reilly meant. Someone he trusted. Like this Bill, working the double shift.

"You and Abbott have a code? Because I didn't hear Dan's name."

"He and Bill generally work partners. It was just a question of who stayed outside."

And Bill had won the nomination because he knew what I looked like. He'd watched me at the office most of today when I'd boogied, which meant he'd be looking that little bit harder tonight for me to leave.

So while I'd been planning to go past Reilly to Burbank, Reilly'd been installing not one, but *two* watchdogs. Tell me we were friends.

"When's Dan coming in?"

"About half a minute."

I still could say no. I could yell about citizen's rights and not having this guy in my house, but that would open up avenues for Reilly that I'd been kind of careful to close. I didn't really want to spend the night in a cell. I'd already given him Mike, so he had what he needed from me short-term, and there was no particular reason for him to indulge me any more, certainly not if I went flaking off about having a cop in my house for protection.

"Dan's only been STU a few months," Reilly said. Helping me find a way to accept it, although I don't know why it would matter to him.

"How old's that rumor about cops and blackmail?"

Kind of a pause.

"Five months."

So he'd brought Dan on since then. Someone he could trust. And they'd been keeping all this to themselves for *five months*?

"Has anyone talked to the Chief, Reilly?"

"Abbott has," he said. End of discussion. Nothing more that he'd say. That final kind of note in his voice.

I shrugged at him then, defeated—what else could I do?

"You need to get some sleep," he said roughly. "I'll bring in Dan and then you go to bed. You and Josh. Leave the dishes for tomorrow."

Yeah. Let the ants have 'em.

"It'll be all right," Reilly said.

I wished I believed him. Really wished that I did. "Come on, Josh," I said. "Let's go and meet Dan."

Dan seemed okay. Male, white. Five-ten, late twenties. One-seventy-five. Blond hair, brown eyes. Worked out some, I'd say, because he had the arms, but that's normal for cops. Called me "ma'am."

Reilly'd introduced us all at the front door. He'd turned off the lights, opened it once, twice, then waited. Dark outside. Dark in. Not as conspicuous as flashing the lights—you'd have to be looking for the door to open and I guess Dan *had* been, because about two minutes later, he'd knocked and entered. Seemed like a nice enough guy.

If it was me, you know, I'd have been kind of ticked at having to babysit someone who'd slipped out on my partner earlier. I don't think I'd have been quite as cordial, but he had a shy sort of eye flicking over me, haggard as I was, and maybe he wasn't as harsh in his judgments as I tend to be. His handshake was firm, warm, friendly.

"Anything?" Reilly said.

"Just that Abbott wants you to call."

Reilly was nodding, not surprised. Looking that tad bit tired himself.

"You can go on," I said. "We'll be fine."

"I'm going to talk to Dan for a few minutes," he said. "Get him situated. No point in you and Josh waiting up."

Go on down the hall, he meant. My own hall.

"It's nice meeting you," I said to Dan. "I really appreciate you coming in for the night. I hope it's a quiet one."

"Yes, ma'am."

"Meg," I said, and held out my hand again. He took it, people do that, makes kind of a bond. "Thanks." His hand was warm and dry. He didn't seem uneasy or nervous or like a man who was planning to search my house on the sly. Not like a man who was planning me harm, either. I've been wrong before, any number of times, but maybe tonight was okay. "Good night, Reilly," I said.

He wasn't offering hands. "Good night." And then, slightly warmer, "Night, Josh."

"Night." Josh wasn't warming to anyone. Wouldn't even look at Reilly. He was standing in the shadows, peaked and small and stubborn, loyalties whipsawed to hell and curled in on himself.

"Come on, tiger," I said. "This'll all be worked out by tomorrow."

Somehow.

He was hall-side already, but I had to get past the two men. Dan was clearing back, well into the living room, but Reilly only moved marginally, planted against the wall. I could brush him or avoid him, so I skirted around, lots of room, distance being the better part of valor, and then I sort of propelled Josh down the hall, shooing him in front of me like a great mother hen. Behind me, there was silence, men watching. A cold, cold prickle down my neck. The Colt was on top of the refrigerator in the kitchen because Reilly had put it there out of the way, very casually, tucked in behind all of the junk, and there'd been no way to get it without making a point. Hadn't wanted to, then. Didn't want to right now. I put both hands on Josh's shoulders and steered him into his room.

"Forget the teeth," I said. "You can double-brush 'em in the morning. Just climb into pajamas and hit the hay."

"I don't have any pajamas."

Because he'd been running away when he came this afternoon. No overnight bag. "Old tee shirts?" I said.

He was shaking his head. A million things stuffed like a rat in his room, but no tee shirts. "I'll get one of your dad's," I said. "Won't be a minute. Why don't you turn on the desk lamp so it won't be so bright."

He was moving obediently into the room and I didn't wait for him. I crossed the "T" of the hall quickly, as invisibly as possible before he reached the desk. Without the hall lights on, it was dark at this end of the house. I live here, though, so I know where the bumping points are, where to put out my hands, how many steps. Through the bedroom door, to the turn, hand on the wall leads you into the closet. Right hand trails the closet door while the left finds the Exercycle, feels past the shirts to the seat of the bike. Clear it, squat down, golf bag in the corner, and behind it are the extra golf balls Charlie kept in their boxes. The third box holds the two-inch, Charlie's backup, his Colt. Takes only a second to heft it, check it, slide it into the waistband, and stand again, glide sideways the three or four feet to snap on the closet light. Half a step, and you're back at the waterbed with the built-in drawers where Charlie keeps his underwear. Kept. Tee shirts and socks, shorts. An assortment to choose from in the spill of the light, a harmless occupation, a task.

No one came looking.

I grabbed the top shirt, turned the light off, and skimmed back down the hall. By that time, Josh had his desk light on, so I was front-lit for anyone watching, but I had the shirt in my hand, and I hadn't been long. "Here you go, babe. Try this on."

"Meg?"

"What?" He looked so young. Tired. Taking the shirt in both hands.

"Is Mike, you know—hurt?"

My throat tight, the breath. "No," I said, "I'm sure he isn't."

Not anymore.

"Was it that guy this afternoon?"

Casing the house. "He could be part of it," I said, "I don't know. We don't know very much yet—just guessing, really, hon, doing our best."

"Would you *tell* me?"

"I *always* tell you," I said, "you know that."

"Everything?"

You can't tell anybody *everything*. "You need to go to bed," I said.

There was only the faint flick, the eyes catching me, and then he was turning docilely, mutely, going to put on the shirt like a good little boy, like a stupid-ass kid, like a slave.

"What?" I said. "*What?* Something *else* you heard, some other great clue?" I don't know why I was yelling at him, it wasn't right, wasn't fair. It's the slave look that eats me. I tried to calm down. "*Did* you hear something else?"

"No."

He wouldn't tell me now. "I'm sorry," I said. "I love you a lot, but I'm beat all to hell. Is this about Mike?"

"No."

"Then I'm going to bed, okay? We can talk about it later?"

"Okay."

Fine. I was essentially out the door when he said, "Are you seeing him?"

Him *who?* But there was only one man acting like he lived here tonight, like he knew me. Had something like rights.

"No."

"I called you on Friday." He was looking very young again. Vulnerable.

"I didn't even *know* him last Friday," I said. "It's just a technique, babe, an interview thing. He's a sergeant, okay?"

"I called all weekend. Called you and called you."

"I've been looking for Mike," I said. "I haven't really been home."

"*She* said I couldn't expect it." He was white, tense. "She said I should know better than to think that you didn't have *friends*."

His mother.

Spent my weekends out, she meant, screwing around. Taking up with God knows who doing God knows what in dirty motel rooms.

Laughing at him.

And he'd understood *that*, all right, was morally outraged, which was why he'd come haring over today to confront me, accuse her of lying.

And found Reilly.

"Oh, honey," I said, "you come and go all the time, don't you think you'd have seen?" but he didn't know, didn't have the experience, what to look for, the signs. He was just a kid and kids live on promises, trust—an eggshell thing when you're dealing with people, with changeable adults. The doorknob was hard in my hand.

"We'll keep it straight," I said, "keep it simple. I may go out once in a while, I won't tell you I don't, but if it's anything more, anybody important, I'll tell you myself. Is that okay? Can you handle it that way?"

He was looking self-conscious. "Yeah."

Someone behind me in the hall. I turned, and it was Reilly.

"You still talking?" he said.

"Josh needed a shirt."

"Needs to go to bed," he said. "So do you." If he'd noticed the bulge in my waistband, he wasn't showing it, and I was pretty well frontally-lit.

And if he'd heard anything, understood it, he wasn't showing that either.

Decent, I guess.

"I'm going," I said. "Good night, Josh. Don't stay up."

"Okay." He smiled a little mistily at me. Uncertainly at Reilly. "Good night."

I *hated* this, wanted to camp by his door, probably would have, but Reilly was moving back, waiting for me to come on, and it was foolish, stupid, because nothing was going to happen. Josh was a kid, not even a player, and these guys were cops, professionals. They wouldn't let something go wrong.

"I should have taken him home."

"Safer here," Reilly said.

"Where's Dan going to be?"

"Front room."

Bill in the back then. Or prowling. We were outside my door.

"Are you going home now?"

"Pretty soon."

Not much to say. Dark there in the hallway and he wasn't leaving. Awkward. Like a blind date waiting for more, and maybe we *were* a little too close standing there in the darkness.

"I'm sorry," I said, sort of low, "about everything. You've been very patient."

I felt him shift then. Take that wider stance, a deep breath. "I've got a man in this house," he said deliberately. "Have a man outside. I don't want anyone getting hurt because you're fooling around. That means you're going to bed and you're staying there—are we clear about that?"

We were pretty clear.

"Don't play with this," he said.

Play with *him,* he meant. I felt unspeakably old. "I was thanking you," I said, "being sentimental. It probably won't happen again."

So I didn't have to say good night to him after all. I just turned and walked through the door, shut it behind me. Stood there in the darkness with my hands on the wood and remembered what it was like to be a fool. It was bad. It was never any good. Eventually I heard him walk away, and sometime after that I crossed the room in the darkness and rolled myself into bed. I pulled the covers straight over me and buried myself in a pillow. Left the sounds of the night to the wolves.

# 20

I don't know what woke me. Bad dreams, a noise.

Someone in the room.

It's terrifying to wake like that, because you can't see, can't breathe, your body won't move. You can only lie like a frozen target, every muscle tense and on call. I hadn't heard the door, didn't think I had, anyway. Someone already here? Mike? I was holding the damn hilt of the gun, but it's no protection in the dark when you don't know where to aim it, can't see what you'll hit.

And I was on the bed, where you'd expect to find me, where you'd naturally look. Hadn't even slept on the floor.

I eased a careful leg left, reaching for the side of the bed, because I sleep too much in the center these days, too far from the edge, and I heard it again, the whisper of weight on the rug, air displaced as a body moved through it. A cautious step. A stop. Listening.

Christ. My own ears humming.

I tucked and rolled sideways, frantically scrabbling, expecting the flame, the jolt, the searing pain. Tried to twist while I was falling so I'd land in position, so I'd have the Colt up, have it snapped, ready. There's no primer for this, no real way to learn it—it's instinct and luck and a thousand yards of gravel, falling over and over till something sinks in. I was face down in the carpet on the far side of the bed, in the lee of the dresser, on my knees and my elbows with the gun out in front of me, no protection, no shield.

Listening.

A thump.

The chair by the window.

And it's a sound that I hear five times every night, don't even think about anymore.

The cat. The damn cat.

Jumping.

I listened for another full minute but all I could hear was her licking herself. If there'd been someone else, she'd be still or uneasy, not settling comfortably into the chair. I moved and she mrrowed at me, being too odd. Hitched myself up, found the bedside light switch. Nobody there but me and the cat, unless they were six inches tall and invisible. What I needed tonight—to be shooting a cat in the dark.

I turned the light back off, but I couldn't sleep then, I just couldn't, there were too many things. What was it now? Three? Two o'clock in the morning. Too many hours till daylight.

It was cold in here, freezing, and I kept hearing silence, kept hearing noises, dogs barking aimlessly, yapping. Electric clock, digital, numbers not turning. How many heartbeats make up a minute? What had Mike said? *"See you tomorrow,"* and I'd just said *"Yeah."* Pissed at him, ticked. No "What are you doing?" "Got any plans?" just *"Yeah,"* and I'd waved, flapped a hand. An hour left to do on the books, easily that, and him taking off, going out. Dressed to the teeth.

He was so *alive,* was the thing, so very alive, eager to be gone, to be meeting someone, but guilty with it, guilty for *me* because I was the stay-at-home stick. The phone kept ringing and it was Mike, *or was it Charlie?* wanting to know where I'd *been* Friday night, wanting to know where I'd gone. *Christ,* I'd said, *I can't even go out?* and this place like a morgue, like a goddamn museum. *I've got friends, you know, lots of friends, good friends, not every-one's after my bones*—and Reilly across the bed looking like sin, with his shirt half off and the holster unslung, just watching the mirror, watching me turn, but Charlie beside me with blood on the floor, on the goddamn walls by the goddamn door, and Mike saying something like "Meg, you be careful," when I woke up tasting the night.

Pillows ajumble. Covers at my throat. Sheet like a snake, like a damned anaconda. Heart going a hundred miles an hour. Three-thirty. Phone?

I grabbed for it, reached, but no one was there. Dial tone stretching forever. As far as the kitchen, maybe. Dan.

If he'd talked, it hadn't been long—long enough to have someone hang up. Mike wouldn't identify himself to a guy who answered my phone. Or maybe it was Reilly, checking in. Or maybe it was nothing, just a dream—heard a sound and built the whole thing in my mind, ten seconds' worth, waking and dreaming. Wouldn't be the first time. I didn't need Freud for some-thing like that. Didn't need anyone.

I just needed Mike.

Needed him badly, desperately, crooking that god-damn shrug as he strolled through the door and said "Hey, I forgot" for the five-hundredth time as in "Sue me." I've never counted on Mike for anything much—I'm the one who keeps *him* straight, which gives me something, some function, and I was realizing, there in the darkness, that I thought he was dead.

Thought that his blood was all over my car.

Because if they'd gotten him Friday night at a beachhouse, they didn't need me. That's what it was, what it all came down to—if they'd found him on Friday, I wouldn't have gotten a call.

Or if I'd been *home* Friday night. If Mike could have reached me.

It was fresh blood on Saturday, a few hours old. Some of it dried.

I'd have said "Where *are* you?" said it first, made him tell me, and then met him or called someone, someone we knew. You don't go without backup, not for something like this.

Because there was blood, and the best I was doing was guessing. Guessing he'd gone A, guessing he'd done B, guessing he might have met C. He'd had time enough to tell me, dammit—he'd had the machine. You protect yourself. You ALWAYS tell someone you've gone.

And you know, Mike's stupid sometimes, but he's not *that* stupid. Even Mike's not that stupid. I'd talked to everyone already, everyone I could think of, and no one had mentioned it, no one had said "Well, he told me to tell you" or "He left me this note," no one had seemed like they knew. And the only odd thing I could think of he'd done was to call from my bedroom.

Because he could have called from the kitchen. *I* wouldn't have known she was married.

It was a small enough hope, the kind the heart feeds on at four in the morning. I couldn't turn on the lights because I didn't want Dan to come checking, but I've got flashlights all over—Mini Maglites, you know, a cop's kind of legacy—and the curtains were drawn.

He'd had three minutes at most, including the phone call. Make it four to meet Josh in the hall.

I started with the drawers closest to the phone, the ones in the dresser and under the waterbed. Lingerie, socks, underwear. I twisted the Mini Mag down to a pencil-light, and checked everything in the beam. It's not as easy as it sounds, in the dark, but I've had some practice. I looked for things shoved into the back, down the sides, underneath. Behind the mirrors. Rolled in a sock. I didn't know how big, didn't know what. That handicapped things just a little, except that I already knew what *should* be there, so I was looking for something that wasn't mine. Something added, something extra. Some damn scrawly note saying "Meg, if anything happens . . ."

I worked my way through the dresser. Nothing, no dice. Turned back to the waterbed. The pillows. Down the sides. He would put it where I'd find it somehow, changing sheets or changing clothes. If he'd left it at all. I went through my basket of odds and ends, sheet by sheet through the box of tissues. Through every other drawer in the room. He'd had four goddamn minutes, and he was standing by the phone. Making his call and looking around. The closet door open, and I was going to have to *lock* that bad boy, lock it or throw things away.

I went into the closet, Charlie's half of it. His shirts

and the coat and the uniform jackets still hanging. His guns still on the upper shelf behind the towels and the cleaning stuff. Videos.

I'm not good about things. It took me more than a year to move into the house, a piece here, a touch there, a box finally opened. Charlie had the silverware out and lined up, towels on the racks, toothbrush holders, everything up and in place by the end of the very first day. I knew what he'd say about this, I could hear him saying it.

I went quickly through his side, brushing down the clothes, the pockets, checking for paper. It wasn't as likely Mike would leave anything there because I wouldn't use it on a regular basis, wouldn't be likely to find it. Same sort of search through the shoes. The stuff on the shelves didn't look touched, but I gave it the once-over just to have done it, the quick lift and poke, and nothing seemed different. I couldn't reach the top shelf without Josh's stool from his room. *Mike* could have reached it, but the logic applies: you don't hide what you want *found* where someone won't find it.

Which meant *my* side. I went methodically through everything I own, shaking out dresses, looking for pins, searching all the pants pockets, the cuffs. Doing it more by feel than by sight because a pencil-light's only for quick little flashes, but I had the advantage of knowing my clothes, knowing the layout of the closet.

No notes. Nothing else.

He'd had four goddamn minutes. Two on the phone. Unless he'd brought Scotch tape, he couldn't have taped anything—but he *could* have brought tape, I didn't know—he could have brought *ten* rolls of tape and some *nails,* a toolbox, a drill. It depends how premeditated Wednesday had been. It depends what Mike thought he was doing, how clever he thought he was being. How much of a threat he'd thought there was.

And the answer was back in my face, where I didn't want to see it. The answer was in the message he'd left on the machine—he *hadn't* thought there was a threat, hadn't thought there was anything he couldn't handle, until Friday night, when something happened, something to tell him this was bigger than he was, something to make him call *me*.

And I wasn't home.

And he hadn't called Jack-Diddly-Anyone-Else, he'd gone on being macho, gone on being solo, because I'd called everyone else he'd have turned to, and none of them would have kept their mouths shut to me. Not with Mike missing. Not with me looking. There'd have been at least some self-conscious hemming and hawing, and I'd been listening for that when I called. Plenty of people surprised I was calling, and plenty of talk about it after, I'm sure, but nobody hiding anything. None of them that good.

I sat a long time on the edge of the bed with the Mini Mag on, waiting for something—lightning or daylight. Inspiration to strike. There was nothing, just nothing. Cold, dark, lonesome nothing. Nothing to do until dawn came, and Reilly, and maybe some news about Sue.

I slept again, finally—woke at six-thirty. Bleary and cramped, forgetting. Couldn't think why I was curled up, wearing my clothes. I saw the Maglite, remembered, *Jesus,* remembered, and I just couldn't stay in the room. Didn't want company, didn't want Dan, but maybe he'd be tired and not in the mood and we could sit reading newspapers or something. I threw myself into the shower, brushed the teeth, brushed the hair, changed the shirt and the pants, the underwear—fresh clothes, you know, not like I'd slept in them—and headed on down the hall. Josh was asleep with his door slightly open, and Dan was moving around in the kitchen.

Not Dan.

*Reilly.*

"Good morning," he said. "Heard you up."

"What happened to Dan?"

"I sent him home."

He was making fresh coffee, knew where everything was. Had a file folder spread on the table. Notes. Box of donuts.

"Weren't you coming at eight?"

"I'm early," he said. Lightly. Easily. "Figured Dan could use the sleep. You want a donut?"

I didn't want a donut, I wanted dry toast and solitude. And I didn't want him there being smooth, especially after last night at my door.

"I got an assortment," he said. "Didn't know what you liked."

"I'm not much on breakfast," I said.

"Did you sleep all right?"

Yeah, I looked it, looked really great. "Reilly," I said, "don't chat, okay? If it's bad news, just tell me."

He was silent. "It's not bad news," he said, "I just want to get started. Burbank can see you at eight."

Rushing me, rushing my play. It gave me no time to call McKenzie or anyone else. "I have to get Josh home."

"Bill will drop him off."

"*We* can drop him," I said. "I'll go get him up." I was already starting out the door.

"It'd be easier if Bill did it."

I swung back around. "Reilly," I said, "I'm not letting Josh go with a stranger, so you can put that right out of your head. I'm seeing him safe home to Caroline before I do *anything*. Burbank'll wait."

He knew they would. That wasn't the issue. He was weighing something, the time or the trouble, whatever he'd planned.

"All right."

"I'll go get him then."

"I'll come with you."

No privacy. No time alone with the boy.

"Sure," I said lightly, "or *you* can just do it. I've got to throw my things together anyway, and that would be faster."

"What things?"

"My bag," I said. "You know, a purse and stuff. Put on some makeup."

"You look fine."

So sweet.

"Not for Burbank," I said.

It was kind of a moment.

"Okay," I said, "what's the deal—no calls? You want to yank out the phone in my room to be sure? I'm just trying to look right, not some tired-out hag. You're rushing me out of here, not even breakfast, and the least you can do is give me five minutes to put on a face and go to the bathroom, for Christ's sake, do some Zen."

"Zen?"

I had him. Amused him. The slight crinkle by his eyes. "*Do* you want the phone, Reilly?"

"Yeah."

Dammit.

"Will you tell me what's wrong?"

"No," he said.

# 21

I don't always think everything through. I try to, but sometimes things happen and you just have to move. Charlie'd get on me for that, but instinct is experience working, the way I see it. Planning suited him, gave him power because he was consciously deliberate, but for me, it's sensing things, acting, reacting, feeling the pulse of the room.

I unplugged the phone and gave it to Reilly, started to close the bedroom door. He blocked it.

"I'll want your bag when you come out."

He knew I had guns. He didn't really think I'd try to smuggle one, come out shooting or anything, but he was making the point.

"Stand there," I said, and turned into the bathroom, took all of three seconds to dig my spare purse out from under the sink where I keep it. Full view of Reilly, no secrets. Dumped everything out on the counter—no guns. I grabbed a handful of pens, an address book, a comb, left the rest of the mess in a heap. Opened my odds-and-ends drawer, snatched a mascara wand, lip gloss, and liner, threw in a blush. Felt the lining of my purse for the twenty-dollar bill, because I wasn't going anywhere without cash. It was there. Fine. "Good enough?" I said. "I'll use the *other* bathroom. You can check it first, if you want to, for poison or knives."

He was looking at me from inside the doorway. Touch of something—regret?—hardening. "All right," he said, and I brushed past him, didn't even flinch when we touched.

I didn't have to wake Josh. He was standing by his door at the end of the hall, watching as I came flipping out. Dammit. "Morning, babe," I said. "You've got to hurry and get dressed, okay? We're going to drop you home early. Get you to school."

He was just standing there.

"Josh," I said, "you've got to get a move on."

He was looking at Reilly behind me, in the open doorway of my bedroom. His dad's bedroom.

"I was getting something and he followed me in, okay? That's his job, to check things."

Josh's eyes cutting left. A polite boy, well-raised.

"Go get dressed," I said.

I went towards him the couple of feet and turned the corner, tucked into the spare bathroom. Shut the door. I had five minutes, maybe less, because Reilly'd have a timer going. I turned the water on to mask it, ripped a page from the address book and scribbled Louis' office number. "Call Louis," I wrote. "Tell him check Burbank at noon *regardless*—Reilly rushing me early, some sort of squeeze." It wasn't much, but it was all I had time for. Melodramatic as hell. Ten o'clock might have been better, and I almost changed it, but Reilly'd be knocking and I had makeup to do, and you need to leave room when you're dancing, not too tight a time frame. I folded the note into a tiny little packet, printed "Josh" across it while I clattered the stuff in the bag, thrust the pen out of sight. Dashed on liner, lip gloss, globbed the blush, and barely had the mascara when Reilly knocked. "God-*damn*," I said, and opened the door. "You must be hell on a date, Reilly."

"You look very nice," he said flatly. "Let's go."

Josh was coming out of his room with his jacket over his arm. No overnight bag. "Josh," I said, "I swear you'd forget your head if it wasn't attached," and pushed past both of them into his room to snatch up his knapsack.

"But, Meg—"

"You know how your mom is. You'd better take it home." I tried not to look like I'd been fumbling with the flap when I turned around to face them. Josh was confused, as well he might be—the knapsack's part of the play stuff he keeps at my house. Never goes home. Reilly's attention was on me, though. He reached out and took the sack from my nerveless fingers and I smiled at him brightly. Harmless Little Woman #8. Housewife. Den mother. "Kids," I said.

"Yeah." He might have been thinking anything.

"So, Josh," I said, "is that it? Your bike, too, I guess, or I'll just bring that by later."

He was still puzzled, but no longer obviously so. Probably remembering how strange adults are. I couldn't help it, I laughed and hugged him despite his embarrassment, despite Reilly, hugged him close and rubbed his shoulder blades, and then stepped back and readjusted his shirt, settling his pants at the waist. "Oh, you boy," I said. "I'm sorry this has been such a mess. I'll let you know how things go."

"About Mike."

"Yeah."

"Am I coming over this weekend?"

"Yeah, sure," I said. "I'll talk to your mom. Explain things." Somehow. I looked over at Reilly. "Were we in a hurry?"

He was holding the sack by one strap, watching me. "We don't want to be late."

Well, certainly *I* didn't. We went around as a group while I checked all the locks. Reilly'd never plugged in the Brewmaster, so that was fine. I left it as was, and then we were out the front door.

Reilly was driving a four-door today, a city-owned car. Parked right out front, straight down the sidewalk, wonderful effort at concealment.

"Where's Bill?"

Reilly settled the seat belt, shifted into drive. "He'll be following us," he said. "Then he'll go home."

Expecting us to be a long time at Burbank—or that the second shift would pick us up there. It was only a few minutes to Caroline's and I didn't spot Bill's car, but then I didn't have full use of the mirrors. Caroline was waiting for us, not rushing out, the curtain snicking back into place in the front window. Watching Reilly, probably, through the lace. She'd be coming out soon, snide or gracious, depending on the side of the bed this morning, but more likely gracious with Reilly there. He could handle it, I hoped, because the house door was opening.

"Goodbye," I said over the seat to Josh. "Don't fret, okay?"

Reilly was reaching back past me, taking the knapsack. He stepped out the driver's door. Josh wasn't moving much.

"You've got to go," I said softly. "Don't have to tell your mom everything, maybe. Not for a while, okay?" Fine example.

Caroline was halfway down the lawn. I swung myself out, introduced everyone, "Sergeant Reilly, this is Caroline Gillis, Josh's mother," as if he didn't know, but we were all being civil and now she could be friendly, chat to Reilly just that bit, while I nattered at Josh. He was finally climbing out of the back seat, but somehow Reilly was between us, blocking me off.

"We're on our way to a meeting," he said nicely, smoothly, over my head to Caroline. "I wish we could stay a few minutes, but they'll have my hide if we're late."

At this rate, we'd be early, but there wasn't much I could say.

"Yeah, we've got to go, Caroline. Thanks for letting Josh spend the night. I'll try to get back to him later, okay? About getting his bike back."

"If there's time," Reilly said, and I wished it didn't sound quite so ominous, so much like he was planning to keep me.

"Right," I said. "Give me a hug, Josh, and go on." Nothing Reilly could do about that, direct request, and we were being polite, so he moved sort of aside and around, shutting the back door of the car while I kissed Josh goodbye. "Jeez," I said, and flicked my hands at his shirt, "you might want to *wash* this before you wear it again."

Caroline stiffened, I could see it out of the corner of

my eye, and she'd opened her mouth before she remembered that she's a Christian these days. "Margaret, you know he always has clean clothes *here*," she reminded me nicely, and sent a maternal smile Reilly's way in case he'd missed it. Considering that she's the original model for most of my Harmless Little Woman line, I'm kind of ungrateful.

I sent a nice smile back. "Yeah, well, he was wearing these yesterday. Slept in the underwear, too."

"Josh," she said rather sharply, "you go on in and change, honey."

"We've got to go anyway," I told him. "Don't fret it. I'll call you tonight if I can."

"Roger," he said.

"Alfred," I said back, and he was smiling at least as we drove away.

Reilly looked over at me at the stop sign. "What was *that* all about?"

"She bugs me," I said. "I can't help it." We were heading straight for the Burbank station, no side routes, no jogs. "Aren't you even going to *pretend* that you're dodging a tail?"

"I didn't want to make you nervous," he said easily, "have you wondering where we were going."

Or make anyone else wonder, I guess. It was a good enough reason. I just didn't like the little curve to his mouth.

He took me in the back way, through the parking structure. I'd been there a number of times exchanging prisoners, and the routine was basically the same as anywhere. Check us in, move us up, second-floor interview room. Largish. More of a conference room, really. It had to be largish to hold all the people. Abbott was standing in the far corner with an older man in a suit, expansive talk like an off-color joke, so they were pals. A younger guy, mid-thirties, was looking at some notes at the table. Another one swung around to see us as we came in, was filling himself up a cup from a coffeepot in the other corner.

And Hubcaps, Mr. Hubcaps, from Mike's parking lot, was standing there, staring. Staring at *me*. I must have stopped in the doorway, stopped in my tracks, because Reilly's arm was hard against my back.

"Go on in," he said.

# 22

There's something about facing a roomful of cops. Abbott was coming towards me, hand outstretched and a friendly smile. Toothy. "Mrs. Gillis, thank you for coming in on such short notice. We really appreciate your helping us out."

So this was just a social call.

And me without my pearls.

"Well, I'm happy to do what I can," I said nicely, "but I wasn't expecting a crowd."

"Yes, well, we all had some questions, Mrs. Gillis, and it seemed easiest to handle it this way, all in one place. We're hoping you can shed a little light, clear up some misconceptions for us."

"Misconceptions?"

Those very sharp eyes and that very bland smile. "About your partner, Mrs. Gillis. Mike Johnson. Can we get you some coffee? You want to sit down?"

Nobody was reading me rights or harassing me. This was just a friendly little chat. "I was sort of thinking I should be talking to Burbank," I said. "Since it's really their case."

The old man in the suit harrumphed. Not so old,

probably, fifties, but lined and thin-haired, half-glasses on the bridge of his nose. Peering at me from across the room. "I'm Lieutenant Pilsner, Mrs. Gillis. Burbank PD. The detective at the table is John Edwards—he'll be handling the case for us."

"John," I said, and nodded at the guy. He nodded back. Two down.

"And you?" I said to Hubcaps.

He didn't seem to like me. "I'm Jones."

"*Agent* Jones," Pilsner said. "And this is his partner, Rick Carlos."

The man at the coffeepot nodded at me carefully.

Agents.

"Nice to meet you," I said. "You're with Beverly Hills?"

"They're with the DEA," Reilly said.

He could have warned me, so I guess he hadn't wanted to. The DEA watching Mike's apartment. That would have changed Reilly's impression of me in a hurry. Right back to drugs. I *did* kind of want to sit down.

"You'll have to forgive me," I said. "I'm just really out of my league here. What exactly was it you all wanted to know?"

"We thought we'd hear your story again, Mrs. Gillis." Abbott, brusquely urbane.

I looked around the room at the assembled faces. "You guys didn't turn out to watch me being booked," I said, "especially at this hour, but you *have* to know I'm not going to talk to you without a lawyer."

"There've been some developments," Reilly said. He'd moved quietly in to the end of the table, was settling himself in the chair there as if I were a foregone conclusion. Pulling out his notebook, a pen, not especially looking at me. And I've been a lot of things in my life, but I kind of pride myself on not being so easily counted.

Versus the notion that the developments had to do with Mike.

Everyone else was focused on me, watching me watching Reilly, and him unconcerned, but he couldn't be *that* sure, he couldn't know what I'd do—it was a play for the others because I was his witness, he was showing them all he could run me. I moved slowly in to a chair.

"What's the deal?"

"Sit down," he said, "and I'll tell you."

I sat, the others sort of finding their seats around me. I was looking at Reilly and he was contemplating the arrangement of his pen and the notebook on the table, very nice view of his forehead and nose. Eyes coming up to me. Grave.

"You were throwing some theories around last night. We want to hear them, ask a few questions. See if anything fits what we know."

"Just the theories?" I said.

"With your input, assessment. Nothing more alarming than that. If you don't feel comfortable anytime, you can say so and we'll stop."

A very fair offer. Not something I'd need a lawyer for, right? Not a reason to hurry me here. "And in return?"

He was looking at Abbott. "We might share what we found out last night."

Deals within deals. Power competing. With two

DEA guys scratching for Mike, and Burbank pursuing. Reilly my port in the oncoming storm.

"Okay," I said.

A faint warmth in his eyes. Abbott nodding judiciously, a man who'd had faith in his judgment. Seemed to me that he was the one who hadn't liked me before— or liked me *too* well, depending how you saw it. Probably *still* liked me that well. Sure as heck Agent Jones did. He was burning holes from across the table, so I sort of wished he hadn't sat there. Not much choice, though. Abbott had moved in to the end facing Reilly, and Edwards was already planted in the chair to Abbott's left. Pilsner had seated himself across from me to the right, which meant Carlos got to sit on my left next to Abbott. No one had taken the seat to my right, between Reilly and me, so I put my bag on it, claimed it, claimed the space, claimed the distance. Still my own person, however constrained.

"Suppose you start," Reilly said.

"Are we recording this?"

"Unless you mind."

I minded like hell—a bunch of guys I didn't know and traps everywhere, but Reilly's eyes were suggesting I just let it go.

"I'll want a copy," I said. "And I want it on the tape, everyone's name and their agency, and why you're all here."

"That's no problem," Abbott said. Edwards was reaching into a briefcase and pulling out a little Sony, battery-powered. Palm-sized recorder, what they won't think of next, and he was pushing the on button so I could see it go down. Very civil, as if they didn't already have an outside one rolling. Put it in the center of the table, ran through the names. Bill Jones. Rick Carlos. John Edwards. We had Lieutenant Abbott already, and of course Sergeant Reilly, and then there was Pilsner.

Detective Lieutenant Pilsner.

Abbott's opposite number.

"Kind of high-powered," I said. "All these lieutenants."

"Lieutenant Pilsner's doing us a favor," Reilly said. "He's not really here in an official capacity."

Wasn't he?

"I made the arrangements," Pilsner confirmed very heavily, "so I thought I'd sit in."

Right. I hadn't even taken out a pen I could play with. Body language. I slipped a little lower in the chair.

"I'm not sure what all I can tell you," I said. "The sergeant got most of it last night."

"We're looking for corroboration, Mrs. Gillis."

"I don't *have* any," I said. "It's just guesswork and supposition."

"We'd like to hear it anyway." That was Carlos. Agent Carlos, quiet Carlos, from the DEA.

"Yeah, sure," I said nicely, because I'm always nice when I don't know who's hunting, "I'll be happy to tell you whatever I can. It's just that if you want corroboration, I'd think you'd do better to talk to Mrs. Haroutunian."

Reilly's face was like stone.

"Lieutenant?" I said.

"Why don't we hear your story first, Mrs. Gillis."

Abbott slipping, kind of sharp, not nearly paternal. Mrs. Haroutunian was the problem, then, and everyone here had known that except me. I was reckoning times. Reilly'd left my house around one, been back before seven this morning. Somewhere in that time frame, he'd talked to Abbott and they'd organized this meeting. I wondered briefly if he'd had any sleep at all. He looked tired. Set.

You don't question solid citizens about blackmail in the middle of the night. You wait for a civilized hour, say nine or ten in the morning, before you knock on their door. It was barely civilized now, which meant nobody'd talked to Mrs. Haroutunian in the usual way. They'd found something or *known* something and had this all hatched before the sun came up. And whatever they'd found had them focused on *me*. Whatever they'd found hadn't cleared us.

So what do you find in the middle of the night?

I had two Detective Lieutenants staring me in the face. *Blood at Mike's place. Blood in my car.*

"Okay," I said, "were you going to tell me she's dead?"

I'd hit it, bingo, right on the nose, and you could have gone through that room and robbed everyone before they moved. Holy Christ. Mother of God.

"So you knew that," Abbott said grimly.

I hadn't known *better,* was the problem, didn't have any sense—not even enough to keep shut in the rain. I was starting to rise, starting to push back, when Reilly's hand moved, stretched out on the table, a motion to stop. Not touching me exactly, but close, very close. He was looking at Abbott.

"I think we might be off track," he said.

I wasn't off *anyone's* track. "Not if you're finding dead

bodies, Sergeant. I don't have anything to say then at all."

He and Abbott were mind-melding. Tele-conferring. "We haven't found any bodies," Reilly said slowly. "We have"—he hesitated—"some information, unconfirmed, about Mrs. Haroutunian. It's one of the reasons we wanted to talk to you, get some feedback."

"I don't know Mrs. Haroutunian."

"You know Mike."

He threw it so casually.

Not "knew" Mike, but "know" Mike.

As if he might still be alive.

"No bodies?" I said.

"No."

He might have been lying. Cops do that in rooms.

"Ask me," I said. Before I changed my mind. He read that, I think, understood me enough. Began asking questions and I answered, ran through everything we'd figured the night before. The Haroutunian connection, Sue. The call from my bedroom. Put it all on the recorder, the chicken-track notes, and it was Reilly I was talking to, the rest very quiet, pens scratching, questions forming but etiquette ruling, giving Reilly the lead. I was his witness. He had the floor. Danced me around ten ways to Sunday, and it's hard to keep track of the turns, all the steps—you can't double-think, you have to feel it, to follow—you just have to trust it and go. Have to trust *him* and go.

And of course, we were talking about more than my theories—a small question here about what Josh had said, another one there about me. Calm questions, quiet, offhand, inoffensive. Breaking-the-ice stuff, personalization: *When that call came in from Mr. Haroutunian Satur-day, what had I thought? Was I worried? Annoyed? So I'd thought it was real? Could I tell them why?* It was tests within tests because I'd told them before, had told Abbott and Reilly *exactly* what happened.

I told them again, what the hell.

And Edwards made marks, Carlos made marks, Jones stared a hole in my skull. At some point, Jones shifted. Came up halfway through.

"We're supposed to *believe* all this shit?"

Etiquette wasn't his strong suit. His mother had obviously given up on his manners, if Jones even knew who she was. I was Weak Woman, Led Woman, so I flinched and looked vulnerable, slightly betrayed. Confused.

"Meg," Reilly said calmingly, "Mrs. Gillis—Bill thinks you might be protecting someone."

About the phone call?

"I'm not."

"Look, honey," Jones said, and he didn't mean sweetheart, "you *knew* she was dead. You're spinning this tale about phone calls and rendezvous like you're thinking we're stupid?"

Well, I *did* think he was stupid, but that wasn't much. Phone calls and rendezvous?

"What?"

"She's four *years* dead," he said venomously. "If your boyfriend was porking her Friday, then we're all in big trouble. You can't tell me you didn't know *that*."

I should have had breakfast. My stomach was turning, was trying to climb. "Four years dead," and no one was contradicting him. "Is there a *Miss* Haroutunian?" I said. "A daughter? A niece?"

"No," Reilly said.

*Unconfirmed information.* "Haroutunian's shown up? He's talking?"

"No," Reilly said. "He's officially missing."

*Officially.* I found half a voice. "Who reported him?"

"His son," Reilly said. "Early this morning."

Early this morning. While I slept with my bad dreams and Abbott and Reilly set up this meeting. "He *has* no son," I said blankly. "I believe I was brought in to your station on Saturday because he doesn't have a son."

"You can see why we'd want to talk to you," Reilly said.

# 23

I could see a lot of things then. I could see that I'd made a major mistake in not waiting for McKenzie. Nobody'd needed to hurry me in here to ask questions about theories. We could have done that anytime, could have done it much later.

"*Was* the son kidnapped?"

"Oh, come *on*," Jones said. Jones from the DEA.

"Was he kidnapped or not?"

"He says not," Reilly said.

"He know anything about phone calls?"

"Not apparently."

"Where's he been?"

"This is bullshit," Jones said.

"*Is* it?"

"*You* called in on the son," he said. "You've been leading us around by the nose."

"Nose" wasn't quite what he said, but I'm sure that's what he meant, with the recorder going and all.

"Haven't been leading *you*," I said. "What's DEA's interest?"

"They got an anonymous tip," Reilly said from my

right, and here I'd been thinking Jones could talk for himself.

"That so? *Yesterday?*"

"Sunday," Reilly said.

"To watch Mike's *apartment?*" I aimed that at Carlos, quiet Carlos, to my left, and he shifted a little bit back in his seat.

"I don't know that it matters," he said, but it mattered to me.

"Did they name names, or just give you his address?"

"We took the call very seriously," he said. So it had come with some detail, some knowledgeable person spreading the oil. Fanning the blaze. Discrediting Mike. Sunday.

"You've got a tape of it?"

"No," he said, and then, because I was looking, "it came in on a private line."

"An *anonymous* tip on your private line?"

"We don't know who it was," he said stiffly, so I guess Reilly'd been asking that, too. Confidential informants are all very well, but when you're dealing with something like this, you want a few names. Interagency cooperation. Of course, I didn't know how much Reilly'd revealed about the problems at Beverly Hills PD— probably not a lot, but surely enough to indicate that they thought a cop was involved. So we could all take our picks—Carlos and Jones were willfully protecting one of their police sources, or some knowledgeable bandit had their private, untapped line. I'd give more credence to a call that came in that way, too, though. Have to figure it *was* someone knowledgeable. Might be thinking it was a cop even if I didn't know for sure and didn't want to say.

I drummed my fingers on the table and Jones glared at me. I wondered if their caller had mentioned *my* name, or if Jones just didn't like women. Wondered what *Carlos* had been doing yesterday about five and if Josh would recognize him as the man at my back door. He didn't look much like Eddie Reyes, but he wasn't a large guy and he was here today wearing a suit. Eyewitness descriptions don't tend to be good. Wondered if I should ask him. What the hell.

"So was that *you* at my house last night?"

Carlos froze. "Froze" is too strong a word—he paused minutely. "No," he said.

Of course, whoever came by was trying to break in. That's what Josh had said, "like with tools and things." Might have misread that, though, because maybe the guy was just writing a note, a card saying "call me." Hadn't wanted to leave it to be stolen by Josh. Didn't care to mention it now in mixed company. Abbott seemed fairly interested.

"My mistake," I said. "I thought maybe you might have."

"No," Carlos said. "Did someone come by?" He was looking at me with a half-flick to Jones, and now everyone seemed fairly interested, except for Reilly, who was studying his notebook.

"I thought Sergeant Reilly would have mentioned it," I said. "Someone came by about five yesterday. Very vague description."

"*Five?*" Jones's voice was grating. I smiled nicely at him.

"While you were watching Mike's back door."

No sound was coming out, but his eyes had that sudden explosive red-rage look. He'd been camping to catch someone and they'd gone to *my* house instead. I revised the scenario. Not Carlos with a note, but unknown A. Somebody working with Mike, say, looking for him? A bad-seed cop? Or one of Reilly's men after all—because he didn't seem even the least bit surprised.

"Were you looking for someone in particular?" I said.

"You *bitch*—" was Jones, and "No" was Carlos at the very same time. He had his left hand kind of raised like he was halting traffic. "We've been working some difficult cases," he said clearly. "My partner's been catching most of the strain. What exactly did your visitor look like?"

A little casual for an apology, but I don't stand on points. "Male Latin, five-ten, expensive suit. Youngish, maybe mid-twenties."

He was nodding thoughtfully, his eyes on the table in front of him. "Not ours, but we'll add him to the file. Identifying marks?"

"Tattoos," I said, "all over his forehead." I was looking directly at Jones. He breathed in sort of hard, but he didn't say anything. Too much like self-control—or like Carlos' hand working, still parting the air.

"Maybe we could go on," Reilly said.

We could do that. I stretched back in my chair so I didn't have to turn my head much to see him. "You were going to tell me where the Haroutunian son was all weekend."

"Berkeley. Visiting his cousin."

"I thought you checked all the flights."

"He drove," Reilly said.

You can do that. I've done it myself more than once, a trip up the coast, but it's the long way to go with the air fares so cheap.

"Drove *himself* ?"

"Yeah."

"Not a child, then," I said. Someone of age. I'd been picturing Josh, you know, or somebody younger, but why?

Because the Haroutunian who was *my* caller, spitting his mangled half-phrases, had said this one thing very clearly, distraught, anguished: *"Why you not send Mike instantly to protect me and recover the boy?"* And then he'd said that bit about honor. That was why I'd gone over there, probably, picturing Josh. We all have our buttons.

Misconceptions.

"Does this guy have gas receipts?"

"He paid cash," Reilly said. "Doesn't like to keep receipts."

Wad those suckers up and throw them away. "How old did you say this kid was?"

"Twenty-one."

Twenty-one years old and didn't use a credit card. From Beverly Hills. The *rich* part of Beverly Hills. "When'd he get home?"

"Last night around midnight."

Technically this morning. Early this morning.

"He called the cops right away?" Because Abbott had wanted Reilly to call, Dan had said when he came in last night to stand watch. Must have known something then.

"Actually," Reilly said, "one of the neighbors called."

It was very still in the room again, Edwards kind of chewing on the end of his pen, Abbott folding his

hands like a minister at lunch. Everyone having someplace to look except Jones. This was why we were here.
"I'll bite," I said. "Why'd the neighbor call?"

Reilly was choosing his words. "Soufi had an accident."

It took me a moment because I'm so slow.

*"Soufi?"*

"S-o-u-f-i," Reilly said. "Mustafa Soufiri Haroutunian. The son."

It was lightning bolts, it was bells. "Sue Something,"
Josh had said, and I'd thought it was a woman, too, with
Mike calling. Hadn't even entered my mind.

"You playing games?"

"No."

"He goes by Sue?"

"Goes by Soufi," Reilly said. "Doesn't like Mustafa."

"What's he saying about beachhouses?"

"Nothing."

"Don't give me that," I said, "he was meeting
Michael there, Friday."

"Says he doesn't know him."

"He the hell *talked* to him Wednesday."

"Says he didn't."

There were too many cops in this room, a tape
recorder. "Did you check my phone records?"

Abbott, so proper again, very smooth. "We didn't
have your permission, Mrs. Gillis."

"You have it," I said.

"Office phone, too?"

A damned sucker-play. McKenzie was going to dis-
own me.

"Yes," I said.

"You understand that you don't have to do this, Mrs. Gillis?"

"I understand that this guy knows something about Mike, Lieutenant. If you need my phone records to nail him, you've got them. What's the deal with this accident he had?"

Reilly was consulting his notebook, back a few pages. "He ran into the neighbor's fence."

"He what?"

"Skidded his car into their gate. Misjudged the turn, he says, in the dark."

Twelve in the morning. "Drinking?"

"Not apparently."

"Drugs?"

Reilly shrugged. "He seemed a little hyper."

But not where they could take him. People misjudge turns. "Neighbors called in on the crash?"

"No," Reilly said. "He woke them up, wanted them to go work out the details for him with his father."

I could feel it coming, everything. "Took them over to the house?"

"That's right."

"And they found the old man missing?"

"Yeah."

All of them there, Christ—Alibi City. And these cops the hell were looking at *me*?

"It stinks," I said. "Does he inherit?"

"Seems like."

"Well, what are you *thinking*?" I said, and it was my old pal Jones who put it into words.

"Think your *boyfriend* had his phone number," he said.

# 24

"Collusion" is a good word, rolls so easily off the tongue. I've always liked it. Means "secret agreement for a wrongful purpose." It sounds like "collision," like a train wreck, debris everywhere.

I'd told Reilly about Mike having Haroutunian's number. They wouldn't have known it otherwise. And Josh had told him about the phone call he'd overheard, Mike's secretive phone call to "Sue." Reilly wouldn't have known that either, otherwise. Little things, little incidents, little damning pieces they were fitting together. What they were all liking, apparently very much, was the notion that Mike was in collusion with Soufi—that one or the other or both of them had caused the wrongful disappearance and/or death of Mr. Haroutunian. The blood in my car.

And what Jones seemed to be liking was the notion that *I* was colluding, too.

"You want to tell us about it?" he said, and you know, if there was anyone there I was going to confide in, it was Jones. I looked over at Reilly.

"Does Soufi live at the house?"

"Says he does."

"Has a key?"

"And a room," Reilly said. "Had a picture."

Pictures again. "Of his old man?"

"Yeah."

His eyes on the table, on his hands, on his pen, moving.

"Was it *our* old man, Reilly?"

"Yes," he said.

The man at the door not an imposter, then.

"Why didn't *your* guys see this on Saturday?" I said tightly. "If he has a room there and all?" and Reilly raised his eyes to me, full on.

"Men's things," he said. "You were saying 'boy.' "

I had been. I was. Thinking "skateboard" and "toys." Josh's age.

"Had to've been more than not home, for the neighbors to call."

Reilly was drawing his squiggles again, on one of his notebook sheets. Calm squiggles, loops. "There was blood in the hall."

Blood.

That little thin man at the door. *His* blood. Maybe. I didn't know. I'm not good about blood, though, the notion of it, the failure. The desperate voice on the phone. *"You hurry,"* he'd said, and I'd hurried, goddammit, I'd done what I could.

"Why'd he say he didn't have a son?"

"I don't know," Reilly said.

Neither did I. You've got cops there, you've got trouble, you turn it all over, right? Jones was still the hell staring at me, and I'd turn everything over to him, too, in a heartbeat.

"Maybe he'd disowned him."

"Maybe you're full of shit," Jones said.

It's hard to be objective about something like that. I rubbed my hands carefully on the tabletop, stroking the wood, and nobody was leaping up to defend me.

"I'm just trying to be helpful," I said.

"You're not doing shit."

He needed a vocabulary.

"I don't think you have a lot you can prove on me," I said. "My only involvement, really, was reporting a crime, and then being the victim of one. Hard to take that to court."

"And you *know* it, don't you?" he sneered. "Think you're too fucking good to touch."

Too good for him. "No," I said clearly, "I think I've been cooperating. And I think you can take what I've told you to any DA, and he can tell you what charges you could file."

*"I'm not gonna be filing a goddamn thing."* He was red-faced, blown, surging up out of his chair and coming across the table at me, out of proportion. I was kicking backwards, away, and then *"Bill,"* Carlos was saying and he was between us, holding Jones back.

"You want to keep him away from me," I said.

He didn't seem to be listening, was communing with Jones, hands and eyes locked. "This isn't the way," he was saying softly, "c'mon, Bill, let it be." As if Jones really *was* a mad dog, as if this wasn't for show. Nobody else stepping in, not Pilsner or Edwards, not even Reilly, so they'd had it all worked out beforehand, agreed. Trial by Jones. Abbott had a thoughtful chin sunk on his chest, was watching me. I didn't spare the glance to see what Reilly was doing, just reached a hand for my purse and started to rise.

"Not yet." Something in Reilly's tone.

"I'm here voluntarily—"

"In a minute."

This was the man who'd sat in my kitchen pinning me about Mike and Charlie and my sleeping arrangements. I rubbed my hands, folded them. Kept my mouth shut. He was looking beyond me at Carlos, who was letting Jones go, stepping back. "Something we should know?"

Carlos shrugged. "We've been tracking her for a while. Bill's frustrated. A lot of stuff going on."

"Tracking *her*?"

"Her partner," Carlos said. "But we don't think he was acting by himself."

"He wasn't," Jones said.

The hell he wasn't. The hell he *was*. I didn't even know what I thought I meant. "You haven't been tracking Mike."

"For what?" Reilly said across me.

"Trafficking."

And drugs all over Mike's apartment. Everything so neat. "I thought you just got this phone tip on Sunday."

"It tied in," Carlos said.

Sure it did. Like a knot, like a noose. "That doesn't *worry* you?" I said. "A case you've been working and someone wraps it all up for you in one tidy phone call? How nice."

He took a long, careful look at me. "We didn't want to prejudge anything, Mrs. Gillis. That's why we're here this morning."

"Your partner's prejudging to hell," I said.

"I apologize for that. We didn't know exactly what the situation was, didn't realize you knew Sergeant Reilly."

"I don't know Reilly," I said, "don't know anyone here, but if he hasn't told you that he's tracking dirty cops, then *I* will. And if that doesn't make you think twice about your phone call and your preconceptions, it should."

"Dirty cops?"

Reilly hadn't told them. Hadn't told them *anything*. He was sitting back in his chair now, very composed.

"Meg has this theory," he said calmly, coolly, "that someone's trying to frame her. Thinks it's a cop."

"A cop?"

That was Jones.

"You know how it is." And then Reilly shrugged, he just shrugged.

Body language, so eloquent, because *everyone* knows how it is. People are *always* innocent, it's *always* a misunderstanding. Someone gave them the stuff or it's a friend's gun they're holding or somebody *else* dropped the dope in the car. Even one of the cops there, maybe, to frame them. God, I was shaking, feeling the web, the strands of it tightening.

"Any proof?"

That was Carlos.

"No. I've been listening to it for a couple of days now and there's nothing."

"You absolute *bastard*," I said.

He looked at me dead-eyed, impassive. "There's nothing."

I cursed him then, yes, I did, so stupid, wasting my breath and my time because he had the badge and the story and the lieutenant to back him up. I was Mike the drug-runner's girlfriend, and there was nobody in that room who believed me, nobody who *would* now. I could see it all like a map unfolding, and even when they were taking me downstairs to book me, there was nothing I could have done.

I'd told Reilly, you know, that I was going to Burbank. Told him they'd be expecting me, that my lawyer had set up the meeting. "*Your* lawyer?" he'd said, meaning Louis, and I'd answered, "No, a criminal guy." He couldn't really ask who, couldn't find that part out without tripping alarms. Smart enough not to try. Smart enough to take me for all I was worth and turn it around on me, walk in, in possession. Nine-tenths of the law.

If I hadn't shown up this morning, Burbank would have contacted my lawyer for my whereabouts, and the lawyer would have flagged me as missing. Given them who-knew-what information that I might have passed along about Reilly and Abbott and blackmailing cops. With the Beverly squad coming out of the blue at Mike's place last night, with blood all over and things kind of fuzzy, Burbank would have listened at least, checked everything out.

So I *hadn't* vanished last night. Reilly'd worked up this meeting instead. Had Abbott call his old buddy Pilsner and lay everything on. They'd moved me in ahead of the lawyer, played some music, let me dance. Asked about my theories, my hunches, let me twirl, showed me off like a goddamn fool.

Because what was everybody doing here?

Listening to me.

And what was I telling them?

My "Sue Haroutunian" theory: Mike's fling with a married woman. Saying it like gospel, preaching it, when they all knew there wasn't one.

Like I thought they were stupid.

No wonder Jones was frothing. No wonder he didn't like me. Reilly'd had this all the way: Burbank and the DEA in one fell swoop. Must have been a shock when I'd told him about the cop in the back at Mike's place, must have worried him some.

Not anymore.

He and Edwards booked me together, prints, pictures, search. Reilly was cool efficiency, filling out the forms at the cage, saying something aside to Edwards. I would have listened, but I couldn't hear him and I was trying to see the clock. Ten-thirty? Eleven? Trying not to look like I was trying to see. They booked me for Obstruction, 148, because they really didn't have anything, but it was sufficient to hold me and I guess it looked reasonable to Edwards.

Still had to look reasonable, you know. It was Burbank's home.

Which was why Reilly wasn't just loading me into a car. That and the fact that he had to know then I'd fight, go absolute Zulu, and with Pilsner there, a lieutenant, it had to look right.

And maybe I should have fought anyway, but I *couldn't* as long as he was just booking me, not doing anything else. You can't win, trust me, in a station full of cops, and I couldn't afford to look unreasonable either.

The jailer was holding the door at the end of the

cage. Reilly'd come around, standing ready, Edwards beside him.

"My phone call," I said.

There're ways to deal with it, always are. Reilly was waving the jailer off, lifting the receiver himself.

"What's the number?"

I gave him Louis' office number so they couldn't say I hadn't and I watched him dial something different, hand the receiver to me. It rang and rang, a long, long time.

"No one there," he said. "You want to try someone else?" and I didn't, wouldn't give him the satisfaction. "All right." He was already signaling Edwards, turning me towards the cage door. They put me in one of the padded cells, all alone, so I couldn't hurt myself, and couldn't make any friends. Left me there maybe an hour. They had my watch, so I couldn't even tell.

I hate small rooms, all closed in, nothing to focus on, just the brain raging. Sat in the corner with my back to the padding, stared at the ceiling, the walls, the monitor lens. I went over and over it, and it came out the same. My one hope was Louis—Louis and Josh. Hope that Josh found the message, hope he'd called right away, hope that Louis believed him. It had to be close on to noon.

Reilly was perfect and I was a fool, always have been—catch me with reason or hormones, blood rising. And Michael, God, Mike—counting on me when I couldn't even see past the trees. "If someone comes looking," he'd said, and I'd thought yesterday about Reilly, I couldn't even say that I hadn't, but it's that old tug, the tie, the trap. "Trust me, trust me," and I used to believe that you *could* trust the cops, but that was before I became one. I punched out the wall to give them something to watch on their monitor. Hurt like hell, hurt my hand, and I didn't feel better but it was something to do. No jailers came running.

It was maybe half an hour when one finally showed.

"They want you," he said from the doorway. No one else with him.

"For what?"

"Interview. Come on."

He was ready for trouble, but I wasn't going to give him any. I'd have hurried *him* there if I could. "Interview" meant something was happening, something besides Reilly wrapping me up. It meant maybe Louis was here, or Pilsner was thinking, or Carlos wanted another look. They could all have anything, everything, I didn't care. Just get me the hell out from under.

It wasn't "they," though.

It was Reilly, sitting alone in the room.

He didn't look evil, he looked tired out, worn—and then he saw me and the mask came down over his face like a shutter and we were players again.

"Sit down."

I didn't move from the doorway. The jailer gave me a shove and then I was in the room with the door slamming shut. Reilly on the other side of the table.

"Sit *down*, Meg."

I didn't have to sit, didn't *have* to do anything, but Reilly was still here, still obviously in charge.

I sat.

"All right," he said. "You have the right to remain silent—"

He was goddamn Mirandizing me. Someone was listening, then, watching behind the mirrored window. Carlos? Pilsner? Hope is a killer. I stared at the walls, the dirty white walls, until he was done. All my rights read and acknowledged. Silence.

"You want to talk to me, Meg?" And I can talk, you know, I can talk to the devil if there's a reason I have to.

"No," I said.

"How's your hand?"

It was fine.

"Josh made it to school all right," he said casually. "I had someone check." Calm, conversational, not even a threat. As if he thought I'd been worried and he was easing my mind.

"I left some very specific notes around town," I said. "If anything happens to me or to Josh, they'll be looking for you."

"Like this one?" He was reaching down beside him and hefting something onto the table.

*Josh's knapsack.*

I must have been looking as sick as I felt. I hadn't seen him take it, he was that goddamn smooth. Unless he'd gotten it later. "You put it out on the lawn."

"I put it back in the car while you were saying goodbye. Josh never missed it. So you could be here a while, Meg."

I could. My hand hurt after all, clenched into a fist. I pushed back from the table, out of the chair, and he wasn't stopping me, he was letting me pace. Like you'd give someone a cigarette, calming their nerves. Like you'd give them a leash. "What d'you want from me?"

Wanted something.

"The truth about Mike," he said, and I laughed, couldn't help it, it just came out that way. Harsh. Humorless. All of this, and he was still on the same dragging line.

"Was he drug-running, Meg?"

"Yeah, sure he was," I said, "or what did you want me to say?"

"Was he?"

People were listening.

"No."

"Anything to connect him?"

Like his drug-dealing friends? "No." Well. "He worked Vice for a while."

"When?"

"Six, seven years ago."

"Made some connections?"

"Yeah, he did," I said, "but it's been a long time."

"Might have kept up."

"Not to my knowledge. No reason to."

He was nodding as if that answered it, as if that was really why we were here. "You know anyone at the DEA?"

"Well, I guess I know Jones and Carlos *now*," I said.

He nodded again. "Anyone else?"

I did, actually.

"No."

"No one there who'd know you, know Mike?"

"I couldn't say," I said. "Is somebody asking?" It was a wild hope, stupid.

"No."

So Jones and Carlos hadn't gone home with my name, mentioned it around at the office. Or Reilly was lying.

"Who's listening, Reilly?"

He cocked his head gravely. "Listening?"

"Behind Door Number Three. The window."

"Abbott."

He didn't look like he was making it up. Didn't sound like it either, but that couldn't be all.

"With Edwards maybe?"

"Maybe."

I laughed then and stretched at him, arrogant, tall. "Having trouble, Reilly? Burbank kind of worried, been giving you flak?" And I should have kept my mouth shut, always my problem, because he was looking at me, caught. Watching me move, analyzing my attitude, my tone. I cut it back instantly, but it was too late.

"It wasn't in the knapsack," he said slowly.

"Excuse me?"

"Your message. It wasn't in the knapsack at all, was it?"

He was as good as I'd seen, examining options, assessing the damage while he waited for me to tell him what he'd already guessed. I could have shined him on. Probably I should have.

"That was window-dressing," I said.

"You didn't have time to get to Josh."

"You'd have spotted it anyway," I said. "Josh tries, but he's not a good liar."

"You going to tell me?"

He was already guessing Josh. Better to tell him so he'd know it was public, that it was too late to stop.

"I put it in his pants pocket when I hugged him in his room. And Caroline's death about him checking his clothes before they go in the wash."

He was remembering the scene on the front lawn with Caroline. He was remembering the *"go in and change, honey."*

"Who's the message for?"

I wouldn't have told him, but he was ahead of me again. "That's all right, we'll just go pick up Josh," he said.

"It was for Louis."

"What'd you tell him?"

"To come screaming in here with all the press he can muster." That wasn't quite true, but I wasn't going to give him everything.

"Dammit." He was looking tired again and pissed off, angry. Angry at himself, looked like, I couldn't tell. "And if I move you?" He was thinking out loud. "Take you to Crescenta Valley or Pasadena?"

"He's got your name," I said steadily, "and Abbott's. The next place he'd go would be Beverly Hills."

Reilly was picturing the scene in the Beverly Hills station lobby, I'd guess, because his lips were a very straight line. The publicity. The fuss. The lid blowing right off his own dirty secret.

"That's *if* he got the message," he said. "Josh is only a kid."

I shrugged at him then and nodded at the window. "Even if he didn't," I said, *"Burbank*'s gotten it now."

# 25

The door beside me from the hall was opening. It wasn't a surprise to see Abbott plowing in.

"Plan B?" Reilly said, and Abbott stopped short, his heavy face fixed on me, sharp little eyes.

"She willing to go along?"

"Not yet."

"Not ever," I said, and Reilly just nodded.

"Come on in, Lieutenant."

Behind Abbott was Pilsner.

Not Edwards, Pilsner.

Another lieutenant. A *Burbank* lieutenant. Abbott's old friend. I was backed up into the corner and I must have been looking fairly desperate.

"You need to think a little," Reilly said, but I needed to think a *lot*. There was a brief sound of conversation in the hall, and then Edwards was coming in the door behind Pilsner. Three cops plus Reilly and me. No room to breathe.

"You forgot Jones and Carlos."

"They weren't invited."

Everyone seemed to know what that meant. I had a Burbank lieutenant, a Burbank detective, a Beverly lieutenant, and a Beverly sergeant, holding me publicly in the Burbank jail. This was either a high-level, multi-city ring of corruption, or I had it wrong.

"I'm not going to guess anymore," I said. "You guys can tell me what's what, or I'm out of here."

"Haven't heard from your lawyer yet, Meg."

A reminder from Reilly, pointed, that I wasn't in charge, but I saw Edwards' head swivel and I knew it was noon. Knew that Josh, bless him, *had* found the note and that Louis for once in his life had put prudence aside and done what I'd asked him without second-guessing, that somewhere in the building he was pounding a desk and insisting that Burbank produce me. It was unbelievable triumph, relief surging through me, and Reilly's eyes were on mine.

"Ask Edwards," I said, and he turned.

"There *is* a guy here," Edwards said. "A lawyer." He jerked his head at the hall. "Dixon was telling me."

"Can you stall him?"

"I can try."

"Ten minutes," Reilly said. "You don't know where we are."

Edwards grinned and was gone. That fast. Trouble.

"Sir," Reilly said, "maybe you and the lieutenant need to get some more coffee."

"I can't have her coerced." That was Pilsner peering over his glasses, sticking up for me. Sticking up for himself, really, because this was his station and he was a lieutenant, retirement age, had a lot more to lose.

"No, sir," Reilly said. "I'm just going to talk to her. Five minutes."

Halving his time.

Abbott touched Pilsner's arm, said something aside in his ear, something convincing, because Pilsner was nodding, and then they were both moving back out the door. It swung shut behind them. Left Reilly and me. Him still at the table and me in my corner.

"Been kind of a day," he said. He was leaning back in his chair, feeling his way. I could have just left him flapping, stonewalled him out, but five minutes was all the time that we had, and I needed to get what I could.

"You did me upstairs."

"Had to."

"Not for Burbank, apparently."

He was tapping his pen. "Carlos would have taken you," he said. "The second it looked like cops involved, they'd have jumped right on you. Federal. Did you want to be riding around with Jones?"

I didn't.

"So you booked me to protect me?"

"That's right."

"Baloney," I said.

"All right," he said evenly, "this is my case."

"Territorial? You the hell sliced my throat upstairs marking your *line*?"

"Something like that."

I know cops who'd do it. Reilly didn't strike me as one.

"Try something else."

*Very* level. "If I'd let them take you," he said, "you'd have wangled your phone call and gotten your lawyer. Sat on your rights until he showed up to spring you, and then you'd have skipped out, gone to ground. Tell me I'm wrong."

I couldn't quite do that.

"Meanwhile," he said, not even waiting, "somebody's looking. Maybe you're *not* in it up to your neck, or maybe you are. Either way, they're looking for you, and maybe you're not as good as you think. Maybe they'd find you before *I* did."

"Maybe they wouldn't, Reilly."

"Maybe," he said, "but I'm not going to spend my time running you down when I've already got you in hand."

"*Had* me," I said. "*Had* me in hand."

He was contemplating his pen, not looking at me. "You won't get bail if I book you for homicide."

He couldn't be serious. *Seemed* very serious.

"You'd do that?"

"Yeah."

He didn't need enough for a case, didn't have to take me to trial, he just needed enough for suspicion. Cops don't like to book on that, tips the hand, and then there're the filings—DAs get very snarky if you don't have the evidence, they throw out the charges and make you start over, but Christ, if he wanted to, Reilly could do it. Tie me up for a couple of days. Keep me in jail.

"This *is* coercion," I said. "Pilsner'll be pissed."

"I don't think so."

He was most likely right.

"What do you want?"

He smiled at me then, full on, a very nice smile. "You probably want to talk to your lawyer," he said. "Probably want to tell him you're fine, that you're helping us out."

"Probably want to tell him I'll talk to him every two hours."

"You probably will." It didn't seem to bother him.

"I had it all worked out in the cell," I said, "how you'd staged the whole thing."

"Me? Why would I?" and I didn't have an answer, not now, not like this, but he wasn't waiting for one anyway. Rising and tucking that pen back away. Man lived in pocketed shirts. "You hungry?"

I was.

"We'll take you to lunch, city's treat. See if things don't look better. After you talk to your lawyer, that is."

And *there* was a conversation. "Louis'll kill me."

That half-glint from him, looking down.

"He'll be standing in line," Reilly said.

I talked to Louis. Louis wasn't happy. Louis had a few opinions about my origins and probable demise which were alarmingly graphic. Reilly had offered us an interview room, but I'd had enough of mirrored windows. He wasn't going to let us stand in the carport, though, so Edwards had finally found us an empty office. Lunchtime, you know, and he and Reilly, I'm sure, were waiting outside in the hall. I was just trying to get Louis to keep his voice down.

"I'm fine," I said, "really."

"You don't even know these guys!"

"Well, unless they've got balls the size of Milwaukee," I said, "it's legit. They booked me in here, they've been walking me around the station—plenty of people to see me coming and going. In company, Louis. I'm not exactly a secret."

"And what do they want from you?"

"I don't know. I'll get it at lunch. They probably just want to pump me some more about Mike."

"They can do that *here*. While *I'm* here."

"You're not a criminal lawyer," I said. "You told me that yourself. And by the time I get Bob McKenzie down here and fill him in, there's another hour, maybe two, when I could have been eating and finding stuff out, gotten a little closer, maybe, to Mike. The thing is, Louis"—I took a deep breath—"someone came by the house last night and saw Josh. He didn't tell you?"

"He was a little upset," Louis said slowly. "Called just before twelve. I didn't get much beyond the note and that Reilly'd taken you off this morning." He was silent then, thinking. Louis likes Josh. "So the notion is that they'll put you in hiding?"

I couldn't tell him that I thought the notion was "bait." He's not as easy with my past as he thinks he is, and he's become very protective since Charlie died. "I'd say so," I said.

He isn't a fool. "You're going to call me?"

"Before five."

"*Well* before five. Should we have a code word or something?"

I *do* like a man who enters into the spirit. I laughed then and hugged him, and he smelled like Old Spice. "I'll call you 'Sugar,'" I said, "if things are okay. My best Southern drawl."

His arms still around me. "And if there isn't any 'Sugar'?"

I pushed back away.

"Well, then you'd best call the cops," I said, and I smiled.

# 26

It was a very nice restaurant. Reilly fetched the burgers from the take-out counter while Edwards and I wiped the table. A lot of napkins right there and handy, so that helped. Soaked up the grease.

"I should have had the salad."

"I don't think so," Reilly said. He was looking under his bun at something that might have been meat. Edwards didn't have the same qualms, he was munching away, but he'd eaten here before and survived, so that was a testament to his iron constitution or total disregard for his health. Total disregard for *ours*, anyway. Reilly took a bite. I dumped a pile of catsup on my plate and concentrated on the fries.

"It's good," Reilly said.

I was willing to take his word.

"You wanted steak?"

"Champagne," I said, "and caviar. When you told me the city was paying, I thought you meant something halfway upscale."

"I had to stretch it to Edwards."

Edwards thought that was funny. I guess we were all in a pretty good mood. *I* was, for the first time in days. It was the prospect of action, and maybe of allies, of not being out on my own. You think you don't need it, you think you won't miss it, but there's a high to this camaraderie business, this sitting around a burger-joint table with large men who handle things, being inside. Reilly was watching me.

"I need to track Mike," I said.

His eyes lidding down.

"Well, I need to do *something*."

"You need to eat," he said.

"You didn't bring me out here to feed me, Reilly."

"No, I brought you out here to talk. A little more comfortable, a little less stressed. Thought we'd run over everything, see what we missed, see what Edwards picked up. That's all."

He could pack that in a bag. "Sure," I said. "Whatever. And then I go home?"

"If that's what you want."

It's good that I've never minded working for things. "So ask me something. Start me."

He did. I talked for a couple of hours at that table, tracing the graffiti carvings, smoothing the nicks. People came and went around us, you keep that eye open, but no one seemed to notice us particularly, except maybe the owner. Reilly got me more fries, another soda. More catsup.

Think I told them everything about Mike but his childhood, and that was because they didn't ask. Didn't tell them about his birthmark, come to that (a delicate issue because how would I know?), and I may not have mentioned every last story because some things are private, but I gave them enough to have a good sense of

Mike, what he'd be likely to do and what he wouldn't. I told them definitely that murder was out. Mike's morals are slipshod where love is concerned, or lust, for that matter, but there was no way in hell I could see him conspiring, whispering in corners about offing some guy.

"So where's the connection?" Edwards said.

"It has to be Soufi. Maybe Mike found him out."

"How?"

"*I* don't know," I said, "it could have been anything. He overheard something or somebody tipped him or he stumbled across it. They were talking about pictures, right, on the phone call Josh heard—so that Soufi could look at some pictures. So maybe he was out snapping hillsides one day, and caught Soufi practicing."

"Sounds a lot more like blackmail," Edwards said.

And, okay, he'd been invited along for his insight, but I was really getting tired of the same one-note song. "It's not blackmail if he was trying to stop him."

Reilly just raised an eyebrow, Edwards looked vaguely away, and yeah, I knew it was stupid. I mean, it's not what you'd do if you found someone plotting a murder, particularly if that someone's a stranger. You wouldn't give them a call and say, "Hey, let's talk, because killing is wrong." What you'd do, what Mike would have done, is to contact the police.

The local police.

Which was Beverly Hills.

Which, you know, had a problem, or at least had a rumor, of dirty cops.

Of dirty cops, and blackmailed Iranians, and possibly murder for hire.

It felt right, very right.

"Mike knows guys on your department," I said to Reilly.

"So?"

"If I were calling your department about a crime like this, I'd call someone I knew."

Reilly fixed on me. Edwards looked caught.

"But that someone might be seeing things blowing up," I said, "on a nice little racket. He'd have DEA's number right there on a Rolodex. He might even have heard you were looking for cops."

"Let's take it in sequence," Reilly said, but I didn't the hell know the sequence. I didn't know anything.

"Mike called Soufi on Wednesday," he said very quietly, "set up a meeting for Friday. We don't know if he kept it. He left a message Friday night, though, on the answering machine at your office. Didn't make it to the office Saturday morning."

"I get a phone call Saturday afternoon," I said, taking it up. "Show up at Haroutunian's house with you. Daddy's okay but he's telling us he doesn't know Mike and that he doesn't have a son. We leave as a group. We don't take him with us."

"No reason to," Reilly said, and I knew that, I did, didn't mean to sound blaming. Hindsight's always so clear, so damned twenty-twenty.

"Anyway," I said, "we go down to the station and my car gets stolen. You drive me home, we reach Burbank seven-thirtyish, seven forty-five. The car shows up at eight-thirty, Point Fermin, full of blood."

"Why Point Fermin?" Edwards asking, and I had no idea.

"Bodies in the ocean. Drugs. Beachhouses."

"Haroutunian have a beachhouse there?" he asked. That was to Reilly.

"Not that we can find. He has one in Malibu."

Malibu?

"Did you check it?" I asked, and Reilly gave me a look.

"Things like warrants."

"Christ, it's Tuesday afternoon already."

That right eyebrow raising. "I didn't hear about beachhouses until last night."

And since then, he'd been kind of busy was what he was saying. I disregarded.

"Josh is probable cause." Enough to get a warrant for the beachhouse, anyway, with bodies missing and an overheard rendezvous.

There was something like a pause.

"Meg," Reilly said gently, "there was a lot of blood at Mike's place." He was talking quite patiently, kindly even, and this is why they don't let friends investigate things. Too much vested interest. Too little regard for the facts. Mike wasn't sitting in a Malibu beachhouse waiting for me to break through.

"I know that," I said.

"We're *getting* the warrant. If there's anything there, we'll find it."

I was flexing my fingers.

"You need to help out, Meg."

"I'm helping," I said. "I'm *sitting* here, aren't I?"

Another kind of pause.

"I've got to call in," Edwards said diplomatically. "See what's shaking on the home front. You want anything while I'm up?"

I wanted the hell to be gone.

"Don't steal my notes," he said, and left his book on the table while he motored outside to the pay phone. Reilly was a lump, impassive, immobile.

"What's it *now?*" he said, as if I spent my whole life being difficult.

"Nothing."

"Yeah?"

Yeah.

"I'm not some candy-ass female," I said tightly. "I know that Mike's dead. I don't need you to point it out, okay?"

He was looking like he was about to respond, so I just rode right on through him. "I'm not somewhere in *space,* Reilly. People die every day for stupid reasons, for nothing, but this wasn't random, it wasn't an accident— it was premeditated, deliberate, and I don't want to hear a bunch of garbage about 'you'll get around to it.' I know you will. I'm saying, *'Do it now.'* I'm saying don't bother to babysit because I'll still be here—you want that on a stack of Bibles, you can have it—but get yourself over to chat with Soufi. Put together a warrant and check out the beachhouse. Do it *NOW* and find the trail, because I have to live with this for the rest of my life and I don't want to be wondering what I could have done or what I should have said or what I should have pushed or your goddamned precious *ego.*"

I could have gone on, *would* have, everything spilling, except the voice broke then, and the tears, and I'm like that, you know. Sitting there hating. I was shaking, mostly frustration, and he was handing me napkins out of the dispenser like he thought he was wise. Maybe he was. Wasn't touching me or anything, trying to pat. Wasn't saying anything. I pushed back in the booth.

"*Abbott's* talking to Soufi," he said. Quietly. No more.

I mopped at my face.

"You want some water?"

I didn't want anything. We were silent a while.

"Ray's doing the warrant."

Escobar. The man didn't sleep. None of them seemed to. Maybe it was a requirement to be on his squad.

"It's just a matter of time, Meg."

It always is. I know that. Things come about in the fullness of time.

"I'm sorry," I said. He nodded. I blew my nose. Took another napkin, wadded it up. "I'll have to call Sammy."

"Sammy?"

"Mike's brother. Sam."

And his mom.

God.

"Not just yet," Reilly said, and, really, what could I tell them?

"Okay."

Craven.

Putting things off. Putting everything off. I took kind of a breath.

"Did you tell the DEA about me?"

He was still, almost shocked, and I realized how it had sounded.

"I don't mean their anonymous tip," I said swiftly, pacifically, "I'm not saying you *called* them, but when they came in, did you tell them about me?"

"Told them some," he said very slowly. "Why?"

"I just wondered," I said.

He was watching me like he didn't even like me, and I get defensive.

"What?"

"I'm tired of this here-and-there stuff," he said flatly. "You *have* something or not?"

I didn't have anything. I shouldn't have started.

"Jones calling Mike my boyfriend, is all," I said. "I thought maybe he got that from you."

A very odd look on his face.

"No."

So he hadn't been dishing me, standing around in some locker room, flapping. I felt vaguely better.

"You think Edwards is renting that phone?"

Reilly glanced that way and then back. Edwards was taking a long time with his phone call, watching us through the window while he shouldered the receiver, chatted.

"What does it matter?" Reilly said.

"Edwards?"

"Jones saying 'boyfriend.'"

Oh.

"It's just—I don't know—I thought, with you talking to Dave—" Reilly's face, very guarded, which told its own story. "He didn't *tell* you?" I said.

"Tell me what?"

"After Charlie died," I said, "he did the investigation into Mike and me." Reilly wasn't moving. Something in the quality of the stillness. "I thought he'd told you."

"No, he didn't," he said.

Oh.

*Christ.*

Dave hadn't told him, hadn't said anything.

"I didn't know Mike was missing then," Reilly was saying. Slowly. Warily. "That was Saturday. I was just asking about *you*."

He'd ask now, though, wouldn't he? Now that I'd said it. Now that I'd gone out of my way to say it. I watched my hands shred the napkin.

"Why'd they do an investigation?"

"They didn't have any suspects," I said.

"Meg."

There are *always* suspects when a cop is killed. Anyone he's ever arrested, every group that's out there. They'd focused on us. Mike and me.

"It was a bad time," I said carefully, because my jaw wasn't working. "Mike stuck by me. One of the lieutenants thought we were maybe too close, and that's how it starts."

"Not how it ends, though."

He wanted everything. Handed to him, there, on a platter. I have moments when I hear myself saying it anyway, over and over to the walls.

"He was shot on the street, point-blank, with a .45, his gun not even drawn. Likely he knew whoever it was or he'd have been ready. And I carry a .45. None of my guns matched, but that wasn't the issue. They didn't figure I'd use my own, that I'd keep it."

"You were having problems?"

It's a small world, a police department. "They thought that we might be."

"Were you?"

"No."

"None?"

Reilly was a cop himself. I watched my fingers, shredding. "It's hard working different shifts, the kind of stuff that we did. Always someone to tell you what the other one said, make a sniggering joke, whatever. You handle it or you don't. We were doing okay."

"What did they hang it on?"

Had to be something.

"We'd had a fight," I said. "Not really a fight. One of those things where no one's quite talking and you don't say goodbye." And five hours later they tell you he's dead, and there's nothing to say then and no one to say it to, not ever, forever, until the day that you die.

"What about?"

There was paper from the napkin shreds under my nails. "The laundry. How I did my hair."

"Not much."

"You find things when you're married," I said.

Reilly'd been married. He knew. A moment or two of shared communion, or maybe he was waiting. Edwards taking a very long time with that phone call.

"He wanted me to quit," I said.

"You didn't want to?"

"And do what—sell Tupperware? It was an idea he had that life would be perfect. Not reason enough to kill anyone."

Anything's reason, though, really. I saw a person once, killed for a pot roast, because it was burnt.

"You quit *afterwards*," Reilly said, and what did he want me to say—that I hadn't? Life's what it is. Always has been.

"Yeah," I said. "It was one of those things."

"I want you to tell me what happened." Short pause. Roughly. "Or I can ask Dave."

Dave could tell him, probably would. And I'd opened the door to this, I'd brought it up. There *are* no accidents if you believe in that stuff.

I didn't want him talking to Dave.

"They cleared us," I said. "Mike was working and they couldn't make a case on me. Tried the first week or two. Tried pretty hard. They kept it quiet—just came in quick and dirty, a handful of people, so it wouldn't get out, you know? Wouldn't get public."

Reilly knew.

"And then word filtered in that it was gangs, a drive-by—not even *meant* for Charlie maybe, just that he was there. Gave me back my badge and my gun, told me what an asset they'd always felt I was. Thought I should take some time off, try to put it behind me. I couldn't seem to do that."

"What about Mike?"

"He told them to go fuck themselves."

"So you both just quit?"

"They offered to settle," I said. "A very generous check."

"And then you started the business."

That's what we'd done, all right.

Together.

*Fuck 'em all.*

"Well, that's pretty clear," he said. He was looking odd. Warily compassionate, if there was such a thing. "You should have told me."

"Reilly," I said, and I was surprised I could talk about it so calmly, "Charlie's gunned down on the street and they look at Mike and me for it. Nothing. Never solved. Three years later, Mike vanishes and I'm running around full of stories about phone calls and stolen cars. You think anyone would've been looking anywhere but at *me*?"

"No," he said shortly.

"Damn straight," I said.

# 27

I don't know what Edwards thought he was doing. Being discreet, I guess. He was standing just inside the doorway, sort of fumbling in his pocket, scanning the menu board as if he'd find something interesting there, some dish he'd overlooked.

"You'd better catch him before he orders again," I said. "I'm not eating any more fries."

"Yeah, I will." Reilly was hesitating.

"I'll be here."

That quirky smile. Beatific. "No other way out."

Maybe not.

I might have been smiling back. Confession so good for the soul. He seemed to think I was okay, so maybe I was, seemed to think we could get by it, so maybe we could. Seemed to think we could unravel this thing, whatever it was, and it's been quite a while since I've let myself believe. He nodded abruptly and went to fetch Edwards.

Something wrong.

He and Edwards weren't coming right back, they were standing at the front, Edwards talking, Reilly listening, intent. Eyes flicking to me and away. Asking a question, a low murmur, a shake of the head from Edwards. Negatory. Something wrong.

I was on my feet without thinking, on my feet and moving, both of them watching me come.

"Is it Mike?"

"No."

"Josh?"

"He's fine," Reilly said, "as far as we know. You all done here?"

There were people around us, jostling people, trying to get through the door. I let him take my arm and steer me outside, head me towards the car.

"Tell me," I said. Edwards on the other side, slightly behind.

"Someone broke into your house this afternoon."

"They what?"

He was crowding me against the car, blocking me in with his body while he unlocked the door, Edwards filling in to the right.

"What the hell are you—?"

"*Get in,*" he said.

I got in. I don't argue with a tone like that. Edwards was climbing into the back seat beside me, Reilly coming around to the front. He opened the door, one swift movement, slid into the driver's seat. Sat low, slumped. Watching the rearview mirror.

"You leave any other messages around?"

"No."

"Nobody else looking for you?"

Josh maybe, but he'd turned it over to Louis. I didn't think he'd do more. Caroline wouldn't, that was for sure, and no one else knew I was missing.

"No. Why?"

"Somebody called the jail."

I couldn't think what that meant, but it sounded bad the way he said it, sounded ominous. "Looking for *me*?"

"That's right."

It didn't make sense. Nobody knew I'd been booked except the group from this morning—or whoever might have followed us to the station, I suppose. Wouldn't take a genius to figure it out, make a phone call to ask.

"He give a name?"

Reilly's eyes on mine in the rearview mirror.

"Mike's."

Like the kick from a shotgun. A kick from a mule.

"You want to tell me what it means?" he said, and what it meant was a joker who knew that they'd ask. You can't get ID on the phone. There was no way it was Mike, there was just no way—even if he was above-ground and breathing, he didn't know I was there.

Unless he'd talked to Josh.

"What time was the call?"

"Two thirty-nine."

Josh still in school. Normally.

"What time is it now?"

"Almost four."

"I have to call Louis by five," I said. "Maybe I should call him early, see if he knows anything, talked to anybody." Talked to Mike.

Except then Mike wouldn't have called the jail. It was uncomfortably close in the back seat with Edwards, with Reilly not turning around.

"Did this guy say anything else?" I didn't know who to ask, his eyes in the mirror, or Edwards, so I aimed it at Edwards, turned slightly right in the seat to address him, slid back for the distance, the conversational space. Out of the mirror. Reilly didn't adjust it.

"Just wanted to know if you were there," Edwards said.

"What'd they tell him?"

"That you were out."

An hour ago. "What's this business about my house?"

Edwards seemed to be waiting.

"Either of you," I said. "I don't care."

"They got your office first," Reilly said. "Your manager called it in this morning. Somebody trashed it."

Trashed the office.

"Last night?"

"Looks like. Manager called the station at nine A.M."

While we were in Burbank, having our meeting.

"A patrol unit took it," he said. "Straight report. Thought it was vandalism, maybe attempted burglary, unable to contact the victim, et cetera. Would have just gone into the pile for tomorrow except that one of the girls in the Record Bureau recognized your name."

"*My* name?"

"We'd had her run a check on you Saturday," he said. "So she mentioned it to Abbott when he got back to the station."

And Abbott had called Pilsner, and Burbank had gone by my house. To find it broken into.

"What time did your guys get to my house?" I said to Edwards.

"Right around two."

"Hot?"

"Hard to say. No sign of anyone hiding in the bushes."

They'd had all morning to break in, though. No need to hurry or to hang around.

"Do you still have a man on Josh?" I said to Reilly.

"Do, now."

He was ahead of me. Everyone was. Someone had called the station at two-thirty. Two thirty-nine.

"Think we'll find you a motel room," Reilly said. He was still talking to the windshield. I could see the top of his head over the headrest, the bulk of his neck, his shoulders. Squared.

Somebody looking for me.

"I need to call Louis."

"All right."

"What do they want with me?"

"Went through Mike's place," Reilly said. "Haroutunian's. Your office, your house. My guess would be pictures."

The ones Mike was going to show Soufi.

"I don't know anything about it."

"Looks like someone thinks you do."

Two someones.

One of them in the front seat.

I'd been crying too much lately, was my problem— you get in the habit, the waterways working, everything primed, lubed. I shut my eyes and there were red spots, little blinding images, the outline of Reilly's head.

"I don't want a motel room," I said.

One of those male kind of pauses.

"We'll see," he said. "You have to make your phone call and I want to talk to Abbott."

I wasn't going to sit in a safe-house, waiting.

"Fine," I said.

# 28

We called from the Pizza Shack on Victory. Not my favorite place, but it had a phone inside, back by the bathrooms, and it was kind of dark, kind of small, only approachable from the front. They had me call first, which was a waste of time because I'd just have to call Louis again once things were set. I'd *told* them that, but no one was listening. Nobody'd called Louis asking about me, not even Mike.

"I don't know what we're doing," I said into the phone. "Are you going to be home in two hours?"

"We're supposed to go out." He didn't sound happy.

"Then I'll call your machine," I said. "It's got one of those timers, right? So you know when your calls came in?"

"What? No, it doesn't."

"That's good, then," I said, Reilly ten inches away. "So you'll know that I called in two hours, or at least within three—let's say three, just in case."

"I don't like this—"

"No," I said, "it'll be fine. It's just to check in."

"I want you to call McKenzie."

I was facing the phone, the Pac Bell instructions. "He doesn't know me, Louis."

"Then he won't get gray hairs," Louis said. "You take down the number."

I took it. I had to borrow a pen from Reilly and I wrote it on my arm. That way I wouldn't be losing it all the time.

"He's working late," Louis said in my ear. "If I'm not back, you call him. I want you talking to a person."

Same views as Mike. Put not your faith in machines, because you don't know who all will be listening. Why Mike hadn't said more.

"I have to go, Louis."

"Are you all right?"

How many times had I heard that lately? "Yeah," I said. And then I got to go sit in a booth with Edwards while Reilly had a private phone conversation with Abbott. It took him a while. I couldn't see around the corner, so I didn't know who was doing most of the talking, couldn't watch his face. Edwards ordered us both another soda. He'd offered me pizza to go along with it, but I'd had the fries, so he just got a piece for himself. Renting the booth, you know—not that they were so busy. Talked at me. He knew a couple of the guys I used to work with, so we chatted about them, eased our way into habits—what it's like getting off graveyard, coming down from the job. He had two kids and a slew of relatives, living with him or about to descend. Used to drink sometimes at the 'Hood. Seemed like a nice enough guy. I was just waiting for Reilly to come back, though, waiting for the curtain to fall. The ax. The other shoe.

He'd been long enough on the phone.

"Look," I said, "I have to use the ladies' room. Do you want to stand guard, or what?"

"Yeah, I'll check it out," Edwards said. He was starting to rise, and I was just sliding out of the seat when Reilly showed up. Magic.

"She needs the rest room," Edwards said.

"I'll go with you."

That way they could chat while I used the facilities. Fill each other in. I wished I had Josh's spy kit with the stethoscope for listening through walls.

Wished I was out of this.

Reilly poked his head into the bathroom first—single stall, single sink, no window, no occupants—and then let me past him, hand light on my elbow. Not entirely distant. I didn't know what it meant. Didn't hurry. They weren't going to talk while I was around anyway. Threw cold water on my face, my eyes, crumpled the paper towels. Reilly had my bag in the trunk of his car, so I couldn't add makeup, couldn't brush my hair. I combed through it with fingers, the best that I could, smoothed it down, but I still looked like something the rats had rejected and my eyes still looked red-rimmed and tired.

All of me tired.

So much for attraction.

When I got out, Edwards was the one on the phone, half turned away.

"Calling his wife," Reilly said.

"Because I *have* to," Edwards was saying, "it's part of the job," and I didn't need to hear any more. *Another* all-nighter, or at least he'd be late, with the in-laws in town. Everybody so happy.

"You tell me what we're doing," I said to Reilly, "okay? Maybe up front."

Reilly'd been here himself. Touched Edwards's arm and indicated us moving on, not to hurry.

Edwards mouthed "bitch," rolled his eyes. "You be nicer," I wanted to say, but it wasn't my business. Nobody'd asked me and I didn't know him.

"Come on," Reilly said.

We didn't go back to the booth, just stood by some empty tables in the middle, watching the front door open and close.

"What's the plan?"

"Edwards has a motel they've used before," Reilly said.

"You're going to keep me in Burbank?"

"Yeah." He didn't amplify. Didn't explain. Either there was some jockeying going on between Burbank and Beverly as to who had the dibs on me or everyone had agreed that Beverly wouldn't be safe right now. If there *were* Beverly cops looking for me, they'd have more options to find out at home.

"So you're turning me over to Edwards?"

He was looking at something by the bar. "For the night."

Okay.

Well.

"Can I go by my house?"

"Why?"

"To get a few things."

"Not much left to get," he said. "Everything's pretty torn up—smashed or cut into pieces."

Sugarcoat it for me.

"Look," I said, "I didn't know about the pictures. Mike didn't tell me anything, didn't *leave* me anything."

"Yeah."

"Reilly, for Christ's sake—I went through the whole goddamn bedroom last night, and there wasn't a thing."

"Less now," he said.

Son of a bitch.

And, okay, maybe I *should* have told him, confided my little heart out, but we are what we are, you know, what we've made of ourselves. Hard words don't change that. And maybe I was supposed to come all unglued now and fall apart at his feet, but I didn't feel much like that either, so I shrugged at him, stared at my own damn section of the bar. If he wanted to talk to me, he knew where I was. And if he *didn't* want to talk to me—well, Edwards seemed like a reasonable man, and Edwards was spending the night.

Spending the night on the phone maybe, because his call was taking forever. Reilly wasn't visibly breathing, hadn't moved.

"Can I at least have my bag from the car?"

"When we get there."

Well, I knew that. Didn't mean he should run out to fetch it.

"Did they trash *everything?*"

"Sounded like it." Like he was waiting for me to ask.

"My guns?"

"They were still there," he said. "Burbank impounded them."

Because I wasn't around.

"Were all of them *mine?*"

"Yours or Charlie's."

He'd thought of it already, then. Burglars who didn't take guns. They hadn't left an extra one, though, by way of apology—one with barrel marks, say, to match the slug in Mike's wall. The thing is, I don't check my guns every day, don't climb up and count them, so any of them could have taken a walk, could have gone for a ride, and I wouldn't have noticed. Reverse burglary. Not to *take* guns, but return them. Tell me I'm paranoid.

"Are they going to do tests?"

"That's the notion," Reilly said.

I touched the phone number on my arm. Indelible ink. Tattooed.

"Any pattern to this?" I said. "Any quirks at the house?"

"Blood."

*"Blood?"*

"They killed a cat, smeared the blood around. Left the carcass by the front door."

*My* cat.

"Someone's pissed off," Reilly said.

Me.

*I* was.

I don't hold such brief for animals, you know, really I don't. I leave them alone, and they do the same. But this was a stray cat that wandered in, that showed up one Christmas and wouldn't go away. Charlie was sneaking it turkey and Josh was putting out milk, and finally I said, okay, it can sleep in the garage, but I won't have the thing in the house. Should have stuck to that, should have goddamn *stuck* to it.

Someone did this to me when I was a rookie, found a roadkill cat and left it on my car, message fairly clear. But they didn't slaughter it themselves, they were just being hateful and I've always figured that kind of mentality breeds its own punishment, makes its own troubles. Comes to its own bad end. It's probably not true, but I've always liked to think it.

Wasn't thinking it now.

"You all right?" Reilly said.

"Why am I going to a motel?"

"Thought you'd be more comfortable."

"*Garbage,*" I said. "You want to get these guys, they want to get me—why aren't I just going home so they can find me?"

"Witness protection."

"I'll waive it."

He was still looking at the bar, but he seemed a little tight. Speaking very slowly. "That would be a problem."

"It's not a problem, Reilly. I go home, Burbank hangs out, someone shows up, they get him."

"It was a *dead* cat."

"So Burbank has to be good."

"They can be the best in the world," he said. "It's no protection against a bomb through the window."

"Nobody's bombed anyone, Reilly."

Very tight. That jaw muscle clamping. "*You* know so much? Who these guys are?"

"No.

"Know what they want? What they're after?"

"No."

"Then you're going to a motel," he said. "End of discussion."

Nothing's ever the end. "Reilly—"

"I'll put you in a cell."

*Almost* nothing.

"Come on," he said. "I want to get Edwards and get out of here."

# 29

Someday I'm going to go to a really nice motel—spend like two hundred dollars for the night and have a fireplace and maybe a heart-shaped bathtub with whirlpool jets. I've always wanted to do that, but I keep ending up in dumps like this one. If you're just going to sleep there, I guess it doesn't need ambiance. Charlie used to tell me that, and I can see the logic, can understand it, but someday I'm going to have satin sheets.

"You going to be all right?" Reilly said.

That question again. "Yeah, sure. Edwards isn't coming in?"

"He's getting his guys squared away."

Okay. I ran my hand over the crack in the wall by the bed. Kind of a small room, with just the bed, two chairs, an end table, and Reilly. A lowboy sort of dresser thing he was sitting on. A lamp. The bathroom was at the end of the room, next to an open closet space with hangers. It had a TV in the corner, bolted up to the wall. Somebody'd hung a Western print, two horses in a meadow, in the space beside the window, so I guess that explained why it was called the Circle Bar Motel.

"What am I supposed to do tonight?"

"Get some sleep," Reilly said.

He'd already checked out the bathroom. There was one thin slider over the tub that looked like it had been painted shut about twenty years ago. Wouldn't give when he tugged on it. I didn't think I could squeeze through it even if I smashed all the glass out, so probably nobody who was after me could get in that way, and Burbank would be watching the front from the parking lot. This was one of the old-style motels, built in a squared-off horseshoe shape with the parking lot in the middle. Two stories. Good for surveillance or for this kind of thing because it had limited access, only one exit. I was on the bottom floor.

I should have felt safe, and I guess I did—*would* have, anyway, if Reilly weren't lounging so casually against the wall as if he were planning to stay. If the room weren't so small. If he'd look at something else. Edwards wasn't spending the night after all. I didn't know if that was Reilly's idea or if they were all just respecting my privacy, because you'd almost *have* to respect it from the outside, with the size of this room. I'd gathered that Edwards was going to sit in one of the cars in the parking lot for a while. I mean, the wife was already ticked off. You wouldn't want to hurry home.

"What are *you* going to be doing?"

"I've got some things to follow up," Reilly said.

"Going back to Beverly?"

"Probably use Pilsner's office."

So he'd still be in Burbank. Closer to hand.

"I didn't mean to mess up your day," I said. His night.

"That's all right."

I traced the crack again.

"Thanks for putting someone on Josh."

He shrugged, crossed his arms. "You'll have some problems with his mother about it."

Yeah, I would. Everything ripples. I fingered the phone on the bedside table.

"I have to call Louis again in a bit."

"It goes through the switchboard."

So they'd know who I called.

"Don't tell him where you are," Reilly said.

I should never have involved Louis—I was being so clever, but if someone wanted to find me, it wasn't a big leap to Louis and Marie. Or to Sammy. Mike's mom. And maybe someone didn't care how much blood they spilled, or whose. So maybe I should tell them *all* where I was so they'd have something to say if someone came knocking, but Christ, you know, there were men outside in a car, too, watching the door. Men with wives. Everything ripples. I wanted to race back to Saturday and slam down the phone. Contain it somehow.

"I can't just sit here, Reilly."

"I'll bring you some books."

I didn't want books. "Bring me files."

He just slouched further down on the wall. Wasn't going to bring any files.

"*Something* started it," I said. "You and Abbott had a reason to be hunting for cops. You can tell me that much. Maybe it'll fit something I know."

Arms crossed, considering. We had to wait for Edwards anyway. Kill the time. "One of our guys had a snitch," he said finally. "Hadn't seen him for a while. He came up one day and wanted to know what it'd be worth to sell cops, 'special cops' he called them. Wouldn't say who. He said the cops were blackmailing Iranians, doing something with drugs, suggested there was murder for hire. The officer was trying to run it, get more information, and the snitch disappeared."

Snitches do that. That's not so unusual. I kept my mouth shut so Reilly'd go on.

"The guy brought it to Abbott," Reilly said.

"Why?"

"The snitch gave him a homicide, and he wanted to check it. It turned out to be right."

And Abbott was the Detective Lieutenant, in charge of the Homicide guys, but that still didn't explain why the cop hadn't gone to IA.

"Abbott have a network?"

"The snitch had implied that the officer knew these cops," Reilly said steadily, "and the guy's pretty tight with some of my squad."

"Special cops," the snitch had said—STU would qualify. And the officer had been sitting on the quandary of believing his snitch or betraying his friends, so he'd sounded out Abbott about the snitch's information—at which point Abbott, I'd guess, brought in Reilly. And somewhere in there, the Chief had agreed that they could check it themselves—in the absence of a verifiable snitch probably. And probably with Reilly putting himself on the line.

"Nothing since then?"

"Not till you."

Five months of nothing. "Five months?"

"Four and a half."

That's a long time for nothing. "Does this cop with the snitch know Mike?"

Reilly was glancing at his watch. "He says not."

One relief. One very small mark in our favor.

"Does he have a wide circle of friends?"

"We looked," Reilly said. "We were close to giving it up until this."

Until *I'd* called the station and Reilly'd heard "Iranian," and then he'd heard "ex-cop." And there was something about the way Reilly was sitting, something about the way he'd been talking. I stared at him.

"Does this guy know *me*?"

"Yeah," Reilly said.

I called Louis, got the machine, didn't tell it where I was. Said I was fine, said I wouldn't get in touch for a while, at least till tomorrow.

Dialed McKenzie. He sounded very sharp on the phone, brisk.

"You all right?"

"Yeah," I said. "This is the deal," and I outlined it for him so that he could tell Louis. I don't know if he was listening. He didn't seem to be. Asked how I liked my coffee.

"Cream," I said, "sugar."

"With chickory?"

"When I'm stuck in the South," I said. Louis was thorough and this guy was all right. I was smiling a little, no very good reason. Reilly had moved in to one of the chairs by the end table and Edwards was in the corner by the door. Everyone watching me phone. Y'all come on down now, y'heah?

"Listen, McKenzie, did you take any notes?"

"Call me Mac," he said. "And I've got a recorder." Taping me. Well, why not? Reilly was probably taping *him*. Us.

"You'll tell Louis?"

"You're cooperating with Beverly Hills of your own free will, you're out of touch until morning, and if anyone calls asking for you, that's what he should say."

"If it's *Mike,* though," I said, "or someone *saying* it's Mike, then he needs to get Reilly, have Reilly get me."

"At the number you already gave me."

He had the recorder. Reilly had a beeper. We were all so high-tech. "He also needs to be careful," I said. "So do you."

"Never even heard of you."

I had his number on my arm.

"You've heard of me," I said. "I just never got around to calling. You've been meaning to get Louis and find out why not."

"I can do that. Anything else?"

Go to ground, Mac. Run from me, run.

"I think that's it," I said. "Thanks for everything."

"Think *you* need to be careful," he said.

Needed something. I hung up on him, rude, what my mother would have said, but, really, we'd finished. And I *had* told him "Thank you."

"Trouble?" Reilly was looking at my face.

"No."

He wasn't going to tell me who the cop was, of course, the one who'd said he knew me, but at least we'd established that the guy didn't know me *well.* I mean, I couldn't think of anyone except Jack Williams, and he was long gone, so maybe this cop had seen me at the meetings or something, some of the classes, maybe even dealing with Jack, but a snitch wouldn't have known that, wouldn't have warned him about *me.* They were grabbing at straws, any connection, and that's what I'd told Reilly. He might have believed me. They'd had three days to check. It was just another one of those things where he was keeping the information to himself, using it to hold me down, knock me off base. I know how it works, I didn't blame him or anything, but I was really tired of him being around. Ready for him to go home.

Not my option.

"What'd he say?"

So I told them what McKenzie had said, not getting into the sugar business, my Southern accent, and everyone seemed fairly satisfied, no questions asked, so they probably *did* have that tape cassette winding. I didn't care.

"You look tired," Reilly said.

Yeah, well, I *was* tired.

"Think we'll call it a night."

Edwards was gathering himself up, too. He'd left a paper sack on the dresser. Dinner for me.

"I'll be out front," Edwards said. "You just yell."

I could do that. I smiled at him nicely. He was okay.

"Stay *inside*," Reilly said.

I kept the smile because Edwards was there and because I don't like to fuss all the time. "Thank you. I will."

He was right over me, looking down.

"You need to go on," I said. "Check out those things."

Something flickered. "You want to give us a minute?" he said to Edwards. "I'll be right out."

He could have just said goodbye. Edwards was clearing out like he thought he knew something, like an accomplice, for Christ's sake, a little quick shrug and a "sure," kind of a lingering glance. My name on the Burbank walls. Reilly waited till he was all the way through the door.

"You having a problem?"

"I don't think so," I said.

"You're acting like it."

I wasn't acting like anything. Maybe *that* was the problem.

"It's been a long day, Reilly."

He was silent, looking. Then: "I'm going to give you my pager number."

I didn't want his number, but he was already taking out the damn notebook, tearing off a page. Writing something. Holding it out to me.

"I'll be home in about an hour," he said. "I'll be at Burbank until then. If you need something."

"I don't need anything."

"Take it anyway."

I took it. Fingered the rough edges where the paper had ripped.

"Watch TV," he said. "Read the Bible. Don't stay up all night."

Yeah.

"I'll be by in the morning." He was moving towards the door and I *wanted* him to go. Wanted him to clear on out.

"Reilly—"

"What?" He had his hand on the knob, turning back, and it was stupid of me, because there wasn't anything, really, that I'd wanted to say.

"I'm sorry for the trouble."

He was looking past me at the back of the room, the open bathroom door. Kind of grim.

"Be here," he said.

\*     \*     \*

I paced, I fretted, I turned on the TV. I looked in the paper sack and it was tacos, my favorite, limp lettuce and cheese. A can of warm soda. That was my fault because it was cold earlier, you could tell from the bag. And probably the tacos had been hot. I doused them with sauce and ate them, personal penance. Hail Mary, Mother of God, and stuff like that. Expiate my guilt.

It was game shows, *Jeopardy!*, Uncle Bill and the family, and all I could think of was Josh. If *I'd* been a kid and this happened. If someone had asked me. Mike and his games. Reilly. McKenzie. The bathroom window was small, I went back and measured and yeah, I could make it if I was careful with the glass, but where would I go? Why? I left the door open for the sound of the TV, took a shower as hot as I could stand. Wasted the little cake of soap, let it swirl down the drain, sat and watched it while the water poured, drenching me, melting me, hunched in the bottom of the tub. It had been a long day. Long weekend. Long year.

California, you know. Profligate water.

I found the shower knob, turned it off, and used one of their towels, like drying with a washcloth. Rinsed out the underwear, hung it on the knob, shimmied back into the rest of my clothes. Like old times, like going camping, but there was nobody there to bump into when I climbed into bed.

I tried to get warm. Shifted pillows. I could see that the door was locked, the safety chain on. Could read the motel instructions. I tried to watch whatever was on the TV, but I kept drifting with the announcers, the commercials, kept snapping awake. Seeing Mike. Reilly. Blood on the floor. Finally I just turned it off. Lay there and watched the outside lights through the curtain, the patterns, the color.

When the phone rang, it was nine-thirty, ten, I don't know. Sharp in the room, unexpected.

"It's Reilly," he said. "You all right?"

"Yeah."

"Did I wake you?" He sounded deeper on the phone. Warmer. Curling into my ear.

"No," I said.

"Everything quiet?"

It was quiet. "Are you home?"

"Yeah."

I couldn't picture him home. "Why'd you call?"

"I'm going to take you by the house in the morning. Thought I'd let you know."

It was nice of him to warn me, if that's what it was.

"I'll get you around seven," he said. "You need a wake-up call?"

I didn't know what I needed.

"You all right, Meg?"

I was fine, so fine, clutching the goddamned pillow and choking on the edge of it. "Yeah."

"You don't sound all right."

Well, I was falling apart just a little, sort of lost in the woods, sort of looking for home, and if he didn't want to hear it, then he shouldn't have called, because I can't be perfect all the time. "It's cold in here," I said. "I should have gotten more blankets."

"Double them over."

Did he think I was stupid? Probably.

"It'll be all right, Meg."

When?

"I know," I said.

"We're going to have you look at some pictures tomorrow, too. Personnel photos. See if you recognize anyone."

I could do that. That would be useful. See if I could spot the son of a bitch who knew me. Any other sons of bitches. Reilly wasn't saying anything else, but he wasn't hanging up and I was gradually loosening, listening to him breathe. Drifting. Floating in the darkness with the lifeline on my pillow. Like an astronaut, sort of. Out in the void.

"Reilly?"

"Uh-huh."

"Do you think Mike's alive?"

There was absolute silence and I had time to hear myself. "Do *you*?" he said. It was his investigator's voice, aware, centered, and I should never have opened my mouth, should have just kept on drifting, because then I wouldn't have to think how it sounded, how *he* sounded, which side of the void we were both really on.

"I have to go to sleep now," I said.

"Do *you* think Mike's alive, Meg?"

I couldn't picture him dead. Couldn't picture *anyone* dead, was my problem, couldn't begin to believe. "You call me around six, okay? Maybe six-thirty."

"Meg—"

"Good night," I said, and I hung up the phone. Gave it ten seconds to disconnect and then I took off the receiver, buried it under the pillow on the floor. I didn't think he'd call back but you never know and I just couldn't talk anymore.

# 30

I slept some. Running from Reilly most of the night and then the banging on the door in the morning was him. I felt like hell. Undid the chain and it was bright out, squinting at him there in the doorway. He came in fast, taking me with him, kicking the door closed behind us, but he was focused on the nightstand, the telephone line to the floor. The phone under the pillow, still off the hook.

I don't know what I thought he was going to do, but he dropped me and moved in to pick the phone up, replaced the receiver, placed the phone neatly on the stand. Impassive as the heads on Easter Island.

"Hard to reach you."

"I forgot you'd be calling," I said. He was so physically there.

"Brought you some breakfast."

"I have to wash up."

"Make it quick."

I did. He was holding out my bag and I snatched it, took it into the bathroom. He'd put in a toothbrush, some shampoo, all the niceties, but I didn't think he'd want me to use them now, take the time, and besides, I'd wasted all that water last night, so I just smeared some toothpaste on the brush, did my teeth. Threw water at my face. Threw makeup. I don't normally use much, but I had to do *something,* because I looked like ten kinds of hell. Didn't want to go out to him. Had to. I put my keys in my right front pocket, and slipped the twenty into the left one so that even if the bag and I went our separate ways again, I could still get home on my own. I hate being helpless. I looked at the face in the mirror and it wasn't me at all, but it was close enough for a stranger.

Reilly took me straight to the house. Had his motor running when I came out, ready to be gone, I guess, not wanting to waste any words. "You can eat in the car," he said. That was that. He drove like an insult, careful, inching, lifting a Styrofoam coffee cup to his mouth.

"After I look at the house," I said, "what?"

He took a right turn. Looked at the rearview mirror. "Edwards wants to run you."

Okay.

"We're discussing it," he said, but what else did we have? Me in a rat-trap or nothing, was what it looked like from here.

"Any progress on who these guys are?"

"No."

And it had to be asked, I guess. *I* had to ask it. "Are your guys somewhere accounted for?"

He took another one of those sips from the cup. "Yeah." Shifted. Sitting real well.

"It's to *clear* them," I said. "That's why we're with Burbank."

"Yeah."

I didn't say anything else. Edwards' guys were in a

white Chevy Caprice about two blocks behind us most of the way. They peeled off just before we turned down the alley, going south one street over. Coming around, I guess. Reilly parked in my spot in the back. I let us in through the gate.

Point of entry was the back door—you could see that without really looking. I'd had one of those key-operated dead-bolt locks, but a crowbar'll get you anywhere. The door hung rather dismally from the splintered wood frame. Someone had propped it closed—probably the Burbank sergeant who'd left his card stuck in one of the cracks. "Report number such and such, please contact us at your earliest convenience." He hadn't known where I was, I guess, or he was covering all the bases. I tucked the card away and kept going.

The back hall didn't look too bad if you didn't stare at the walls. A fair amount of dried blood. The house itself felt foreign and silent, violated, waiting. I wished I had my Colt, didn't want to front the open doorways, even with Reilly behind me. The laundry room off the porch was a mess. Soap powder dumped, machines pulled out, hoses slashed. I store lightbulbs in one of the cupboards and shards were all over the floor. Cupboard doors hung open, battered. The next room down is my home office and somebody'd taken my files and thrown them. They were crumpled, stepped on, torn, and the drawers were all ripped out, upside down in a heap in the middle of the room. My pictures, all my certificates, were next to the drawers as if they'd been piled and jumped on, frames skewed sideways and the safety glass shattered. Rings of safety glass. I went rapidly on down the hall.

Storage room. Everything slashed, scattered.

Pantry. Boxes torn open and dumped, thrown around.

Kitchen the same, a pile in the middle of the floor. Flour sacks, jars, canisters emptied. Mess everywhere. You couldn't walk through the room without getting stuff on your shoes, and people already had. Tracks everywhere, coming and going, heading out to the dining room. Probably the lab guys, taking their pictures.

"Mike's place look like this?"

"Yeah, pretty much." Reilly was waiting behind me, not pushing himself on me, letting me see.

"What do you hide in a spice jar?" I said.

"Negatives. A roll of film."

Somebody'd junked them. Emptied them all. It *did* seem to come back to pictures.

"And the eggs?"

"Negatives can fit in a shell."

Well, they can, you know, but I didn't think so. I thought someone had gone into Smash Mode. Two dozen eggs, individually, lobbed at the walls. That takes more time than stomping the cartons. All of my glasses shattered, the dishes—you can't hide negatives in a plate and mine were in bits on the floor. I went around the bend in the hallway and stopped by the outer dining-room door. The tracks were coming towards me there, petering out. Little dried marks under my feet, heading towards the living room, and there wasn't much in the dining room I wanted to see, so I followed what was left of the prints.

You don't think you have anything irreplaceable until somebody trashes your house. You think "If I lose this, oh, well—at least I'm alive," and "I could walk away from it all tomorrow if I had to," and "Thank God for insurance," things like that. And it's true that you *could* walk away, even true you should be thankful, that the safety net we have is enormous compared to someone in Kenya or the streets of LA, but the cold selfish truth is it's *your* things destroyed, and as I looked at the mess, the arbitrary meanness, I wasn't *thankful*, I was angry and sick, shaken. They'd slashed the couch, the stuffing spilling out, and *nobody* hides things in couches, come on. They'd smashed all the knickknacks on the fireplace mantel, stomped on the candles where they'd been knocked to the floor. Somebody'd kicked a hole in the wall, had used the straight-back chair to batter the mirror. Tell me they thought I had something underneath it. I looked at the front door.

Reilly was still sort of pokeying in the kitchen. I guess one of the lab men had removed the cat's carcass, bagged it for evidence, because it was gone. Big splotch of blood on the wooden floor. I didn't waste any time getting down the hall, didn't look left or right, at the bathroom, or Josh's room, or the spare bedroom. Went straight to *my* bedroom, the door. It was standing wide open, but the room was dark, a dim trail of sunlight coming in through the blinds. Takes a second for the eyes to adjust. I was reaching for the light switch, had my hand out and froze. There were piles of clothes and drawers thrown around, same as everywhere else, but I was looking at the bed, flipped the switch, took a long, hard, *good* look before I went to get Reilly. He was just coming into the living room.

"Is this another test?" I said.

"What's that?"

"There's a body on my bed, R—"

He was strong, Reilly was, and bigger than I am. When he started moving, I was swept on along, his hand kind of clamped on my arm. Back down the hall to my bedroom. Stopped in the doorway.

"You didn't know it was there?"

"No," he said.

"Wasn't here yesterday?"

"No."

He dropped my arm, stepped carefully in, leaving me there.

"Should I get Burbank?"

"In a minute."

There wasn't any question that the guy was dead. He'd been shot once through the back of the head with what looked to be a hollow-point, large caliber, so he'd have no face left to speak of. Most of it was splattered across my bed and upwards towards the mirror. No question at all that he'd died where he lay. His arms stretched down along his body, palms up, fingers limply curled. His hands had been behind him when he fell, was the way it looked to me, and because I have that kind of mind, I figured he'd been cuffed. Somebody'd removed them, taken them back. Markings on them, maybe, police issue. Or they hadn't wanted to get another pair.

Small guy. Thin. Dark. Youngish, judging by the amount and texture of his hair, the look of his wrist. Olive tone to the skin. Nice clothes, a Rolex watch that nobody'd bothered to steal. Leather shoes. There were traces of flour on the sides, so I'd guess he was one of the people who'd walked through the kitchen. Not just the lab guys after all. This one looked more like Beverly

Hills, and I'd bet almost anything that this guy was Soufi. Young Mr. Haroutunian.

Reilly was done looking, was stepping carefully back in his same tracks to me. He hadn't taken long, just enough to check rigor—making sure that the guy had been dead for a while, you know, that I hadn't just killed him.

"I'm going to call Abbott," he said.

Not Burbank.

Dead's dead, though. A few minutes more wouldn't hurt.

"We'll call from the kitchen," he said. "The phone there still works."

How did he know? Checking things, I guess. The phone in here was ripped out, torn apart, completely unusable, and I'd have thought the other was, too, dangling as it was, you know, by its wires, half pulled from the wall.

"Come on," he said. He had his hand on my arm again, like a Boy Scout this time, helping me back down the hall. I'm not good with dead bodies, tend to focus on things. Little things, anything. Time enough to smash eggs, but they hadn't torn out the phone. They? More than one. The house was too big for the time, the destruction. Josh's room didn't look bad, but *mine* had been trashed, someone in a frenzy. Slashes in the waterbed, the water slopping over. They'd pulled up the sheets first, looking for pictures, had sliced up my clothes, ripped them, scattered them, smashed all my figurines, the little ones that Charlie always bought me at Solvang.

My dragons.

I was shaking, I guess, which was stupid, so useless. No one to see. Reilly was reaching for the phone in the kitchen and he'd replaced it, rehung it on its base in the wall. Still working. He was turning around to look at me, keep an eye, and I moved off to the nearest counter, the one by the sink. The one where we'd played push-and-parry. I fingered a knife. It was bent all to hell like they'd pried something open, but really, there was nothing to pry. Not here in the kitchen. Back in my den? When they'd gone through my files, maybe. Jacked the thing open. Probably not, though, because they'd had a crowbar already, coming in through the back.

Reilly said something behind me into the phone, something like *"What?"* or *"All right,"* but it was the tone, and he hadn't even told Abbott yet that we had a body. I turned back to face him and he was looking away, but he'd been staring at me. His eyes were a study, speculation, lids coming down.

Christ.

I wanted Edwards, normal Edwards, who bitched about his wife and who had no connection, no history, no axes to grind.

"I have to get Burbank," I said.

He covered the receiver.

"I'll call in a minute."

"*I* want to call, Reilly. I want to do it now."

Another ten seconds. "All right," he said, and into the phone, "We've got a body here, Lieutenant. Looks like last night . . . Yeah . . . Yeah . . . No, she's here with me. We haven't called it in yet . . . Right." He clicked down the button and held the receiver out to me. "Burbank."

I had to cross the kitchen to take it, had to go to him.

Managed. He was standing on top of me, watching me dial. Nine-one-one. Shaking like a goddamned tree. "You need to send someone," I said into the telephone. "Please."

They sent a lot of people. Edwards came and a Homicide detective named Burroughs. A couple of uniforms. Pilsner. The Bureau Captain. Everyone. Burroughs took a statement from me in a corner of the living room while Edwards and Reilly went off with the lab guys to check the body again. Still dead, I guess. Still there.

"You know him?" Burroughs said, and for a second I thought he meant Reilly. I had to pay attention, had to stop wandering, because there was a dead guy in my house, in my *bed*. Kind of made me the prime, you know, in spite of the watchdogs last night. My phone had been off the hook—Reilly could attest to that. I'd been unreachable most of the night.

"No."

"You don't know him? Why he was here?"

"No," I said. They'd ripped the drapes off the window. Killed my cat. Burroughs probably hadn't been here yesterday, probably none of them had. Maybe the lab men. "Do you know if anything's different today? If the rooms look more rummaged?"

"Why?"

"It's not adding up right," I said. "He came through the kitchen, but there's nothing on his hands."

"What d'you mean, 'nothing'?"

"No flour," I said. My own were streaked. I was rubbing it off and that was just from holding the knife. The kitchen was covered.

"You're saying he didn't touch anything?"

Or he'd washed his hands, how the hell did I know? Burroughs *had* to have talked some to Edwards. Reilly. Pilsner. They wouldn't have brought him in cold. "Burroughs," I said, "I'm running kind of ragged, okay? Every time I turn a corner, there's something else there. Someone searched my house yesterday, tore it right up, not like professionals. I was thinking it was cops, doing it sideways on purpose, but maybe it was *this* guy. Maybe he came back again, looking."

"For what?"

They'd put Burroughs with me deliberately— Edwards could have stayed. Change 'em off, check the stories, that's how it works. "For negatives," I said. "That's what your boss thinks it is anyway. Me, I don't know. I just think it's odd that his hands are so clean."

As if they'd been behind him when he came through.

Cuffed already.

Not found and cuffed after he'd entered my bedroom.

"And you don't know anything about negatives, is that right?"

"I really don't," I said. "I'm sorry."

We went through it about ten more times before Edwards and the captain came out. The coroner's team had gone in long since, and I guess they'd all been busy taking pictures and measurements, angles of fire.

"Well, young lady," the captain said. Dresden.

I didn't feel very young.

"Sir."

"I've been talking to your department, Lieutenant Drogemuller. You remember him?"

"Yeah." Mule was okay.

"He remembers *you*. Gives you a good report."

That was nice. "Captain," I said, "can you check with the guys who were here yesterday? See if any of them can come back and go through the house?"

"Why?"

Edwards was watching me, too, but Reilly was still in the bedroom and it was a tight little quiet group we made there in the corner. "It doesn't feel right," I said. "It's too personal. Could you just have them walk it without making it obvious? See if there's anything different, anything that might have been, well, rearranged?"

The captain had those eyes aimed right at me. "Without telling Beverly Hills?"

"For the moment," I said, "sir. If you don't mind."

"Get Holchek," he said to Burroughs, and Burroughs faded through the hallway door towards the back. The captain harrumphed at me sternly. "You understand, Mrs. Gillis, that I'm not playing favorites?"

"Yes, sir," I said. I'd have said anything he liked and maybe he knew it, but he had a bona fide homicide here and he didn't mind giving me rope. And besides, Mule had vouched for me—that might have counted for something.

The coroner was coming down the hall with the stretcher, two men kind of steering it behind her. Life ends in a plastic bag on a cart. Dresden was moving out to see her off and Reilly was coming around the bend from the bedroom. I was starting to walk, thinking I'd go out, too, I guess, but Edwards had a hand on my arm. Everyone grabbing me these days. "We have to talk," he said. "You and me and the big guy. You want to stay here?"

I sure as hell didn't.

"I'll protect you," he said, and he might have thought he was kidding.

"Can we do it in Josh's room? Gets us out of the way."

"Yeah, sure, why not? Don't have to watch them all coming and going then, huh?" He was tugging me through the pileup by the front door, dragging me right into Reilly. "Kid's room, okay? It'll be quieter there and we'll have someplace to sit."

"All right."

Reilly agreeable. As long as I had Edwards on my arm. We pushed on down the hall, breaking clear, and turned into the corner room. Edwards let go and I found myself by the bed, so I sat. Edwards took the desk to perch on, and Reilly stayed by the door. Dividing me.

"So, Mrs. Gillis—"

"I think we're beyond that," I said. "You can call me Meg."

"Sure. Meg. You leave the motel room last night?"

"Past your guys in the parking lot?"

"They're human. Gotta scratch, drink, answer the call."

"I didn't," I said.

"Okay." He was smiling.

"You should know about Mike," Reilly said. Ping-Pong. His serve.

"What about him?"

"He's alive," he said.

People have lied to me all of my life. Cops have lied to me most. Small lies, big lies, whoppers. Mike was dead and I knew it. Reilly was playing off the stupid thing I'd said last night, when I was tired, when I was vulnerable, when I'd had no guard to speak of.

"Sure he is," I said.

"He is, Meg. They found him near Palm Springs this morning."

Palm Springs. I was looking to Edwards but that was useless, because Edwards was part of this game, sitting there on the desk.

"What's he saying?"

Edwards's eyes slid away. Wrong question. Wrong person.

"What's he saying?" I said again, louder.

Reilly. "Not saying much."

"Neither are you."

"He's in the hospital there. Intensive care."

The room kind of moved, the walls closing, and I was going to be sick. Violently ill. "Where?"

"Not *why*?"

"It doesn't matter why."

"It should."

Well, maybe it should, but it didn't. "The doctors'll tell me," and Reilly was shaking his head.

"You can't go," he said.

I couldn't go. That meant Mike was under arrest or *I* was, because there was no other way in hell he could stop me. "You guys are reading me rights?"

"If you want them."

Not under arrest. Edwards still here. Protecting me. I took another kind of breath. "Okay, what happened to Mike?"

"He went off a cliff."

"He *fell*?"

"His car ran off the road."

"You're saying he had a goddamn *car accident*?"

"You don't think so?"

He knew what I thought. "When?"

"They found him about six-thirty this morning."

"I meant 'When'd he go over?' "

Eyes flat as glass. "They're working on it."

Last night, then. Maybe. Because Edwards had asked if I'd left my room. I guess I could have made it to Palm Springs and back.

"Was he *in* Palm Springs?"

"Not apparently."

A lot of desert outside of Palm Springs. "Was it a main road?"

"No."

"Someone stumbled across him?"

"Dirt-bikers out for a ride."

So somebody'd cleaned house. Popped Soufi. Dropped Mike where he wouldn't be found. I was staring at Reilly's feet, at his shoes. "How bad is he?"

"We don't know."

And I couldn't go.

"Guarded?"

"Sheriff's department has him covered. San Bernardino County."

Not Palm Springs PD? San Bernardino was taking an interest, then. Found in their jurisdiction.

"Who knows it?" I said.

"Abbott. You, me, Edwards. Pilsner. Both captains."

And whoever else they'd told. I *couldn't* go—it'd be a straight line to Michael if someone was tracking me. Maybe Reilly had thought of that. Maybe that's what he'd meant. He had a little dusting of flour on the sides of his shoes. Like Soufi, walking through the kitchen.

"Was the body Soufi's?"

The shoes shifted.

"Yeah," Edwards said. "You *guess* that, or have you seen him before?"

I never had. Was tired of saying so. "You might want to show Josh a picture of him, if you can get something reasonable. See if he's the five o'clock shadow. He was dressed fairly nicely and he'd look kind of Mexican."

"Yeah, we thought of that," Edwards said. "Yesterday."

Yesterday. *"And?"*

"Kid picked him right out. Nice kid. Observant."

Observant, hell. "You've been sitting on this since *yesterday?"*

"Not exactly sitting. Did you talk to Josh at all?"

"You know I didn't—you were running a tap on the motel phone."

He shrugged. Just business, you know. Part of the go-round, like this was.

"Let me spell it out," I said. "Josh picks out Soufi yesterday and Soufi eats it last night. Who the hell knew?"

"No one," Edwards said.

No one but him and Reilly. "You think it's coincidence?"

"I believe in coincidence," he said blandly. "I hear about it every day. And you want to reach a little further back, girl, it was just yesterday *you* disappeared from the running. Made someone very anxious. There's cause and effect, if you're looking."

Okay, maybe so. Maybe I was just the hell out there. "What happens now? To me."

Edwards scratched at his eyebrow. "Can't really keep you."

He could, you know. Or I could ask for protection. Both of them watching to see how I'd go. I wanted to run, skip out of town.

"I'll stay here for a while," I said. "Clean up."

"You want me to leave a guy?"

He'd leave one anyway, visible or otherwise.

"Yeah, sure," I said. "That would be fine."

# 31

I had to wait to find out about Holchek. Edwards was kind of busy wrapping things up and Reilly seemed to be welcome, right in there with him, so I stood around in the kitchen with one of the cops. Poked at the mess. Tried to see what was bothering me, aside from it all, but if there was something in the room, it wasn't speaking to me. Too much of a crowd.

"What d'you want?" Edwards said.

"Holchek. The captain was going to have him walking the house, I thought, while we were in Josh's room talking. To see if anything looks different from yesterday."

Edwards didn't look over at Reilly on the other side of the room. "No problem. I'll find out and get back to you."

He wasn't going to let me talk directly to Holchek, of course. I was a suspect. It wasn't personal or anything and it's not so much that I minded, it was just that I needed to know.

"Pretty soon?" I said.

"Yeah, in a while."

He had cases to work on, plenty to do. Reilly catching his eye and coming across. "Okay," I said.

"There's one other thing."

"What's that?"

"Massoud."

It sounded like something. "Excuse me?"

"Massoud," Edwards said. "Soufi's cousin—you know him?"

I sure as hell didn't.

"His alibi."

Berkeley. The cousin Soufi'd been with over the weekend. I remembered now, from the interview room.

"I don't know him," I said.

Edwards seemed satisfied. Can't say Reilly did. He was looking at the same counter I was, frowning, his face kind of grim.

"I'll call you," Edwards said.

It took me hours to clean up the mess. Not cleaned up, exactly, but dented, the rooms at least worked through, stuff shifted aside. I swept the glass into trash bags, salvaged some papers, some clothes. Edwards hadn't hurried to call.

"Holchek says it's the same" was what he said when I called him. "A little bit more in the bedroom, but not very much."

"The phone was ripped out like that? Taken apart?"

"Yeah, he didn't say any different. Why?"

I was on the phone in the kitchen, the one working phone. Edwards' cop was out in the living room, parked by the mantel, watching the door and the windows. He'd been by a few times checking up on me, making sure I was there, but otherwise left me alone.

"They didn't take apart *this* phone," I said.

"They didn't have time."

Time enough to toss eggs. I'd thought that before and I was looking right at it, the egg whites, the smears, the dried bits of shell on the wall. Nothing much on the phone. They'd dusted for prints, but of course there was nothing. Wiped clean or gloved, it didn't much matter.

"Or they needed a warning," I said.

"Maybe so."

It seemed okay for a reason. I don't know why it shimmied, why something said no.

"Anything else?" Edwards was kind of impatient and I couldn't think what to tell him, or to ask while I had him.

"Any word yet on Mike?"

"Yeah. Guess he's coming around."

I wanted to believe him. It's the way that he said it. "Guess he's coming around" isn't really a lie—you can guess and be wrong, could mean "turning the corner," not your fault it sounds like he's conscious, about to start talking.

"Don't do me," I said. "Not on this."

He thought. He decided. "He's breathing," he said.

It was little enough. Little enough to hold on to.

"I've got another call, Meg. Are we done?"

Really, we were. I just didn't want to be out here alone.

"Yeah," I said. "Thanks."

"I'll get back to you."

Sure he would. And I'd be here. I cradled the phone, went on with my work, let Edwards get on back to his. Scrubbed and wiped. Swept. Washed the blood off the walls, all the flour, the egg. I'd have to repaint. The cop came through, checking, and I must have looked tired, bedraggled or something.

"You all right?"

And I wasn't, you know, I honestly wasn't. "It's the mess," I said, "the meanness. They didn't have to do it like this," and it was bells going off, or a bomb. I was scraping a piece of dried shell from the floor, glancing away from him, straight at the phone. At the god-damned, unbroken phone. What do you hide in an egg? He'd said "negatives." What do you hide in a *phone*?

You can get that stuff cheap, all sorts of devices. Miniaturized, broadcast. Can pick up the sound in a hundred-yard circle with nobody using the phone. So you'd know I was here, you could hear me. You wouldn't have to risk a man on.

Define paranoia.

"Mrs. Gillis," the cop said, "hey," and I guess I'd been out of it, staring.

"I'm sorry," I said, "I'm just tired."

"Maybe you should quit for a while."

Maybe I should.

"Come on," he said. "You can sit in the living room."

I stood up obediently, stumbled, the world kind of spinning. "Maybe I'd better lie down."

"You want me to call Edwards?"

Not with that phone.

"I'll be okay," I said, "really. Just give me a minute." Give me twenty or thirty. I wiped a hand past my eyes. Wavered towards him there in the doorway, paused. He'd stepped back to clear for me, arm's length or more, but I wouldn't have taken him anyway, armed. He had a radio on his belt. Police band—easy to monitor if someone was troubling. Define paranoia on the edge of the jungle.

"Listen," I said softly, leaning in, "I'm going back to my room. You want to get Edwards on the radio, see if he'll collect me in an hour or so? I can keep on cleaning if he's not in a hurry, but I don't want to spend the night and I don't trust the phone."

He was looking over my shoulder at the kitchen wall. Strike the right chord. "Okay," he said just as quietly. "I'll walk you down."

He could do that, I didn't mind. Keep the goblins at bay. So we single-filed it down the hall to my room, and he went in, checked around, nothing different or striking.

"You're going to stay *here?*" He was looking at the blood, at the gore, and I guess I could have fainted, but there wasn't a good place to fall.

"I don't *have* to stay here," I said. "I just thought it'd be safest. Farthest from the street."

He couldn't be everywhere. I didn't think he'd want me around when he was talking to Edwards—radios aren't private—but he *did* have an interest in keeping me safe. Wouldn't want me to be shot through a window if he could have helped it. Captains don't like that.

"Okay," he said. "I'll be back in a minute."

A couple of minutes, at least. I looked around at the room, at the phone torn apart, listened to him walk down the hall. Things were clearer, lots clearer. I knew what was wrong with the house now, the feel.

Inside information.

Because my *bedroom* was trashed, pulverized—everything I had that might mean something to me—and the rest of the house was for show.

Even the cat, killed.

To cover the fact that they'd known about the bedroom. That they'd been in here searching and someone had lost it, vented his temper when they'd come up stone-empty. Because they *had* come up empty, or they wouldn't have been looking for me.

Calling the jail. Thinking I had it.

I couldn't *swear* that my house was untouched before the weekend, couldn't have told you that. I don't walk around setting traps, leaving hairs on the doors. So someone could have wired the phones before Friday, a professional, and I wouldn't have known it.

I just didn't think so.

No reason to.

Nobody was involving me until *Saturday,* and I wasn't even sure about that. The call had come in for *Mike*—Haroutunian didn't want *me.* Then he'd changed his mind and said yeah, I should come, and after that, well, then everything *was* me. My car stolen, the blood, the cops. As if somebody couldn't get Mike, but thought that *I* could get him, that I would if the going got rougher. Nobody was searching offices then, tearing houses apart.

Because nobody'd heard about pictures until Monday night. Josh across the kitchen table. Talking about Mike and pictures and someone named Sue. Describing the man he'd seen hanging around. Soufi.

Sometimes things click, you know, like kaleidoscopes turning, snicking down into place, a new way of seeing the world. I was staring at the wall across the room, the dried streaks of blood, the matter. The little bit of starred, broken mirror still hanging over the dresser, forlorn in the frame. I could see myself in it, my hand.

Soufi was driving back down from Berkeley on Monday, didn't get in until midnight, one o'clock in the morning. Except that Josh placed him *here* about five.

Which meant his alibi sucked—that cousin, Massoud—and somebody'd figured that yesterday, before Soufi got killed.

Because they'd heard that Soufi'd come here.

Not trying to get *at* me, maybe, but *to* me.

Because I was Mike's partner? Because he'd been by Mike's place? *Because he'd already been home, earlier Monday, and found his dad missing, found blood in the hall?*

If he'd set it up as a murder, he'd have called it in then. And if he didn't know *anything,* he'd have called in then, too. Was a little bit hyper, Reilly'd said, and I'd figured drugs, not desperation.

He'd crashed his car, gotten neighbors involved, lots of neighbors, protection. Can't take you off in a crowd. Not very smart, because yes, they can, when they're cops, but maybe he knew who they were.

Knew that Reilly was *here.*

Soufi could have seen us through the kitchen window if he'd come back Monday night again, looking. If what he'd wanted to say to me was important.

Somebody'd thought that it was.

And someone had thought that I'd *know.* That was the point here, the purpose. They thought that I'd found the picture or pictures, so they'd marched Soufi in here, a message, a warning, left his brains on my bed and my wall. They were *sure* I'd know why. The pictures would have told me why.

If Mike had actually left them.

If he'd goddamn made copies.

If he *wasn't* just making a call.

And it was irrational, really, I knew that it was—I'd already *been* through this room. A truckload of people had been poking and prying, lifting this, bagging that, they'd gone through it twice, four times, altogether, there was nothing I could possibly find. So I started at one end, shuffling and sorting, making neat little piles. It was *my* stuff, you know. Maybe something would tell me.

The cop had come back, stuck his head in. "Edwards'll send a car in an hour."

Fifty minutes. I still didn't have my damn watch. "Yeah, fine," I said. "Any word on the phone?"

"Someone'll come check it out."

"From the bomb squad?" I said.

He looked kind of jazzed. "Yeah, that's what they're saying."

I wondered what this guy did for kicks. Airplanes, maybe. Jumping out of 'em. "I'm going to stay here, then, okay, for a while? I want to get a little more done."

He didn't care. No skin off of his nose. None off of mine. He wandered back down the hall and I was going to skip out the window, get the hell gone, but it's being in the *middle* of something—another five minutes, you know, maybe ten. I had fifty to spare. I was holding half a picture, a strip, really, ripped, part of Charlie's brag wall. Someone had smashed all the glass in the frames, torn out the photos, certificates, scattered them everywhere. Looking for hidden pictures, I guess. The old purloined letter. I put it on the heap by the bed. Maybe I could tape it, glue it or something. Maybe Mike could make me a print. And I was thinking about that when I picked up the next piece, had turned it over before I really saw what it was.

This piece was part of one of *my* pictures.

It usually hangs in the den.

I did a major quick inventory. Everything else in the room belonged to the room, as best I could tell. This was the only thing imported.

I found the other half, thirds, really, straightened them out. An earnest young group of cadets in a pose. The picture was here, it was ripped up like everything else, not me circled in ink or blood smeared all over it, not pinned to the wall with a note. What the hell did it mean?

I hadn't even noticed it missing when I'd cleaned up the den, hadn't even considered it. Why would they bring in my Academy picture? The young Mike stared solemnly back at me, Mike, and it *had* to mean something—a clue. Had Mike brought it in for a message? He'd had plenty of time to be more specific—to say "Look at the wall in your den," for example, which still wouldn't mean worth a damn. One of our classmates gone bad? There was no one I recognized there as from Beverly. No other connection, and I didn't have time. Look up each of these guys? Turn it over to Edwards?

But if this was the picture . . .

Something clicked down again, shifted the view. It *couldn't* be the picture Mike was showing to Soufi, because it was here in my room.

So what *wasn't*?

I scrabbled around then, dug out all the pictures, arranged the scraps in front of me. I hardly noticed Charlie's brag wall these days, it was there like the furniture, a part of the background, and I couldn't remember exactly how it looked now, where everything went. This certificate here, that small one in the lower left corner. The class nurse award somewhere halfway down on the right. I had it mostly assembled, the best I could manage, a few pictures jumbled, the shape not quite right. Rearranged things a little, called it up in my mind.

Charlie's uniform picture.

That's what was missing. The same shape and size.

I'd have noticed a hole, a blank on the wall, a different-looking frame. Mike must have thought of that, worked it all through. He'd invited himself over for dinner that Wednesday. Been right there by the den, on his way to my bedroom.

Ten seconds to let Josh clear the back door, another ten to whip down there, lift off the picture, five to get on down the hall. Come in, swap the pictures, makes it forty-five seconds, tuck the frame in his windbreaker, pick up the phone. Less than a minute and Mike had had four. Could have goddammit strolled.

I was flashing, you know, because Mike had pictures already, lots of pictures of Charlie and me. Like the one at the office, that no one had stopped for, the one ripped in half—Charlie on one side and me on the other, cozily warm at the beach. Ripped apart. Down the middle. So symbolically torn.

I'd been listening to Reilly's fixation on Mike, and I'd let it affect me, color my judgment. Rule number one, and I should have known better, known better about *Mike* anyway. I've known him for twelve years, god-dammit—thirteen—the bond wasn't sex anymore.

Because the picture had been in his *desk,* not his wallet. Not where I wouldn't be able to find it. Not where you'd keep a treasured memento. In his desk at the office. Crammed in there.

Torn.

As if he'd only been showing one half around.

It's hard to detach from emotional things. I was staring at the pictures and it was Charlie on a gurney, Mike at the door. That goddamned IA man. Dave. I knew why Mike hadn't told me, why he never had said. Because I was a basket case, eaten alive. A little bit crazy. There was only one reason I could think of why he'd need a uniformed picture of Charlie, the head-front-and-shoulders shot.

If Soufi hadn't been sure.

If he hadn't quite recognized Charlie in a beach shirt because the only time he'd seen Charlie was when Charlie was working.

Some kids, they'd said. Mexicans. Running away.

Mike had found the missing witness to Charlie's murder.

Witnesses, plural.

That cousin, Massoud.

# 32

I should have just run for the high ground. I'd intended to, Lord knows, but there I was, thinking. I found the cop in the living room, got him quick down the hall.

"Your unit's outside?"

"Yeah."

"How fast can you drive it?"

He had one of those jaws. "Fast enough."

"I have to get to the station," I said. "I think we'll be hit when the car comes to get me and I'm not hanging around. I'm going out the side window in about half a minute—you want to come with me? Take me to Edwards?"

Was he going to say no? This was the man who thought bomb squads were fun. "Out the window to the car and then I drive you to the station?"

"Fast," I said.

He was looking up the hall at the door of my bedroom. "You were a cop." It wasn't really a question, or maybe it was, what Edwards had told him.

"Nine years," I said.

"So you can run?"

I smiled at him then like a kid out of school.

"I can run," I said.

We kicked out the side screen, the hell with the damage, dropped onto the small patch of lawn. I let him go first, but not so far ahead that he'd get perturbed. Raced across the yard to the car, stretched for the handle, threw myself into the back, flat out on the seat. He already had the transmission bucking and the doors slamming shut as we barked from the curb.

He could drive.

Didn't see much of Burbank, but I already knew it. I was busy ducking and weaving, looking for tails. Hanging on to the seat back, the belt, anything I could hold while he cornered and jogged. It's only five minutes from the house to the station, but your heart's kind of racing, you know, when you're revved, and time's not a factor. Could have taken two minutes, could have taken an hour. I was wrung out when we got there and jazzed, like stealing home plate while the batter's still swinging—God, what a rush, what a high. Sliding in past the catcher, the ball in his glove coming down. Safe.

Had my hands on the cop's arm walking into the station, and I was grinning like a fool, practically dancing. Man, he was good, he could sure as hell drive. He was grinning at me, too, comrades in danger, and we ran smack into Reilly at the top of the stairs. Stopped short when he saw me. Flicked to the cop. Stupid to feel so suddenly guilty.

"Christ," I said, "what d'you, live here?"

He was still looking at the cop, and it seemed like the

good time to drop the guy's arm. Reilly observed it, expressionless.

"We weren't expecting you for another half hour."

We? "Well, you know how it is," I said. "I didn't want to be late."

"Yeah?" Eyes still on the cop, who was starting to bristle, and the thing was, he didn't have to answer to Reilly. Neither did I.

"You want to get out of the way?"

He stepped back, silent, so I pushed on by. I couldn't stop him from following, but I had to find Edwards, get to Edwards, and I was grateful that the Burbank cop came on with me, showing support. We left Reilly trailing, but Christ, I was shaking again, all the blaze gone.

We found Edwards in the captain's office down the hall. The cop had asked someone when Edwards wasn't at his desk, and the someone had said go on down. Reilly still with us. Edwards not especially pleased.

"Hey," I said, "I figured out this business with the pictures—you didn't want to hear it?"

One of those dead kind of silences, everybody looking at each other and none of it changing anyone's attitude.

"Fine," I said. "I'll come back."

They weren't going to let me go—it was stupid of me even to have said it, gets the backs up. I could feel Reilly shifting behind me and I just wanted to call it all off right then, wanted to have skated out the window and run. The cop still there, though, the Burbank one who'd driven me. Sharing the ride.

"Mike was looking for witnesses," I said, "looking for leads on Charlie's murder. He found Soufi and his cousin and got somebody upset. He didn't *leave* me a picture, he took one, okay? For Soufi to identify. And now Soufi's dead and Mike's in the hospital, and I really think you need to get to Massoud before something happens to *him*. That's why I'm here, why I came."

The captain was the first one to move. Military man. Marine. "Why don't you sit down, Mrs. Gillis. In that chair."

The one in the center of the room. I could drag it back a little bit, though, getting myself settled. He was dismissing the cop with one of those captainly nods, Reilly was coming on in, Edwards fetching a chair from the hall. Another small room. Knee to knee. The captain behind his desk.

"You willing to talk for the record?"

Or I could wait for McKenzie. "Yeah, sure," I said.

He had a handy recorder. I was forgetting his name, but it was Dresden or Dreiden, something like that. Stocky man, in good shape, his hair combed precisely. Fiftyish. Making sure I'd heard all my rights. Always reassuring.

"Why don't you tell us, Mrs. Gillis."

So I told them. Backed it up a little bit more, laid it out the best way I could, the way I'd figured it, the deal with the pictures, Soufi, the phone. Nobody interrupted me—the captain upright in his chair, military fingers tapping, Reilly very intent to my left, Edwards taking notes. I was talking more towards Edwards and the captain, I guess, keeping Reilly peripheral. It was Burbank's case. I couldn't lose sight of him, though, couldn't afford to, because he and Edwards had a rapport, something I seemed to have lost.

"So it's Massoud," I finished. "If the killers are clearing their tracks, he's more of a target than I am."

"You don't know him, Mrs. Gillis?"

I'd said this before. "No, I don't."

"He knows *you*."

Pussyfoot games. I looked straight at the captain. "How?"

"He says you've been blackmailing him."

Well, hell, yes. In my spare time. I should have been surprised, but really, I wasn't. "Did Beverly Hills find him for you?" I said.

"Mrs. Gillis?"

Feeling so calm. Not looking at Reilly. "Sergeant Reilly or any of his men? Were they the ones who brought him in?"

"Mrs. Gillis—"

"It's *inside* information," I said. "If the phone wasn't tapped, then Reilly's the only one who was there Monday night to hear about Mike and the pictures. Reilly was at the door talking to Haroutunian, Reilly's been following me around. Did *he* find Massoud for you?"

"Sheriffs did," Reilly said.

"Sheriffs?"

"San Bernardino County."

I blinked at him then, at the group of them. The captain was looking annoyed, Reilly impassive, and I couldn't read Edwards at all.

"The desert?" I said.

Reilly was nodding.

"He was with *Mike*?"

"It doesn't matter," the captain said, but it mattered to me.

"Was he hurt? In the wreck?"

"He wasn't in the wreck," Reilly said, and it didn't make sense. Unless Mike had stashed him over the weekend, told him to hide. But Mike *couldn't* have stashed him, because Massoud had been with Soufi, was Soufi's alibi, Monday.

Tuesday, Mike crashed. On a desert road.

And Wednesday, the sheriffs had Mike, had Massoud, and Massoud was claiming I'd been blackmailing him.

"This guy took out *Mike*?"

Reilly wasn't saying anything, which gave me my answer.

"*He* hurt Mike?"

"In fear of his life." If it was a joke, no one seemed to be laughing. They seemed, if anything, very intent.

And Tuesday night, Soufi was dead. In *my* house. In *my* bed. You get so utterly paranoid.

"This is wrong," I said. "Why would we kill a witness we were trying to find?"

"It depends what he would have said, doesn't it?"

It did, yes. God, I was going to be sick. In the nights after Charlie died, those first awful months, I had dreams like this—one cop pursuing. It didn't matter what I did, how I twisted or turned, he was there. I shot him a thousand times, point-blank, emptying, and he just wiped the blood away and came on.

I was looking at Reilly. Charlie's friend.

"You want your lawyer?" he said.

I wanted to smear him all over the walls.

"He'd have said that I *did* it? Is that what this is? You've got this whole thing worked out that *I* murdered Charlie?"

"Meg—"

"There was a woman," I said tightly. "It's in the reports. She saw the boys running and the car going after them. A drive-by, rival gangs."

"No."

"We know it all, Mrs. Gillis." The captain in charge. "Massoud's told us everything."

"Not if he's saying that *I* killed my husband."

"Oh, he's not," the captain said. "He's saying that Soufi did it."

Soufi?

The killer?

Everything turns.

"They were witnesses," I said.

"He was the shooter. It was outside a drug house, Mrs. Gillis. *You* knew that."

I *had* known, but not until later.

"What was your husband doing there, Mrs. Gillis? It wasn't his district."

"I don't know," I said numbly.

"Don't you?"

Everything unreal. Maybe I did.

"I'll tell you." Warming up, because he was a captain, not used to holding his peace. "You were outside the drug house that night, you and your partners. Waiting to take off the boys."

I was picturing the street. Know that street well. "In the car?"

"That's right."

" 'Partners' plural?"

"Your husband and Mike." Captain had it all worked out. "A neat little racket. I think you were just planning to shake 'em down, a couple of rich kids caught buying dope, might pay a little something so Daddy wouldn't know. But then Charlie got shot and bam—the golden goose, huh? Motherlode. Homicide. You've been raking it in ever since."

Everything tidy. "Massoud's saying that?"

"Word for word."

"How'd he know it was *us*?"

"You followed them home."

"Followed them home," I said. "To Beverly Hills?"

"Yep. Broke in, slapped them around, laid it all out."

"Right away?"

"What's that?"

"Did we follow them straight to the house?"

"You know that."

"I know a lot of things," I said. "Was it the *same* night or later?"

Reilly stirred in his chair. "That night."

Right.

"Well, I don't want to throw any water," I said, "when you've got such a nice fire burning, but we couldn't have done it that night, there just wasn't time. Charlie was shot at one fifty-five, the call came in two minutes later. By two oh-five, the street was closed and the lieutenant had Mike. Mike was working Three's district, so they got him up fast, got a look at the scene. By three, they were all at my door. In company, Captain, and there I was, home. I guess I could have made it to Beverly and back—depends how easy they were to beat up—but it sure wasn't *Mike* I had with me."

"Mrs. Gillis—"

"You didn't check with my department? Get the reports?"

He hadn't checked anything, hadn't had time, and besides, he was a captain, but he wasn't going to let it just go. "Massoud's making a positive identification. Two cops, he said, and he's picked you both out."

"Then you'd better start asking him why."

Reilly so quiet over there in his corner. Nobody even looking at him. Two guys in a car.

"*You* knew this," I said. "You've been looking into me since Saturday—you didn't know the time frame that night?"

Those eyes coming up.

"I knew it cleared Mike."

Yeah, fine.

"A woman called it in," he said, and something caught in my chest.

"So?"

"Gives you a motive."

I could hear every tick in the room.

"For what?"

"Soufi."

Dead in my bed.

"He was killed with Mike's gun, Meg. They found it in a trash can two houses away. Ballistics made it a match."

"Christ, Reilly," I said, "I'd have thrown it into the ocean," but he wasn't even listening.

"You had access."

I did have. Both places—Mike's place and mine. Motive and access. Opportunity. Because I *could* have gotten away from the motel last night without being seen. Minutes away.

"A woman called it in," he said again, and I could hear it the way it was on the tape, the dispatch tape from that night. The thin female voice, hysterical, screaming. *"Oh my God, they shot Charlie . . ."*

"It wasn't me," I said blindly. "Dave knows. You could have asked him."

"Dave's not talking to me now."

The long goddamn loyalties. The chain. Because Dave knew about Mike now, and me, so he was clamming up, too late or too early, depending. The pain flaring, the anguish, and it was all I could do to push it on down.

"You *tell* me," Reilly said.

Charlie's friend. Not mine.

"He was meeting someone." I could talk that way, to the floor. "That's why he was there that night."

"At the drug house?"

"Next door. Nobody knew it was a drug house then, *we* didn't know—at the department, I mean. It was in the 'good' part of town. They were flying the drugs in from Bogotá, to LAX or to Burbank, driving them over to the million-dollar houses in Chevy Chase Canyon. Safer. They could afford them, you know, and rich neighbors aren't out and about much to get in the way."

"Who was he meeting?"

At one in the morning.

A woman.

I looked at them then, all of them cops and all of them knowing, with that look on their faces and they could all die.

"You want to hear it?" I said fiercely. "About what happened that night? No major fights but maybe I *should* have, maybe that would have kept him. He'd been wearing me down, aching about this and bitching about that, turning forty-one, getting old. Nothing right, not me, not the job, and I'd been putting up with it because that's what you do, you try to get through it, but that night I'd just had enough. That night as he's dressing for work and running his mouth one more time, I said, 'Christ, Charlie, give it a break.' Nothing big, not even raised voices, but he's slamming when he goes out the door. Fine, then, forget it, but at three in the morning, there's two cops and a lieutenant and Mike there to tell me he's been shot, that he's dead and he's not coming home."

Not ever coming home.

"And then the captain comes wanting my guns, 'for safekeeping,' but he's been shot with a .45, you know, what I carry. And Homicide's coming around. Was it true we'd been fighting, had I gone to make up, and no one will tell me exactly what happened. Just question after question and my friends not talking to me, none of them, but Homicide's zeroed on me. I don't have an *alibi*—I was home, for Christ's sake, in bed by myself—but they're looking to do me, won't even say why. It took me three frantic, scrabbling days to find out that the coroner had said Charlie'd been with a woman just before he was shot. They thought it was me. That I'd lured him up there and shot him, because no one had trouble thinking *I* screwed around, but Charlie was the one faithful man."

And he *had* been, he was—I should never have started. Should never have told them a word.

"How'd it come out?" Edwards said. Reilly wasn't saying anything.

"Twelve days into it, it all clamped down. Reports were being pulled and lost, IA backed off, and the word came out to be looking for gangers, a drive-by, two witnesses. It took me a week more to learn that the woman had finally come in. Came in with her husband, a city councilman, you know—cried on the Chief's shoulder, confessed the affair. The Chief has to consider his political obligations, what he owes to the city, the council, the bad press if all this gets out—am I drawing a good enough picture? So I'm cleared, no hard feelings, welcome back working, but don't go near the street, Meg, don't talk to the woman, it wouldn't be good for the department."

"Did you stay away?"

Reilly asking. I just looked at him.

"The thing was," I said finally when no one else spoke, "there was a jackoff upstairs who was still hunting me. He figured I knew Charlie was stepping out, because any fool could have seen it, especially a cop, and that I'd gone up there to shoot him because of the woman. He just couldn't find the weapon."

Or the witnesses.

"What's the guy's name?" Reilly said.

It was none of his business. He was looking quite grim.

"Archer."

"Not Dave?"

"Dave led the first sweep." Sitting there asking me questions, like him. As if we'd never been anything. Were never connected.

"You should have told me," Reilly said.

You can't tell everyone everything. I was godawful tired.

"I didn't kill Charlie," I said. "And we'd given up

looking, a year, year and a half ago." I had, anyway. Pretty much.

"You didn't know about Soufi?"

I didn't. I hadn't. We'd been looking for Mexicans, gangers, maybe Colombians. I never would have made the leap to Beverly Hills and Iranians.

"What were they doing there?"

At a drug house.

"Buying crack," Reilly said. "The kids were all hopped up to be big-time dealers for their buddies, and suddenly there was a cop right there on the sidewalk. He says Soufi panicked and shot him."

Panicked. Almost an accident. Charlie in the wrong place at the wrong time.

"What was the car, then? Shooting at them."

"Not shooting," he said. "The woman got it wrong. Those were the cops who followed them."

Followed them home. "Extortion?"

"They said they had pictures of the shooting."

Pictures again. Of Soufi shooting a cop.

"Massoud doesn't know what they looked like?"

"They were masked," Reilly said. "Black hoods. One big and one little. He swears it was you."

"No," I said.

Mike hadn't known, *couldn't* have known. He'd been looking for witnesses and stumbled on Soufi—contact or contract, I couldn't tell, but he wouldn't have gone after a killer himself.

"What's Massoud's version of taking off Mike?"

"He says Mike had come around upping the price, so Soufi worked out a plan to grab him and leave you a note."

Upping the price? If they'd been jockeying, maybe. It happens that way when you work undercover—you don't always know exactly what it is that you're saying, but you have to finesse it, seem to imply. Act like you know so much more than you do so that people will come to you. There must have been some delicate half-conversations if Mike thought he'd found the reluctant witnesses and Soufi thought he'd found the blackmailing cops.

"They left me a *note?*"

"Saturday was a regular payoff drop. They thought they saw the end of their problems."

"Jesus," I said, " 'Nyah, nyah, we've got your partner and we'll only exchange for the negatives'?"

"Something like that. With Mike's driver's license tucked in for proof."

So someone had gotten it Saturday, been kind of pissed. Gone to the Haroutunian house to get Soufi and found Haroutunian Senior instead. Thrust the driver's license under his nose. Asked him what he knew about Mike.

"Haroutunian must have hired Mike on the side," I said, "asked him to check something out. He knew to call on the private line."

"The bank accounts maybe," Reilly said. "Soufi'd been tapping them pretty heavily, covering it up."

"Massoud's just been *saying* all this?"

Reilly looked sort of odd.

"Reilly's got a friend on the sheriff's department," Edwards said. Everybody much looser, even the captain. As if the room had relaxed.

"I didn't kill Soufi," I said quietly. "It wasn't revenge, I didn't even know."

Edwards sort of patted my knee.

"Soufi had Mike?"

"He and Massoud," Reilly said. "Something happened, they didn't know what, but Mike didn't show at the beachhouse Friday night. They'd been using a little, very full of themselves, and Soufi knew where Mike lived." Reilly's face was expressionless. "Guess Mike wasn't as careful as he thought."

He never was. Rarely.

"So *they* took him off, then? Friday night?"

"Yeah."

Blood all over Mike's place. I hoped *some* of it was theirs, surely did hope so.

"And they tore his place up? Left the dope kit?"

"They forgot it," Reilly said. "They sat there for a while, refreshing the high. Congratulating themselves."

High-fiving. *God.* And I'd been drinking myself into oblivion that damned Friday night.

"They had Mike all weekend?"

"At the beachhouse in Malibu. Trying to find out about you."

"Me?"

"They thought they'd get you, too, since Mike was so easy."

Both of us. It made a cracked kind of sense.

"By Sunday night, it was urgent. Massoud had gone back to the house to check in, found the mess and the blood and thought it was you, that you'd taken his uncle. They stuck a needle into Mike, got him talking about Charlie, describing the house. They were doing some of the needles themselves, so it was quite a night."

Christ. "You *had* to know it wasn't me when he was

saying all this. There's no way I could have done Haroutunian. I was with you Saturday night."

"I don't know all your friends," Reilly said.

And Massoud had already told the sheriffs that Soufi'd killed Charlie. Gave me a motive for a double-cross. Haroutunian's murder. Soufi's murder. Revenge.

But I'd been sitting pretty in Alibi City—everyone at the station on Saturday to see me there. *And* in the motel room last night. Ms. Machiavelli, with one of my rene-gade cop friends doing the deeds for me while I sat in the police eye, under guard.

"I'm not that good," I said. "I've just been ducking and dodging, the best way I can." While Reilly tailed me. While somebody else did. I couldn't think. "So Haroutunian was what—a mistake? The two cops found *him* instead of Soufi and so they just *did* him?"

Reilly was looking at me. Me cracking open.

"He *called* me," I said but I was remembering *"No, no, must be Mike." I* was the one who'd offered to come, and Haroutunian had been saying no. Until that fumbling silence, that gasping, that choke. Then *"Yes, you must come,"* in despair.

"They were with him," I said. "Had to be." With a gun in his face, most likely. A hand on his throat. "You tell her to come," and that little man still trying, only I hadn't known it, trying now to protect me, to give me some warning: *"You get Mike,"* he'd said. *"Hurry."*

And *"I have no son,"* because he'd thought I would know that he *had.*

I'm not good about bodies, picturing things. Blood in his hall. The back seat of my car. My car at Point Fer-min on Saturday night.

Reilly was still watching me, starting to stir, moving to shield me, I'd guess, from the others. He'd been there, too, you know, standing in the doorway with that scared little man. Surrounded by uniforms. Cops everywhere.

"They must have said you were *theirs*," I said, "something like that, when you came pulling up. They had to have *somebody* answer the door or you'd have blocked the place off maybe, getting no answer." Trapping them there.

"Maybe," Reilly said.

*"Am I doing this right?"* Haroutunian's face, so silently pleading. He'd been doing it right, God, yes, *more* than right, but I just hadn't seen it, didn't know.

Off a cliff at Point Fermin.

I had to refocus.

"Massoud's saying 'two cops,' " I said. "One big cop, one little?" Mike wasn't that big. I wasn't that small. "What's the size on Massoud?"

"Five-eight," Edwards said. "Thin."

He'd have been shorter three years ago. Twenty-one to eighteen. So the cop didn't have to be *huge,* might just have seemed that way to a hopped-up kid—especially at night in a mask.

Masked.

Like a drug raid, sitting on a house.

The captain's scenario: cops waiting to shake someone down? Beverly cops could have followed them there, but the thing was, they'd followed them *home*.

As if the target was the *house* and the boys were a bonus, not the other way around.

Something was niggling, bugging me, something I couldn't quite pin. We had masked cops on houses, cops

on the take. Murder for hire. Bodies. A body off the
cliff. Sitting on a rock in the California sun, *and you'd have
to know it was there . . .*

*Have to know that the drug house was there,* to be sitting
on it in the first place. *Our* guys hadn't known, not until
later—not until *after* Charlie was dead— and it was our
town.

*"Special cops."*

Like a task force, a drug raid.

Drug *haven.*

Point Fermin and Glendale. Bogotá. Burbank.

All different towns.

And who the hell else had been coming around?

"Reilly," I said, "your cop with the snitch—he ever
work with the DEA?"

# 33

After that, it was easy, more or less anyway. Reilly's cop had worked Vice, so he *had* come in contact—did, in fact, know Carlos and Jones. I had a side-chat with Edwards while Reilly was calling.

"They'll walk," I said.

"Maybe."

"No maybe about it. Massoud's at the sheriffs claiming it's me, and Mike doesn't know anything—if he knew it was DEA, he'd have said so. Most likely he snuck up on the cousins at the beachhouse Friday night and heard enough to learn there'd been cops at the scene, that we'd all read it wrong. He'd be thinking *our* guys, a set-up on Charlie from one of our own, because that's what *I'd* think if I didn't know better—and I'd guess that's why he was going away, to try to think through the roster, figure who to approach. He *couldn't* have known DEA."

"So maybe he didn't."

"So they'll walk," I said. "Drop operations, sit tight. You can watch 'em a while, or the feds can, a year or two maybe, going through records, trying to build up a case, and meanwhile I'm looking over my shoulder, hoping my kid'll come home."

"You've got a plan?"

"They wanted *me,* Edwards."

"They wanted your partner."

I moved impatiently. "No," I said, "they were tearing my bedroom apart looking for pictures they thought Mike had hidden. We horned in on their action, Edwards—*that's* what they're thinking. If I were them, I'd be wondering how they'd slipped up, how Mike had found out. They were sitting in one of your conference rooms while I told everyone that Mike has a camera, that he goes out and shoots, does a little surveillance for fun. If I were them in that meeting, I'd have been rethinking the last six months, how many times I'd been to a drop, sat in a car."

"You're talking a shakedown?"

"I could do it," I said. "I'm already Mike's partner. Gets it done, maybe. Gets 'em on tape."

He was looking at Reilly on the phone at the other end of the room, all the desks in between. "You don't want him to know?"

"He doesn't have to."

"He *has* to," Edwards said. "I've got to work with him yet. Don't think I want him pissed off."

All how you look at it. More or less easy.

"No," Reilly said. Just no.

"Reilly—"

"They won't talk on a wire."

"Okay," I said, "then they won't. Then I've wasted my time, so what's the big deal? You think it'll tip them we're *on* to them or something?"

"They'll want to meet."

"So I'll meet."

He was silent. Edwards leaning back in his chair.

"Look," I said, "they don't know if I'm dirty. What they saw was you running me, beating me down. Maybe Mike and I were going to make some quick bucks—we're entitled, right? Share a little of the wealth for our pain? They know how it works. And I'm a suspect, for Christ's sake, you won't tell me anything—let's say I don't know that Massoud took out Mike, let's say I'm thinking it's them. I'm a little fish swimming out of my depth, anxious to patch it all up, give it back."

"Give *what* back?"

"Mike left me an envelope. A couple of pictures and a whole lot of details. Notes on activities—places and times. I'd be willing to turn it all over, forget it, if they'll just please back off and leave me alone."

"You don't have any activities."

"Your snitch," I said, "had a homicide."

"We don't know it's the same."

Well, we didn't know *anything,* did we? "It's a *taste,*" I said, "if I'm selling the package. Lots more where that came from—theirs for the taking. I could do it, Reilly."

He was shaking his head. Goddamn it anyway.

"We can cover her in Burbank," Edwards said.

"They'll want to meet someplace else. How would she get there? Why would I let her?"

"I ducked out," I said.

"From the jail?"

"You wouldn't have to be keeping me in *jail,* Reilly. Maybe I've got *favored* dirty status. Maybe I'm negotiating with *everyone* for the envelope." He gave me a very old-fashioned up-from-under look. "Okay, so you wouldn't do that—*they* don't know."

"We're going to have to talk," he said meaningfully, but that could come later. I can always talk later. The point was I *had* him. He was starting to work it. "I want a wire on you."

"Okay." They wouldn't talk on a wire, but what the hell? Risk my life.

"You'll only meet in Burbank. Someplace crowded."

"The Spoon would be good," Edwards said. "Always busy at night."

It's a diner on Olive. Some tables, some booths, swivel seats at the counter. It has the kind of rough-edged food that tastes really good around midnight when you've been working too hard.

"I'll need their phone numbers," I said. "I don't want to call Jones. Maybe Carlos at home, do you think?" He should be there now, dinnertime, sixish. Had to be tired. He'd been running all weekend if we were right, he and Jones looking for Mike. And they'd have had to put in some time at their DEA jobs, not something they'd want to be absent from if the eye of suspicion was glancing their way. All the webs.

"I'll get the numbers," Edwards said.

That would leave Reilly with me.

"I'll just go put on a wire," I said, "if you'd get me one first. Might as well have it ready." And that way I could sit all alone in the ladies' room until Edwards was done.

More or less easy.

Edwards handed over the phone. I tried the office, in case they were there, but the guy who answered it said they were gone. I made up a name and left it.

Carlos picked up the home phone on the third ring.

"Carlos? Rick Carlos?"

"Yeah."

"I'm sorry to bother you," I said. "It's Meg Gillis. We met yesterday."

"Yeah?"

Very guarded. Someone talking in the background. A woman.

"I got the message you left," I said, meaning Soufi. Soufi's body. Let my voice tremble a touch. "This is getting out of hand, you know? We didn't mean any harm, we're just small-time."

"What message?"

"And now Mike's in ICU, they won't let me see him."

*"They found your partner?"*

He didn't know.

"I just want to stop it," I said. "I don't want to get hurt. Mike should have known better."

"What are you talking about?" Very clipped. Wary.

"The pictures," I said. "Always using that camera—I told him to leave it alone. He was thinking a little bit extra, you know? To get by on, from Soufi. He wasn't going to go after you. He was just interested, that's all."

"In what?"

"I found an envelope," I said, "over the weekend. Tucked down the side of my bed by the phone. I guess he'd been doing surveillance or something—there were a lot of notes and some pictures, going back quite a while. I didn't really look at it, you know, just put it somewhere safe in case anything happened. I recognized *you* right away, though, at the station. From the pictures, I mean."

"Mrs. Gillis—"

"Really," I said, "we didn't want a lot of money. We don't even need it, you know? It just kind of mush-roomed. But I've got to make a choice here, pretty quick. Reilly's after me all the time, kind of keeping me close. I just got out now because he's gone and the cop didn't know."

"Where are you?"

"At a pay phone," I said. "I'm not going to hang around long, though. Gotta make my choices, but I thought I should call you. See what you thought I should do."

"If you've got some sort of evidence," he said very slowly, "then you ought to come in. Where's Reilly now?"

"I don't know. Out." And then I just felt like it, it just seemed so right, so "I think you need to keep an eye on your partner," I said.

Silence. "How'd you get this number, Mrs. Gillis?"

Dammit, too much. I always go over. "It was in with Mike's stuff." As if I didn't know why Mike would have had it, what kind of blackmail tricks he got up to. Reilly was watching me, listening in.

"I'll want to see the envelope."

Sure he would. "You can look at it—can you meet me tonight?"

"I don't think so."

"Okay, then, I'm gone. It won't do me a hill's worth of beans if Reilly's already gotten through to your part-ner."

"Wait a minute."

"I can't, man, I'm here on the street." I wasn't on the

street, I was in a damn office, should have called from a pay phone outside. Wrong kind of noise. "They'll be closing this building soon," I said, "and I don't know when Reilly'll miss me. Look, there's a diner called the Spoon, on the back side of Olive. Meet me there in, like, half an hour, or forget the whole thing. Just *you*, Carlos, okay? Don't tell Jones."

Carlos had a lot to think about, was trying. "All right."

Fine. Reilly already had another phone going, dialing Jones's number. I hung up on one and he was getting a recording, an answering machine. Hung up on that one, too.

"Maybe he's not home," I said.

"You'd better hope."

I was hoping.

"It would really be safer without the wire."

"It'd be a *lot* safer," he said straightly, "because you're not going without it."

Men. Edwards was being part of the wall. "Yeah, okay, whatever," I said pacifically, "are we going to go do this or what?"

Easy.

More or less, anyway.

Last-minute instructions in the van. It was getting dark outside, headlights coming on, shining in, the three of us crouched by the rear doors.

"Keep it simple," Edwards said. "You didn't bring the envelope, you don't trust anything, you want some assurances."

"I'll give him the homicide," I said, "see how he looks. You guys going to be watching?"

"Don't get too eager."

I'd been here a thousand times. Hey, batter, batter. Huddled with the coaches.

"Signals?"

" 'Jackpot,' " I said.

"Don't forget it."

"Let me play it," I said, "okay? Just back me up, however it goes."

"It's going to go fine."

Yeah, sure it was—fine.

"Got a line yet on Jones?"

"He's not home," Edwards said.

Wonderful. Reilly so silent beside me. Feeling it maybe, like I was, the pull of the night. Anxious to go. Or maybe, like me, wishing things could be different, not wanting to have all the bad blood between us. Edwards was moving up to the driver, the cop in the front, just the two of us there in the back. Quiet. Close. "I'm sorry," I said softly, "about all of it, all the trouble."

Reilly didn't care about bad blood, I guess. Very curt. Hard. "Don't do anything stupid," he said.

Made it easy a little. Easier.

Carlos was sitting at a booth towards the back, facing the door. We were friends, old friends, so I smiled and went towards him. "Thanks for coming so late," I said clearly. "I hope your wife isn't upset about this."

"Part of the job."

In case someone was listening, he thought he'd come out to meet an official informant, had no other reason to be here. I saw the metallic flash in his hand, though, before he curved it under the table. A goddamn sweep meter, smaller than I'd ever seen, and the chill in his smile was nothing to that in my stomach, because we were in it for real now and it all came down to the game.

"She must have been put out," I said, while I slid in across from him, shook out a paper napkin, fumbled for an obvious pen in my bag.

What a sweep meter does is sense electrical current, like the kind a battery-powered wire produces—the kind, you know, I was wearing. They sell sweep meters in fancy catalogs now so you can protect yourself against espionage, with a portable version for the businessman on the go. The DEA doesn't usually carry them because *they're* usually the ones with the wires. I wondered where Carlos had gotten his, but it didn't matter much now.

"We should order something," I said, and opened the menu, shielding my hand from the rest of the room. Scribbled frantically on the napkin: *"I'm wired—Reilly—only way—don't know who's watching."*

Carlos was geared for a trap.

*"Deal,"* I wrote. *"Please."*

"I'll just have coffee," he said. He was sitting back in the booth, watching me. Thinking. He looked like he had at the meeting yesterday, a nice guy out of his league, uncomfortable with the cloak-and-daggerness going on around him. I'd have believed him, too, if I hadn't seen that flash in his hand. "You said something about an envelope when you called me, Mrs. Gillis."

Christ. I wagged my hand frantically. *"Notes,"* I said, "so we could compare notes," while I tried to write faster. *"Didn't tell R. about env."* He was glancing at his watch.

"I'm not sure I know how to help you, Mrs. Gillis. This isn't a DEA case."

Playing the lie to the limit, that all he was here for was *me*.

"Where's your partner?" I said.

"I don't know." That seemed to be true, the eyes kind of shifting. Disturbed.

"It's just that he might be involved." This pen stuff wasn't going to get it—I couldn't write fast enough and he wouldn't sit still for it. Take the bull by the horns. I shredded the napkin, chucked it, propped the menu on the table like a wall. "I didn't think you knew about it— about your partner, I mean. That's why I called you, to see if you'd help."

"I think you've got the wrong guy." He was starting to rise.

"You can't leave me for *Reilly*." I sounded desperate because, really, I was. Had my hands where Carlos could see them, on the table, moving. Brought them in to my chest. "Reilly scares me," I said. Ran my hands down my breasts, pulled the shirt very tight. No gun, Carlos, no weapon. "He's just so unreasonable, so violent." Drew the cloth partway up like a tease. Carlos was watching me, blank-faced and frozen. No gun at the belt, see? Not armed. Held the shirt up with one hand, moved the other down slowly, rested it there on the skin. "He was pushing me around," I said, "in the motel room last night. Just look at this bruise." Lifted my hand, exposing the tape, the battery pack, the wire. "What could I do?" I said. "A woman alone." Ripped at the tape. Jesus, it hurt, but I had to be quick. "And he's so suspicious, he wouldn't trust his own mother. He probably followed me here." I was fading my voice in and out like a transceiver gone bad. "But you could help me, Carlos, you

could take me on in. Protection, you know? DEA." I
had the cord on the table now, stretched. Carlos watching my hands like a lynx. "You could *snatch me*," I said,
"when we're done talking. Make it official. Come in
heavy-handed and just take me out." Had the butter
knife sawing. Crude but effective, the thin wire parting.
"He doesn't have anything provable yet," and the cord
separated, split, two ends. "Check me," I said.

He was just staring.

I smiled to remind him that someone was watching,
looked around, brushed his hand, his sweep-meter
hand. "We don't have all night. These things can break,
but he's edgy as hell, he could come anytime. Check me
out, do it fast."

He dropped his hand to his pocket again, looked at it
there in the shadow of the table. Kept his eyes on it.
"What's going on?"

"Reilly caught me coming out of the building," I
said. "I had to tell him I'd called you, but I said I did it
for protection—it was the only way I could think of to
meet. I didn't tell him about finding the you-know-what,
but he's been *at* me about it, so I'm sure he suspects. You
tell me how you want it to go. Do I give it to Reilly or do
you want to deal?"

"Blackmail?" He was very quiet. "You think that's
smart?"

"You can't take me out," I said. "There are cops all
around."

He still had those eyes on his hand. "Where's the
envelope?"

"Well, I couldn't get to it with Reilly right there."

"That's too bad."

He didn't believe me. Didn't think that there *was* one.

"I wouldn't have given it to you anyway," I said, "till we'd worked out the terms."

"But you don't even *have* it."

He was planning to walk, that pasty-mouthed smile.

"Let me give you a taste," I said, please, God, be with me, and I threw out the details the way Reilly had told me, the homicide the informant had spilled. We *could* have been wrong, it might *not* be the same, but there was a certain satisfaction in watching his lips turn that little bit paler. Not a different bunch after all. The same crooked cops.

"I'll have to talk to Bill."

"You do that," I said. "Just don't let him near me. I had all I wanted of his act yesterday."

"He gets carried away."

"He's psychotic," I said.

"I know." He was quiet, very quiet. Almost regretful. "I should never have gotten mixed up with him."

Well, we all make mistakes. Reilly was coming in through the door.

"You just have to help me," I said fairly loudly, "take me in," sweeping the pieces off the damn table, trying my best to re-tape. I looked up then and saw him, right on top of us. Guilty. He was looking ferocious.

"Evening," he said tightly to Carlos, but he was homed in on me.

"Reilly—"

"Think we're going outside now to talk."

"No," I said, "please—"

"There's no 'please' about it," and he had a hand on me, dragging me up.

"You can't just *do* this," I said, "Carlos—"

"It's not his damn business. You're under arrest," and he had my arms up behind me, Christ, cuffing me.

"Listen, you son of a bitch—"

"That's enough," and he sort of half-shoved me, sent me flying into the next table before I could balance. I hoped someone there would report him.

It wasn't going to be Carlos.

"She's been saying some things."

"That's what she does. Don't take it to heart." Reilly had his hand fastened back on my arm. Hauling me up. Very tight.

"They found her partner?"

"Yeah, Palm Springs. He didn't make it, we just got the word. All we've got left now is *her.*" He was sounding disgusted. Ticked off. Kind of mean. "Move yourself," he said in my ear, "I'm taking you out—and then you can tell me what games you've been playing." Like he meant it, you know, and maybe he did.

"Carlos," I said. Desperate, looking for help.

"You have to go with him, Mrs. Gillis. I'll try to work something out."

"There's nothing to work," Reilly said. "This one's ours."

"She wanted my help."

"She's playing you, man. Did the same thing with me. Have your chief give Abbott a call." We were already moving, aimed for the door, and I was going to need surgery if he didn't let go of my arm. I sagged back on him, whimpered, but he didn't ease up.

"Reilly, for Christ's sake—"

"Be quiet," he said.

*   *   *

Not all of it easy.

He stopped me before we got to the van, turned me around. Had a hand on my shoulder kind of holding me against the brick wall of a building. *Maybe* Carlos was watching. I shrugged at the cuffs. "You taking these off?"

"I don't know," he said. "What was the trick with the wire?"

"He had a sweep meter on me. Knew I was miked the second I spoke."

Those lips very set.

"You should have come out, then."

"The point was to snare him," I said. "I tried writing notes, but he wouldn't sit still for it. It took too much time, and I had to do something he'd believe, that I was conniving past you, grabbing my chance."

Eyes fixed on the bricks beside me.

"Well, it worked," I said. "I think it did."

Reaching back for his keys. "You can explain it to Edwards."

"What are *you* going to be doing?"

"Finding Jones," he said.

Maybe not easy at all.

I'd told Edwards everything two or three times.

"It makes you a target."

"I was a target *before*," I said. "Now there's an urgency, now they can't just sit and pick me off when they want to. That's how it works. You rush 'em, they make a mistake."

"Not many so far."

So I *wasn't* perfect. So Reilly was pissed, Edwards not

happy. "I wanted to get them, okay? How's Mike doing really?"

"Better. They'll say that he's not, though, for now. Professional courtesy."

Nice of the sheriff's department. Nicer of Edwards.

"I'm sorry," I said. "It just seemed pretty good."

"Oh, it was good." He was chewing a pencil. "Left us a little bit out of the water."

I knew what he meant. You can't always scramble that fast. "I was trying to tell you."

"We heard it," he said. "Reilly did. I was watching the show."

Oh.

"It was good," he said. He might have been grinning. Thank God I hadn't been wearing a leg wire, had to strip all the way. The other cop was keeping his back turned, had the earphones on, the radio. Maybe he hadn't heard.

"What happens next?"

"We're going to let you go home."

"Home?"

"It should be safe enough now and I can't keep affording motels. I'll send Pedersen with you. We found Jones at a girlfriend's, so we think that's okay, and Carlos went straight back to his own house, still sitting there with two of my guys—probably trying to reach Jones. They debugged your phone, by the way. You were right about that broadcast—good range, the tech said. He was really impressed."

Great.

"What if these guys have some friends?"

"Do you think?" Edwards said. "That's what Pedersen's for."

# 34

Nothing is easy. Pedersen went through the house looking for danger, but he didn't find any the first time
through, just the picked-over mess I'd left. I wished I had
that other cop with me. I'd liked him. Wished I'd asked
him his name. Pedersen was okay, very good, but I hadn't
done anything with him and there's less of a bond.

Wished I could just talk to Reilly.

Wished I could just have my gun.

"Can't," Edwards said when I'd asked him. "You
aren't going to need it, for one thing, and it's all locked
up, for another. Evidence."

"Then let me have one of yours."

"Are you kidding? Pedersen's there. I've got guys all
over, coming and going. You'll be shooting somebody,
and then I'll have to explain to the captain."

"Edwards——"

"You won't need it," he said comfortably. "We've got
this thing wired."

Had *me* wired, that was for sure. I liked *him,* too, you
know, him and his wife, the notion of it. He was a
prince. "Put not your faith in princes," my dad used to
say. Very biblical, Dad was. Put his faith in his guns.

So I scrounged up some sheets, sort of straightened the guest room, the one in the middle. Could have slept in Josh's room, but that didn't seem right, and my own was a long time away. Too many memories. Too much debris. Pedersen was camped down the hall.

"Listen," he'd said, "you call if you need me," but I'd seen his eyes when I was ripping off the last of the tape and I was pretty darn sure that I wouldn't need him. Wouldn't need *anyone* that bad.

"Thanks," I'd said, and went off to the room. Closed the door.

Wished now that I'd left it open.

It was cold, very cold. Didn't really have blankets left, just a couple of strips and a coat. Piled them over me, sat on the bed. Wondered if Charlie could see. This whole business had started with Charlie, or further back maybe, I didn't know. Maybe it had started with me. I'd tried so hard to be perfect. It had taken me years to get used to Charlie, the fact of him breathing, lying beside me, the notion of loving him. Him loving me.

Define reality, beauty, the eye of the beholder. Everything's easy if you *want* it to be, and maybe I hadn't, I just couldn't tell. Because what was that blonde bitch, that mealymouthed whore?

I could hear the phone ringing down the hall in the kitchen, ringing and ringing, so they'd left it plugged in. Pedersen wasn't hurrying any to get it, and I was watching my door handle, watching it turn, door pushing in towards me, seeing the gun.

"Hello, Carlos," I said.

He had gloves on, white latex, surgical type, and he stopped just inside of the door.

"How'd you lose the tail?" I said. It didn't matter, it was reflex, conversation. Buy another minute, maybe two. The phone finally stopped ringing. Started again.

"Obscene calls," I said. "I've been getting them lately."

He still had his sweep meter and I wasn't wired. Wished that I had been, that I'd kept the tape on. I wondered if an electric blanket would have confused him, but that didn't matter now either.

"Put your hands where I can see them," he said. He was moving into the room, cautious gun first, and I put my hands out open-fingered, on top of the coat. Was I going to bluff him? Pretend to be aiming? "Look at that bird over there"?

"What happened to Jones?"

"He's with Reilly," he said, and I should have known better, should have looked at his eyes, but I was busy watching the gun. It was closer than he was.

"We can work this out," I said. "Honestly, Carlos. You can turn state's evidence. I'll testify. You couldn't have known Jones was going to go crazy, and once you were in, you were stuck, just deeper and deeper."

"Don't play me," he said.

"I'm not," I said, "really. Just pointing things out."

"You *knew* he was talking to Reilly. If he got there first, you said."

"That was a bluff, Carlos—who's going to believe a psycho like him?"

"*Exactly,*" he said.

I had enough of a glimpse to start rolling, but he was already leaping and slashing at me with the Sig .45, the barrel connecting with my cheekbone, pain high and inside. I might have yelled, I can't really remember, but I know I kept moving, kicking up as I went. I landed on the floor by the inside wall and I'd gotten him somewhere, because he was bent over, grunting, as I came crouching up. The problem was, he was coming up, too, and he still had the gun.

Sighted on me.

"Carlos," I said—gasped, really, winded—"I'll give you the envelope."

"There isn't an envelope." His pupils were pinpoints.

"Swear to Christ, Carlos, on my mother's grave."

"You'll be buried before her," he said. "Stand up."

He had the gun, so I stood. "Look," I said, and I was trying to think faster, "Reilly can't prove anything without it. It's your word against Jones."

"I know that," he said softly, and I'd painted the corner. Carlos didn't need to *have* the envelope, he just needed to be sure no one else did. Just needed me dead and then he couldn't lose. If there *was* an envelope and I couldn't tell anyone where to find it because I was dead, then he was home free. If there *wasn't* an envelope, then he was still clear, and I was just dead. Poor stupid Meg. Thought she was smart.

"Reilly knows where it is."

He smiled at me, the chill smile from earlier. "Then he'd already have it."

"He's talking to Jones first. Thinks it's safe where it is."

"Too bad."

He was going to kill me anyway. "Please," I said, "Carlos, you don't have to do this. Five minutes, you can check it all out."

"Turn." He was closing on me and I measured the

distance, but he had the gun shielded, close-quarters position, and I couldn't get to it. He couldn't miss. Couldn't lose. "Turn."

I turned.

It was like this at Auschwitz, all the world over. Each compliance buying you time. Microseconds. Nanoseconds.

I turned and he cuffed me like Reilly had earlier, but *this* man was wanting to hurt me. I knew it before he'd finished clipping the cuffs, before he drove his fist into my kidney and the numbing, shrieking pain ripped my legs out from under me, before he twisted me up and slammed me back into the wall. This man liked to hurt people. This man had killed Soufi. Killed Haroutunian. Left Haroutunian's blood in my car.

I'd been thinking the mad dog was Jones. I'd been wrong.

"Now we'll talk," he said, with a heavy satisfaction. Feeling better, I guess. Not nearly so frustrated. "Where is the envelope?"

I couldn't even speak.

"The *envelope*."

"I'll show you," I started, tried to say, but he was already smashing again.

"That's not what I asked you."

I'd caught the wall with my cheek this time, blood coming down, and I didn't know how long I could do this. He was going to keep on, though—he liked it too much. Paying me back for being a woman, for having the gall to think I could play him.

"It's in the garage," I said. Mumbled through my puffing lip.

"*Where* in the garage?"

"I'll have to show you." He was moving again, but I'd felt him this time, threw myself desperately sideways, turned towards him, talking frantically like I thought it would help, like I thought if I cooperated, he might not kill me. "That was Reilly on the phone—he keeps checking because he doesn't trust me, and I didn't answer. He'll be here any minute. For God's sake, let me get it and then you can go."

He stilled and I thought I had him. And then the steel mouth of the Sig came up to my neck, drawing a line that ended in the hollow beneath my left ear, just behind the jaw. I could hear the snick as the trigger pulled back. "Where in the garage?"

I stared at him for half a second, at the light in his eyes. "Behind the workbench. Taped up."

He smiled, a full-lipped, sensual smile, and I'd been so wrong when I'd counted Carlos the safe one. He was going to have his orgasm watching me die. Not yet, though. Not when he could prolong the foreplay, the pleasure. He was easing the trigger back and I was holding my breath for it, listening for the round to click through. "Now you can show me," he said.

Show him what?

"*Now.*"

"Yes, okay," I said. He was pushing me towards the dark hallway. I stumbled slightly, over something, and somehow I caught the light switch with my elbow, clicking it on. All the lights coming on, blaze of glory, and Pedersen a bundle at the end of the hall. Carlos was chopping at me with the flat of the gun. I twisted, dodged away, and he followed, drove the other kidney. I didn't even scream this time, I couldn't, I just fell like a nerveless sack. I'd be spitting blood soon, coughing it out, and Carlos stood over me, loving it. Loving me. Stretched out his hand very slowly. I watched, mesmerized, helpless, and he smiled down at me as he changed its direction, reached to flick off the lights.

"Get up," he said in the dimness, the spill from the bedroom, and I struggled to my knees, leaned weakly against the wall. I was still trying to plan, trying to do anything because we'd get to the garage and then I was dead. That *might* have been Reilly calling. Maybe they knew they'd lost Carlos and he'd wanted to warn me.

"Get up," Carlos said again, softly, so softly, and I forced the foot under me, willed the body to move. I jacked up slowly, pushing against the wall, and somehow I was standing, weaving. Carlos hadn't put the gun away, it was in the small of my back, his other hand tight on my cuffed wrists behind me. He was pressed up against me, letting me feel him.

And me, so demoralized, cowed, moving down the hall like a fluttering shadow. Clinging to the hope that if he got what he came for, he'd go. Outgunned. Cowering like a pale weak woman. "Don't shame me," my father was saying, his ghost, but shame's what you make of it, Daddy, and pride isn't just dying well. I come from a long line of women, *surviving* women, who knew you spun wool for the devil if that's what he wanted, if that's what it takes to keep you from harm. He's bigger than I am and he's got the gun and I don't want to die now, please, Daddy, okay? Forgive the dishonor, but I don't want to die.

We were at the back porch, the one Charlie and I had

enclosed. He hadn't come in through the door, it was still propped shut, but he'd brought his burglar kit with him, cut out a window so we wouldn't hear the glass break.

"Out," he said.

It's hard with your hands cuffed behind you. I sort of stuffed myself through the window and fell. He dropped on the deck next to me, the Sig at my neck. "Go on."

I could see the backyard, but barely, a clouded moon. The side door to the garage has a spring-loaded lock. Carlos made quick, silent work of it while I thought about kicking him, thought about screaming, thought about trying to run. He motioned me in with the gun.

"You'll have to turn on the light," I said through my lip. "I can't see."

He had a pencil flash. It speared through the darkness from beside me, lighting up parts of the garage, settling on the workbench, the tools. "That it?"

"Yes," I said, and he moved us both in, the door closing behind us.

"Where?"

I had the one chance. Wavered quickly to the far end of the workbench, sank there to my knees facing him, my back to the sink we'd built opposite the workbench so long ago. "It's under here. If you'll uncuff me, I'll get it for you. It's kind of hard to find."

"I'll get it," he said, and he could have moved me away, but he was too smart for that. He'd seen me glance around, noted the workbench, the wrenches, the hammer. He wasn't going to leave me free to smash him over the head, and he wasn't going to let me pull an unknown something out from under the workbench. He was a cop.

He had the flash on my face, watching me closely, and I could have wept from frustration, from fear, from the dreadful paralyzing knowledge that he had me cornered. I was kneeling in the space between the workbench and the sink and all he had to do was throttle me and I was gone, couldn't move, couldn't fight.

Or he could just shoot me, not wait for the envelope.

I was working my fingers desperately behind me, crouched in the corner, not caring anymore that he saw my panic, that I was a rabbit before him. I could feel the built-in shelf of the sink behind me, backed myself further against it.

He was smart, Carlos was, and he knew I had plans. Despised me for them, my transparency, my attempts at deception. "What's under the workbench?"

"Nothing," I said, and it was a wisp, a thin reed of sound. "The envelope."

His hand flicked forward, his left hand, and he slapped me into the side of the sink.

"What's under the workbench?"

I shook my head, fighting for consciousness. He'd driven my bad cheek into the wood and all I could see were the stars. "Nothing. I swear."

He slapped me again.

"Carlos, I swear."

And again. Twice more, putting his weight into it. It was dark in there, pitch, and the pencil-light dancing every time that he hit me.

"What's under the workbench?"

I was slumped in the corner. Mother, I hurt. He was

too smart for me. Hard. Reilly wasn't coming and I'd never make it. Couldn't stall anymore.

"A gun," I said numbly.

"Cold?"

There were two of him weaving there in the pencil-light, and I couldn't think. "Charlie got it. For emergencies."

"Is it *cold*?"

Time running out. His hand up to hit me. "Yes." I was weeping. "It's not registered anywhere."

"You stupid bitch," he said, sneering, and he was right, I was stupid, because now he'd kill me with my unregistered gun. Why waste his own, don't you see?

He crowded in on me then, contemptuous, shouldering me into the corner while he reached up past me under the workbench, and there was no chance and no time. I twisted sideways, stretched desperately, strained against the cuffs. The first muzzle-flash blinded me, inches away, and the gun bucked and burned in my hands. I was blind, I was deaf, echoes in the garage, and there was no room and no time. He was moving, I could feel him, and I clutched in a panic, jammed the gun up against him, the trigger pulling all the way back. Again. Christ, again. I could smell the cloth burning, the plastic bag and the flesh. I was point-blank on him, emptying, and the son of a bitch wouldn't die. He was turning, I was crying, the barrel too hot, searing my wrist, and the trigger so stiff, please, Mama, please, God, and I wrapped my fingers around it and pulled. Again and again. Nine shots, all I had, and it wasn't enough, would never be enough, but I couldn't miss, couldn't move. He convulsed right there in my lap, and I was trapped with the stench and the sounds as he turned his face towards me, as he choked on his tongue and he died.

Deception, Dad—*that's* my legacy, all that I have, more useful than pride, because I kept the gun under the sink, not the workbench, and he would have killed me with it if he wasn't so smart, if he hadn't been sure I was a weak, lying woman. I don't know *who* I was crying for, then—all of us, maybe. I was pinned by his weight, in the blood and the offal, with my hands cuffed behind me and his body on top, so I couldn't lever up or get free.

They kicked the door, Edwards and Reilly, coming in hard and low. "Too late," I said, "too goddamn late," and I meant it *all*, useless, but I think Reilly thought I'd been shot. I looked pretty dreadful, I guess, with the blood everywhere and some of it mine, and just the thin pencil beam glowing till Edwards found the switch for the overhead lights.

"Take it easy," Reilly said, very tightly, and I *was* taking it easy except for his hand on my arm. I winced away from the bruise, from the grip, and he loosened.

"Do I have to stay like this till they come and take pictures?"

"No," he said. "Where's it hurt?"

It hurt everywhere, but I couldn't think now, I just couldn't do it, I still had to focus. "Where's Jones?"

"Burbank jail."

So Josh would be safe. And Michael was better. I might have said that part out loud.

"Take it easy," Reilly said again, and I *could* take it easy, because things were okay now, things were all right. Edwards was talking to people on the radio, doing the cop stuff, while Reilly stayed with me, so silent, a shadow. The circus came to town and dusted around me, drew its diagrams, asked me its questions. I told it mostly the truth, an edited version—the taped-up envelope story, me stalling for time till opportunity rose.

The only bad moment came when the captain, Dresden or Dreiden, held up the cold gun in the bag. "Where'd this come from?"

They were all cops there, just needed an answer. Easy, really, you know.

"I guess he brought it with him," I said.

# 35

Friday, I went to see Mike. I'd slept most of Thursday away in a coma, but no one had called to see how I was. Well, Edwards had, and probably the policewoman he'd left had checked in on a regular basis, but nobody else had bothered to call. I was okay, though. Some nasty bruises all over, aches and pains, but the doctors hadn't found anything broken. Nothing for anyone to concern themselves about.

And my cat showed up, I don't know where she'd been. I went down to take a look at the other one, the body on ice, and it was my neighbors' cat, Princess. Jane Balfour's. She liked to sun herself on my deck if my cat wasn't there to drive her away, and I guess Jones and Carlos had thought she was mine. She was stupid, you know. She'd go to just anyone because she'd never known anything but petting and being made much of, so she'd never had to learn how to hide. Not her fault, though, really. Not a reason to die. I cried with Jane, telling her.

Mike looked like hell.

He was drawn and bandaged, his face very white, in a hospital bed with the curtains around it. I sat on a chair by his hand. He'd been talking, they told me, a little bit yesterday. Reilly'd been down. I just sat where I was, watched the rise and fall for a while. To know he was living. I'd have to call his mom pretty soon, do fifty other things. Clean his place, clean the office, call the insurance. But Mike was alive.

"Meggie," he said.

"Michael."

He smiled at me mistily, drifting. "Screwed it up, 'Gie."

"Not really. Except for not telling me." I leaned in, and touched his face. "How'd you pay for the Porsche, babe?"

"Sammy got a second." He seemed to think that explained it, so maybe it did. Mortgage. A second on the house out in Riverside.

"He paid you back?"

"Yeah. I should have invested it. I knew what you'd think."

*I* didn't care.

"You should have *burned* it," I said. "You're such a turkey sometimes. They told me you'd been running drugs."

It hurt him to laugh, but it did me the world. Something to count on again.

"A sergeant was here," he said, "what's his name— Reilly? Asking me stuff about you."

"It's okay," I said.

"I didn't tell him."

"That's good."

"You having a thing with him, 'Gie?"

I wasn't.

I wouldn't.

"No," I said.

"Seemed like a pain in the ass." He was drifting again, floating away. "I didn't mean to get you hurt, though."

"You didn't," I said.

"*He* thinks I did."

"Hell with him, babe. You go to sleep, Mike, okay?"

He went. I could see why the nurse had said not to expect much. He was drugged up and injured, so weak. I spent some time sitting by him. If it hadn't been a weekend, and a Josh weekend at that, I'd have stayed in Palm Springs, but I'd promised Josh on the phone again yesterday, and I knew he was anxious, so I packed up at three and went home.

It was nine-thirty when Reilly called. Josh was in watching *Star Wars* on the brand-new TV set and I was throwing away what was left of the kitchen.

"It's Reilly," he said, his voice close and curling. "How are you?"

I was fine.

*Very* fine.

"I wanted to come by," he said. "We won't be done till eleven. Is that too late?"

It was, you know. Much too late. "Josh is here."

"He'll be in bed by then, won't he?" and when I didn't say anything, "Meg?"

"Yes," I said, meaning "Yes, he'll be in bed," but Reilly was already saying, "Fine, then, I'll see you," and I was left holding his dial tone like a fool.

Josh didn't want to go to bed, as it happened, he wanted to stay up and talk, but I was talked out and crabby, so he finally gave up, wandered away down the hall. When I checked on him later, he was asleep, sacked and gone, one arm hanging off of the bed. I closed his door softly, and went back to pace by myself.

Lights through the living-room windows. Headlights. Swinging up and around, parking in front.

Reilly.

I went to stand in the doorway. He was climbing out of an El Camino, hefting a couple of brown grocery bags.

"Where's the Toyota?"

"It's my son's," he said easily. "We'd traded for a few days till I could get it fixed up for him."

He had a son old enough to drive.

And he'd been laughing at me about the Toyota, had read my assumptions. The amusement was there in his eyes.

"You have any other kids?"

"A girl," he said gravely. "Fourteen. Were you going to let me in?"

I hadn't been, no, but he was already to the door, so I held it open. "What's in the bags?"

"You said you wanted champagne."

Had I? I couldn't remember. He was making himself right at home, down the hall to the kitchen. The bags on the counter. "That one's for you," he said, pushing one towards me. "A present." Fished through the other. "I wasn't sure if you had any glasses."

So he'd brought me some Styrofoam cups from the station. "Reilly—"

He was already opening the bottle, fingers untwisting the wire with a minimum of movement, compact, very able. He stopped, was still, watching me watching him, and we were too close.

"You should open your bag," he said casually, as if I were always a statue, and then he pushed the plastic cork off the champagne bottle with his thumbs. It frothed up and over. "You want to give me a cup?"

I wanted to run. Reached for some sense. Handed him cups. Tried for something like normal conversation. "What were you working tonight?"

"Had to pick up a guy," he said. "We'd left him alone for most of the week, so I thought he'd be surprised." Grinned at me like a wolf. "He was."

That satisfaction. That leaping excitement when things have gone right.

It was good champagne, sweet.

"To you," he said. Toasting me. "You all right?"

I was okay.

"Josh asleep?"

He was asleep.

"Can we sit down, Meg?"

Laughing at me. He'd bullied me in this room, pressed me against the counter. "The living room would be better," I said, and went down the hall so that he had to follow. I stood by the armchair next to the fireplace, which basically left him the couch. Suited him, I guess. He settled back into it—sank into it, really—propped the bottle on the coffee table. Took a sip from his cup.

"So you're all right?"

Looking at my face.

"It'll heal. I thought he broke the cheekbone, but the doctor says not."

"That's good."

He seemed to be waiting for more. "You don't have to do this," I said. "Deprogram or anything. I've been in shootings before."

"I know."

Reilly knew everything. "You've been reading my file?"

"Dave told me."

Dave Yarrow.

"When do you have time to do *police* work?" I said, and he laughed at me comfortably.

"I hope to get back to it soon." He was stretching his legs out—an invitation, a lap. Looked at me again, my eyes, and his own eyes changed. Narrowed.

Stillness.

Very softly. "Why don't you come and sit down, Meg."

Because I was a coward. Because it meant crossing the room. He could read me, you know, like nobody had. He was rising and coming towards me, easy so I wouldn't run, taking the Styrofoam cup from me, setting it on the mantelpiece, out of the way.

"Meg?"

Husky, asking, and I could feel his warmth very close. I put my hands up against him, to clutch or push away, I couldn't have told you, and his jacket was rough against my fingers, hard seams and snaps. He was nuzzling my ear, lips soft and seeking, and *God,* it had been a long time. I put my arms around him then, and kissed him as if he were all I had left in the world.

"All right," he said after a while, "all right, that's better." He was smiling again, I could hear it in his voice, but I wasn't looking at him, I couldn't. He had my head tucked in under his chin, and his arms were tight around me. "Mary Margaret," he was saying richly, warmly, rolling the syllables over my hair, and no one calls me that anymore, I didn't even know where he'd gotten it because I haven't used that name in years. There was something possessive about the way he said it, though—as if he thought he'd found my hidden heart, as if he'd been thinking of me this way all week, had been biding his time.

Except that I *wasn't* Mary Margaret, and I'd thought I could do this, but I had been wrong.

"Reilly, let me go."

"Why?"

He *didn't* know everything, didn't know I was crazy. His hand moved up to the nape of my neck, under the hair, and he was rubbing so gently there in the hollow. Back and forth, back and forth, until I was dizzy with it, pressing my face to his chest. "Why?" he said again softly.

"I need some champagne."

I needed some air. I needed to be across the room where his touch couldn't find me.

He laughed, but he wasn't letting me go. "I have a new ambition," he said into the hair by my ear. "Do you want to know what it is?"

I shook my head but his voice was still there.

"I want to hear you say *'Please, Reilly, please.'*" He mimicked me softly, teasing and warm.

"I've already said it."

"But I'm going to make you *mean* it," he said, and he wasn't talking about "Please, Reilly, let me go." He was hard up against me, moving in, and I was already back against the wall.

"Reilly—," I said, and then his mouth had me, drawing me deeper. He tasted of salt and champagne, and sweet, raw man. I was trembling against him, under his hands, his hands sliding under my shirt. "Ah, Mary Margaret," he murmured, kissing my throat, and I exploded then, pushed away from him, frantic and scrabbling, until I stood all alone in the middle of the room.

"I'm sorry," I said, choking, "I'm sorry, I can't do this."

He was still, wasn't moving.

*"Why?"*

Someone had skinned me—*he* had—Reilly had, nerve endings exposed, everything tingling and ready to bleed. He needed an answer, deserved one, and how could I tell him I was stark, staring twisted? How could I say "There's a ghost in my bed"—a ghost who stank of cordite and sweat, who'd loved and betrayed me and just wouldn't let me go.

"I'm sort of seeing someone," I said. I couldn't look at him, so I didn't, I stared at my hands. Blurring hands.

"All right," he said finally on a long grim breath, and he moved past me, cleared, but he wasn't going to the front door or even back to the kitchen, he was heading determinedly left to the bedroom hall.

"What are you doing?"

"I'm going to wake Josh up."

"Reilly, *Christ*—why?"

"Because," he said, "I think you promised to tell him when you were seeing someone, and he doesn't seem to know about this guy. I already asked him."

One cop pursuing.

"For Christ's sake," I hissed at him, "can't you take no?"

"I can," he said evenly. "When I hear the truth about it."

"There *is* no truth about it," I said. "It was a *kiss*. You want to hear it was the best kiss I ever had, well, then, fine, you were great. Gosh, I wish I could go to bed with you, but I've just joined a monastery, so you'll understand that I can't."

"Nunnery," he said.

"Whatever."

"You done?"

I was, yes. A basket case, nuts. Trembling and sick and I don't know how I'd ever thought I could handle him, because I couldn't even handle myself. "I'm sorry," I whispered, to him or the ghosts.

"What's going on, Meg?"

"I'm turning you down," I said. "I'm not doing it right, I'm sorry."

"I don't want to hear 'sorry,' " he said tightly. "Is this to get me back for the week?"

"No."

"*What*, then?"

I couldn't have him thinking it was spite. I was seeing him again, kind of tough, kind of hurt, and maybe he deserved the truth if only I could find it.

"Where'd you get Mary Margaret?" I said.

He studied me a moment. Waved a hand.

"Sit somewhere."

I was closest to the armchair, so I took it. He sank onto the couch across, watched me huddle.

"Mary Margaret's how I think of you."

"Well, don't."

As if I hadn't spoken. "That's what Charlie used to

call you up in Sacramento," and it couldn't be, wasn't.

"He didn't even *know* me then."

"Well, he sure as hell wanted to," Reilly said. "That's all he used to talk about on the stakeouts, this little girl back at the station named Mary Margaret. A mouth on her, he said, but a whole lot of guts."

"Not so little," I said, and he was wrong about the guts part, too. He was doing it again, though, talking me down—making it easier, making me a present. Reminding me of the way Charlie'd loved me at the start.

"Charlie's dead, Meg."

I knew that.

"It's been three years."

And six nights. I knew how long it was.

"If you were his bitchin' great friend," I said fiercely, "how come you never came around?"

"I meant to." He was looking at his hands. "We'd run into each other at the meets sometimes, and I always meant to. And then when I heard . . . I saw you at the funeral, but you didn't know me and there were a lot of people around."

There had been. And Caroline wearing her grief like a badge, clutching Josh bravely to her side. "It was a zoo."

"I admired your courage."

He meant it, really meant it, and I laughed at him bitterly, all the days and the nights, what men mean by courage. Don't shame me, girl.

"There *is* no Mary Margaret," I said, "and you're a cop."

"I don't sleep in my uniform."

"You don't have to, Reilly, it's the way that you breathe, the way that you think. Double-checking everything, looking for weaknesses. Lies. I can't live like that anymore, I can't be around it. It makes me too crazy."

"I don't think you can judge by the last few days."

He was being very calm, but I wasn't having any. "All your friends are cops, Reilly. You go to cop parties, cop bars. Everyone knows everyone's business. If you want to know something, you just pick up a phone and call Joe Doaks in Glendale or LA or Burbank, because that's how it works for you, that's how it is. But not for *me*, not anymore. Not checking mileage and rearview mirrors, not checking drawers and collars and stories. I can't stand it. I can't be around it."

I was tearing myself up for him, strip by strip, but he wasn't moving. Maybe that muscle by his jaw. "You're very dramatic," he said evenly. "But, you know, I would have said you'd been enjoying yourself parts of this week."

I didn't say anything.

"And I would have said you liked me, liked me a lot. I would even have said that you wanted to kiss me."

Maybe I had.

"Drugs make you feel good, too," I said down to my hands, "and then they steal your soul."

"I'm not into soul-stealing, Meg. *Body-snatching*, maybe. *Your* body." He was laughing at me again, I couldn't believe it. "Stay here," he said.

And then he was down the hall to the kitchen, coming back with that other bag in his hand.

"Open it."

He was standing right over me, so I fumbled with the staples until he took it and ripped the bag open, dumped it out on the coffee table.

It was a gun.

I managed to speak.

"You couldn't find any flowers?"

"I try to suit the presents," he said.

It was a .38 blue-steel Smith, curves glinting in the half-light, beautiful, deadly. I could have someone run the numbers, but it wouldn't be registered anywhere. Reilly had brought me a goddamned cold gun and I couldn't breathe for the ache in my throat.

"You'll want to be careful with that." He was settling back onto the couch.

"I'm going to throw it into the ocean."

"No, you're not," Reilly said. "You're going to tape it up in the garage where the other one was."

I reached out with my index finger, touched the barrel, the grip.

"Not the garage," I said. "You already know about that."

He laughed out loud then—a man who had me and knew it, thought he knew *me*. Maybe he did. We are what we are, I guess. Me such a coward.

"I don't know how to do this, Reilly." I was meaning everything, really, and the voice wasn't mine.

"It's easy," he said. "You just come here and kiss me. I can take care of the rest."

So right. Capable. I was trembling on the edge and I couldn't quite go.

"One touch from you and my troubles are over—is that how it works?"

"Well," he said thoughtfully, "I don't know if I'm *that* good."

He was smiling at me with his eyes, so easy, and I

went down to him then like a candle in the wind, flaming, burning, and he *was* that good, he was every bit that good, he was so damned good it scared me and even *that* was exciting. Baptism by fire and saltwater tears. Not reborn, exactly, but come back to myself. Charlie's ghost was still there, always would be, I guess, but I couldn't hear it as clearly with Reilly's voice in my ear. I didn't even care that he was saying "Mary Margaret" as if I were a nun or a schoolgirl, because he knew me, he'd found the heart of me after all, and what's in a name? He'd seen me bitchy and evil and crying like a fool, and it was *his* chest I was hiding my face in, *his* hips that were pressing me down, *his* name that was on my lips when the moment came.

"*Please, Reilly,*" I said just for him, "*please, please, Reilly,*" and he looked down at me and laughed, and then he drove me home.

# Acknowledgments

I'd like to thank my parents, Barb and Cliff, who haven't understood every choice that I've made, but whose belief in my abilities has never seemed to waver. Thanks for the courage, folks, and all of the values!

Next is my honey, the Red Man, whose expertise and advice have been bedrock to me in shaping this world and the real world we share. I couldn't do it without him—or without C. and R., the short people in our life who help keep me grounded. (Dinnertime *again*?)

I owe special thanks to Evan Marshall, renowned agent, who was willing to take on this book, and to his assistant, Nancy Bandel, whose powers amaze me. Love and kisses to Susanne Kirk, equally renowned editor, and to *her* assistant, Elizabeth Barden, who so cheerfully and tactfully have steered me through the publishing maze. It's been fun, you guys, really! (The next book's due *when*??!)

Hugs to my Library Moms: Vickie, Debi, Katie, Jana, Leesa, Corey, and Lillian, too. I really appreciate the support and the cheer—let's do breakfast, okay? (I'll bring the pie. . . .) And Vivian T., your unabashed enthusiasm is a lesson for me. Life to the fullest, girl! With you all the way!

I want to thank the "other C.J." (Chris Caracci), and Mark, Denny, Colonel Gerry, Harry, and Hershel. You guys were fantastic, VERY generous with your time and your talents, and it still means a lot to me.

And as long as I'm listing: thanks, Clint, Robbie B., Ken Murphy, and Terry—*excellent* training out there in Texas, some of the finest. Chuck T., you were great; Brad and Naish, see you soon. A special thanks to *mon cher* Richard G., who's been beating me up regularly so that I could learn knife fighting. (And he's *enjoying* it so much, which worries me some. . . .) There's Leslie A., my good friend and my shining example, and of course, Erick G. (Kudos to you, boy! Watch out for those gangs. . . .) It wouldn't be right to leave off Tracy N.—twenty years friends, girl! Who would have thought it?—or Lisa and Vera, my neighborhood carers (Yes, good things *do* happen)—or my big sister, Kathy, her husband, Frank, and my small sister, Tam, who read *Bait* several years ago and swept me away with their positive responses.

A special place for my Glendale guys: Bill H. (who first taught me the Weaver), Ron A. (*and* his helicopters), Big Mac, Randy P., Jerry R. (and gal Carolyn), and of course, Tom Terrific.

And lastly, to all of my Lost Boys out there: Trust is a hard thing, but I love you, too. Yes, I'm still here, and yes, I am keeping the faith for you, hoping with all of my heart that you find a way home. . . .

CJS